even small birds fly free

Pádraig O'Gorman

Icon O'Clast Press

First Published 2024

by Icon O'Clast Press,

29, Bamba Street,

Clonakilty,

Cork, P85FP60

Ireland

ISBN 978-0-9957843-0-7

Book cover by Emily Catherine.

www.emilycatherineillustration.com

First print December 2024

Thank you for supporting independent publishing

*For Ezra, Enid,
Shae and Orrin*

Foreword
by Author

When Irish refugees arrive in America in the middle of the 19th century, they come face-to-face with racism and slavery. Irish people commonly share the same neighbourhoods with African Americans and intimate relations are common between the two races.

I listened to an interview Percival Everett gave about his magnificent novel 'James' which is extracted from 'The Adventures of Huckleberry Finn' by Mark Twain. Everett, however, in his novel gives voice to the escaped, enslaved man, Jim. Hence the title of the book. In the interview he suggested that Twain had no capacity to write an African American in the original as he could not have any real, intimate insight into how Jim (James) would feel, see, react. Hence the one-dimensional character of Jim in Huckleberry Finn. While I am not comparing myself to either of these accomplished, brilliant writers, I have also written African Americans into my narrative and equally struggle like Twain to understand the awful plight of an African American in the institutionally racist country that America was in the 19th century. Yet I felt compelled to write the story.

I faced many challenges when writing this book. I would like to draw your attention to two. When writing a piece of historical fiction, I believe it is essential to travel back in time and seek to be as authentic as possible. This requires hours of research. It also requires in my opinion that one uses terms in use at the time, no matter how offensive they may be today. And some are extremely offensive. I refer to one term in particular. African Americans were commonly called Negroes in the 19th century and that is how they are largely described in this story. I apologise for any offence this may cause. I also direct my readers to a letter written by the great philosopher W.E.B. Du Bois faithfully recorded in teachingamericanhistory.org under the title 'The Name Negro'.

The second challenge I faced was following through on an essential element of my story which is a rape of a woman and its consequences. I have been challenged that this is a woman's story to tell and for a man to write it usurpative. Yet the incident is central to my fictional narrative. In a real and figurative sense. Largely both the incident itself and its aftermath is told through the eyes of men who are either bystanders or family and intimate partner. In this way, I am, also through the story, coming to terms, as a man, with the consequences of such a violation. I hope, as a reader, you can allow that.

Thank you,

Pádraig O'Gorman

Cast of Characters

Townships of Graigue and Grenville, County Cork, Ireland

Peadar O'Brien. A widowed schoolmaster, lives in Graigue with his eighteen year old daughter, Mary. He is the grandchild of Péigín. He founded the hedge school which serves the townships of Graigue and Glenville.

Péigín O'Brien. A matriarchal figure in the village of Graigue steeped in Irish culture, history and tradition. Mother of Peadar.

Mary O'Brien. Peadar's daughter and his close companion. Her mother, and Peadar's wife Brigid, died at Mary's birth.

Cormac McCarthy. A seventeen year old boy living in Graigue. He is a graduate of Peadar O'Brien's "hedge school" and is forced, through hunger, to work for the Landlord's Agent, Robert Kincaid.

Robert Kincaid. The agent of the absentee Landlord of the Graigue township who receives a commission to manage the tenancies on the Landlord's behalf.

Eileen O'Sullivan. A native of Ballyhooley, she moves to Glenville to work on the Famine Road.

Canon Ryan. The Parish Priest of the parish of Glenville.

Justice Crawley. Presiding as magistrate for barony of Duhallow and Fermoy

William Hudson. Son of Lord of Glenville Manor

Skibbereen, County Cork and Kenmare, County Kerry

Pádraig O'Donovan. A Spailpín Fánach or wandering landless labourer like his brother. He is a native of Skibbereen and an accomplished fiddle player.

Caelan O'Donovan. The younger brother of Pádraig. He is an accomplished Melodeon player.

Alex Somerville. Alexander Somerville (1811-1885), - a real life character, a British journalist of Scottish parentage, wrote his Letters from Ireland during the Famine of 1847 for the Manchester Examiner, which published them serially.

Ship Cambridge

Nora Flanagan A widow who befriends Mary O'Brien on board the ship travelling to New York and her four daughters, Méabh (13), Nóra (11), Alannah (8), and Bríd (6).

Liverpool

Johnny Dolan. A workmate of Caelan O'Donovan on the docks.

Finn. Owner and barman in Shebeen on the Scotland Road.

New Orleans

Johnny McEvoy. A workmate of Pádraig's in the Levee's.

John Roberts. A Patty Roller who befriends Pádraig.

Solene. A free woman of colour (femme de couleur libres) who meets Pádraig.

New York

Annie. Sex worker who befriends Mary in Five Points.

Biddy Mulligan. Madam who runs the brothel in Five Points.

Sister Agnes. A Sister of Mercy. The Irish order of nuns founded in 1831, followed the Irish diaspora, providing essential care particularly to vulnerable women and children.

Samuel Williams An African American, former enslaved man, who is handyman at the Sisters of Mercy convent.

Cora Mary's daughter

Abe Mary and Samuel's son

Mima Samuel's mother, an African American enslaved woman

Boston

Bridie Mulcahy. Married to Seán Mulcahy, with her six children, befriended by Caelan O'Donovan on board the Caledonia on the way to Boston.

Seán Mulcahy. Married to Bridie. He helps Caelan settle in Batterymarch Street, Boston.

Ambrose Cutting. A early photographer, who tutors Caelan in the art of photography.

Frederick Douglass. An American social reformer, abolitionist, orator, writer, and statesman. He became the most important leader of the movement for African-American civil rights in the 19th century.

'A nation has the ability to recover from trauma, even if it has been the perpetrator, it has time to regenerate and learn from its mistakes, if it has the will to do so. Because if you try and continue without really facing big parts of your history, then, are you building something very fragile and breakable on bad foundations?

Kazuo Ishiguro

Low lie the fields of Athenry
Where first we watched the small free birds fly
Our love was on the wing,
We had dreams and songs to sing,
It's so lonely 'round the fields of Athenry

From the song by Pete St John

part one
the great hunger

the humble prátaí

Graigue, County Cork,

In which 9 year old Peadar O'Brien learns about the customs, history and beauty of his local culture. His Dúchas.[1]

Samhain, October, 1810

It's little Peadar's favourite time of the day. Sitting next to the hearth as Péigín, his grandmother, sets the fire. Her effortless economy of movement enchants him. She stokes the dark brown, earthy sods of turf and releases orange-blue flames licking up each side. He loves breathing in the sweet smell, of turf burning. Today, she hums a song to herself, her delicate voice filling the small room with the comforting sound that embraces and surrounds his childhood.

> *"Sé mo laoch mo ghile mear[2]*
> *Sé mo Shéasar, gile mear*
> *Suan gan séan ní bhfuair mé féin*
> *Ó chuaigh I gcéin mo ghile mear"*

She looks up at him kindly.

"Would you ever fetch the pail there, Peadar mo stóir[3], and fill it for me."

Now he is eight years old, she trusts him to fetch water from the River Bride. Eagerly, Peadar grabs the pail and heads out the door of their small, simple bothán[4]. He makes his way, with an assumed air of resolve and purpose, glad to be counted as a helper at last, past the ten dispersed houses of the village. He can't help but notice and absorb the low hub of conversation from neighbours, gathered as they are by Seán Murphy's house; The daily ritual of smoking pipes and gossip. The evening melody of birds, the blackbird, thrush, robin and wren punctuate this chitchat with animated song as if mimicking the serious and intense interaction of the men gathered round.

On the boreen out of the village, he is overcome by the rich smell of honeysuckle and hawthorn, the evening air augmenting the scent. On either side of him, fuchsia dominates the hedgerow and at one point clambers and piggybacks on two beech trees and forms an archway through which he passes with élan. It's a glorious Autumn evening.

In five minutes he is by the river. He pauses for a moment to look upstream. He is always captivated by this view. Large rocks and boulders seem to have been placed strategically, even aesthetically as far as his eyes can see and the river tumbles over them, round them, swirling with abandon and creating a chiaroscuro of light and shade that always lifts his heart. He dips the pail to collect the crystal clear water and rests for a moment.   He's a gentle, reflective soul is Peadar.

Through the overhanging boughs, he looks out over the expanse of meadow beyond and is enthralled by the daily murmuration of starlings, flocking in their thousands every evening at this spot, at this time. Swooping in the darkening sky, they weave charcoal patterns as they coalesce and diffuse. It's enough to take his breath away.

On the other side of the meadow, he can just make out the Glenville children playing Tig, eking out the last pleasures from the day. Their cheerful voices and squeals of laughter travel uninterrupted over the valley towards him, almost beckoning him to cross over. He takes a deep breath of satisfaction and turns for home struggling with the now heavy pail.

At the brow of the hill and through the thickening gloaming, he sees Micheál and Séamus, outside the Seanachaí's[5], practicing tunes on their fiddles for the céilí[6] by the big bonfire at the Glendule crossroad. Tomorrow. The feast of Samhain[7]. The end of the Celtic year.

Micheál sees him and shouts out across the divide,

"Aren't you the grand lad to be helping your grandmother like that, Peadar O'Brien. Fair play to you boy,"

He smiles to himself embarrassed at being singled out and confused by the unsolicited praise.

When he arrives at the bothán, Péigín has the prátaí[8] ready. She fills the pot with them, handling the light, brown tubers with reverence and asks him to cover them with water from the pail.

Most days as he sits beside her, she tells him a story. It's often the same tale, but he doesn't mind. He loves to hear her voice. It draws him close to her. Envelops him. Something they share together, alone. And she delights in the way he is all ears for her.

"You'll go far in the world if you listen to and heed your old seanmháthair[9]," she says with a twinkle in her eyes.

"These are God's gift to us, mo stóir," She continues, pointing at the Prátaí simmering gently in the pot. "We need to honour them. They're the thing that's saving us. Since the Penal times[10]. When the English took our land from us."

                    even small birds fly free

"How did they manage to do that, Seanmháthair?" He knows this question will prompt her, will get her going and is delighted when she responds.

"Sure, they passed a law that made it illegal for a Catholic to own land, a horse, go to school, attend mass, vote, be a member of parliament. If they could have made a law against breathing, then as sure as you're sitting there, they would have done. They wanted us all to turn Protestant. And then when we defied them and stayed true to our faith, they insulted and exploited us by leasing the same land back to us again in short tenancies."

"But why do we only sow prátaí? Is that something they ordered too?" He knows the answer to this question. It's deeply implanted in him. But he loves to hear Péigín expound on it. He imagines it helps to bring the best out of the food. Like a blessing intoned over its preparation. A prayer to improve its taste and texture.

Péigín regards him closely. There is a curious, amused look on her face.

"No, we are blessed. It's because the prátaí are so good for us and they give such a bountiful harvest. I remember, when I was a little girl, the first year of our planting of the prátaí. It was a big risk. But when we saw the harvest, it made our hearts glad. We couldn't believe how big a crop we raised. We knew we could plant and feed ourselves from our small two-acre tenancy for the whole year. They were our only comfort when the rebellion failed in '98[11]"

As he sits, the warm glow of the fire captivates him, its flames enhancing the telling of the tale. He gazes into its flickering light and it becomes a vessel for his imagination.

"What happened then, in '98?" He is provoking her to tell the story of courage displayed by his heroes. Their pikes against the guns and might of the English army. Robert Emmet, Wolfe Tone.

"We rose in force against the crown. Catholics and Presbyterians together. Probably the last time we will ever join forces. Against their tyranny. But we were crushed. Again. Our hopes of following France and America and forming a Republic cruelly thwarted. The English empire too strong to stand against. They would surely always defeat and frustrate us. We had to resign ourselves then to our fate and to our small, rented plot of land. For our sustenance and survival. Without the prátaí, we would have been lost."

She reaches into the small cupboard for the salt and sprinkles some into the boiling water. She is in her stride.

"But you have to take care of the prátaí," she continues, "They don't just grow by themselves. We had to learn how to plant them in the best way. Fertilising the beds with manure and sea shells. Then banking the sides at the right time. To prevent the tubers turning green and poisonous. And weeding, keeping on top of the drills. But once we learned, we were away on a horse's gallop. Tons we harvested and stored. I saw a huge change in our menfolk. They grew strong and tall, so nourishing is this food. Handsome and proud, they became. It was only then we could find time for ourselves. To relax. To listen to stories from the Seanachaí. To play and dance. Sure, folks made up songs to these little things - our prátaí."

At this, she stops talking and concentrates on lifting the pot from the fire with the iron bar and lays it gently on the floor, exposing the beautifully floury and creamy texture of the potatoes nestling inside. She pours buttermilk from the jug and he watches, exuberantly, as it flows down through the mound of potatoes, enriching their creaminess at every step. Steam rising from the pot.

"Dinners ready, Peadar. Be a good lad and call them in from their idle chatter."

The family gather around the pot and tuck into the rich feast prepared by Péigín. A quiet contentment spreads among them all. No food has ever been eaten with such relish and gratefulness. Peadar notices, as always, that Péigín has taken some prátaí and placed them in a side pot by the fire. Almost as a ritual, he can't stop himself asking the question,

"A Seanmháthair, why are there still prátaí left in that pot?'

"That's for the man coming over the hill, Peadar, a stóir."

The man coming over the hill. And she was right. Many the evening, when darkness fell, they would hear a polite knock on the door, to reveal a Spalpeen, a wandering labourer on his way to Cork city. 'Our man coming over the hill'! He would receive a warm welcome, a place by the hearth, and the prátaí which had been set aside would be warmed for him. And if they were lucky, when he had his fill, he would reach into his bag and pick out his tin whistle and give them a couple of tunes or a few stories. These wandering, welcomed strangers often regaled them with an impromptu performance, as they gaped open-mouthed in wonder, bringing a quiet, contented joy to the long, winter evenings.

    even small birds fly free

death of the liberator

Graigue, County Cork,

May, 1847

In which Mary O'Brien sees the desolation of her father by the death of Ireland's un-crowned king and becomes exposed to the landlord agent, Kincaid

Mary O'Brien

As he comes through the lintel of our small bothán these days, I study him, stooped and bowed as he is by his years of struggle. I find myself doing that more and more lately, watching his movements, seeking some form of reassurance in his mien. The strong shoulders and arms that picked me up with gusto as a child, seem to hang loosely by his side. He is cowed, defeated in a way I have not known. The last two years bringing a hunger to our people as the crop rotted in our small fields.

His deep, brown eyes, however, still hold his soul, and his wise and searching intelligence. And they always shine when he comes across me, a smile of greeting lightening his face and chasing the years.

"Cén Scéal, mo chuisle[1]"

His usual greeting, 'what's the story' melting my heart every time. I love the fact that he sees me as the pulse of his life, standing as he tries to, between me and danger.

Women in the village told me he had been broken by Ma's passing, at my birth. "They were a couple apart, Brigid and Peadar O'Brien, somehow entwined and in love. Her death almost destroyed him. Coming so soon after his seanmháthair, Péigín."

"You saved him, though. He fell for you and after that there was no stopping him. We never saw a man like him for the nurturing of you. The two of you were inseparable. He would carry you on his back as he went about his day."

The image of my infant self on his back moves me deeply. Just the two of us. Sadly there was never anyone else for him.

"That's gone from me now, Mary," he said when I asked him a few years back why he never married again. "Sure your mother was the love of my life and I felt it would be unfair to anyone who followed her. I was always happy and content with you."

Today when I enter the bothán I find him by the hearth, on his chair, sunk into it, spent. He had gone to the market house in Rathcormac to see if he could pick up some work.

                    even small birds fly free

Only once before, have I seen him like this. I was a small child then. It's a distant memory. It frightened me all the more, then, because I didn't understand what had overtaken him. It was years later before I learned of the Rathcormac massacre[2]; The Worcester regiment opening fire on villagers from Gortroe for refusing to pay the tithe required by law to the local Anglican Vicar. Shooting them and killing eleven whilst injuring a further forty five. Nine of these dying later. Many of them close companions of his youth.

Looking at him now brings all that back. I know him well enough to let him come to himself. So I stop everything just to sit by him.

Eventually, he says, "He's gone from us, mo chroí[3]. O'Connell is dead."

"Oh," I gasp and reach over to him and hold him in to me as he begins to sob and wail, pressed against me for solace and comfort, his body racked with keening.

Eventually he continues, "He died in Rome yesterday. He has asked for his heart to remain there and his body to be returned to Ireland. But he's gone from us now and in the midst of this, I don't know how we will ever recover."

Daniel O'Connell[4], the liberator, the "king" of Ireland. The man who single-handedly raised a people, crouched over, broken down, ashamed, overcome from centuries of defeat.

He often told me stories at night by the fire on winter evenings. Of the time, in '28, two years before I was born, when he and Ma travelled to Limerick to hear the great man speak after he was elected as member for County Clare. The miracle of it. Opposed by one an all, a Catholic, who could not take up a seat in Westminster. There was no law against him standing for office though. And stand he did and with the power of his voice and words defeated all and won the people. They had returned him by a landslide and he and Ma had gone to Limerick for his coronation.

"They wouldn't let him speak," He retold this tale many times over. "They cheered him for a full hour or more, your mother and me in the middle of them. Many a cap was tossed in the air that day, ne'er to be seen again. In the end the great man could do no more but laugh and raise his hands in salute back to us."

Those same memories must be coursing through Da as I hold him and as grief overtakes him; For every once in a while he lets out a loud wail that shakes our small home.

"We have lived under the shelter of his voice and words, and he is gone from us. He has become an absence now. A shape difficult to fill."

It was O'Connell's influence which gave Da the resolve to found a school. To repay the village and surrounding neighbourhood for the care and attention he had received from them when I was a baby. To take his part in the raising of the people. His natural intelligence and quick mind gave him an easy facility to learn and he set about readying himself to teach and guide the children of the area, girls and boys. A hedge school. Mirroring Penal Times. When it was illegal for Catholic children to be educated. Although in this case, he found an old abandoned clochán[5] and rescued it. Its beehive shape providing shelter as he and the children, me among them, conjured up worlds of imagination together. Faithfully, week by week, year by year, he sat with his books in front of him and in a lilting voice transported us all to places we could not have conceived or dreamed up.

All that has changed and our circumstances have been reduced by the blight. It has devastated our landscape turning it from green to black. It's been a long time now since the villagers could afford the farthing a week he asked for the learning. The people have retreated into themselves and a great fear has gripped them all. Stories are told and passed on, one to the other. Some blame the crop failure on the change in the air from the new locomotives spreading smoke around the countryside. Others hear of what they call mortiferous vapours spreading out from volcanoes around the world. Most, however, take it upon themselves as a great punishment for the many sins they have committed.

Da knows differently. From early on he was aware of a disease which had spread from Mexico and America to Europe. Penetrating devastatingly across Belgium, France, Germany and Holland, farmlands lay black and putrid in it's wake. A fungus carried on the wind and thriving in the mild, wet climate of Ireland. Inexorably sweeping over farmland until it arrived in Cork, two years ago. The disease affecting the beloved potato. Other places in Europe could mitigate its destructive sway with substitute crops and other means of income. But in Ireland, it laid us waste, solely dependent as we are on this singular produce for our sustenance. The annual, rich harvest which has allowed us and our

even small birds fly free

neighbours to live in the small tenancies we occupy, providing us with nourishment year on year, flourishing as it did in our tiny acreage, and allowing us to hope for a future different to our past. Its nutritious essence ensuring our people were among the most healthy, tall and strong in Europe.

Now its diseased tubers has brought us once again to our knees.

I sit with him for a long time that evening, comforting him. I bring in fresh hay for his bed to provide him some solace. I make soup for him and as the day passes into night, he eventually sleeps.

Kincaid arrives. Like a skilled predator, a vulture, an eagle scanning horizons, he senses and thrives on weakness and debilitation and knows when to strike. A big bull of a man, he barges through our door into the sanctuary of our little home, something he would not have dared to do in normal times. I immediately feel violated. Our small, one-roomed harbour, breached. He scans it voraciously. I watch his face change as he sees the skill evident in the repairs deftly made to the sods of turf and grass on the roof and the expert craftsmanship of the dry-stone walls. I can see he is surprised. Taken aback by the small, few items of wooden furniture which Da made in the long winter evenings.

As our landlord's agent, I know he likes to rule over us and make sure he imposes his will upon us. His black eyes are sharp and narrow as pinpricks. His mouth twists in cruelty, a physical metaphor for the words that pour out of his spiteful and maleficent heart. I observe him carefully from the corner of the room. For once, I feel glad of the solitary window letting in the little light the bothán allows. I remain invisible to him in the shadows away from his gaze. Da's presence usually an asylum in which I take refuge.

But today I feel stripped bare. Da, grief-stricken, has retired into himself and has no energy for this beast.

"I don't think I need to remind a man of your wit that I am your master, O'Brien," Kincaid blasts out. "I have the power to dispose your future. What I want, I get. Understood. Now as to the small matter of your rent. Small to me, big to you. I have not received it. I see no reason why you should be treated differently to the others. In fact, I see a very good reason why you could be made an effective example. As the most insightful man in the village, some would even say the leader, I expect you to show the nature of things by your actions. Lead the way so to speak, so others don't get foolish notions. So they don't get a run of themselves and assume the absence of their fucking potatoes means I have to do without my due income and just desserts. What's more, the government wants to tax me so they can provide for you lazy, feckless eejits. Not on my life."

I can see he enjoys lording it over Da. With others he is reduced to shouting and monosyllables as he has no grasp of our language. But with Da he can give full reign to his invective and I see conquest in his eyes. Here is a man in front of him whom he needs to diminish. His status depends on it.

When Da does not respond, I see disappointment cross Kincaid's brow. He enjoys mastery over the 'intellectual' of the village. The closest to his 'equal' he will come across. It is obvious the derogatory nature of the encounter boosts him, helps him stride about in his cock-a-hoop way. Usually Da allows him this frippery. Da's meaningful, pregnant silence exposing the buffoon in Kincaid of which Kincaid is comically oblivious.

Today is different, however. Da's grief renders him listless and lethargic. Then from my refuge in the corner, I see Kincaid switch. He turns fully towards me, like a cat with a prey and gives full reign to his lechery. I feel him regard me lasciviously, running his eyes over the length and breadth of my body. At this moment, I feel unclothed, burnt within the elemental ferocity of his gaze. And it isn't only me, our place and the objects around me, pregnant with meaning and intimacy, the room I adore is violated by his presence. The walls crumble and I feel revealed, exposed, laid bare in powerlessness and vulnerability. For an age, he lingers wallowing with impunity in his salacious lewdness and I feel abased and degraded by it.

"I will take what I want and what I need, O'Brien," he mouths, carefully looking at me as he addresses Da. "It's in your interest not to get in my way. The ditch is not a pleasant place to be these days. You have been warned. Play ball or face the consequences."

He turns on his heels and throwing one last, cruel look in my direction he storms out the door. The air which had changed on his arrival retains its raw, dismal, bleak, sombre mood as he leaves. Our home, my sanctuary has been disturbed. I feel like an animal, frightened out of my wits. I understand from now on, vigilance is an imperative.

even small birds fly free

taking what I want

Graigue, County Cork,

Late November, 1847

In which Cormac McCarthy is burdened by his cowardice and complicity and through a be-loved horse risks all to escape his master

Cormac McCarthy

I feel a trembling come over me both inside and out. For the life of me, I can't say if it is the cold blast of wind or the icy weather or my perilous thoughts which are shrivelling up my insides.

Dark clouds, thick with snow, have changed the landscape. Like last winter, we have never seen anything like it. Its monochromatic, ghostly whiteness accentuating the beauty of the gentle, rolling hills but bringing little solace. The freezing temperature has at least obliterated the sickly, sweet rot of the potato crop that has clogged my nasal passage for as long as I can remember. But the bitter weather is also a herald of the next wave of devastation. The land, our people's land, seems dead set on its betrayal of its occupants; Nature not noticing the sorrow that has come over the people.

I am supposed to be at work but I cannot move. I finally see and am confounded by what is required of me. If Master O'Brien could see me now he would be horrified, disappointed. I miss school and those moments when he would transport me, in thought and reflection. Events have conspired to take me away from days where I could think deeply about things, inspired by his gentle encouragement. I have compromised so much.

My co-workers are busy. Desperate men, willing to do anything to survive. Ropes have been slung over the rafters of the tiny cottage. They are dismantling the beams and pulling them dramatically to the ground. A tumbling, it's called, as if it is something joyous. The landlord deciding it's better to evict the family rather than be taxed for their upkeep. Since the Poor Law Act[1], which taxes the landlords to pay for relief, there has been a spate of evictions every week throughout the county.

A makeshift fire has been lit and I can see beams which have already been razed burning brightly, but I get no comfort from the flames. This wreckage is an insurance demanded by the landlord; rendering the bothán uninhabitable. The eviction will then be final, condemning the Crotty family (whose tenancy is being revoked) to homelessness and the ditch.

     even small birds fly free

I am in a catatonic state and I cannot move. And I think it isn't a result of the cold or the eviction; My mental state is overwhelmed by recollection and guilt. How did I end up here?

When the crop failed last Autumn, my family had no means to buy seed potatoes for the planting season. Ma and Da, in a desperate measure, sent me to work for Kincaid, the landlord's agent. That was six months ago.

Kincaid is a brute of a man, all muscle and menace. He fills me with terror and apprehension from the very first encounter. Of course he only speaks to me in English. It's all he knows. I often think this language fosters superiority, sophistication and duplicity. It certainly does in him. It suits his oppressive manner consummately. It's so different to the softness of our everyday vocabulary.

"Right, Cormac McCarthy is it. Ha. You're a skinny little rake for saying you're fifteen. Are you sure about that?"

I nodded.

"Well, you've joined the takers now, lad," Kincaid snapped, "Lets see if you're up for it."

Those words, cruelly spoken, burnt into me. I had a deep sense of foreboding. At fifteen years of age, I could see my life was going to change and I wondered then in what way.

A month ago, in late October, when I was following Kincaid to serve notice on a tenant, we stumbled on Mary, Master O'Brien's daughter near Lackendarragh woods. Now a young woman, she was foraging for berries and mushrooms. Her deep auburn hair catching the fading light. It's unmistakably her. Kincaid turned and looked at me. "This ones for you, boy. Let's see what you're made of." I could see terror come over Mary's face and it dawned on me that this was not the first time Kincaid had ensnared her. Next to Kincaid's enormous physique she was no more than a slip of a girl, her frame exuding a raw vulnerability.

"Lie down," Kincaid shouted at her. I saw her slump to the grass, weighed down by fatigue and hopelessness, resigned to her fate. Then he turned to me 'Take her boy, she's yours". I was stunned into immobility.

I realise I have buried what happened next. And this morning it is overtaking me. As I stand here rooted to the spot, by the Crotty's dismantled home, I feel traumatised by memory. And I am wrestling with myself to explain what overtook me that day, in Lackendarragh woods. Right now, I am powerless as the stark facts replay in my consciousness, condemning me in every frame.

That day, bewildered by what Kincaid was suggesting, I remained rigid, full of dread and consternation. He cursed and moved past me and dropped on Mary. I heard him grunt, "This is for August's rent." She did not utter a word. She did not resist him but turned her head to one side, her only act of freedom not to see his face. She seemed to have accepted the idea that she had no choice, abandoning herself as someone who was shutting herself down to escape from a terrifying situation. Frightened and full of shame, I remained motionless, unprotesting, as he took her.

The same smell of fear fills my nostrils now. Of a frightened animal mixed with the rich dank aroma of the cold, dark earth. I realise it is lodged in my olfactory nerve, from that ignominious day. The mortification I felt standing by as Kincaid finished with her, will stay with me embedded, to trigger, capriciously, a vivid recall at any time. It will plague me for the rest of my days.

The fortnight after, Kincaid began to act in force on evictions. Happy to use the Gregory Clause for his own ends. There would be no harvest even though there was no blight. People not being able to sow in the Spring. They have no money to pay the rent. This he knows. This he is happy to exploit.

Three weeks ago Ma and Da, already weakened, succumbed to starvation and disease. How I miss them. I'm on my own now. The O'Brien's were evicted the week before and I now recall them passing through the village, knocking at doors in the middle of a long, dark night, pleading in hope of some sustenance and shelter; Firmly locked out by their neighbours terrified of catching something from them. The image of Mary outside haunts me. The following morning they were gone without a trace.

Suddenly Kincaid arrives. My languor is abruptly interrupted. As usual, he shows up towards the end of an eviction, so sure and certain is his grip over his lackeys. His subjugation guaranteeing that the removal and demolition will be completed to his exacting detail. He dismounts from his horse, Capaleen and strides into the ransacked building.

Capaleen moves towards me in her strong, self-confident way. Kincaid has only ever seen her as a mere beast, oblivious of the ghastly irony of that observation. I love her. I delight in the task of grooming her and

even small birds fly free

we have formed a deep bond over the six months I have been with her. When she reaches me, she buries her muzzle in my chest. I am suddenly overwhelmed by energy flowing from her; Strong, knowing, convicting. As I look into her deep brown eyes I see the reflection of my troubled soul. How I adore her. The moment is held. I feel the dark entropy of my complicity in all of Kincaid's actions, but particularly his violation of Mary, envelop me. Enfolded by Capaleen, bathed by her tender breath and revitalising power, my shame dissipates. It is as if she knows the depths of my despair and guilt and moves to expiate it.

At this, liberated, I drop the felling axe to the ground, hug her, walk to her side, grab her reins and mount her. She responds immediately and we gallop up the boreen. Shock registering on the faces of the bystanders as they witness an act of insurrection they find imponderable and impossible. Together, in front of their eyes, Capaleen and I are shattering the hegemony and hold of Colonisation, Imperialism and Empire.

At the top of the hill, I reign her in and look back. Kincaid is striding out of the bothán and looking up the lane at us. Horrified I see him become enraged and strike the two nearest bystanders with his cudgel, screaming at them all for their inaction and complicity.

The die is cast now. As I turn Capaleen and gallop away, away from this life, away from Kincaid, back over the line I have crossed, I realise that I have made a very dangerous enemy. I do not have any idea of where I am going. Stripped of any reason to live, bereft of Ma and Da, ashamed of my complicity in the rape of Mary, I do not know what is in store for me. But I feel ennobled, moved by the animal's simplicity and extraordinary sensitivity and the only thing of which I am now certain is a resolve forming within me that I will seek a different life for myself, a way of expiating my desecrating crime.

I feel one with the animal in a way I never thought possible. I have joined 'the takers' all right but not in the way Kincaid understood. Speaking softly to Capaleen, I need her assurance now more than ever, we move together in the direction of Cork city and beyond.

the tumbling of lives

Graigue, County Cork

Early November, 1847

In which Peadar O'Brien reflects on the destruction of his home, village and Dúchas and is separated from his beloved daughter Mary

Peadar O'Brien

This is breaking my heart. Seeing those I know, some I taught in school and there they are pulling down our home. Dismantling a lifetime of memories. Stone by stone; Sod by sod; Beam by beam. That building is part of me. I remember choosing every stone in the wall. Carefully selecting the right one for form and stability. The thought of that, and of Brigid all those years ago. Full of hope and joy we were as we thought about our future together. I took great care over it, I remember. It was our own little bothán and we built it together with pride. Every part of it brought out Brigid's creativity and personality. She knew exactly where I should carve the neat cubby holes into the walls to store the pots and pans; She helped me design the falling table, the hanging dresser and the clevy above the hearth. It may have been a small, humble one-roomed place but it was ours. Now piece by piece it's been taken apart as I watch, hopelessly, from the roadside.

It was in the early morning they came, Kincaid swaggering at the front of them. He had managed to bring the constabulary with him, a show of force more to magnify himself than anything else. He took great pride in bellowing out the eviction notice he had gained from the magistrate. It was his moment of triumph. At long last, I could see him think, he was bringing me low.

But I have no time to regard him or be bitter. I was never going to resist of course. That would have been pointless. And I knew it was coming for a long time. Since the day he barged in after O'Connell died. He somehow had the upper hand after that. And of course the Poor Law Act making him and others liable for relief was all he needed. He was never going to stand for that. He's being going mad about the place, evicting those who have been tenants for years, clearing the land and reducing his liability at the same time.

I was not long waiting, late last month in fact, when he appeared at our door, again, after racking the rent, shouting,

"What the devil do I care about you or your black potatoes? It was not me that made them black. You will get two days to pay the rent, and if you don't, you know the consequences. Peadar O'Brien former schoolmaster. Pretentious Fucker. Ha-ha."

My only thought now is Mary. She seems curiously changed these days. Locked inside herself in a way I have never seen. The last two years have got to her, I suspect. The slow demise of our common life. Bless her, she is growing up into a strange, apocalyptic world. She needs my support now more than ever.

But at this moment, I need time. To absorb this. To say goodbye. I look at my friends, neighbours, companions and I see that a great fear has gripped them all and they have been broken. There is no music among us, no dancing, no celebration. All is quiet. And I feel it is up to me to stand here now for them. To look at this physical dismantling. To watch those who are busy tearing down, razing. To reflect on our passing. And to think deeply, to mourn. Things will never be the same again around here. The life we have shared together is gone now. The Fairs, the Markets, the Races. The companionship, the shared struggles, joys, births. Our wakes, the way we consoled one another in death. The strength we drew from our communal life. Péigín, Brigid, the Seanachaí, it would break their hearts to witness this. I see our bonds torn and atrophied in every stone removed from its perfect location and cast to the ground. This life, this precious life we have lived, and God knows did we take it all for granted, will be no more. It's gone.

And so I grieve in this moment for myself, but also for others who have not the strength to do so, for our memories, our ties, our connections. Those of us that survive will wonder if what we had was all a phantom. I see my neighbours so traumatised by this that they have forgotten who they were, who they are and who they can be. In deep silence, slow tears, wordless prayer I acknowledge and remember. For us all.

I have to sit down now on the stone wall on the other side of the boreen, Mary silent beside me. The day is passing and the late afternoon, autumnal sun is coruscating in its transcendental, exquisitely ethereal, incandescent light as it radiates across the meadow beyond the now broken house. Reaching the hill and wood in the near distance. Presciently, it picks out the crossroads at Glendule, and sparkles at the meeting of the Bride and Glashanabrook rivers.

Memory overtakes me and I am sitting here with Brigid, pregnant with our child in a late October evening just like this one, many years back, like a different epoch except the same light is gracing our horizon. The sounds come rushing back as swallows and swifts get ready for

     even small birds fly free

their great migration and we hear children playing across the valley, the peal of laughter lifting our spirits and acting as a precursor for our own as we await the birth of our child. It is a memory to hold onto. One I need to harvest. A promise of a future which can overcome the present.

Dusk has suddenly fallen around the both of us as I have been reflecting and it has become bitter. I am disturbed in my reminiscences by the nightly congregation of crows in the valley, our own valley, called from ancient times 'Gleann an Phréacháin'[1], the birds, as in the last act of every day, pour into the air above their rookery, a vast mass of thousands, roiling as if been tossed about by a storm. It's a thing that we have taken for granted here in our little valley. But now, today, it has a sombre air. Is it the last time I will see it? This tumult of thousands of crows in a mercurial swirl, with their gigantic roar, almost in protest at what is taking place below. But of course this is an illusion of my own creation. The crows have enacted this same spectacle daily for thousands of years, oblivious and without a care of what is taking place in the world below of us humans. What they have seen come and go. Stirred by this, I realise I have waited too long. We have to move.

"Thank you, Mo Stór. I needed to do this."

We rise together and move up through the village. Mary asks me to knock on doors. I know it will be futile. Our neighbours, our people have long since closed their homes on one another fearful, as they are, of the famine fevers. Each knock is hollow and empty; My voice comes back to me unconsoled.

We move together up the boreen out of the village and strike out for the road to Cork. Late in the evening, we huddle together, like we have not done since she was a small infant. Desperate for warmth under our shared blanket, we spend a night in troubled sleep.

Cork City,

December, 1847

I can't settle here. We've been here three weeks now and there is sickness all around. The snow has come. The same as last winter. That was like nothing we have ever seen. Bitter in its whiteness, it covers the streets and rooftops of the city. The buildings themselves, the many bridges over the river form ghostly shapes, widespread arms, beckoning us to our doom.

At every street corner, huddles of families lie prone, emaciated, dying. It's not the hunger that's killing them, though God even that's bad enough. It's the fever. There's a listlessness and apathy as whole swathes of people, particularly around the workhouse on the South Douglas Road, battle with vomiting and diarrhoea amidst the biting cold.

It's Mary I'm worried about. The longer we stay here the worse it's going to get. We queue every day at the Quaker's soup kitchen in Barrack Street. It barely keeps us going. We separate every morning looking for work, even for a place to stay, but so far it's been hopeless.

Today, however, something happens to give me hope. Walking on the quays, I am hailed by Cormac McCarthy riding a horse. It shocks me to the core. Firstly, why is he here and secondly on a horse? As he gets closer I recognise that it is Kincaid's horse.

When he dismounts, I reach out to him. He looks hesitant, tentative with me but I put that down to me being his former master and the strange times and big city.

"I was sorry to hear about your Ma and Da. They were good people. I'm sorry for your trouble."

He then tells me his story of escape from Kincaid and I whistle softly to myself in anxiety for him.

"You're a marked man, Cormac. That fella will hunt you down to kingdom come."

"Sure I know, Master O'Brien." Quaintly calling me by my schoolteacher name. "But I'll take my chances. I've been looking for you and Mary. It's no accident I found you. I want to give you this."

He reaches into his purse and draws out five sovereigns.

"Where in heaven's name did you get those," I ask.

"Well I sold Kincaid's saddle. I want Mary to have the money I got for it. It will pay for her passage."

    even small birds fly free

As he says this, I notice a troubled look cross his eyes. I can see that something must have passed between the two of them. But I also pick up that he is not going to tell me.

"Will you do that for me, Master O'Brien," he pleads.

"Sure I will. But what about you. What are you going to do now. It's not safe for you here in the city. There's no doubt in my mind that Kincaid won't rest till he finds you."

"You never said a truer word, sir. I'm off to join the Booleymen[2]. I think I will be a lot safer up the hills for a while. If you don't mind, I'll be off now. And thank you so much, sir for all your kindness towards me."

When Mary comes back and I relay the story to her, she has no words. I find this strange but know I should not pry. Anyway I want so badly that she does not protest but will take the money for her passage.

"No Da," she wails, "I can't leave you. We have to stay together."

"Mary, mo chroí, I can't protect or help you here. Your best chance is to take the money and buy a passage to New York. I can look after myself so much better, if I am not worrying about you. This will be the best for both of us. I can follow you later when things get better. We'll go to Cove in the morning and buy the ticket."

I have to admit it is a great relief to me that as we lie in a doorway on Carey's Lane that we now have the opportunity to get her far away from the devastation around us. That she accepts. I sleep better than I have in weeks.

Cove[3], County Cork

December, 1847

I break down when the Cambridge' moorings are released and she moves away from the dock. I have been strong up to this point. When I held her, frail and small as she seemed to me, for the last time. Alongside hundreds of others we were saying goodbye. The harbour full of desperate people looking to flee. Many left behind, forlorn, having missed the passage or unable to afford even steerage. A disconsolate, heartbroken melancholia overtaking them as they huddle together waiting for the next boat. The sun incongruously shining on this cold December morn.

When she had boarded and disappeared from view, I look out over the vast expanse of the cove, its beautiful coastline curving around towards its mouth, the lush green, verdant hills sweeping down to the bay. The land of her birth. She will never see it again.

She won't even have this last vista for consolation and comfort, cooped and locked as she is with the other passengers in steerage for her long voyage across the ocean. I cannot protect her now. I lost that capacity a while back. And I do not have the luxury of tears.

She was strong. Stronger than I expected, when we held one another for the last time to say goodbye. There was a grim determination about her. After the ticket was purchased, we had just enough to buy some oatmeal for the journey. And a few shillings for the moment of her arrival on the other side. She's in God's hands now. And I can do no more. Mary, mo Chuisle.

I heard this morning that some public relief works are starting in Glenville near home. So I will walk there and see if I am able for it. We made a promise to one another that we will try and survive and I will do my best by her in that.

even small birds fly free

leaving it all behind

Skibbereen, West Cork,

September, 1847

In which Pádraig O'Donovan tries to convince his brother to leave their homeland forever and has the good fortune to run into a radical Scottish journalist.

Pádraig O'Donovan

We've been talking about whether we should leave or stay for hours and getting nowhere. I'm not much of a one for talking myself. That's Caelan's way, really. I just want to be up and doing. But I have to listen to him, nonetheless. If I want him to come with me.

"They don't give a fuck about us. And we see that in every move they make. Just look at what their papers say. The Times. Punch. The Illustrated London News. They see us as ingrates. Lazy. Feckless. They're even depicting us as Apes.[1] So it's small wonder they keep changing their minds. About everything. One week they are championing relief works, next they're abandoned. And when they begin again we're paid by piece-rate. The fucking chaos. At the end of each day, the foreman measuring the ditch, sending his measurements to Dublin and us waiting four weeks for the calculations and the measly balance of our wages. Measly because we didn't have the tools in the first place and then the most of us half-starved and sick with the fever. Trevelyan worried we are taking him for a ride. As for soup kitchens, in the beginning they are there every day for all and then they disappear."

He hardly stops to draw breath, but continues on with a passion that always defines him. I regard him more these days. He has become precious to me. His young, slender frame, shock of long, curly brown hair, handsome face, deep-set brown eyes in which people often say they see his soul. My brother, Caelan O'Donovan.

"They even made a profit distributing the corn donated from America which was supposed to be for us," he continues, "Peel's fucking brimstone[2]. Inedible, giving us all stomach ache. But at least his government had a mind to bring some relief. This new lot, Russell and Trevelyan, they have it all worked out. Seeing the blight as an act of God, a benign judgement as far they are concerned, to teach us 'fucking peasants' how to take our nostrum. A good dose of hunger the very medicine to get us to knuckle down. They are claiming they have God on their side. May the devil make ladders out of their spines. My God, but O'Connell, the Lord have mercy on his soul, got it so wrong in giving support so that crowd could form a government. Leaving us powerless. In our own country."

I am deliberately letting him rant. I can see he needs it. We are sitting at the pump in the centre of town. The two of us. We have to hold on to one another now, be together. We're all we've got left. I see fear and frustration in his young eyes. He has to grow up fast.

The town itself has metamorphosed. It's no longer the bright, friendly, welcoming, musical town of our youth. Its long, winding streets and back-alleys used to team with life and 'divilment'. The town a jumping off point for Baltimore and the islands of Roaringwater bay. Its market days a time of revelry, gaiety and conviviality. And Caelan and I at the centre of it.

Death and desolation has marked its passage over the last two years. The longed-for harvests failed everywhere in the county; As night following day. Each Autumn, in a tumultuous twenty four hours, the rich, green tubers of the potato crop, pregnant with hope and sustenance, collapsed overnight into a fetid, black, gooey stench. A smell that inhabited our worst nightmares. It signalled the end of hope and consigned the town and surrounds to an uncertain future. The land itself had turned its back on us and spewed out its guts; Vomiting its entrails in nausea.

Of course, the havoc attracted voyeurs from afar. We had our fair share of them. Newspaper men from all over the world. In fairness, parts of that invasion did some good for a while. Drawing attention. In the beginning. But people soon get tired of compassion and they have reverted to type. Caelan is right in that. No one wants to be reminded of death and sickness for any length of time.

Now looking down the streets of our town is a grim prospect. Each doorway is filled with the spectre of skeletons. Families are wandering about in a daze. Lost and forlorn. Caelan and I have witnessed our fair share. We have often been recruited, in the last year, to transport emaciated remains of towns folk to the graveyard in Abbeystrowry. Carrying the coffins in a cart, the false bottoms opening at the grave pit to despatch the remains; The coffin taken back to town to be refilled. Soul destroying work.

It was in Abbeystrowry, we buried Ma and Da and little Aoife in April. It pains me now to remember it and then to look at Caelan, the only one left of kith and kin. We stood together that day, alone, on that ground. Incongruously, Spring breaking around us - Furze in full bloom

                    even small birds fly free

and a lark incandescent in song in the clear, blue heavens above. The gentle hill on the other side of the river Ilen and the woodland beyond dappled with light. The river coursing below us, wending its way to the Atlantic. For all the world, beckoning us, as a sentinel, to leave this god-forsaken place while we have a chance.

"O'Connell fucked up for sure," he continues, "Cancelling that monster meeting at Clontarf because he was afraid it would end in violence.[3] The English don't respond to anything else but violence. The only thing that will shift them is insurrection. My voice is with The Young Irelanders. We need to join forces and revolt."

This, of course, is what I'm afraid of. His passion and idealism leading him to revolutionaries and unrest.

"Caelan, for God's sake. That's not the answer. Look around you. People are broken, hungry, emaciated. There isn't strength in them to raise their voice. Not to mind respond to a call to action or violence. It's a pipe dream and it will only get you into trouble. Draw attention to you. Our task now is to survive. You can't change this system. Much though you might like to. Most times we can manage to make our way in it. But right now it's stacked against us. We have to get out. Look, we used to see emigration as banishment, as exile. We have to change our view on that. Now it becomes our passage to a better life. We have to take it."

I see him sink low on hearing me say this. I think he knows in his heart and soul that what I am saying is correct. His resolve breaks in front of me. It is hard to watch. Painful. Necessary. The light going out of him. I wonder will I ever see it there again. But from this moment on, we can make plans. I know now he will come away with me.

On the road, West Cork - Kerry,

September, 1847

A few days later we hear of a scheme of assisted emigration in Kenmare, over the county border in Kerry, and we set out on foot. We'll become Spalpíns again, like in our teens.

It took all my energy to keep Caelan stable as we trek through Bantry. The town suffering as badly as Old Skibb. We go by the Quay Road to avoid encountering the chaos around the Workhouse, overpopulated as it is, a crucible of disease, sickness and death. Caelan's hunger for justice will become inflamed again if he hears the barbarous cruelty inflicted on the townsfolk through Whiggery[4].

We make our way out the old mountain boreen up towards the Priest's Leap. And as we do, a weight falls off our shoulders. I feel grateful for the beauty of the landscape. The ruggedness of rock formations, the grasses wispily swaying, the rich and vibrant colours of the heather, the wind in our hair, the solitude, the extraordinary life that teems about us. It seems as if nature is in mockery at the failed and dismal civilisation below us in the valley.

For almost the whole journey, the whole time, we see the wild Atlantic beyond the rolling hills, beckoning, calling us. It strikes me that this is a pilgrimage, a saying goodbye to the countryside, the province that has nurtured us and we know instinctively that we should slow down, take our time, allow it to seep into our souls, our beings. We will need these moments, these memories for the tough days ahead.

Caelan comes into his own. His deep knowledge of our folklore, passed on by our Seanair[5], enriches our journey. All those days he spent foraging in his childhood make perfect sense now. With humour and bright intelligence, he points out and gathers wild asparagus, wild carrots, sometimes called Queen Anne's lace he tells me on account of the delicacy of their little flowers and the feathery divided bracts which surround them. Praiseach buí[6]-charlock he finds to enrich our porridge. And then he grounds broimfhéar[7] roots to add its succulent, sweet, liquorice taste to our oatcakes. Every evening we light a fire and cook and consume our simple meal. Then we lie back on the ground, contented, to take in the shape of clouds, marvel at them and see the stars roll around the heavens above us.

      even small birds fly free

Kenmare, Kerry,

September, 1847

After our sojourn on the mountain road, we arrive at the suspension bridge outside Kenmare on a beautiful, sun-kissed, September morn. The sight of it always takes our breath away. This morning we waste some time looking out toward the Atlantic beyond. We dream of being on a ship out there sailing to the new world. Caelan acting the fool jumping up and down on the timber struts to see the bridge sway. The cool air is enriched by the smell of seaweed from the bay and cut grass from the meadows sloping down to the ocean.

After some time, we move on into the town. Our memory of arriving here on market days is of bustling and vibrant thoroughfares; The town set out in its ornamental triangular shape of three streets. The carefully designed shop fronts, with their cornices, capping and mullions. Their fanlights, bright and decorative; each shop boasting a carriage lamp and ornamental sign. Standing in the square, it's always a joy to look down Main Street and breathe in the wide vista and proud shop fronts. The bustling crowds of market day, drovers, cattle and mayhem.

Today, however, it is eerily busy, populated with people from the surrounding districts, ragged, lean and emaciated, huddled in groups. They are awaiting the arrival of Tench, the Landlord's agent. Rumours abound of offers of assisted passage to North America. Many farmers of five acres or more have abandoned their homes in desperation, conscious that they will only qualify for relief by doing so. Gregory's clause[8] stipulating only those with less than a quarter acre will qualify for relief and assisted passage. Compelling farmers to give up their land or die of disease and hunger. Most seem to be reaching out to this slim hope of survival. An escape. A forfeit of dreams for a life away from their homeland.

The sea air invigorates the town. Its prominent position at the beginning of the Kerry peninsulas, its proximity to the mountains and the Killarney lakes still attracts the moneyed class and they can be seen in carriages leaving and entering - the grocers, drapers, ironmongers, saddlery, apothecary and bakers still thriving in the gloom. One world, divided in two.

"Dia Dhaoibh a chairde.[9]" We both turn at the same time to see this stocky man come towards us across the square.

"I'm Alex Somerville," he says as he gets closer. His accent strange to my ears. "And where are you gentlemen from. I can see you are not from the town."

Caelan laughs. We are used to Kerrymen wanting to know our business as soon as we cross the county border and turn up somewhere in their kingdom. But your man is not from round here from the cut of him. He must have assimilated fast. He has bright eyes and an inquisitive, gentle face. I decide to indulge him.

"We're the O'Donovan brothers. I'm Pádraig and this is Caelan," I gesture with my hand and ruffle Caelan's long, curly hair. "We've come over the hills from Skibbereen. We heard there may be a chance of assisted passage here in the town. Have you any knowledge of that?"

"Well. All the way from Skibb. Is it? You look like you could do with a pint of stout and a hearty meal. What would you say to me standing for you in the Arms itself. And you can tell me your story and I will tell you what I know. Is that a deal?"

I look on him with suspicion. It's a strange offer and I wonder what kind of a chancer he is and what we have to do to earn the grub.

"Don't worry, lad," he says, "I'm on your side and I've got scars to prove it. You're safe with me."

Thinking we might as well be hung for a sheep as a lamb, Caelan and I move with him down Main Street, weaving in and out of congregating groups; A look of fearful, vacant desperation evident in their eyes. We make our way to the Lansdowne Arms hotel.

The owner, Thomas McCarthy, greets him warmly as an old friend. Surveying us in tow, I can see hesitation in his eyes. However, it's clear Somerville has some clout as he gestures towards the snug and tells him it's free. We make our way there, past the oak-panelled door and bright stained glass windows of the partition.

"Proper introductions then," he says as we sit down. "For my sins, I'm a reporter and I write for the Manchester Examiner."

I can see Caelan freeze at this and I'm sure he's thinking the same way I'm thinking. Why would we want to furnish this man's coffers with stories of the pain of our people.

He laughs at the expression on our faces.

"I see it's not the first time you've met reporters. I know we are not everybody's cup of tea. But I have to make a living somehow."

     even small birds fly free

He chuckles to himself and at that moment the pints arrive on the table.

"If it helps I'm from poor stock in Scotland. My people are experiencing the same blight, famine and clearances as your people here. The big difference is that when they lost their homes they could move to the cities for work. Here you have nothing to fall back on."

I see Caelan fidget with the leather corner of the seat absent-mindedly, preoccupied with his thoughts.

"Is that what you mean when you tell us you have scars to prove your mettle." I hear him say.

Somerville regards him. I see him taken by the bright intelligence of my little brother. With that he takes off his jacket, turns around and lowers his shirt down from his back. We see lines, welts, deep scarring running diagonally from his left shoulder down his back.

"Ouch," I say, "Where did you get those?"

"Opening my big gob. I was in Scots Royal Greys in my youth. Before you were born I should say. When the Reform Act extending the right to vote was passed. There were riots. You've heard of the Chartists?"

We nod our heads, silently.

"I was with a battalion despatched to quell them.[10] I wrote to the newspapers at the time. My first bit of journalism so to speak. I said in the letter the army was more taken with protecting property than supporting people's rights under the Act. Naturally, they took a dim view of that and they court-marshalled me. I got a hundred lashes for my trouble. But the good thing was I was able to buy myself out of the army soon afterwards through the generosity of supporters who saw my punishment as politically motivated."

"Bloody hell," I say, "That's some story. It's like something out of a Dickens novel. I can't imagine going through that."

"A long time ago now. But you can see from it I have no truck with the English Establishment. Us Scots can be a belligerent lot."

His openness did the trick. Caelan and I free up and relax into the conversation. Maybe it's the porter but we begin to tell our stories of the last two years. Sometimes the memories catch in our throats. I think it's the first time we have acknowledged to ourselves the full horror of what we have been through and seen. And I see in Somerville's eyes and the way he listens to us that he understands and is truly sympathetic.

"I think it's important for you lads to know what has being going on here," he says, halfway through our stories. "The English government are more interested in seeing a massive social change in Ireland than in saving lives. By and large they think that you are lazy, that because you only grow potatoes, which in their eyes takes no time at all, they think you spend the rest of your days drinking and sleeping. They really don't spend any time thinking of you. Ireland, for them, has been one big experiment in conquest by plantation for hundreds of years. They gave your land away to their own people. And you have no security of tenure. So why in God's name, I'm thinking, would you try and improve your tiny couple of acres, if you can be evicted on a whim."

He represents a curious specimen to me. This man. To hear him, in his Scottish accent, reflect back to us in eloquent words what we already know ourselves. There's a strange comfort in that.

The food arrives at this point. Slices of beef, succulently arranged on the plate, heaps of gravy with potatoes and turnips. Caelan and I look down at the plate in wonder. God, I haven't seen meat in three years. It seems strange to the both of us, I'm sure, to be eating so well, while outside on the street people are starving. As if prompted by the food, Caelan says,

"But why won't they at least feed us? Why do they make it so difficult to even get relief work? And the pay hardly keeps one person alive. Not to mind his family."

Somerville was now in his stride. The passion which had got him into so much trouble in his youth lies undimmed, it appears to me, as he holds forth with us in that cosy snug, comforted as we are by the meal and pints lying, invitingly, before us.

"As I see it, there are two reasons. They think by giving you food, you will become dependent on them and then you will never change. And they will have to carry you as a burden indefinitely. But also they truly believe they have God on their side. They have this God-like idea of the market. They think it should not be interfered with. Most of them see the potato blight as an opportunity to change Ireland. Many even believe it comes directly from God to teach the Irish peasant about self-improvement. A providential act. If you like, in their opinion, you are the undeserving poor."

This strikes a sore point in Caelan.

    even small birds fly free

"But surely a wander down any street in any town in Ireland over the past couple of years would disabuse them of those notions."

"Sadly, most of the people we are talking about have never set a foot in the country. They see your landlord class, of course. Many of them absentee landlords. Swanning about London. The ones who historically were given your land. By the very same people who now despise them. All they see in them is indulgence and wastefulness."

Caelan now fully engages him.

"This new Poor Law is to make those landlords liable for our welfare. They want to tax them. Setting the amount by the number of tenants they have. If they know these people so well, how come they don't see straight away that they will immediately duck out of that accountability?"

"There's a simple answer to that. Politicians are stupid. And they are primarily only interested in their own and their party's welfare. There's been an economic depression in the last year and that has put a lot of strain on cities in England. They think if they have to continue to bail out Ireland, then they will have a revolt on their hands. English people in general have lost interest in the potato blight by now. And they have been told, correctly of course, that there is no blight with this year's harvest. They now think the famine is over. The ordinary English person doesn't know or care that you were so famished during the last God-forsaken winter that you were forced to eat your seed potatoes. And that you have no harvest. Government has decided the best way out of this is to make the Irish landowners pay for relief. They win both ways because they both avoid the bill themselves and dump it on these landowners whom they despise anyway."

Personally, I am tired of this continuing analysis of what is going on. Caelan is the one who wants to keep talking. I want to get on with our quest. So I chip in and say,

"What about this Lord Lansdowne? Here. In Kerry. We heard he was prepared to pay assisted passage to America. Did you hear anything of that?"

"Yes. But it won't help you. It's only for his tenants. And it really doesn't help them either. It's mostly a way for him to clear his land. The landlords have worked out that the income they get from farming the land themselves is double what they get from rent. So this potato blight is a Godsend to them. It means they can get rid of the lot of you. Off their land, so to speak."

But Caelan is not finished. He wants to plummet this thing some more,

"Tell me this. The blight has been everywhere in Europe. France, Holland, Germany. I hear in Belgium they lost ninety percent of their crop. What happened in those countries? Did they suffer the same way?

"No. Very early on their governments bought grain on the open market. To feed people who lost out."

"And why didn't the same thing happen here in Ireland?"

Somerville lies back on his seat. We've finished our meal. He is invigorated both by the food and the conversation. The snug with its oak panelling and windows, the green-leatherbacked seats, its warm enclosed cosiness has become the crucible of our thoughts.

"It's back to the same old story of economics. The English didn't want to compete in the open market for these foodstuffs as it would drive the prices up. So they didn't buy any grain then, thinking they could import enough Indian corn. When that didn't work out and they had to go back to the market, it was bare. There was nothing left. Bought up by other countries that had acted quickly. They had left it too late. As I said in the beginning you were not a priority for them."

"I'm tired of this," I say, "And I want out. As quickly as possible."

Caelan pounces on me. The conversation has again kindled his revolutionary spirit, "Pádraig, we can't let them get away with it. We have to fight. To protest."

"I'm inclined to agree with your brother in this, Caelan. It's a long way from Kenmare to Westminster. And you have no voice. You've had the most charismatic man of the 19th century in Daniel O'Connell on your side and they still haven't listened. What makes you think they would listen to you. It's a scandal, of course. In that you are correct. How the richest, most powerful Empire in the world can let people die like this. But you are dealing with a people who have perfected the art of ignoring what is happening to the people they have colonised. And they wallow together in illusory amnesia and blissful ignorance. Perfected over centuries of colonial rule. Their ordinary people brainwashed into thinking they are a civilising force. This will never change. It has been perfected for centuries and will run for centuries more. Your best bet is to leave, I'm afraid. Work your passage on a ship to Liverpool."

Caelan sinks again at this. Somerville looks at his forlorn state and as if to lighten the mood says,

                                even small birds fly free

"Tell me a bit about yourselves, lads. What did you do before the blight came along."

"We were Spalpeens really," I say, "Going from town to town in West Cork. Filling in wherever there was work. It was a great life. Carefree. And we're musicians, playing in Shebeens and Crossroads for our keep at times."

"Oh and what do you play?"

"Melodeon and Fiddle. I play the fiddle and Caelan plays the Melodeon."

"Well, well, well. I'm sure Thomas has instruments behind the bar. Your own are gone a long time ago I'm guessing."

"Sure enough. They were the first things to go. We haven't played in two years."

"Would you play now? I'm sure I could raise some interest and maybe you might get a couple of lops." Somerville gets up and leaves the snug. He isn't gone for long. When he comes back it's with both instruments. He tells us Thomas would be happy for us to play for his customers. We tune up and then move into the main lounge.

It's early evening by now and a fair group of wealthy people have come for a meal. They look expectantly at us. It's been years since we've done this and we are nervous. We've never played in front of such an audience. We start the performance slowly with a couple of reels and polkas to set the mood. I look across at Caelan and see his brow is wrapped in concentration. But I also see his spirit rise with the music. He's in his element. Captured by the thing he loves to do more than anything else in the world. The diners warm to us and very soon there are people on the floor dancing. Incongruously in a depleted town, there is some joy for the moment. It's as if we have released a pressure valve like on one of these modern steam engines and the mood of the evening and the faces of the diners metamorphose into a Bacchanalian frenzy. We play and play, digging into our repertoire. Jigs, Kerry slides, hornpipes, reels, polkas

Towards the end of the night, Caelan reaches into his jacket pocket for his tin whistle. I leave him to it as he plays this new song 'Sliabh na Mban'. Halfway through he breaks into song and tears well up in my eyes. When will we do this again, I wonder, as he sings with a full voice and heart,

"Alone all alone by the wave-washed strand
And alone in a crowded hall
The hall it is gay and the waves they are grand
But my heart is not here at all
It lies far away by night and by day
To the times and the joys that are gone
But I never will forget the sweet maiden I met
In the valley near Slievenamon"

Somerville leaves his seat at the end and amusingly circles the lounge with his cap. Collecting 'lops' for us as he calls it - Where did he learn Cork slang? Is there no end to the man? We see him stop at each table and engage. He appears shameless and the diners are embarrassed and cajoled into parting with a farthing, half-penny or penny.

When he gets back to us, he has collected a full twelve shillings, so persuasive is he. He is as happy as we are. There in our hands, by the grace of God, the fare for our passage to Liverpool. We look at one another. We don't know how to thank him.

"Off you go lads," he says, "Safe passage to you." And with that he claps our backs and is gone. Our Saviour. We will never see him again.

even small birds fly free

in the mountains

Sheep's Head, West Cork,

April, 1848

In which Cormac McCarthy finds refuge in the mountain on Sheep's Head peninsula and communes with the many who did not survive the Great Hunger

When he leaves Cork city behind him, Cormac breathes a sign of relief. He feels safer, travelling by night along back roads, westwards towards the mountains and peninsulas in the west of the county. He remains fearful of being discovered, however. After all, he remains an unusual sight. A Gasún[1] like him on a beautiful mare like Capaleen. During the day, he rests in hidden copses or in small valleys, away from the misery and from prying eyes. He learns to trust Capaleen's intelligence and give her freedom to graze.

The horror of what they pass during those nights on the road almost overwhelms him. His people reduced to starving, fever-struck wraiths populating the boreens. It is impossible to determine whether the bodies he passes are dead or alive, huddled as they are, often, together in a ditch. He needs Capaleen then to keep going dependent as he is on her strong, compassionate energy to give him courage.

He heads for the Sheep's Head peninsula. He knows from tales told of old that it is there he will find Booleymen, Drovers, who use the vast acres of the hills of the peninsula to graze their cattle in the summer and host their sheep and goats in winter.

He has been here for four months now. Living in these hills. In a small Booley[2], hidden by a cairn. It is sheltered from the prevailing winds most of the time. The booleymen had taken him in but looked at him suspiciously wondering what his story might be. In the beginning before he gained their trust, he was always accompanied by one of their number, Éamon. An often-silent, wizened old man but fit as a fiddle. When it was recognised that Cormac was hard-working and honest, they left him to it and Éamon returned down the mountain to pass the harsh winter months in his permanent home on the shoreline.

Cormac settles into his life easily in the hills. It becomes his retreat. From the place he settles at the top of the mountain he can see both sides of the peninsula, Bantry Bay on one side, Dunmanus on the other. Next to the Booley is a field in which Capaleen grazes. The Booleymen provide supplies to help tide him over the winter months.

"We can't give you any wages," Éamon had told him, when he asked the booleymen for work. "We can give you food, shelter and hay for

          even small birds fly free

the horse." They see the value of Capaleen of course and recognise that on horseback Cormac will be much more able to account for their small flock of sheep and goats. Simple people, they never ask him questions about himself and more importantly, the horse. Conscious as most of them are of their own chequered past.

The landscape beguiles Cormac. It feels daily as if he has entered an elemental world. Lost from man and human habitation, he is content in a way he has not been for some time. The rhythm of each day is different. The weather sees to that. Sometimes, stretches of tempestuous storms, hail lashing against the mouth of his Booley. On others, the sun rises and sends a beckoning light through the clump of furze which acts as a door. He keeps himself warm. There is an endless supply of gorse to light fires and turf from the surrounding peatland to give comfort from the howling gales. He makes a fresh, soft bed of heather to lie on and the booleymen have given him a sheepskin for cover at night to keep him snug.

He does not lack companionship. Wildlife surround him and as winter gives way to spring the comfort it provide grows each day. He has his favourites, the song thrush and the wren. On the horizon, in both bays, he sees cormorants, guillemots, razorbills, shags and seals. Swallows and swifts have returned in the last couple of weeks. On the odd day, when the sea is calm, he can pick out a pod of whales, their tail fins beating the waters out on the ocean. There are a pair of hares on the other side of his hill. He loves to surprise them in the morning as they race to the haven of their form. At night, he can hear owls calling.

The landscape is a profusion of colour. Bell heather, gorse, sedge, furze, moor grasses and bracken. Even in winter the warm prevailing wind off the Atlantic brings early arrivals, daffodils and primroses. But it is the sky which transports and intoxicates him. The low lateral light of the winter sun generating rainbows in raindrops. Cobwebs glisten and sparkle in the hedgerows, proudly illustrating their filigree shapes like the most exquisite lace. There are times in each day when he sees the transcendent face of God mirrored in the small and beautiful details of his new neighbourhood.

He cannot escape his phantoms though. It's almost as if he is drawn to them, inexorably. They appear before him as the mist rises from the sea in the morning. Thousands of faces, calling out in anguish, begging him not to forget, to remember. Mary O'Brien is often prominent among them. He sees her prostrate on the ground, helpless; Only this time not with her face turned to the side to eliminate presence. Now she silently looks at him and her sea-green eyes have a haunted and haunting expression in them and face him daily with a question mark. Why did you stand and stare at my defilement? My violation by this man?

Nightly he is also visited by the same terror. Whether at those moments he is awake or asleep he cannot say for sure. Then visions of Mary appear again with the same wild, questioning of his complicity; His feet are locked into immobility and his mouth is struck dumb. He feels like he is being submerged and it takes all his energy to force himself back into consciousness. This leaves him afraid to sleep as each time he lies down, exhausted by his labour he can only anticipate another journey into hell. But in the end, he is always so tired at the end of each day that he slips quickly and fatefully into another tryst with his demons.

Each daybreak as morning arrives the phantoms dissolve but his heart and spirit remain heavy. He seeks out the waters of Glanlough and sits there, waiting. He discovered early on, apparitions which bring him a strange sense of commune and certainty at the lakeside, in the mist. His people often come to him there, veiled in a mantle of fog. In this assignation he embraces them and he hears stories of their abandonment and rejection. Neighbours turning their backs in fear; friends, relatives left to die without comfort, prayer. He speaks out loud about the need each had to survive the tumult but he knows his words are without substance. The common life they had previously shared, which had enveloped them has been torn to shreds. The poison of reproach and self-hatred, seeps out of him and into the soil. He knows he must make his peace with the common neglect he was part of, with his people, with Mary. He needs forgiveness. The pain and despair of this gripping him. Firstly, to forgive himself. But he also knows, it will take a lifetime.

The world is raw to him in the mountains but that brings with it its own enormous comfort. There is no pretence among these rocks. Here, he can reach out and touch the elements. There is a profound intimacy in his interaction daily with the cosmos and it is in those encounters that he seeks redemption.

As Spring moves towards Summer, he realises his time on his own is coming to an end. The Booleymen and women will come up on Mayday. They have already told him that this is a cause for great celebration. He is not sure if he is ready for company yet. But he knows

            even small birds fly free

now he will endure. And then he also takes comfort that come November, just six months away he will have the mountain back to himself again.

Just days before the Mayday celebration, a strange thing happens to him. While riding Capaleen and searching for a sheep that had wandered, he found himself moving towards the edge of his usual boundary. He took himself up a nearby hill to scan for the missing sheep. When he reached the top, he saw fall away from him, on the other side, a long beautifully constructed dry-stone wall travelling down into the valley and up an escarpment on the other side. Shaped like a piece of art it seemed to him like a monument. A folly. There could be no useful function to it. It simply separated one field of gorse from another. He realised immediately of course that this was one of those famine relief projects he had heard about. Where poor, starving evicted tenants were given work for corn and a small stipend. What was it they got? Fourpence a day he thinks.

Looking now at the architecture of this wall, he is overwhelmed. Whether it was because of his own trauma; His many culpable acts of betrayal; His own need for forgiveness. He cannot tell. But he finds himself gazing across Dunmanus Bay. The horizon seemed to fall away and he travels in his mind's eye to Schull, Baltimore, Clonakilty, Kinsale, beyond Cork, Waterford and Wexford; Across the Irish Sea until it comes to rest in Westminster. There before him are arraigned men, entitled men who make up the rules. The English Parliament. And their Queen - Elizabeth. Who couldn't find it in their shrivelled hearts to reach out and provide assistance, simple charity, basic food to survive until his people discover better times. Hearts which had been shrunk by years of Empire, years of seeing themselves as some kind of master race who looked on mere natives with disdain and turned their backs. Men who had profited from two hundred years of making slaves of other men. Across the world. Somehow, magnanimously, he feels sorry for them. For their narrow lives. For the cancer of bitterness that has devoured them and will eventually, he is sure, engulf their nation.

As he rides down beside the wall, he is enthralled by its beauty and craftsmanship. Each course of rocks balanced on the course below, each stone chosen and selected and keyed in so well that this shrine will remain in place for centuries. A cromlech for those who slaved and died in its construction.

He dismounts from Capaleen and kneels beside the wall and with all his heart cries out to the heavens beseeching mercy for those obdurate, callous men and their Queen, hundreds of miles away, over the sea,

"Lord forgive them for they know not what they do."

Mayday eve, Éamon arrives, up from the coast. His retreat is over. Éamon looks him over and with more words than he had ever uttered before, says,

"I see you have been communing with our dead. You went to Glanlough and saw them in the mist of the mornings. That's not where you will find them, of course. That's not where they are waiting for you. They're inside you now, a bhuacaill. They survive only in you. And you will survive only through them. From now on, you will find your strength only through them. No-one will be able to take that strength away from you. With their memory you will be able to do things you never dreamed of."

Éamon's words resonate powerfully within Cormac's soul. He is strangely comforted by them.

Later, the rest of the booley men and women arrive. It's May Day. In the evening they strike up their instruments, fiddles, banjos and bodhráns. There is joy, laughter, music, songs to welcome in the coming Summer. The men are strong and agile, even carefree. There is beauty, charm, grace in the women. One of their number, a young vibrant Cailín catches Cormac's eye and elicits a tenderness and desire in him, which is devoid of all self disgust and reproach. Maybe there is hope for him yet. He becomes bewitched, charmed, captivated, spellbound and finds himself moving towards her.

Surely, he thinks to himself "I can make my home here among these graceful men and women and through that keep my own people alive."

        even small birds fly free

from anywhere to nowhere

Glenville, County Cork,

March, 1848

In which Peadar O'Brien joins a working gang building a useless road and finds unexpected joy

The haggard, emaciated, hollow-eyed group had been cutting into this rock face for two months now. They are unrecognisable as human, poorly clad, slow in movement as they clamber through each day. Rising twenty feet above their heads, the rock face stretches for a hundred yards into the distance.[1] The men hammer at it, daily, with iron mallets striking wedges until large pieces give way and hurtle to the ground. For days afterwards, these large, fallen boulders are broken into smaller, more malleable pieces. The women gather the handiwork into baskets to spread on the road some ways up ahead. The road is being cut alongside the river Coom and Bride. Rocks quarried from the cliff face providing its foundation and stability. This road starting anywhere, leading and ending nowhere.[2] A metaphor for the villagers lives right now. Pointless yet making an important point. Trevelyan will not trust them with charity, thinking if he gave them alms, they would never lift a finger or work again.

On his arrival, on his first day here, having made the difficult journey back from Cove, the foreman Jones gives him a quizzical look. Peadar recognises him, of course. One of Kincaid's henchmen.

"Well if it isn't Peadar O'Brien," he declares. "I thought we had seen the back of you. How the mighty have fallen."

There is cruelty in his behaviour. He carries a whip which he likes to crack over the heads of the workforce if he thinks they are slacking. All the while and known to all that he pockets the balance of wages which are calculated at piece rate in the Dublin office of Public Works and meant to be disbursed. It is received weeks later. So, with equanimity, he sees it as his. For his trouble. There is little anyone can do.

Peadar refuses to let his mind rest on these dismal thoughts, on any form of protest. He knows that in a crisis, in a new dispensation, it is those who accept the new reality who will survive. Those that rant and rail against the prevailing conditions capitulate and are consumed by it. He promised Mary he will survive and that's what he plans.

Daily, he looks for some meaning in the mundanity of what is expected of him; From dawn to dusk, every hour, every minute. Beating large rocks with a hammer until he creates a mound of smaller rocks; Which are then loaded into the baskets of those charged with laying the road. The road to nowhere.

He also shuts his eyes to the misery around him. He refuses to engage. Unusually for him he ignores whole families, emaciated and desperate, labouring for their four pence wage and a handful of Indian corn. A pall of sickness envelopes the workforce and regularly people keel over and die, to be dragged onto carts and taken to Doonpeter cemetery on the other side of the river and up the hill; Overlooking the valleys of Graigue and Glenville. The place he called home.

The landscape has changed beyond recognition in the last six months. The people on the neighbouring Glenville estate have all left. Bought out by Hudson the Landlord, who also paid the passage to America for each of his tenants. Now as Peadar looks over the land, nothing is left of that village. The ten houses were tumbled soon after evictions took place and their dry stone walls used to build a majestic enclosure circling the Manor House. The foreign nature of the new landscape helps him shut off his feelings. There is nothing left to remind him of what has been.

His immediate neighbours in Graigue were not so fortunate. By a cruel twist of geography and birth, their absentee landlord, unlike Hudson in Glenville, abandoned them to their fate. Kincaid, of course, wasted no time. Families he had known for years, long gone. If he thinks about it at all, Peadar fears for all of them. They were left with nothing and most he heard died on the roadside in the frozen, wet ditches of the bitter winter that followed the mass eviction. There's nothing left of the village structure either. Kincaid cleared the land and Peadar can already see cattle grazing on it. Determinedly he eliminates these thoughts. He knows to entertain them will drain him of energy. Benefiting no-one.

The workforce are strangers to him. He recognises no-one. Most travel from districts as far away as Mallow and Macroom. Many walk eight or ten miles a day before they even start work. It's difficult to look at their gaunt and haggard state so he deliberately keeps his head down and keeps himself to himself.

Today however a woman catches his eye. He is mystified and can't explain why. There is something about her that captures his imagination. Her quiet dignity. He sees deep suffering etched in her face. Yet she carries herself with immense grace as she goes about her work. Twice this morning she arrives at his side to fill her basket. And he is taken

                    even small birds fly free

by surprise. Both times. He has not had feelings like this for decades. The second time she picks up the stones he has broken and places them in her basket, he looks into her eyes, azure blue, startling, with a depth of soul that seizes his breath. Shaken, he is, for ten minutes afterwards. He cannot account for what is happening to him.

He watches her often during the remainder of the week. She is largely unaware of him or indeed anyone else and seems to work as if in a dream. Yet there is a lithe sensuality in her mien which captivates him. At the end of each day he notices she moves away from the site in a different direction to everyone else. She crosses the river at Black Stones and seems to be heading towards Doonpeter Well. She looks broken as he watches her cross the meadow on the other side of the river. Mystery surrounds her. Part of him wants to follow her and find out more about her but he knows that would be an encroachment. She deserves her privacy. So he exercises restraint and turns away, moving to his own place of refuge.

He has built himself a small Scalpeen down by the river. There are some big rocks there and he used the indent of one to provide the shape of a small dwelling. Gathering large branches, he made a simple, waterproof structure. Hay he stole from the barn in the Manor, late one night. He spends the early evening and each Sunday stockpiling firewood, knowing it is essential to keep the Scalpeen warm and dry. Sometimes he raids the bog and carries back some turf. Each evening he cooks a simple porridge of Indian corn. He forages for wild greens every night, lucky to discover a spot nearby where he can harvest winter chanterelle and hedgehog mushrooms. He religiously keeps some of the mash he makes for the morning, which he eats cold before moving up the hill. Back to the point where work was left off the evening before.

On Saturday, she doesn't turn up at the relief works. Peadar is disturbed by her absence. And alarmed that he is. Without drawing too much attention, he discovers that her name is Eileen. Surprisingly a number of people know her. The women whisper silently of her tragedy.

"..............Her husband dying of fever in '45 and leaving her with a young son and daughter," He overhears one of the women.

Another takes up the refrain. "Both of them died a couple of months ago when fever swept over the township of Ballyhooley. He hears local people say they were her life and soul. She bore them late, in her thirties after a long wait."

This explains the deep sadness he sees in her piercing, blue eyes.

It being Saturday, Jones calls it a day early at four o'clock; Eager, Peadar imagines to head off to some Shebeen or other. Peadar had always seen him as a drinker. A way to deaden the perversity of his life.

As soon as it is down-tools time, Peadar heads for the stepping stones, following the pathway he had seen her take each day. His immediate instinct to head for Doonpeter. He climbs the hill slowly. The late March sun on his back. The air crisp and bright. Spring announcing itself in the loud, sweet cacophony of birdsong accompanying his steps. Primroses, daffodils are strewn throughout the meadow.

When he reaches the surrounding wall of the cemetery, however, the atmosphere changes. He clambers through a gap in the ditch. Spread over the graveyard are small rocks driven into the ground, a poignant reminder of grief and loss. Gravestones of the poor. Each one committed to memory by loved ones. Many are of unbaptised children who were not permitted to be buried in consecrated ground. Parents forced to bury them secretly in the dead of night. A sadness overtakes him at the lack of fáilte, welcome, charity. He rails in his spirit at this heretical notion of the Creator.

Then he sees her lying on the ground, prostrate, by two small rocks which are driven into the grassy soil. On the other side of the graveyard. His first thought that he is too late. She is gone from this world. When he reaches her, though, he finds her weak but breathing. He presses his hand to her forehead and is relieved that she has no temperature, no fever. She is barely conscious. Her condition due to exhaustion; mental and physical; Hunger its relentless driving origin and force.

"I am going to carry you, mo stór," he whispers into her ear. "Be patient with me. To where it is warm and dry. Where you will be safe. Trust me."

He lifts her gently on his back, discovering that she is as light as a feather. As kindly and tenderly as he can manage, he bears her down to the hill, taking his time, humming a lullaby as he walks.

'Tis the last rose of summer,
Left blooming alone;
All her lovely companions
Are faded and gone;
No flower of her kindred,
No rose-bud is nigh,

  even small birds fly free

He shuffles gingerly over the stepping stones until he reaches his Scalpeen. She is conscious now as he props her carefully on the straw bed, her back resting against the rock.

"I am going to light a fire, mo stór, to warm you up. I will make a little soup for you and then you must rest."

He sets to. Busy with the firewood and turf he scavenged from the bog. Soon he has a simple soup prepared with as much nourishment as he thinks she can handle. Surprisingly she responds well and eats enthusiastically. When she is finished, he lays her on the straw bed.

He feeds the fire during the evening, bringing a temperature to the Scalpeen that it has not been at before. He thinks he needs to get the chill out of her bones. He cannot take his eyes off her. She is so beautiful, resting there. When it is time for his rest, he is embarrassed. At first, out of decorum he thinks he should try and sleep sitting by the makeshift door, his back against the structure. But as the night gets colder, he knows, practically that their bodies will be warmer together.

"Forgive me, mo stór, but I think I should hold you," Shyly and discreetly, he lies beside her. He feels her melt into his arms. He is taken aback, Surprisingly there is an ease, almost a recognition, between them. Within minutes they are both sound asleep.

When dawn breaks, he wakes, rises and feeds the fire. She sleeps on and he is glad. As it's Sunday, he has the day to take care of her. He makes some more soup and when she wakes he takes it to her. She receives it gratefully. There is a serenity in her presence. It's as if they have been together for some time. After she has eaten she lies again and sleeps soundly for the remainder of the day.

At four in the afternoon, she wakes with a start. With a look of terror in her face.

"What's the matter, mo stór," he whispers.

"I must get to my children for I have abandoned them," she says and rises immediately and moves towards the door.

He knows he cannot do anything to stop her and follows behind as she makes her way to the stepping stones. He calls to her softly, letting her know he is following her. But she is preoccupied in thought and seems not to hear him.

Within ten minutes they are in Doonpeter again. Surprised as he is by her pace and energy. He watches her make her way to what he now knows are her childrens' graves. He watches her, solicitously for a while, fearful he is intruding on a private tryst. Then she speaks to him.

"It breaks my heart to be apart from them. There are times when I want to rip up the soil between me and them to hold them just one more time in my arms. It is all I can do to stop myself. I am afraid wild animals and dogs will dig them up. I have seen too much in the last two years. It's all I can do now to protect them."

This stuns him. He can see her pain and is powerless to ease it.

After some time, he whispers to her softly, "It's important you stay well then, mo stór. So you can protect them. You will not survive out here in the cold. You need to stay warm and be able to sleep."

He watches her to see if what he is saying is reaching beyond her debilitating grief. He is caught in conflicting thoughts. Is what he is saying helping or trivial? He does not want to hurt her, yet it breaks his heart to look at her so vulnerable, in this cold makeshift graveyard, on the top of a windswept hill presiding over a now godforsaken valley. Yet he presses on helplessly. When he thinks she is ready to hear more he says,

"Tonight, I can cover their grave with rocks. We can be confident that no animal will be able to violate them after that. Would you let me do that?"

He waits for her to absorb what he is saying. Eventually she looks up at him with those beautiful, yet sad, doleful eyes and nods in approval. A sob catches in his throat. He is touched she trusts him.

As she watches and sensitive to her every movement, he begins to gather rocks from the field beyond. Large granite pieces. These he places reverently, thoughtfully and solemnly on their graves. The act itself further making him aware of a deep sense of her loss. Is he locking her children further way from her? A deep commitment forming within him that he wants to bear it with her; To somehow, if he can, nurse her through this crucible of pain, this circle of hell that life has prepared for mothers who have lost their children.

When he finishes, he looks over towards her and says,

"Eileen, you can come here every day as a vigil. I can take care of the work. I would like to take care of you. And next Sunday, when I have time again, I will move the Scalpeen up the hill next to the graveyard."

even small birds fly free

After a few moments, she looks up at me. Tears are brimming in her eyes.

"You would do that for me, Peadar?"

"Willingly." He moves towards her and places his arms around her. She slumps towards him and begins to sob, her body heaving with the effort. After some time she begins to ease. The evening is drawing in and it's getting cold.

"Eileen, mo stór, we need to go back to the Scalpeen now. We need to eat and sleep. You can return in the morning."

He waits with bated breath. Hoping against hope that she will have the courage to leave. After some time, she moves her head away and looks into his eyes and agrees. She rises slowly and moves towards the graves, now covered with a mound of dark grey, granite rocks. She bends to kiss the pile, turns, reaches out for his hand and together they make their way down the hill to the Scalpeen.

They settle into a rhythm during the following week. Waking early and after eating the leftovers, he makes his way up the hill from the river to the Relief Works. He cannot stop himself from looking back towards her and sees her gather herself and make her way towards Doonpeter.

His day now takes on a different level of meaning. He is working for Eileen. He is supporting her to survive, grieve and gain strength. He looks forward to the short evenings they spend together, arriving, as they often do, at the same time at the Scalpeen. The ritual of lighting the fire, preparing and cooking the basic meal forms a bond between them, deeper than words. They lie together at night. His immediate sense of her difficulty being separated from her children and often comforts her with words and soft lullabies. He learns their names, Ciara and Oisín and he loves to listen to her as she talks about them and remembers them.

On Sunday, they set about building another shelter near the graveyard. Eileen discovered a fallen Elm tree in the copse near Doonpeter during the week. The absence of tenants in the surrounding district means it has not been stripped bare since it was felled by a thunderstorm. The wide girth of its bole lying on its side provides a perfect foundation shape for their handiwork. They gather and break saplings, careful to measure size and girth. Often she points out tiny details of shape and texture which need correcting and Peadar adjusts. He recognises Péigín in her and is conscious of the deep, hidden, practical wisdom women pass on to one another through the generations. As an osmosis. As they work, he tells her about Péigín, Brigid and Mary. The women in his life. She touches him gently as he reminisces.

When the architecture is complete and they can stand back and view its simple lean-to shape, they take a break. He lies on the grass of the meadow and Eileen makes her way to the grave. It's her necessary moment of private reflection, a vigil she has promised herself she will keep.

In the afternoon, they set about making the roof secure and waterproof. The woodland is rich with various mosses; wavy-beard and wavy-leaved, broom-moss; spike and stone mosses and sphagnum. Following her example, he finds himself decorating the roof. He amuses himself thinking how differently he approached the covering on the Scalpeen down by the river. With Eileen it becomes an adventure in artistic expression. At one point, as she is foraging in the woodland for moss, she comes across an old Birch stump. She summons him and explains that the bark peels easily and can be used it as roof shingles. They set to work together stripping the bark in long sheets.

Towards the end of the afternoon as they finish, arm in arm they look at their creation; a rich tapestry of colours and textures. In an extraordinary way the simple structure exhilarates them. They search the copse for dry saplings that are shaped and wedged to create a makeshift floor. As evening approaches they carry the hay and logs up the hill to their new home. Exhausted they light a fire, cook a simple meal and collapse in sleep.

The following weeks take on a graceful pattern. He leaves her in the morning and on return, she is ready to greet him with a fire and hot food. Three weeks on, he returns and she is nowhere to be seen. He immediately moves through the gap into the graveyard but she is not there. He searches the copse thinking she may be collecting wood. But he does not find a sign of her anywhere. After an hour and in the gathering dusk, he begins to panic. Where is she? With a dawning realisation, he knows now he cannot live without her. In such a short time, she has taken hold of his life and turned it upside down.

As night begins to fall, he sees her climb the hill. With an overwhelming feeling of relief he rushes down to help her. She is carrying a bag of turnips.

"I'm sorry," she says, "I heard that there were turnips going cheap in Watergrasshill and I thought I should go."

		even small birds fly free

He laughs in relief and joy at her courage and energy.

Later in the night, he is wakes with a start. She wakes also and looks at him with concern. He tells her, haltingly of the panic that he felt in the afternoon when she was nowhere to be seen. The overwhelming realisation that he has fallen in love with her. His dear, sweet Eileen. And the thought of her disappearing; Of never seeing her again? That would have broken him. As they lie together, he confides all this with her and more, tears streaming down his face. She reaches for him tenderly and kisses him warmly.

"Sure where would I go, Peadar, mo muirnín[3]. My life is with you now. We are bound together, for better or worse."

There is a release between them then and their bodies reach for one another, hungry to coalesce, to express vulnerability, to be intimate. They make love gently, tenderly secure in the tiny Scalpeen they had built together, just three weeks previously. As sleep overtakes them, Peadar thinks of the outrageous words of Saint Augustine; His 'felix culpa' and reflects that in an extraordinary way this plague, this great hunger is also a 'happy fault' that conspired to bring her to him. He has not been as full of joy as this for years.

part two
emigration and refuge

the wretched refuse

The Hold of Ship Cambridge

December 1847, January, 1848

In which Mary O'Brien develops strategies to survive in the hold of a coffin ship, makes a discovery and has a disastrous arrival in New York.

When she leaves her Da's arms on the docks at Cove, Mary knows she must not weaken. Resolved, she withdraws from his embrace and walks away. She knows she cannot even look back at him for just one last time. That would not change her into a pillar of salt like Lot's wife. But something far worse. She would become a broken, disintegrated creature who would take others with her to hell. No. She knows she must stay strong. If her dear Da knows he has not been able to protect her from his nemesis, Kincaid, it will break him. Just another few steps to fulfil the charade. She counts them determinedly. For his sake. If he is to survive, he has to believe that she will also and this is the best way to prolong that hope. Afterwards she can crumble and let go. She knows she has been living in a dream world, a kind of non-existence, a nether region of reality. Blotting out from memory what happened in Lackendarragh woods. Keeping Da content and herself with the appearance of a dour sanity. All that can collapse when safely away from her Da.

The crew shepherd the passengers on board. It all happens in a blur. Later Mary can't recall much of it. Her Da gone from her; Cork and Ireland a memory. At the top of the gangway, they are commanded to stick out their tongues for an examination. Goodness knows, she wonders, what these people are looking for. Then they are herded down into the hold. Immediately the dank, fetid, lifeless air engulfs her and in the dim light, she tries to make sense of where she is. Slowly shapes begin to be distinguished. She can make out the form of makeshift, wooden bunks which are already overpopulated and cramped. Passengers who boarded at Liverpool. Wan, sickly faces peer out at her in the gloom. Mostly hostile in their demeanour, she finds it hard to look back.

She circles the hold many times looking for somewhere to rest. These people will be her neighbours for the next six weeks. She can hardly recognise them. Irish faces all, without a doubt. But without the grace, verve, winsomeness of her people. Stripped of hope, contact with the land and without the common rituals of celebration, they all look reduced; forlorn, empty shells. At that moment, reality implodes on her consciousness. What folly to undertake this journey on her own. How

                    even small birds fly free

can she survive in this inhospitable environment if she cannot even find space to lay her head.

After several trips round the dark and cavernous hold, she hears a kindly voice say, "A stór, tar isteach anseo linn" ("come in here with us, pet.") She looks over and sees the bright, round face of a mature woman in her forties, surrounded by four children, encamped on a six foot by six foot, lower bunk. "Go raibh maith agat," she gestures to her and with relief climbs on board their little platform, a life raft in a sea of abandonment. "Tá fáilte romhat." (You're welcome). She wonders at the miracle of her kindness. To surrender what little space she has for her own and give comfort to another.

The dream state in which she has been immersed is plunged into a nightmare shortly after she makes herself comfortable in the small space. With a loud, scraping sound, the door access to the deck is shifted into position and the hold is plunged into total darkness. For all the world she imagines it like the closing of a giant coffin lid on those who have passed on. Screams of terror erupt from all corners as people try to grasp what has taken place. The suffocating air, the lack of light, the fear of a future in this blackness all conspire to invade Mary's own defences and she breaks down in an anguished sobbing from what has overtaken her these past few weeks. Yet even still, conscious and in a way grateful for the children on the bed beside her, she stifles her sobs. She turns her back on the family that have given her shelter and expiates her anguish as quietly as she can, her head firmly pressed against the upward stanchion of the bunk; Digging into the post, the pain of the pressure an anchor to reality and survival, lest she be consumed altogether by memory and loss. The whole structure of the ship starts to move as it leaves the dockside. Mary lies down eventually and the gentle sway of passage out of Cork harbour lulls her into a comforting slumber.

She awakes, hours later, to high-pitched screams of terror, the ship roiling in all different directions, upwards it seems almost to the perpendicular and swaying side to side like it will capsize. In the blackness, which is now semi-lucent, oil lamps flicker and sway frighteningly. Here and there, she can make out terrified faces; some sprawled over the side of bunks to retch and vomit violently. The acrid, acerbic smell of sick and hysterical fear overwhelming her senses. The children in the bed beside her grasp their mother for comfort and security. Their mother looks at Mary with kindness.

"Ná bí búrtha leanbh. Níl ach an ghaoth 's na tonnta i gcéist. Ba sheacht measa ar dtríall o Learbhall na é seo." (Don't worry, my child. 'Tis only the wind and the waves. The crossing from Liverpool was seven times worse.)

Mary marvels at the serenity of this stranger. She can see she is being strong for her children. And generously she is also extending that shelter and comfort. They get to talking. Nóra Flanagan her name hailing from County Roscommon. It is clear early on in the conversation that she doesn't want to say too much about what has happened to her and her family.

"Níl na leanaí gafa leis, ní thugann sé aon suaimhneas ar bith dóíbh." (The little ones don't want to bother with it, it doesn't give them any comfort.) After some time, in sheer exhaustion, the children settle and fall asleep each clutching her fiercely as if to a life raft.

Later in the evening, Nóra opens up to Mary telling her that her husband was shot dead by the R.I.C.[1]

"They were looking for an excuse really. They knew he was very active in the Young Irelanders[2] movement and convinced he was involved, a few weeks earlier, in the killing of Major Mahon, the landlord of Strokestown House[3]. He wasn't, of course, but he did rejoice at the execution of a man who was responsible for the eviction and death of thousands of our neighbours. Worse than Cromwell, he would say. When they came to sack our little cottage, they gave us no time to collect our belongings. We concentrated on the children. Trying to comfort them. Seán was furious of course, boiling. I could see in him the impotence of trapped rage. He was a proud man and very protective of me and his family. Among these thugs he felt emasculated. They eventually grabbed a hold of him and held him, fearful of his strength. The Agent's name was Ross Mahon. Seán saw him pick up a wooden box, a precious heirloom from his mother and fling it with contempt into the fire which was already consuming our rafters. Isn't it extraordinary that it's the small things that mean so much to us in the end? Maybe Ross Mahon knew this for it seemed to me a deliberate act of provocation. I can still see the evil sneer on his face as he turned towards Seán in the act of throwing. I felt sick to the stomach. For I knew immediately what would follow. With superhuman strength Seán shook himself free of the men holding him and bounded across the divide separating himself from Mahon. My God, I think they were waiting for this because immediately one of the RIC officers fired his pistol and Seán, my dear

   even small birds fly free

Seán, fell to the ground, dead, on his own soil, in front of me and the poor girls. It broke our hearts. Since then we have been trying to forget."

Mary regards her for a long time after this. This strong woman. With all her heart, she wants to gather her in her arms but is restrained by the thought Nóra will not be able for such a show of affection.

"The Society of Friends[4] rescued us. They gave us shelter, fed us, nurtured us and gave us ferry passage away from Ireland and so here we are now."

"The Society of Friends? Who are they?"

"Oh you may know them as Quakers. They are amazing people. They helped so many people all over the West of Ireland. Providing food and shelter. Without any judgement. And no proselytising. So we didn't have to worry about being vilified as 'Soupers"[5]. We owe them our lives really. They took pity on the girls after what happened to their father. Seemingly a group in Philadelphia heard our story, had compassion on us and sent money for our passage all the way to there. So that's where we are going."

At this the two women sink into a silent reverie of gratitude. Mary looks at the sleeping girls. And not for the first time is enthralled by their beauty, the tranquillity and trust they have in their mother. She can't help thinking of all those other families who were not so lucky. Those who did not survive. Who were wiped out by the pestilential storm of the last three years. Her own villagers in Graigue. And those across the valley in Glenville.

Later she reaches out to Nóra again.

"Níl mórán Béarla agat." ("You have no English").

"Beagánín" ("A little"), she says, a slight blush appearing on her cheeks. Mary's heart goes out to her. Her simplicity, her bravery. Their conversation effortless, their connection easy as they continue to talk together 'as gaeilge'.

"There's no shame in that. But you know we have to survive now. And see the English language as a gift that may very well save us. We have to let the old tongue go I'm afraid. I'll tell you what. Why don't we spend the time on the way over with us all learning the new ways. Sure Da was a schoolteacher and I'm sure I can copy some of the tricks he taught us all as we were growing up."

"Oh my dear, that would be grand. Would you do that for us."

"For all the kindness you have shown me, that would be a small thing to do. And sure, it will pass the time."

"I'm so grateful to you. I can't wait to tell the girls when they wake up. You are a dear, dear cailín."

In the morning Mary is greeted by the girls surrounding her with whoops of laughter and unrestrained joy. They are going to set up a school on the bunk. Surely this will provide the bulwark needed to survive the gruesome circumstances in which they find ourselves.

Over the next few days and weeks, Nóra and Mary settle into a rhythm, a conspiracy of sorts, to keep the girls buoyant. They create a haven, an oasis in the midst of an inferno, a refuge from the abomination, the atrocities of what takes place around them, hourly and daily. As if intuitively, they surround the girls with activities every morning when the crew arrive for the macabre task of lifting bodies of people who have died overnight, swept away by the famine fevers, and carry them up to the deck to be slung overboard; The euphemism of burying at sea never managing to eliminate the profound sadness of it all. After a week, they lose count of the number of those pitiless journeys that need to be eliminated from their consciousness. All the while not sure if they are succeeding in their distracting activities. Mary often wonders if the girls are just playing along with their mother as much to protect her as they themselves.

All sorts of games are invented to help swap English words for the Gaeilge, the childrens' evident joy at their increasing proficiency demonstrated by the smiles which wreathed their faces. All in the end are beneficiaries. When each of them think back on those days (in later years), days wherein they all should have been consumed with dread and trepidation, all they can individually remember are; The dimpled grin of Méabh, the shining eyes of Nóra, the pride beaming from Alannah or the joyful glee from little Bríd as each one of them conquer the language. Mary realising that those girls saved her life even as she set about preparing them for their future.

Every second day, in small groups, passengers are allowed on deck to cook on the fire at the aft of the ship. This becomes a blessed hour when Mary, Nóra and the girls can look at the sky and horizon as they cook their porridge. The taste of cooked food helping them swallow the foul, bitter-tasting water drawn from the barrel provided in the hold.

Three weeks in, Mary is consumed with sickness and nausea. Long after the queasiness brought about by the turbulent seas has left her.

 even small birds fly free

Morning after morning she wakes and her first instinct is to retch. Fear grips her soul. She can only think it's the Famine Fevers assailing her and she knows she has very little strength to fight the disease crippling her body.

Three days into this debilitating state, Nóra blurts out,

"I don't want to pry, a stóir but where is the father?'

Mary can hardly make sense of what is being asked of her. Surely she has explained painfully enough, her leaving of Da on the quayside in Cove.

"Not Da, oh, you don't realise," Nóra exclaims when she sees the look on Mary's face, "sure I have been through this too many times to not recognise the inescapable signs. You are with child, my dear. And I simply want to help. Who and where is the child's father?"

The words hit Mary like a thunderbolt. She collapses in despair

"It's OK, my dear. I will take care of you. You will be alright. Not to worry now. Just rest."

Mary lies down on her corner of the bunk consumed by the knowledge that Nóra is correct in her diagnosis. She is "with child" as Nóra puts it. No longer just trying to survive on her own, she has the dawning realisation that she now must carry the burden of a child growing inside her. Overwhelmed she has no energy to contemplate his or her origin. To bring that to mind will devour her altogether.

Later that night when the girls are asleep, Nóra holds her in her arms. "I don't want to probe, my dear. It's sufficient just to know that now we must look out for you with even greater care and diligence."

The following morning the girls surround her. It's obvious Nóra has told them of her condition. Their collective faces are rapt with excitement. Mary looks over at Nóra and can see her smirk. She knows the medicine needed. To look at the vibrant lives of these siblings and see the hope in them and capture a vision for the child growing inside her. They will become a sisterhood together, a little village of their own for the remainder of the journey. To protect and nurture their unborn member.

They become so close through the voyage. As they approach the end, when word goes out that land is in sight and they will soon dock in New York, Nóra says,

"Mary, my dear, why don't you come with us to Philadelphia. We are being met in New York by a member of the Society. It will be much safer for you to travel on with us."

After some time, the path ahead becomes clear.

"Thank you, Nóra, but I feel I must strike out on my own. I also want to stay close to New York. To the harbour. I am frightened that I might lose Da. Where we're going. It's such a big country. I haven't given up hope that I might be able to earn his passage and I want to be nearby when he makes the crossing. To greet him. To be reunited with him again."

"I suppose I have to accept your wishes against my better judgment, Mary, but if you ever need us, please write to me. At the Quakers. They have a meeting house on Arch Street. They will make sure I get it."

That is one of the last conversations they have together.

On arrival day they are herded up onto the deck. The passengers needing to be out of the way and off the ship as soon as the ship docks. In quiet relief, they each draw in the clear, salty air into their lungs and relax. There is something quite overwhelming, gazing across this beautiful and wide harbour as they approach land. The sun is setting and the horizon can be seen away to the west, golden against the fading of the day. Tall, stately, red-bricked buildings dominating the waterfront. The sixty or so packet ships moored at the dock, masts reaching to the sky, their square rigging framing the geometrical city streets, the light diffracted through the cordage creating a kaleidoscope of colours and shapes on the skyline. It is exhilarating. This place of their new home. Their new lives. They have made it.

Very little space is evident among the tens of ships already berthed and the passengers watch and marvel at the skill of the captain and deckhands as they guide the Cambridge into its moorings. As they draw closer to the shore they are astonished at the level of frenzied activity on the docks. Carts, horses, people milling around at a bewildering pace. An utterly unfamiliar world awaiting them.

As soon as the moorings have been made secure, a group of twenty or so men in red tabards sling a gangplank onto the side of the ship. And in a simultaneous, almost choreographed movement, spring onto it to race upwards. To be first on board. To ensure they get the best portering assignments. But as the lead group reach halfway up the gangplank, it tips over and disgorges all of the them the full fifteen feet below to the dock. Those on deck watch in horror. Almost immediately however, and undeterred it seems, the men pick themselves up and laughing sheepishly begin, once again, to right the plank and resume the mad scramble to be first on board.

     even small birds fly free

At the same moment hold passengers are being ushered off the deck. On another gangplank. The pushing, shoving, elbowing which follows is frightening. Almost as one organism they are driven down the gangway to the dock. The dockside feels no safer. Dray men usher their horses and carts closer for loading. Other men, with large handcarts, also race to the side of the ship. At any moment those disembarking can be mowed down by the aggressive rivalry underway, the mad scramble for the most lucrative competitive advantage. The noise is overwhelming. Most of the shouts and roars from the men are unintelligible. It's impossible to distinguish English from all the other languages being uttered.

Miraculously within it all, Nóra is found by her benefactor and the moment comes for the tearful goodbyes and separation. They are boarding a barge on the Hudson river to catch the train to Philadelphia.

It's a sickening, lonely feeling for Mary to watch them walk away. Bringing back to her that moment of absence in Cove. Now she is truly alone, again, despite being surrounded by a sea of aggressive and inhospitable faces, animals, carts, buildings, noise. In the fast fading light, she retreats and finds a spot among casks and barrels, away from the crowd, to reflect. She sits for quite some time on an upturned wooden crate, gathering herself for the next stage of her odyssey, unconscious that the harbour is thinning out of people as she procrastinates, deep in thought. She needs to gather courage, strength to look up and take in her new surroundings.

"You look like you are away with the faeries, mo stór[6],"

She is jolted back to reality by the Tipperary accent and looking up, finds herself being scrutinised by a young, cheerful-looking gasún.

"You wouldn't want to be hanging around here for long. There's some dreadful chancers in the docks and it's also going to get fierce cold in a short while. Is it someone you're waiting for? Did they let you down?"

The light of the day is gone and an ethereal glow gives the dockland and narrow streets running from it a very strange way. Mary finds herself fighting a sinking feeling of terror, holding at bay an intense paralysis of movement brought about by the dread and panic she feels in this strange, unfamiliar environment.

Afterwards she cannot reconcile or credit what gets into her. Whether it is the dreadful loneliness, the surprising and welcoming lilt of the man's Tipperary accent, the sense that she has the good fortune to meet one of her own here, miles from home in these new and unfamiliar surroundings, the strong putrid smell of the docks, the oppressive close-knit buildings and narrow streets leading from the quayside like an unfamiliar path through a dense wood. Whatever it is, she surrenders herself totally to his care. Sure what could be the harm? He is one of her own.

"You'll be needing somewhere to stay, first things first. I'll take you up to Five Points. That's where we've settled. It's safer there. You wouldn't want to run into any of them Proddy Know-Nothings.[7] They'll savage you as soon as they'll look at you. Do you have any cash at all?

"I have a few shillings," she answers, meekly.

"Sure that's the very thing. But its no good to you here, mo chroí. Here we have the mighty dollar. You'll need to change it. Come with me. Sure I know the very place. We'll have you rich in Dime and Dollar in no time."

He leads her up one of the side streets running from the docks. Catherine's Slip she learns it is, afterwards. He doesn't stop his running conversation all the way to the top of the street and Mary finds it strangely comforting. After walking for five minutes, they stop at a crossing and he points up the hill running away from where they stand. About a hundred yards up, he points to a group of rough-looking men leaning against the wall, smoking outside of what appears to be a shebeen.

"Those are the very boyos," he says, "But they would skin you alive if you approach them to change your money. If you trust me, I can take your shillings to them and get a fair few dollars for it. I think that would be your best bet."

No sooner have she handed him the shillings, her last precious coins, no sooner has he turned away from her to walk up the hill towards the men, than she realises in the pit of her stomach, she has made a terrible mistake. She watches hopelessly and helplessly as he strolls past the men and sure enough, just five yards beyond them, bolts down one of the myriad of side streets in this forest to which she is a complete stranger. Duped, taken for an amadán by one of her own. It has come to this. Irish people have become prey to one another.

Forlorn and heartbroken she is left with no option but to continue on up the slip, putting one foot in front of another, penniless, looking for somewhere she can rest. Darkness is now complete and enveloping and

     even small birds fly free

the air has turned bitter. Within minutes it begins to snow. She finds a small overhanging shelter near what appears to be a closed market and slumps to the ground. Hugging herself to keep warm, she recalls the last time she was in this position outside Graigue village. Then she had Da to comfort and protect her and give her his warmth.   Immediately she is gripped by a sense of failure. She can't protect her own child, growing inside her and utterly dependent on her. This night, she is alone, on the other side of the Atlantic Ocean, in a strange city, which she has already experienced as dangerous and unsafe. Disconsolate and desolate, she succumbs to a overwhelming sense of melancholy as she slips into a fitful sleep in the doorway on that deserted side alley, snow falling heavily on the streets around her. The white darkness carrying her to a blessed oblivion.

Liverpool, England

March,1848

In which Caelan O'Donovan witnesses the full extent of the pernicious nature of the English government policy, makes a friend and hears from his brother

On this cold, bleak morning before the sun rises and as Caelan O'Donovan makes his way to work, the seafront takes on a eerie, unearthly quality. He loves this moment, before the real day begins. It becomes his escape from the narrow, oppressive streets and lanes of the city. The joy of seeing a horizon. There is a beauty to be found here in the morning twilight. The panoramic night skyline, the constellations shimmering above seem to be enhanced by the bumptious display of prosperity; The elaborate outline of various buildings highlighted by the many fires which drive the steam engines below; The smell of coal pungent in the morning air. The imperious dome of the Custom House rising above the magisterial frontage of the warehouses surrounding the docks underlying and emphasising the wealth of this city. Dwarfing men, scurrying about underneath, like ants with a logic all of their own. The montage of African heads, both men and women, carved into some of these buildings give broad hints as to the ill gotten gain of which the city fathers are ostentatiously proud.

When they arrived in Liverpool at the end of December, his brother Pádraig took one look and decided they needed to get out as soon as possible. Such was the misery that greeted them. Caelan realised this was typical of Pádraig. Always practical, not much room for reflection. They got a tip from a fellow traveller on the boat over from Castletown Berehaven, that there were contractors in Liverpool who would pay passage to New Orleans. But only to strong men willing to sign an indentured contract to work for a year. Twenty dollars a month plus board and lodging. Pádraig was keen to try it for himself.

"Sure I can earn your passage in no time there, Caelan. It's better only one of us go first. There's no point in both of us signing up for a year. You keep your head down here for a while and it won't be long before you're also on a packet ship and we're together again. And the year will pass in no time at all."

Caelan couldn't argue with him. Pádraig was dead set on it anyway, convinced as he always was that his perception in the way things worked was to his advantage. He had forever looked at the world and found his place in it. A Pádraig-shaped space. Caelan supposed that was why

even small birds fly free

he was so frustrated by his brother, who was oblivious of the difference between them. Caelan carried within his heart a vision of the way things should be and used all his focus and energy to direct his life that way. This was the source of all their arguments and disagreements. "It's a waste of time trying to change things. Best to accept the way things are," Pádraig would say. This time however, both felt it best not to argue as they braced for their parting, unsure as they were of when they would, if ever, see each other again. Sure enough, Pádraig passed muster with the contractor and within a week he was gone, leaving Caelan behind in this city, to make his own way, for a while.

Like the other men, he stood in line looking for work on the docks every morning, trying to appear strong and capable. That's what Johnny Dolan tells him on the first morning they meet.

"Put a smile on your face, boy. That's the way of it. They don't want anyone miserable."

They get selected together in the same team. And become inseparable after that. Caelan so grateful. Old enough to be his Da, but strong as an ox, Johnny keeps him going day after day.

Most times they get portering jobs, carrying cargo onto carts which are pushed to the vast warehouses lining the docks.

"Would you take a look at that!" Johnny whispers regularly and conspiratorially to him, "That's coming in from Ireland."

Then gazing open-mouthed, like gormless gombeens, they would see vast tons of wheat and other grains unloaded.[8] Some days, they are engaged to herd hundreds of heads of cattle. On others, they shift gallons of butter. Caelan outraged, has to bite his tongue. It's hard for him to comprehend. How can his people be left to starve? How can he reconcile the things he has seen in Skibbereen and among his own family over the last few years and now look at this food, the wherewithal which would have kept them alive, arriving here in England and being unloaded by the same, half-starved workers that managed to escape? His blood boils often and if it isn't for Pádraig's exhortation ringing in his head, he'd be plotting murder and insurrection.

Johnny laughs at him. The only way he can guide him back to his station.

"Sure, boy, there's no point in getting excited about it," he says, "That's the way the world is. You and I aren't going to change that any time soon. And look around you, would you. The authorities hate us.

They see us as disease-ridden vermin. They are just looking for an excuse to beat the tar out of us. No, boy, your best bet is to keep your head down until your brother writes to you."

Two weeks ago they witnessed the worst encounter. Police, out in force, in Clarence Dock ordering those who had just landed, traumatised, emaciated and weak as they were, back onto the ship from which they had just disembarked; Deported back to where they came from;[9] Their last hope of survival, extinguished like one would casually snap the flickering flame of a candle. Caelan blots it out of his mind. He really can't think about it, or else he would go mad.

Cautionary tales abound to instruct him as he makes his way back to the dormitory in the boarding house each evening. Many, men and women, wandering the crowded, filthy back streets with crazed expressions, muttering to themselves, wailing into the night. He regularly sees them being picked up and he hears later that they are carted off to local workhouses or to the asylum.[10]

Those singled out for work at the beginning of each day toil silently together. No friendships are formed. They are working alongside men who have no memory, no light. The songs, the jokes, the laughter, which would normally be common among them, absent. At the end of long days, in the evenings, hordes of men and women, drunk and staggering, incoherent and wild, crowd the streets. Their behaviour a desperate attempt to forget. To reach oblivion. To bury memory.

Caelan is grateful for Johnny. He's a tonic. In a way, they don't really know each other. But every morning, Johnny arrives at their meeting point at the corner of the Albert Docks, six o'clock sharp, ready to begin their search for work as companions, together. He is always cheerful. It lifts Caelan's spirit to see him.

Two mornings ago, however, Johnny didn't arrive. Caelan waits until he couldn't stay any longer, but there is no sign of him. Abandoning his friend he makes his way to the spot where the gangers were picking the men. He rationalises it as being for Johnny's sake as much as his own. If they don't show up on any given day, they would be at the back of the queue when they turn up again.

At the end of the day, Caelan makes his usual visit to the Shipping Company on the Waterloo Road. As things would have it, he receives word from Pádraig who has purchased a ticket, steerage class on the Boston Packet, leaving the following Tuesday. It makes finding Johnny all the more urgent.

          even small birds fly free

In the evening he goes searching for him, with only a vague idea where he lives. He makes his way up the Scotland Road to the Shebeens in Everton to ask about him. About ten o'clock at night he finds him, slumped in the corner of one, in a bad way.

"Johnny, I've been looking for you all evening. Are you alright?"

Johnny looks at him directly. Surprised. The light gone out of his eyes.

"You don't want to be thinking of me, lad. That's not going to help you. Best thing you can do is leave me here. I'll be fine. You just need to look after yourself."

Caelan can get no more out of him. He turns to see if there is anyone around who can help and sees out of the corner of his eye the barman gesturing to him.

"Are you Johnny's friend?" He asks, "He's been telling me of a young lad that's been doing him a power of good down at the docks, day after day. Is that you? Are you Caelan?"

Caelan is taken aback. The barman knows his name. "I am indeed. Though it's definitely the other way around. Sure I would never have made it in this city if Johnny hadn't shown me the ropes."

"I'm Finn," The barman continues, grasping his hand in a warm, friendly handshake, "It's been a bad couple of days for him. On top of all that's gone before. Two days ago, his wife went mad. Not surprising really. She lost her four children to the Famine Fevers. Two in Ireland and two since they landed here."

"Oh, I didn't know that."

"Era sure, that's Johnny all over. He would never burden a young fellow like you with his worries and woes. He has a real grá for you. Talks to me about you all the time. Anyway, the missus broke down two days ago when you were both at work. She was screeching and roaring up and down the street outside, running from child to child. Looking into their eyes with a mad stare. Bystanders say she was calling out her childrens' names, asking all and sundry if they had seen them. She was peering into those new prams you see on the street. The women were very frightened, terrified by it. We couldn't control her. It was desperate to watch. In the end, the Police were called. They came upon her up in St Anthony's. By the paupers' grave. Where her two are laid to rest. She was scraping the soil away with her bare hands. I suppose digging down towards her little leanaí. Lord have mercy on her and their souls. Inevitably, the authorities took her away to the Asylum."

"My God, did he get home before they took her away?"

"No, Son. That's the worst of it. She's in Lancaster Moor asylum. Sure what chance would a man like him have of making it all the way up there? He came in here yesterday and hasn't left. The life's gone out of him. Sure now he's only drinking to forget. And in all honesty, I don't think it's right to take that away from him. What else has he got?"

Caelan turns to look at Johnny collapsed in the corner.

"I can't leave him here, Finn. I have to help."

"Caelan," he says, "I've been running this place for ten years now. And I know our people and I know how far they have sunk. Sure the majority have no memory at all of a time when they were happy. All the everyday things that brought them joy, a session around the fire, stories from the seanachaí, the look of their child's face, the crop flourishing in the field; all these things are obliterated. What faces them now are things that cause them pain, that rip their souls from inside them. I have heard all their stories when the poitín has freed their tongue and they are all the same. I have come to the conclusion that for most of them, anything that helps them forget is a blessing. That's the kind of place I have here. Johnny Dolan will be fine with me. I'll give him some work and some food to keep his body and soul together. Possibly he might make it up to Lancaster one day. Here he will have the poitín to deaden the pain. This is not a place for you. You will serve him best by getting the hell away from here. By finding a life somewhere else. He tells me you have a brother in America who is sending you your passage. Johnny loves to tell me that about you. That's what he wants for you now. To get away."

Caelan leaves Finn with a heavy heart and sits down in the corner with Johnny again. This time he looks up and smiles,

"You met Finn. A powerful man. Salt of the earth. Did he set you straight?"

"He told me about your missus."

A stab of pain comes over his eyes.

"I couldn't save her, Caelan. When she lost the children. They were her life. She doted on them. She left me and the world as one by one they were taken away from her. I tried to bring her back but there's

       even small birds fly free

nothing here for her anymore. And the awful truth is that with her gone, there's nothing for me here either."

"Don't be saying that, Johnny. You have to be strong."

"Ah bless you son. Thanks for your concern. But the truth is, there's a different kind of strength asked of me now. You know there comes a time when being strong is about accepting the reality of your situation. I can do that. Now. But tell me something I've been wanting to hear, son. Did you hear from your brother? Did Pádraig write to you yet?"

"Yes, I got word today. He has paid my passage on the Cunard line on Tuesday to Boston."

"Well isn't that great altogether."

For the first time the light comes back into his eyes. He reaches across the table and takes both Caelan's hands in his. His skin and flesh are hard from the years of toil as he grasps them firmly. Looking straight at him he says,

"Caelan, this gladdens my heart. That I can sit here now in an evening and know that you are far away. That you have escaped all this misery and are off somewhere in the new world building a new life for yourself. Like a small bird flying free. That some of us managed that. Right so, and on a serious note, I want you to promise me something."

He looks across the table searchingly.

"Of course, anything for you Johnny. Anything. What is it?"

"That you'll say goodbye to me now. That you won't come back here again to look me up. That you won't look back. You can carry me in your heart where you're going but not as a heavy burden. Will you do that for me?"

Caelan's heart sinks. How many more of these painful goodbyes must he endure. He know of course that Johnny is right. He has him captured with a promise. Tears well up and stream down his face.

"There, there, boy. I'll be fine. Sure I have Finn to keep me company."

He stands up. Johnny Dolan does and walks around to the other side of the table, reaching out, they grasp one another, like the son and father they truly have become and hold on to one another, this one last time.

"Beannacht Dé ort agus slán" (The blessing of God and health go with you) are the last words Johnny utters.

One of the hardest things Caelan will ever do in his life is to turn from his friend and walk across that Shebeen to the door. He can feel

Finn's gaze follow him. He is leaving them all behind. His people. How many will survive? Will they be able to start again here? How much of themselves will be lost along the way?

His heart remains heavy with remorse and guilt during the days that follow in Liverpool and breaks when he walks the streets towards the docks and the Caledonia to start his journey for Boston and the New World.

    even small birds fly free

To Caelan O'Sullivan
40, Vauxhall Road
Liverpool
March 1848

Mo Bráthair Caelan,

At long last I get a moment to write to you. I am sorry for the long time you have been waiting. And wondering, I guess, if I made it at all and whether I am still alive in the world. I'm here alright but that's a long story.

As I write this, I can hear your voice in my head. Your sweet, gentle voice; Tomás plays the uileann pipes behind and you strike out with Do Bhí Bean Uasal. I am singing it now as I write;

> *But the sea is wide and I cannot swim over*
> *And neither have I the wings to fly*
> *I wish I had a handy boatsman*
> *To ferry me over my love and I*

I made it to New Orleans as you can see from the postmark. And its not something that I'd be recommending to you. That's why I'm passing the money on for you to take the shorter passage from Liverpool to Boston. Its too long this way and I barely survived it. It seemed to take forever, the voyage. We felt tossed about like rag dolls on the high seas and at times it felt like it would never end; Hundreds of us cooped up as we were in a cramped, airless hold and with only one stove. Days went by without cooked food and the water was sparse and fetid.[11]

We lost forty people on the way through typhoid; They were thrown overboard without ceremony; painting a picture that none of us mattered.[12] It was awful brother and something I do not wish for you. In fact the only good thing about it is that I can now save you from the same fate.

I miss you, you know, and you are the only one left in this world for me now that Ma and Da and Aoife are gone. So I want you to take care of yourself. This is no time for high-flying idealism. I know you too well. You're always out to help somebody else. You have to survive, Caelan. That's your mission now.

So that's why I want you to take the shorter Boston route and prepare for it well. I have arranged your travel with Train & Company on the Waterloo Road. They organise travel on the Boston Packet. Talk to them. They have promised they will look after you.

I know you may be disappointed about this. That you are arriving at a different part of America. But it will be fine, Caelan. We will soon be reunited.

It's important you prepare well for the journey. Bake some oat biscuits before you board ship and store them, well hidden. They will keep you going when you can't cook porridge. And fight for the water every day. Don't get involved with the misery around you. It will only drag you down.

When you arrive in Boston, please God, ignore the bastards who come on board offering you jobs and lodgings. Even our own are involved and they will fleece you for everything you have.

Just make your own way into the town and God be with you. Write when you get there,

Le Ghrá,

Pádraig.

even small birds fly free

New Orleans

April - August, 1848

In which Pádraig O'Donovan is plunged into the fetid, asphyxiatingly clammy nature of the Louisiana swampland and seeks to be rescued.

It's the heat that first hits him when they moor. He thought escaping from being cooped up below deck would allow him to breathe easily but the oppressive, humid air shocks him. The exuberant colours and sounds all around are exhilarating, an assault as a cacophony of blurred impressions, leaving him disconcerted as he stumbles with others from the ship when it docks; Desperately looking for stability, the ground seeming to float before his eyes. His legs tottering and rickety. The air hot and clammy. Breathing a chore. He is shepherded with the other indentured labourers to a particular section of the quays. The charge hand, a burly, intimidating fellow calling out the names - Pádraig O'Donovan; He almost misses his name as it is bellowed out; The sound of it unrecognisable. From that moment on, he knows he should call himself 'Paddy'.

The bustling harbour takes his breath away. Tall stately buildings lining the dockside; The hive of activity frenetic as men push carts to and fro with no discernible pattern but are full to overflowing with cargo; Horse drawn carts heavily laden vie for space to move, the horses nervously nickering amid the bedlam. When he looks out over the wide expanse of the river, he finds the spectacle difficult to absorb. Huge ships pour smoke into the skies, their structure artfully designed and painted in exquisite pastel shades with strange enormous wheels straddling their sides. Steamboats he learns they are and is surprised at the ingenuity of wheels driving their huge frames.

The five men who had signed up for indentured labour are marshalled quickly and marched in file away from the scene. They make their way through the city, this new home. Pádraig is in awe at its beauty. Elegant homes decked in mellow colours, built in peerless architecture. Balconies strewn with plants and flowers; Ornate shop windows denoting the affluence of the population. Women in long flowing gowns walk confidently on raised pathways shaded by umbrellas. They look like a different species altogether.

After walking a mile however, the very air changes. Belching fumes from tanneries mix with the pungent smell from the knackers yard as bones are boiled; thick smoke spewing from the brick factories gel into a noxious concoction that makes it difficult to breathe. Here are ramshackle buildings teeming with people, all looking dishevelled and downtrodden. This is the Irish quarter, someone says from their ranks.

They continue their march and are taken outside the city to camps in the swamplands. The air is thick with an earthy smell. As they march through brooding, ancient trees and sombre foliage which overhang the backwater, nothing looks familiar. They arrive at sodden grounds where tents are pitched and populated by rough-looking men, who stare at them, inquisitively, with eyes that barely register any human emotion. This place, this alien, exotic place is to be his home now. Cypress and Mangrove trees, girthed as big as houses, hauntingly draped in ghostly moss, catch the evening light and enclose the encampment like so many gigantic, chimeric banshees. The landscape, the smells, the heat so different from his beloved West Cork. He is overcome with homesickness.

They are shown to their billets. The large canvas tents are blessedly cool inside and narrow bunk beds occupy every inch. The kitchen tent where they will be fed is in the centre of the compound. At the edge is the whiskey store which they are informed will open every evening. Then they are read the riot act. Their contract is for a year and will be honoured, 'by hook or by crook'; even using the Irish saying. They will be paid monthly and are warned that absconding is punishable with a jail term and an extension to the contract. Assurances are declared that any absconders will be hunted down. Just by looking at the swampy terrain in which they are camped, Pádraig resigns himself that he will have to serve the year out.

That night, at dinner, they learn what they will face. Most of the people in the camp are from Ireland. People from Clare, Mayo, Galway, Cork and Kerry. Many of them have been digging canals for years, boasting work on the Erie and Ohio canals. Joe McEvoy, a small, stockily built fellow from Ballyhaunis, with an impish face, becomes Pádraig's instructor.

"You've decided to hop out of the frying pan into the fire, too, I see" is his opening gambit. "And this sure enough is the fire."

"What's the work like?" Pádraig asks naively.

"It's brutal. We're digging the canal. The whole city where you landed is built on water. It's tougher here than other canals I've worked on. It's our task to drain the water out of swamp to build ridges, which will hold the canals and keep the city dry. The ridges are called levees here. Like dykes. Backbreaking work. But that's not the worst of it.

There's fellows dying by the dozen. The place is full of alligators and snakes. And then there's the swamp fevers. The yellow fever which comes on us every summer. Sure, there's thousands of us buried in the Bayou's."

"What's a Bayou?"

"Its this whole region - a bog, so to speak."

"I notice there's mostly us Irish working here. Why's that?"[13]

"Well we've always worked on canals. Sure haven't we built this country. But there is a story that goes that plantation owners who hire out their slaves, don't let them anywhere near these swamps or this work. It's too dangerous you see and their slaves are too valuable. As for us, they can hire us for a dollar a day and at the drop of a hat. And if they lose one of us, then sure, there's another anniseoir arriving on a boat the very next day. They don't give a fuck about us. We're a dime a dozen."

Pádraig hardly sleeps that night after this conversation. The fear of what he is facing fills his imagination and leaves him terrified. The following morning, at sunrise and after a hearty breakfast they are led down to the work-site. There they are plunged into water up to their knees and with pick and shovel and wheelbarrow are told to empty the sludge from the basin. Steam-powered pumps on the side of the ditch siphon the water to enable them to have access to the muddy depths. The noise is deafening, the heat oppressive. But despite all this Pádraig is happy to be on Terra Firma and in no time at all he is confident he will have the money to pay for Caelan's passage. Surely he thinks he has the willpower to stick this out. It's better than dying in a ditch back home.

Day follows day in monotonous regularity. The men slog and toil until they are led back to the camp in the evening for food. Pádraig does not blame the men who bolt their food and head for the whiskey store, religiously, like clockwork, every evening where they drink to ease their pain and to forget.

On Saturday evening, he makes his way to the bars of Bourbon Street. It costs him. But he needs to reconnoitre. He needs to find out where he is, where he has landed. What are the rules? Passing through the district called the Irish Channel on the way to the bars, he is shocked by the derelict, dirty and decrepit conditions of its occupants. As bad as

Liverpool. From these first moments, he resolves to find a way out of here, to escape, lest he also gets sucked under.

The bars are lively. He ends up in Alexis Coffee House. Music, song, whiskey and women freely dancing with a confidence and abandon he has never before seen. The men talkative. He finds himself enjoying these evenings of laughter and conversation; Meeting new people. But it's the music that sweeps him away. Bringing joy and tears in equal measure. As soon as he walks into the first bar, he is captivated. They are playing the same instrument that he and Caelan play - the humble fiddle. But unrecognisably. The phrasing, The rhythm, the plaintiff notes as if they are coaxing sounds from another world. The fiddles respond singularly and distinctly in their hands. It's intoxicating and electrifying. When the vocalist begins to sing he produces a melancholic sound so strange and unique, and in a language he has not heard before. He is transfixed and transported. Tears come as he thinks of Caelan and knows he would be hopping alongside him here, with the joy of this discovery. At this moment, in the middle of the poignant song he misses his brother, his family, he misses old Skibb, home. The plaintive notes of the song, the phrasing of the instruments seem to be in tune with his mood, evoking grievous memories and reluctant recall. He turns to the fellow next to him.

"What's this music I'm hearing?"

His neighbour, a strong burly man with broad shoulders and piercing eyes laughs at him.

"They call it Cajun[14]. It's from French-Canadian people who settled here and brought their tunes with them. Good stuff, isn't it?"

"I've never heard anything like it. I play fiddle myself but not like this. It's just so uplifting, so evocative. It pierces me through and through."

"John Roberts," with a hand reaching out, "I come in here when I can to get my fill."

"Paddy O'Donovan," He says as he watches the dancers take the floor to a vibrant tune. "What's this they're playing now?"

"'Allons le Lafayette'. It's a song in French about a woman coming to Lafayette and the place changing her character. This place changes all of us. You're Irish, right?"

"Yes. I'm working in the Bayou on a contract for a year."

"That's a hard slog. I don't envy you that. I'm a Patty Roller[15] myself."

                    even small birds fly free

"What's that when it's at home," I joke.

"We are hired to hunt fugitive slaves and return them to their masters or the auction houses. There's good money in it."

Pádraig is stopped in his tracks with this declaration. Such a new thought to him that he doesn't know how to engage the man about it so he lets it lie.

They spend the rest of the evening listening to the bands and chatting. It brings enormous comfort to Pádraig to find a friend and that he can come to Bourbon Street as an escape when the work gets him down.

He leaves the bar that first night on a cloud of euphoria. Maybe there is a future for him in this country after all.

A few months into his stint, the gang move to work on virgin territory. Pádraig is not settled. The terrain with its swamps, ancient trees, hanging moss instil in him caution and fear. He has by this time graduated and is in a vanguard of labourers. The job to carve a line through from one established Levee to another. They work in groups of five, two in the water at any one time. Using the pick to create a clean line on the dyke. One mid-morning, Pádraig raises his pick and when he hits the bank below the line, the water convulses and erupts around him like a mini-volcano. At the same moment, he feels excruciating pain as something bites his leg and thigh. He passes out. The rest of the men act quickly and pull him out of the water. Its clear to them that he has hit a nest of cottonmouths. Quickly they strip the clothes off of him. One of the gang, Chatan, a Choctaw takes control. Laying Pádraig on the ground, he washes and binds the wound with a poultice made of plantain and applies a loose tourniquet to his leg.

He lay in a stupor for two days, in and out of consciousness and in fever dreams he hears voices,

"You're a lucky man to be still with us Paddy."

"You disturbed a nest of cottonmouths with your pick and they sprang at you."

"One of the Choctaws saved you. Otherwise you'd be a goner."

"When we pulled you out of the water and stripped the clothes off you, we found you had been bitten four times, so it's no small wonder you passed out."

"The Choctaw fella knew to wash your wounds and then made a poultice of leaves he gathered."

"Many of the lads were sceptical but I reckon it's why you're alive"

"Blueflower coyote thistle and plantain leaves. Acts as an antidote to the snake poison."

The delirium lasts for two to three days and he slowly recovers. But through it all a resolve grows in him. He's had enough of this. His people also populate his dreams. They look weighed down and broken. Pádraig determines to separate himself from them too. Otherwise he will be dragged down with them.

When fully conscious and on the road to recovery, he decides to change his story, his destiny, the narrative waiting to be written for him. Everywhere he looks he sees his people wearing suffering like a badge. Persecuted at home, unwelcome in Liverpool, set upon and exploited here in America.   At St Anthony's, on a Sunday morning, preached at by priests who tell them to accept this suffering as redemptive, as a blessed affliction that will one day secure them a place in the hereafter. Damnation on them, he splutters to himself. If this horrible event is to have any good outcome for him, he will have to leave all this 'affliction' behind and start afresh.

Five days later, he is back in the swamp. It isn't the same anymore. Stepping into the water is fearful, traumatic. Every swing of the pick leaves him shaken. He tries his best to hide what he is going through but the others look back at him like he has become a wraith, a Púca[16]. He knows he won't last long here. He needs to find a way out.

He thinks of John Roberts in the bar in Alexis Coffee House. He just needs to make it to the end of the week and then go and find him.

It's three weeks however before he runs across him. Three long weeks. Days, hours and minutes of horror, flashbacks, imaginations, hallucinations. Every move in the water spelling danger, terror, setting his heart, pulse and imagination racing. At night he barely sleeps. Spectres, phantoms haunt his nightmares and slithering water moccasins dominate his consciousness gliding along the surface of his murky dreams, their fangs bared and ready to strike. He is at the edge of myself, the end of his tether.

It is with great relief then when he eventually spies John Roberts in his usual, nonchalant pose propping up the bar in the Coffee House on the first Saturday night in August.

              even small birds fly free

Five Points, New York City

January - May, 1848

In which Mary O'Brien is saved from death by her countrywomen and finds a kind of refuge in their company in Five Points.

"You'll catch your death of cold trying to sleep out here, love."

Mary is woken from deep sleep by a gentle shaking of her arm. A bright, beautiful, smiling face looking down at her. She can't think where she is. Nothing looks familiar. She immediately feels the extreme cold in her bones and doesn't want to be woken up, the bliss of forgetfulness ruptured.

"C'mon Annie. Leave her there. We'll all be in trouble with Biddy if we don't get a move on." A chorus erupts from three other young women standing by and ready to set up the hill.

"For God's sake girls, how can we leave her here. She'll be dead in the morning. She's one of our own. Weren't we all rescued in one way or another. Where's your compassion?"

Mary realises she has only been asleep a short while but it feels like a lifetime. Indeed it is a lifetime, she thinks, so unfamiliar is the air of this city on which she has just stepped foot. She can just make out all four of the women. They are dressed to the nines. Ample breasts popping out of frilly blouses and long flowing dresses decked out in the brightest of colours. For a moment she thinks she is in some sort of weird dream.

"Can you get up on your own, love?" She hears the first woman speak again.

"I think so but I'm not sure I want to,"

"You can't stay here, mo chuisle, mo chroí. It's only going to get colder through the night and then you'll never wake up as sure as night follows day."

"Maybe that's for the best."

"Era whisht out of that, cailín. That's the devil talking. Here give me your hand. You're coming with us up to Biddy Mulligans. Sure, that's the only place for girls like us. That's the only place we'll be looked after."

"While we spend our time looking after the shillelaghs of men." Roars one of the other girls who all fall about in a ribald chorus of laughter and glee.

"Cop onto yourselves, girls and give me a hand here. Sure this poor one is long past caring."

They lift her together and when she finds her feet she is able to walk alongside them, with Annie and another girl propping her up.

After a surprisingly short time, a few minutes really, they turn onto a junction of intersecting roads. Immediately the world around them slips into chaos. Mary's senses are overwhelmed. In the middle of the night, it's like daytime. A cacophony of noise, laughter, shouting, loud music teeming from the bars and taverns that populate each of the buildings. Men and women with their arms slung around one another stagger across the square. She encounters the first black man she has ever seen as this strong, muscular, handsome fellow approaches one of the girls and she throws herself at him in a passionate embrace. Suddenly aware, Mary see scores of Black men throughout the square, nonchalantly wandering and mixing, Black men and what can only be Irishmen casually engaged in easy conversation in front of the various bars and taverns.

Pigs run riot over the whole street, seeking rotten food, noisily eating. In one corner, a cock fight is taking place with the bystanding audience boisterously committed. Three men brawl in the mud nearby. Tar barrels with wild flames leaping from them occupy the area as so many sentinels of scurrility. Throngs of dishevelled people gather round them. Here and there, in marked contrast, men of impeccable bearing, besuited in the highest of fashion, top hats crowning their highfalutin appearance, strut about with a superior air, among their obviously despised minions. It's the closest thing to bacchanalia Mary has seen in her lifetime.

"Welcome to Five Points[17], mo stóir," Annie gesticulates at the scene opening up in front of them. "This is your new home."

They don't stay long in the street. As they near one of the large buildings on Anthony Street, a large bosomed woman leans out of a broken window on the second floor.

"What's kept ye, ye floozies. There's customers up here waiting on ye."

"Sure we were bringing you a new recruit, Biddy. Aren't we your best girls."

"Another mouth to feed, ye mean. I'll give ye "best girls" if ye don't make it up here quick, sharp." She roars in reply.

even small birds fly free

They make their way up the narrow stairway. From a long way down Mary hears bedlam from the room above and when they burst through the door they are greeted with an overwhelming mix of raucous conversation, music from a fiddler in the corner and fellas and girls swinging off one another as they make an effort to keep in time with the jig that's playing. 'Am I being rescued or sent to hell', Mary wonders to herself.

Annie takes her to a windowless room down the hallway where she tells her they all sleep. Basic straw mattresses are packed into the room. She gets her some food and tells her to rest. She won't be disturbed 'til morning.

Over the next few days Mary settles in. The girls have created a small community of laughter and fun. Her defences slowly dissolve and she joins in. Beautiful Annie takes care of her, making sure she is part of the group and gets enough to eat. Mary falls in love with her vivacious, generous heart. In the evening, the main room is taken over as a dance hall by men who arrive in their hordes. It's the job of the girls to make them feel at home, dance with them and make sure they have enough to drink. During the course of the evening and at different times each one of the girls disappears. When Mary asks Annie about it, she tells her it's not something she has to worry about.

On the fourth night however, Biddy Mulligan summons her over to where she is perched, like a queen, at the doorway of the room. Standing next to her is a big, burly man who is looking at her in a way that makes her feel uncomfortable.

"Time to earn your keep, lass," she says. "Take this man here to room number four and make him happy."

She is stunned and rendered numb, as it dawns on her what is expected. How could she be so foolish, so naive? She immediately recognises the look of the man as the same salacious look Kincaid gave her. She is trapped. The man grabs her roughly by the arm, drives her out the door and down the narrow corridor to 'room number four'. She is gripped by terror. Abandoned. Why didn't Annie warn her of this? Why didn't she see this coming? Conflicting and alarming thoughts render her paralysed.

The man has the strength of four. 'He could snap me in two', she thinks. 'How has it come to this that once again I find myself powerless in front of another human being?' Inwardly she chastises her own stupidity as despair grips her.

He flings her on the narrow bed in this tiny room and is, in no time, suffocatingly astride of her. The searing pain of memory, the hopeless sense of abandonment, the cleft of body and spirit as she is violated one more time, her sense of self rived. Conscious of her unborn child, she lies listless, without struggle, as he mercifully finishes with her within a short minute. It feels like a lifetime.

Afterwards he rises quickly, this perfect stranger and without a word departs.

She lies on the bed for some time after. Forlorn, broken. Staring at the blank and dirty ceiling, Kincaid appears as a phantom smirking lasciviously. Darkness overcomes her. She has never hated or despised herself like this before.

Eventually Biddy Mulligan appears at the door.

"You have to cop onto yourself if you want to stay here, girl. I can't have my customers going away unhappy. I'm not some charity. I have a business to run and I can't take any passengers on board. He says you lay there like a lifeless doll, like a dead crature. You have to show some enthusiasm for this game if you want to stay off the streets because there's loads more where you came from. Take the night to think about what I'm saying. Go back to the dorm and let me see you arrive tomorrow evening with an appetite."

She makes her way to the dorm and falls on the bare mattress in desolation. It's there Annie finds her later in the night.

"I've been looking for you Mary. Are you alright, mo stóir."

Mary falls into her arms and sobs.

"I can't stand it Annie. I'm losing the sense of myself. I wish I was dead. It's only my baby that's keeping me here."

"What? You're pregnant? How far gone are you?"

"Four months."

Mary howls at the uttering of confirmation coming from her lips. Somehow it makes her situation permanent, more real. Confiding in Annie. And her prison perpetual. Annie holds her for a long time until the pain and grief is expiated. Then she whispers softly.

"This is a game here, Mary. We have to play it in order to survive. And you have all the more reason now. Sure I'll help you. We're the best actresses in the whole of New York. The best burlesque vaudeville is no match for us girls here. And it's our salvation. I'll teach you how

 even small birds fly free

to do it. And I'll take you under my wing. I'll make sure Biddy doesn't send the rough fellas to you any more."

"But I'd still have to do it, Annie. I don't think I can survive letting another man inside me. I'm sure it will rip me apart."

"And you won't have to if you take lessons from me, mo stóir. Most of the fellas who come in here are desperate. They have such little money. They save up for weeks for a shot at us. And in a way we provide them with a great service. They are so lonely and lost, the most of them. Real sisters of mercy we are. Here's the trick. We play along with them. Like the consummate actresses we are. Moaning and saying the most outrageous things to them. They are so easy to stoke up. We give them the impression that we are dying for it too. Like if they hadn't turned up that night, we would explode and self combust with desire. A few wiggles here and a shake there, you just reach out for their mickey and bobs your uncle, they explode, right on cue. The poor cratures don't have the cents or the sense for a second round and have to leave kind of satisfied and empty and frustrated all at the same time. The thing is to keep up the pretence all the way, showing disappointment after and the hope that they will come back again. And that you can't wait for that. Otherwise they can get violent. But when you get it right, which I'll teach you, it's a triumph and you'll be an expert in no time. Sleep now, my cailín deas and we'll have our first class in the morning."

The following morning, with all the other girls gathered round, they begin her 'class'. For the first time in months, Mary is overcome with uproarious laughter convulsing in two as the girls enact various techniques designed to manipulate the notional fancy man in front of them, using words and phrases and actions that would make a Bishop splutter and blush. Eventually, they prevail on Mary to perform. She loses her inhibitions in the midst of their clamorous encouragement and uproarious laughter and cavorts in front of them. The gathered women respond with cheers to every suggestive thought that comes out of her mouth. She swivels her hips languidly, seductively, voluptuously to loud and riotous applause. She didn't realise she had it in her. In the end, eventually, she capitulates in surrender to the mood and slides to the floor overcome with laughter until all her muscles hurt.

It's hard for her to comprehend. 'How is it possible that these wonderful women have saved my life twice in as many days? I haven't felt such joy or love for months.' Thoughts flying through her. These women together, separated from their homes, their culture, the villages that nurtured them, are now free of convention, of having to watch themselves or their behaviour and suddenly find liberty to be different, here in their own, small, tiny, joyous community. Mary thinks 'It's impossible to imagine it.'

When she calms down from splitting her sides in laughter, Annie eventually says,

"A sexy, beautiful woman like you, Mary. You'll have no trouble getting them to spill their load. You'll be teaching us your tricks in no time."

In the following days and weeks, she learns and practices well. Annie is true to her word and keeps the rough ones away. Mary comes to understand the situation she is in and delights in the remarkable and glorious companionship and support of these women. They even become a force to be reckoned.

Annie says one day,

"We can be our own gang, girls. Why should the fellas own the streets? Look at the "Dead Rabbits"[18] and the "Forty Thieves"[19] how they keep us all safe from the "Bowery Boys"[20]. We have our own bowery boys to fend off."

"We could call ourselves Biddy's Best Girls," Mary says, remembering the words Annie shouted at Biddie the first night she arrived.

"A sound idea. And we could steal the motto from the three musketeers 'one for all and all for one'."

It is a special moment for them all. Naturally and organically the situation they are in forges a strong and binding commitment to each another. An oath of loyalty, so to speak. In a strange way, Mary feels safer than she has felt for quite some time.

The summer arrives and mornings are a joy. They feel free then, to enjoy the place. A bunch of girls all dressed up and promenading Five Points. The hubbub of activity exhilarating. Hawkers set up in the square. The shouting and the humour of the vegetable sellers. Outside the various tenements, women are sewing and mending; Menfolk are carving and shaping wood or drinking tea and smoking pipes; Shoemakers, tailors toil in the sun and the two blacksmiths on either end of the street sweat over their forge. The stench from the slaughter-houses, tanneries or knackers yard cannot dampen their enthusiasm on those glorious days. This corner of New York city is an island apart.

          even small birds fly free

To; Nóra Flanagan,
The Quakers House,
Arch Street, Philadelphia

From: Mary O'Brien,
Biddy Mulligans,
Five Points,
New York City
10th May, 1849

Dear Nóra,

I am writing to you in desperate circumstances. I know you won't judge me. I am here at Biddy Mulligans in Five Points. As you can probably guess, it's a brothel. In all honesty, I am well looked after by the other girls here. All Irish. They are the salt of the earth. But as you can imagine by now, I am well gone. I'm six months almost and I'm afraid the madam won't keep me when I'm really showing which although I've got away with this up to now, will not be able to do so much longer. And I know she will throw me out on the street then.

I should have asked you earlier in the letter. How are you and the girls? I hope you are well.

I'm in a bad way, Nóra, as you can see and you said I should write to you. You're my last hope, I'm sorry to say. And I know you probably have heaps of trouble of your own. But do you think one of the Quaker people could help me out?

Thank you Nóra for being my friend

Love

Mary O'Brien

Doonpeter, County Cork

Spring, 1848

In which Peadar O'Brien has a fateful meeting with Kincaid which ends with him being thrown into jail and despair but is miraculously rescued

Peadar O'Brien wonders often to himself if there isn't an obscenity to his happiness. He now goes about each day with a deep, unfettered joy, transfixed by this beautiful woman who has become his companion. Like a teenager in love, he greets the morning with exhilaration. Bewildered that he is allowed the gift of such a love at this time in his life; That he gets to enjoy the privilege of another minute, hour, day in Eileen's company. That this love is located in a time of great misery and sorrow for others does not escape him and yet bliss, rapture best describes the mood that being with her brings.

They have their difficult moments. Deep in the middle of the night, Eileen awakens regularly with the awful realisation that her precious children are gone. Then, overcome with grief and hopelessness, she wails in his arms, clinging to him, bereft, that she will never again be able to hold them close, smell their sweet breath on her cheek. Her tongue thick with heartache, words desert her. "Peadar," her speech slow, halting, thick, her words broken with sobs of woe. "I took my children for granted. Their birth. Their life. This loss, though. Their absence is not like that. It's a deep, conscious, wound, a chasm that I have to negotiate every day in order to keep going."

At those times, her anguish is so raw, her abandonment to it so complete, that he wonders if she will lose her mind and reason. Yet even then, in the midst of torrents of such pain, as he holds her, Peadar still feels blessed that it is he who is gathering her up, that it is to him she turns for comfort. With all his heart, with his whole being, he desperately wants to be strong for her then, as waves of desolation wash over her. And in it all, within those desperate moments, he is acutely aware that there are so many, too many mothers wrecked by this plague. He thinks there is a grotesque section of hell reserved for bereaved mothers.

After these moments have passed, it is usually then that Mary appears in his mind's eye. He misses her terribly but he knows he is not alone in that. All on those working on the relief road endure the absence of a loved one, consoling themselves with the thought that no matter how much hardship their loved ones are experiencing wherever they are, it cannot be as bad as the homelessness and hunger endured by being

even small birds fly free

marooned, stranded, stuck in this god-forsaken country. Nevertheless, at moments like this, Peadar would love to know she is alive, that she made it across the ocean to the new world. He has no idea how he will discover that.

As Spring takes hold, Eileen and he, together, have a good rhythm going. When it moves into early summer and the days get longer, they stroll together in the evening alongside the River Bride. New life taking shape around them, forming an incongruous backdrop. The gentle Spring air enveloping them both. The sweet, yet frenetic mating song of small birds calling out, delighting: The chirruping thrush, the lilting sing-song of the blackbird, the staccato echo of the wren, the glorious celebration of the skylark dominating the skyline. There is a fragrance in the hedgerows and a gentle warmth from the evening sun on their faces.

Near the bridge up towards Doonpeter, a shimmering carpet of bluebells captivates with its honeyed sweetness, drifting in a lake of blue and violet, flickering ephemerally in the dappled sunlight. The evening sunsets from the prominent position of their scalpeen on Doonpeter hill casts a lateral light over the fields and hedgerows for miles around, illuminating patterns and shapes of rich greens, vibrant blues, scintillating yellows. These transfiguring events provide huge consolation and healing for the losses they have both sustained.

"You must be worried about Mary, Peadar. Sure it's only natural."

"Well in many ways there's not much good in worrying if I can't do anything about it, so I just let it go," he lies to her, "God knows what I would be like if I didn't have you, Eileen. You are the thing I cannot account for. You have changed my life. I am so grateful."

And with these words, he reaches across and embraces her, thrilled by her presence and the intimacy of her touch. There is a stabilising consolation to be had by her very presence.

He is at work, head bowed and thinking of Mary the following morning, when Jones summons him from way down the road. As he makes his way towards him he makes out the figure of Canon Ryan, the parish priest in Mallow, sitting astride a horse beside him. His heart skips a beat. What's the priest doing out here so far away from his usual beat. As if recognising the disquiet featuring in Peadar's face, the Canon shouts from afar,

"There you be, Peadar, I haven't seen you for a while. This came for you last week," he says, handing him a letter from his satchel.

"My God," Peadar thinks, "if it isn't Mary's handwriting" as the priest hands him a letter.

He rips the envelope open with an urgency he has never felt before.

Da,

I made it to New York.

I will write again when I am settled.

I hope this finds you, and finds you well.

I thought Canon Ryan would be the best bet.

Love,

Mary

Those simple lines lift his spirits exponentially. A wave of relief courses through his body and the burden he has borne silently, quietly, drops from his shoulders.

"Is it good news then, Peadar"

"The very best, Father. It's from Mary. She made it safely to New York."

"Well God bless her. That's great to hear in this day and age."

In the evening, Eileen shares his delight. They can think of building a future now, together, knowing Mary is safe.

   even small birds fly free

The winter took its toll on the work force and it is a very different contingent of people that Peadar now works alongside as the summer finally arrives. He acknowledges to himself the wisdom of his decision to keep his head down and keep himself to himself. God only knows what his state of mind would be if he had got involved and suffered the painful loss of so many as they succumbed to fever, hunger, the cold. They continue to be engaged in this tough part of the work, carving the road out of the huge rock face which hangs over the Bride river. The mindlessness of it all never ceasing to amaze Peadar. But this he also puts to the back of his mind. Hubristic imperiousness truly an apt description for the imperial power that has colonised his country for centuries.

In the middle of the first week in June, he stands up from the task, mid-morning to wipe his brow. Gazing around him, he spies in the distance the brooding presence of Kincaid on a huge black stallion, travelling towards them. The horse, a replacement for the one McCarthy stole, he thinks. He watches Kincaid tentatively guide the horse as they gingerly find their way through the partly made road; The carved rock face providing a significant hazard.

What is Kincaid doing here he wonders? He can see Kincaid has his stare fixed on him from a long way off.

"O'Brien," Kincaid bellows, still ten yards away, lording it over all from this great height astride his mount. "I heard you were here and I want a word with you. I am searching for that little guttersnipe McCarthy. The fucking horse thief. I have an idea you might very well know where he is."

Peadar looks at him blankly.

"And if I did know, why would I be telling you? Haven't you wreaked enough havoc in your little life already?"

A pall of unconcealed rage crosses Kincaid's face

"Hmm. So that's the way of it, is it, O'Brien? Well now, you might be wanting to find him yourself after I tell you my little story. Didn't the two of us, McCarthy and me, have great sport with your girl Mary last autumn, green-gowning her up in Lackendarragh woods. My goodness, a great little ride she was. Lying there begging for it, as horny as a rabbit. Your little friend McCarthy is probably, to this day, making himself go blind stroking his John Thomas with the memory of it. Such a harlot she is."

The words cut through Peadar as a flaming spear. In a blind rage he rushes towards the mounted reprobate. But before he can get to him, the black stallion rears up, spins and in one movement tears down the partly-made road. Within a few strides, Kincaid loses his hold and with one leg caught in the stirrup he is flung at full speed from the saddle his momentum carrying him into the rock face. There is a loud hollow-sounding crack as his skull hits a jagged, jutting projection of the escarpment. The horror convulses those around into paralysis. Kincaid's lifeless form is dragged by the horse another fifty yards, the clothes and skin being ripped off his back by the sharp stones, until finally his foot disentangles and he, this despised landlord agent, the man who has caused so much distress in this valley, is cast to the ground, blood springing from his shattered scalp and mangled body.

The suddenness of it all, the horror of the outcome shakes those standing there, riveting them to the spot. Peadar is overcome with torrential conflicts of emotion; Horror, panic, hatred, rage, pity, sorrow and despair. He can hardly speak.

The events that follow are beyond his consciousness. The constabulary are summoned from Mallow town and they arrive in two horse drawn carts. Kincaid is laid out in one and Peadar is handcuffed to walk alongside the second.

"It'll be Van Diemen's land[21] for you now, O'Brien," Jones retorts as he helps load Kincaid's body onto the cart, a cruel, rasping chuckle escaping from his mouth. "We won't be seeing you again. And good riddance to bad rubbish."

Peadar is sick with the dread of it all throughout the slow, tortuous journey to Mallow police station and the cells. Life changing in a matter of minutes. He tries to think of Eileen for comfort but all he finds inside himself is recrimination. Wanting to be someone who will bring her solace, he is now the cause of further heartbreak.

The hearing is two days later at the Mallow magistrates court. In his cell, Peadar remains in shock. The cell walls provide the blank tapestry for his beleaguered state. Kincaid's leer and his sunken mangled face the stuff of haunted nightmares. He cannot think of Mary; He cannot recall Kincaid's words about her. This he suppresses with all his being. To do otherwise, he thinks, would send him insane.

On the morning of the hearing, he is taken up from the cells to the dock. The sombre mood of the court and the solemn face of the Justice provides no comfort. When the hearing begins and the case is read out,

	even small birds fly free

he discovers that he is charged with causing an affray which brought about the death of the respected businessman, Mr. Robert Kincaid.

Justice Crawley, is about to read him the riot act when there is a kerfuffle at the back of the courtroom. A tall, elegant man strides confidently up the aisle. Peadar recognises him immediately as William Hudson of Glenville Manor. He cannot comprehend why this esteemed man is here, at Mallow court, at his arraignment.

"If I may, your honour," he starts to say.

"Who might you be," Crawley demands.

"I'm sorry, your honour. My name is William Hudson. I am the son of the Lord of Glenville Manor. A number of things have come to my attention in respect of this case which I think you should hear before pronouncing judgement."

"I'll grant you permission to address the court properly. Please step forward and take the oath."

The courtroom is astonished at this turn of events and an air of expectancy settles over the watching gallery.

"I have been aware of the accused for a number of years, your Lordship. He is a man who has made an enormous contribution to the township of Graigue and to my own township Glenville. He established a school from his own resources and has been teaching all ages of schoolchildren for the past fifteen years until the recent plague hit us all hard. The deceased on the other hand, and I rarely if ever wish to speak ill of the dead, has caused immense hardship, heartbreak and death among my neighbours by his great haste and little compassion evicting, last summer, all the villagers of the township of Graigue, of whom Mr. O'Brien was one. Most of the villagers have died of starvation since their eviction. Also, in the last couple of days, a number of the workers on the relief road have reported to me that Mr. Kincaid made scurrilous and vile remarks about Mr. O'Brien's daughter prior to the incident in question. Remarks, I hasten to add, which could not be repeated in this court of law. And if I may say so, your honour, would guarantee to inflame the passions of any man here present. It is my proposition therefore that it was this undue provocation which caused Mr. Kincaid's death. Witnesses have also told me that Mr. O'Brien did not touch either the stallion or Mr. Kincaid but that the horse reared up on its own accord. It is a stallion I may add which was known only briefly to the late Mr. Kincaid. He had purchased it just a few weeks ago."

"That's all well and good Mr. Hudson. But what am I to do with the accused. I can't have him running amok in the countryside. Justice has to be served."

"Yes, your honour. If it please your honour, I would be happy to take him into my care. I have need of a bookkeeper to manage my estate and would be happy for Mr. O'Brien to fulfil that role. As a schoolteacher, he is well equipped. And if I may make the point your Lordship, there has been so much suffering in this Barony in the last three years that I think some mercy would not go amiss."

"You're overstepping the mark there, Mr. Hudson. I thank you not to lecture me on how to balance the scales of justice and mercy."

"I'm sorry, your honour."

There is a long pause. All eyes are on the magistrate as he closes his. There is a suspenseful silence in the court. Justice Crawley keeping all guessing for an age as he deliberates. It feels like an eternity for Peadar. Eventually, Justice Crawley looks long and hard at Peadar and commands him to rise to his feet.

"You're a lucky man, O'Brien, to have someone to speak eloquently on your behalf. I am minded to bind you over for the next three years into the care and keeping of Mr. Hudson here. Let me not see you before this court again. This case is dismissed."

Loud gasps ricochet across the gallery. Peadar can hardly believe what he is hearing. He is free. He has a second chance.

Mr. Hudson takes him by the arm and leads him outside to his horse and trap tethered on the side street of the courthouse.

Peadar remains silent beside him out of awe, respect and disbelief as he guides the horse through the crowd milling around by the clockhouse and they make their way over the Blackwater bridge out along the back roads towards Monee. After ten minutes on the road, Hudson turns to him and says,

"That's an exceptional woman you've got there, O'Brien. A man is very fortunate to have a wife like that."

Peadar is stunned and says nothing.

"I wouldn't be here in town at all if it wasn't for her. She came to me two evenings ago and implored me. Placed all her energy and arguments in front of me. She is an irresistible force. A rare combination of beauty and intelligence, I might say. In the end though, it was when she told me you were to have a baby that opened my eyes. After all the losses

   even small birds fly free

you've both sustained. That was the thing that swung it for me. We've had so much disease and death in this valley. I thought to myself, 'let's have the joy of a birth of a child'. And lets also make sure this child has her father to take care of her. Don't you think so?"

Shocked, speechless, Peadar does not know how to respond. Hudson looks at him queerly.

"Cat got your tongue?"

Peadar spends the rest of the journey in a state of ecstasy. 'Can it be true? He thinks, or is Eileen making up a story to convince the man. Hardly, he says to himself. That's not her way. I'm to be a father. I'm to have a child with Eileen. This man next to me is my saviour. He has given me a job and my freedom.'

"I have the old gatehouse free at the moment. I thought you and that wonderful woman could move in there. I'll give you a couple of days and then I expect you to turn up at the Manor where I'll show you the books. Does that sound fair to you?"

Once again, Peadar is stunned into silence and can hardly speak.

"You're a man of few words, O'Brien. But maybe that's for the best. I'll leave you off at Doonpeter bridge here and you can move into the lodge tomorrow. Slán leat as they say."

And with that he reins the horse in and Pádraig is left on the road sheepishly waving him goodbye, but avid, eager to find Eileen and make sense of this new world into which they have been plunged together.

Oh joy. Oh joy.

Eileen sees him from a long way off. Peadar watches her running down the hill towards him. They rush into each others arms. Sobbing with joy and relief.

"Is it true, Eileen? Are we to have a baby?

"Yes, dear Peadar, we are. I couldn't be sure before. The last morning, after you left, I felt the baby kick inside me. And I know for certain now. Are you happy?"

"Gosh, I couldn't be more happy Eileen. Thank you so much."

That night, he awakes suddenly and is immediately overcome with thoughts of Mary and of the last words of that man, Kincaid. Guilt, powerlessness, anguish defeat him. Something breaks deeply inside him. The one task he was dedicated to, gave his life up to, had made a solemn vow to his Brigid that he would take care of their daughter; This he has failed in. The spectre of Kincaid sneering at him in triumph reduces him completely. He feels emasculated. Eileen wakes to find him sobbing.

"What's the matter, Peadar?"

Peadar recounts to her Kincaid's parting shot.

"I feel I have failed her, Eileen. If it's true what he says, I feel she was so alone in the last weeks before she left. I did notice she was different but thought it was a result of the devastation which surrounded us all. Why would she not tell me?"

"Cause she knew it would break you Peadar. Listen to me now. It's very important that you understand what I am to say. That Kincaid raped Mary the onus is totally on Kincaid. This is what every woman has to know. We can torture ourselves with guilt and recrimination. We can tell ourselves that it's the way we looked, our dress, our manner which caused this and all of that is just devilish lies. If Kincaid set about taking her by force, that has wholly come from Kincaid's evil heart. There is nothing any of us can do to protect one another from that malevolence. There is only one person who is responsible for that terrible act and he is no longer with us. Mary kept the knowledge from you because she knew you would suffer with it. You must honour her now and not let it harm you."

Her words and touch bring him some comfort.

After some time, they fall asleep in one another's arms.

Try as he does though, his self indulgent mood overtakes him. During the next days, as they move into the gate house; which should be a time of great joy; and as he works alongside Hudson in the Manor House; he sinks into a deep depression. Images of Kincaid rise as an eldritch before his eyes, shaking him to the core. Kincaid's visage lords over him with a leering mouth and those fateful, last words echo loud and clear, issuing horror, pain and guilt.

Peadar's thoughts also migrate towards young McCarthy. How could he take part in that? And then afterwards, the bare cheeked nature of the boy to come to him in Cork with money for Mary's passage. As if that would compensate for his complicity in Kincaid's degeneracy? At times Peadar's thoughts cause him to spit with rage and bitterness.

He is overcome by his own sense of failure. Failure as a father. That his Mary was let down, exposed. That he even allowed Kincaid access to their home. He remembers and dissects that morning like a physician,

even small birds fly free

looking for clues as to Kincaid's evil designs, seeking clues he failed to see then. The internal dialogue consumes him and he is also haunted by the fact that Mary couldn't approach him, tell him afterwards what had happened. Could not come to him for comfort.

Self incriminating thoughts catapult at him incessantly, encompass him compounding his wretchedness with a reproachful examination of his life's work. The teacher of the valley? Huh! How can he now look at his life anymore with any sense of achievement and pride when he couldn't inculcate in a young boy, one he thought was his brightest star as well, just basic decency and courage. Thoughts of betrayal, anger, hatred well up in him towards young McCarthy. He is consumed with it all.

Mary reaches out to him daily but to no avail.

"Come back to me, Peadar, come back to me. Don't allow that man to achieve through his death what he was not able to do in his life.. Come back to me. Leave that place you go to."

Her words fall on deaf, lifeless ears. He is gone from her and the joy they shared has dissipated. He struggles through every day at the Manor. Mechanically doing what is asked. Fortunately he is good with figures and the work is easy for him. Hudson, preoccupied with other demands, does not seem to notice anything. Otherwise he would not last.

His hourly thoughts are dominated with continuous and revisionist conversations with Kincaid; Raising him from the dead to challenge him, stand up to him, demonstrate Kincaid's scurrilous character for its cant and affectation, exposing him for the bully he is. Round after round they go together in his head as he dredges up courage and arguments he never found or thought worthwhile while Kincaid was still alive.

These thoughts swap places with brawls with young McCarthy as he unleashes his fury on him, grabbing him around his slender neck and slinging him to the ground, endlessly choking the life out of him. He has barely room for anything else in his life, the arguments with Kincaid growing louder and more strident as the loving, compassionate voice of Eileen whispering 'come back to me' becomes ever more faint. Disappearing into the distance.

In the few sane moments he snatches, he is in despair. 'God, even though I have had to endure a lot in my life and have come through so much, I see no way, no path on which I can be delivered from this awful torment.'

The Caledonia & Boston, USA

April, 1848 - end 1848

In which Caelan O'Donovan first meets Bridie Mulcahy[22], is enraptured and travels with her and large family to Boston, meets Seán Mulcahy and settles into the Irish ghetto in Boston.

The first time Caelan O'Donovan sees Bridie Mulcahy will live forever in his memory. On the morning of his departure from Liverpool, as he queues to board the Caledonia, he picks her out among the throng of refugees on the dockside, surrounded by her six children; struggling as she is to keep them together. He is overcome by her spirit and beauty and it has an immediate effect on him, lifting his mood like a tincture of opium. Her long, flowing black hair, her mesmerizing almond-shaped, green eyes and beautiful face set his heart racing in a way he has never experienced before. He wonders if it's the excitement of the journey. He can't help himself though and nervously approaches her.

"You look like you might need a hand," he suggests tentatively, knowing how vulnerable she may feel at being approached out of the blue like this.

She looks at him with a broad, gracious smile and answers, 'as gaeilge',

"Tá tú an-chineál," (You're very kind.)

This is how they meet and start their story together. As simple as that. As most stories begin. And this is what makes the journey across the Atlantic, three weeks on the shores of heaven, as far as Caelan is concerned, so easy. Pádraig always says he's a soft touch with women, but this is different. He has never felt like this before. Spring and the voyage and a new start all coalescing to form the perfect background for their tryst. He willingly capitulates to the beauty, charm, courage and energy of this extraordinary woman.

Caelan helps her with the children and what little they carry with them and they make their way on board finding bunks adjacent to each another.

"I'm Bridie" she says, when they have settled, "and these are my children. Gráinne, is eight and these four are two sets of twins, Finbarr, Aine, Liam and Eoin. My youngest, this toddler is Patrick."

Caelan is astounded at her courage taking on such a journey with her whole family in tow, all on her own.

"Where are you from?"

even small birds fly free

"We had a tiny place just north of Cork city in the village of Glenville. Do you know it?"

"I don't know that part of the county well at all. I'm from West Cork, Skibbereen.

"Oh Skibb. You have had it tough there."

"You never said a truer word. I lost my father and mother and little sister in the first year."

"We were lucky really. With our landlord. The second year of the plague, my husband Seán left for America. To see if he could raise money for passage for all of us. He's been gone a year now and settled in Boston. In the end, it wasn't needed. Although many of our neighbours, my friends, on the other side of the valley are all lost to the plague, our Landlord, Mr. Hudson, bought us out a couple of months ago, paid for our bothán even though it was legally his and stumped up for our passage. It's Boston we're bound for, to be re-united with Seán."

During the glorious days that follow, Caelan loves helping her. He wins the friendship and trust of the children through careful and judicious rationing of the oatmeal cakes he has in his sack. 'Well done, Pádraig,' he says to himself, each time he doles them out and watches the glee on the childrens' faces and more importantly, the look of gratitude on Bridie's.

They have the evenings together, on their own, just the two of them; stolen evenings, with the children fast asleep. They swap stories, hopes and dreams. The ten years difference in their ages obliterated by their common energy, the ease with which they share in one another's company. Caelan is enthralled. Somehow the days are too short for him and he thinks he's the only man, the only person on board, who is sad to hear the call 'land ahoy' being bellowed out as the Caledonia nears the other shore of the Atlantic.

He is nervous, of course, meeting Seán. He's easy to pick out. A tall, strapping man with a handsome face and wide smile, who waves vigorously at his family from the quayside, as they dock. The moment of reunion is moving. The children overcome with excitement and Caelan looks on, enviously, at the love and affection evident between Bridie and Seán.

After a while, Bridie turns to introduce the both of them and Seán generously grabs Caelan's hand.

"Have you got plans for yourself, Caelan?"

"Not really. I'm just glad to be here. I'm sure something will work out."

"Hold on a minute, there," He says, "This is a very dangerous place to be Irish. We're not liked here. Despised in fact. So you need to be cautious."

"What do you mean?"

"Well, we all gang together. It's the safest way. So I think it best if you come along with us. I've settled in Batterymarch Street. I'm sure I can find a place for you. There is a fierce gang of louts ready at all times to bash our heads in. A secret organisation called 'know nothings'. If you try and make it on your own they will destroy you. They plan an attack on us at regular intervals or when they get stoked up with drink. It's all we can do to hold them at bay, away from our women and children. A strong lad like you will be an asset to us."

"I see. It's very kind of you to take me under your wing. Are you sure it's no trouble?"

"Well, it's the least I can do after you helped take care of my family on the way over. I'm obliged to you."

With that they shake hands again, gather their stuff and make their way into the city.

Despite Seán's gloomy observations, the steps Caelan takes away from the docks are full of hope, leaving him buoyant, carrying him along on a wave of optimism. The docklands and bay feel sumptuous on this gorgeous summer's day. The stately buildings on the shoreline which run into the centre of the city amplify his thoughts and mood. Regal, brownstone buildings of different shapes and sizes, their deep, ochre colour reflecting the morning sun of this June day.

He is in America. He has made it. The land of opportunity. Here there is no King or oppressor. The land belongs to all. A republic. What he dreams for his homeland. What are the words of the song; 'The land of the free and the hope of the brave'. And that great declaration of independence from the British Empire, something he so longs for his own people; What are the words of that? As he walks along the lanes of the city following Bridie, Seán and the children, he sets his gaze on everything with wonder and awe and tries to store all these images in his imagination, his first impressions of this great land. All the while trying to recollect that bold rallying cry, that impressive vision.

                    even small birds fly free

Yes, he shouts inwardly to himself, as if there it is, painted in bright colours on the azure blue skyline before him; As if the words were written especially for him - the great declaration, stroking all the colours out of the sky, "*We hold these truths to be self-evident, that all men are created equal, that they are endowed by their Creator with certain unalienable Rights, that among these are Life, Liberty and the pursuit of Happiness.*"

These words are going to be his motto from now on. Let the 'know nothings' deprive him of that, if they can. Fuck them. This is his country too. Now and from this point on. He can make it here.

His animated disposition does not deflate when they arrive at Batterymarsh Street.[23] In the backyards between the houses, he sees a shamble of roughly constructed huts, families teeming in and out of them. The houses themselves full to overflowing and children are running wild everywhere among the pigs and chickens. The place feral in its spirit. The stench awful.

"This is as much as we can afford at the moment," Seán says. "But it's not wise to move too far away from here, anyway. There's safety in numbers. We're among our own here. And we manage pretty well."

Seán finds him a bed in a shed. There are three others in the room, staunch lads from county Galway. It's good to be with his own people as he sets about starting his life in this great country.

The following days remain positive. He turns up at the docks every morning and whether it is the sense of presence he carries over from his Liverpool days or not, or whether it's Johnny Dolan's advice ringing in his ears - to smile broadly, he is chosen by the ganger for work every day. A dollar is the daily rate and he is thrilled to have this money. He tells Seán he wants to help out his family and make a contribution every week. Seán protests a little but Caelan reminds him of his own words that they are all in this together, and that they are safer in numbers. Seán reluctantly accepts, unaware of the sheer joy Caelan feels at being able to give to Bridie, secretly, as a gesture of the unkempt devotion raging in his heart.

And they are good to him in turn. Including him in all their social gatherings and pretty soon that part of the alley is the place people meet in the evenings. Despite the misery all around. Among the common possessions are a few musical instruments and Caelan begins to feel at home, picking up the melodeon again. It becomes an essential vehicle for the unexpressed and inexpressible fervour he holds secretly in his heart. He loves to play 'the girl I left behind' with a twinkle in his eye.

There are extra skips in his heart seeing Bridie, smiling along, as he resurrects some of the old tunes 'She moved through the Fair; 'the Rose of Tralee'.

But there is also accompanying heartache as he watches Bridie and Seán in one another's arms, so obviously deeply in love. He seeks consolation where he can find it and is happy with where he lives, with his new-found community and that he has the privilege of living his life as proximate as he can to the woman who has won his heart. He goes to work each day for her. The energy he expends every day he does joyfully. In his fantasy, in his fertile imagination he sees himself fulfilling the same apprenticeship that Jacob served for Rachel.[24]

Towards the end of the year, when he is coming home from work he observes a very strange sight. It's late afternoon and the sun is setting. There is a gorgeous light reflected on some of the warehouses which captures the delicate frames of masts of the many packet ships moored at right angles to the dock. On the street in front of the Commercial Coffee House, he sees a horse hitched to a stationary cart. The cart itself is covered with a makeshift, little cabin perched on the back. And across the street there is a fellow crouching beside a strange box-shaped instrument. He watches him for a while and from a distance before he decides to approach. When Caelan eventually walks across and is about to greet him, the man throws a black cloak which is pinned to the box over his head and disappears. Caelan is taken aback by the sudden, comical nature of this action. He is confronted with the strange, hilarious sight of a man's backside and legs; The rest of him hidden under a hood like some preternatural ghost. He does not know whether to laugh or be disturbed. Very shortly the man reappears and stares at him.

He is an older man in his late forties. His appearance looks very like paintings Caelan has seen of the Pilgrim Fathers, the first European arrivals in this city. Stern, biblical types. Not given over to much humour. Surprisingly, however, this man's face breaks into a warm smile.

"Hah," he says, "I guess you are wondering what this crazy fellow is up to. The funny thing is not many people notice me. Either they are scared when they watch my behaviour or they are too absorbed in their own little world. So what catches your attention, young man?"

Caelan is unsure now. He didn't expect such a response to his approach. He had thought he could sneak up and watch this strange fellow and be largely unobserved, but the stranger is sharp and to the point. Caelan tries not to be defensive.

     even small birds fly free

"Oh, I'm always curious. That's what my Seanair would always remark about me. If something is happening, Caelan wants to know what it is."

"Caelan, is it. My name is Ambrose Cutting[25]. I am making a photograph. Do you want to see how it works?"

"I'd love to," Caelan is excited, somehow realising this is a pivotal moment in his life.

"Well you have to be very fast. That's the main thing. And methodical. Otherwise the moment will be gone."

"If it's a photograph you're after, are you able to catch that light?"

This startles the stranger who looks back quizzically.

"Are you an artist yourself," he asks. Caelan laughs at this.

"It's not many people who know that is the trick of it all; the light. Keep that curiosity going, young man and you will discover a world worth seeking."

With that he invites Caelan to cover himself with the cloak and look into the box. What transpires amazes and overwhelms him. There in front of him is the Coffeehouse Building perfectly framed as an image to be grasped. It's almost better than the thing itself, the frame drawing attention to the exquisite detail of the building; The perfectly shaped windows, their shutters, all evenly spaced and immaculately positioned to highlight its overall simple, elegant design; the canopy blind in front providing a gorgeous relief to the flawless symmetry of the architecture.

"The most important thing is to get your image right before you start," He says, "You will not be able to change it afterwards. Come with me."

With that, he crosses the street and disappears once again through a tiny door he has made in the cabin-like structure on the cart. Caelan follows him in. It's a tight squeeze and they are immediately plunged into darkness.

"This is where the magic happens."

After a while their eyes adjust to the darkness. Cutting is holding a sheet of glass in is hand and is polishing it with a rottenstone mixture. Caelan recognises the mixture from polishing the wood frontispiece of his melodeon.

"This is to help the collodion chemical adhere to the glass plate. Watch and learn. This is the beginning of a new science.[26]"

He takes a bottle of a thick, viscous mixture and gently pours it onto the plate, tipping the plate expertly in his hand so the viscosity allows the liquid to cover the whole of its surface. Caelan is enthralled. He then reaches for a sealed tin which is sitting on a wooden draining board. Opening the lid of the tin, he slides the plate in so it stands vertically on its edge. He closes the lid.

"In there is a silver nitrate solution. It will stick to the collodion spread on the glass. Silver nitrate is light sensitive and that's where we will get our image. But we have to be quick as it only lasts ten minutes. We'll leave the plate in there for three minutes and then I'll whip it out and put it in this casing here. It's sealed so no light gets in."

Watching all this, Caelan is fascinated by the man's skill and his generosity in letting him see the work.

When Cutting has the plate safely in the sealed case, he gestures to Caelan to go out again into the evening light. Emerging from the little tiny structure, the sun is blinding at first. They move swiftly and economically towards the box which first drew Caelan's attention and Cutting clips the case to the back of the frame.

"You see this here," he says, pointing to a tab on the top of the casing holding the plate. When I pull this, it will expose the plate in the box."

He pulls the tab and a black curtain screen is drawn from the top of the box and clipped to the bottom.

"Now," he says, "The final bit of magic. And this is why you must have the picture you saw at the beginning perfectly as you want it. Because I am going to take off this cap."

He points to a circular, large plate on the front of the box, like an oversized bottle top.

"When I remove this cap for a couple of seconds, the light will flow into the box and land on the plate. The way the light hits these buildings will be reflected onto the plate and interact with the silver nitrate. And hopefully we will get an image. The thing is, you never know what kind of an image you will get. Sometimes it's beautiful, sometimes I have to start again."

He removes the cap and then deftly replaces it after five seconds. He then moves adroitly around the back, releases the tab and the black curtain screen moves up and over the top of the casing.

     even small birds fly free

"When I unclip this now, no light will get into the case. But we have to be quick."

He removes the case and gestures to Caelan to join him once again in his makeshift, dark cabin. He removes the plate and lays it in a tray of liquid.

"This is developing fluid. It will help reveal the image. I'm still working on its constituent parts."

Caelan watches open-mouthed as slowly the image of the Coffeehouse Building appears on the plate. He feels privileged to be watching the wonder of modern science at work.

"The next trick is to know when to stop this process," Cutting says as he dextrously removes the plate from the tray and lays it in another tray.

"Simple water," he gestures, "To remove the developer and stop the reaction."

Then he takes the plate and places it again vertically in a different tin. This, he explains is full of a mixture he is still experimenting with but is designed to stabilise the image they have just seen.

Finally he lights an oil lamp and expertly pours varnish over the image and seals it with the gentle heat from the lamp. They then move outside again and he holds the plate against the fading light of the day. Caelan is astonished at the exquisite image he is shown.

"There you go Caelan. Have you ever seen anything more beautiful than that?" Cutting grins widely.

"Oh Mr. Cutting, I am so taken. Can I come and help you with this when I am not working. I would love to learn more."

"Ha ha," he laughs, " I could see it would have that effect on you. Sure thing, boy. Here's my card. Come along here tomorrow evening and I will set you to work.

Caelan leaves him with a spring in his step. When he arrives home, Seán and Bridie and others crowd around him as he regales them with an account of what he has just seen. He can see in their faces and lack of real enthusiasm that this is a secret for himself alone, a revelation, a pathway to a future. Much like the manifestation he received from his recollection of the promise of the declaration of independence, Caelan sees before him, here in America, a road to follow, a covenant of opportunity. This he knows is what he has been looking for. A lifetime of perfecting the image shown to him by Mr. Cutting. This now is his dream, too. It grows inside him. Like the discovery of gold in California that he has been reading about in the papers, this represents to him, in this land of opportunity, his American dream.

To: Pádraig O'Sullivan

10, St Thomas Street,

New Orleans

July 1848

Pádraig,

I made it. Go Raibh Maith Agat.

I am here in Boston on Batterymarch Street. I am living in a small shed in a back alley and pay rent for the space. There's all sorts of people on the make here, but "needs must" as they say. And I got work on the docks. Its not great but I am managing. I'm dreading the winter but let's see what I can do between now and then. We have regular visits from No-Nothing gangs and I don't like the violence at all but I have to play my part. You know me, not great with the fisticuffs.

Most of my neighbours are desolate and uncontrollably sad, but we still try to keep positive. The plague has ripped the heart and soul out of us and people are numb with grief. Even though there's often no appetite for songs among us, we try our best. I like to have a go as we have a stock of instruments among us but the words of the songs now take on a different, deeper meaning. Sometimes they stick in my throat. I think we have changed forever.

I notice people grouping together with their own lot - people from Cork on Cork Hill as its become known. And Galway people in another neighbourhood. Its a funny thing, you know, many don't know that they are Irish, at all. They just know they are from Limerick or Cork or Clare. They and their families have lived all their lives in the same small village before this upheaval. I don't know how many of us will survive, bless us. The disease and sickness here wipes out families week after week.

You will be angry with me of course when you hear that I didn't obey your instructions about the passage. How could I Pádraig? When I got on board I found myself befriending a woman, Bridie, from a village north of Cork City who was travelling, on her own, with her six young children. I couldn't believe her courage and desperation. Her husband had gone a year before to prepare the way.

She told me something strange. She came from a tenancy in Glenville. Their landlord bought out their tenancy and others when the crop failed and paid the steerage passage for all to America. It suited him of course. That he was able to clear his land. Their neighbours in the adjoining township of Graigue had no such luck. Their homes were owned by an absentee Landlord and his agent, Kincaid, a terrifying man by all accounts, cruelly evicted the lot of them, clearing the land, leaving them to die in ditches and the workhouse. Families and friends she had known for years, poor woman; Helpless in their suffering and passing.

Anyway, we became friends. And you guessed it and what could I do, Pádraig but my store of biscuits barely lasted a week. The kids were so hungry. We managed though. And I am so grateful that we took the shorter route. I don't think we would have survived the extra thirty days crossing to New Orleans.

Her husband Seán met us when we got to Boston and so I was able to ignore the wasters who promised us gold at the end of a rainbow. And that's how I got to here.

Bridie had a great reunion with her husband. Seán helped me find the place I have now, such as it is.

I'll write again when I am more settled.

Go Raibh Maith Agat mo Bráthair.

I am forever in your debt.

Caelan

even small birds fly free

To: Caelan O'Sullivan,

Batterymarch Street,

Boston

November 1948

Caelan,

I hope this finds you well.

As for me, I am in a swamp entirely, go huile agus go hiomlán, ó thus go deireadh. (Absolutely). The heat in New Orleans is a killer and disease is rampant. The only job I could get is labouring in the ditches, clearing the levees in this swamp engulfed place. I discovered pretty soon that the reason that there were jobs available at all is that Plantation owners won't sub-contract their slaves to do this work as its too dangerous. I heard one contractor say "If I lose a slave, that's my investment gone, an Irishman only costs me a dollar".

So I set to work and it was tough, knee deep in the mud, picking and digging in the oppressive heat, under fierce sun, in these pestilential swamps, wading among stumps of trees, mid-deep in black mud, clearing the spaces pumped out by powerful steam engines, wheeling, digging, hewing, or bearing burdens. It even exhausts me telling you about it.

I was told to be on the lookout for snakes and alligators. But either I'm blind or I can't see, for a few weeks in, I sunk my pick, unknown to myself, into a nest of moccasin snakes and was bit a few times. I can still see the head of one raised to strike me now and I find sleeping difficult with that image. Some of the lads pulled me out. They told me I was lucky to survive as I was bitten by a nest of them.

I was very sick for a week. After that, there was nothing for it but to return to the dyke. The first day back was terrible. I shook all over. I learnt that Irish immigrants have been building these canals for thirty years now and no-one knows how many have died. Some say its as much as twenty thousand. For myself, I've seen things I don't want to repeat.

Telling you all this, I know you will understand that I am desperate to climb out of this pit. I have made friends with a Patty Roller, an English guy. Patty Rollers are hired by plantations to recapture escaped slaves. I think he watches me to see how I am getting on and I am optimistic of landing a job. He tells me you need to be tough. There's no room for soft stuff as the slave needs to be kept under control for his own good and not get notions above himself.

Now I know you won't like this, but I think I am quite capable of helping him run a tight ship. I know Americans despise us, seeing us all as wretched, disease-ridden papist bastards but I think I can be accepted by him. I hope by the time I write again I will be away from here.

I'm glad to hear you keep singing. It's what keeps me going. Some days I get overwhelmed with memories of the old country and our life there. I get paralyzed and breathless with the pain of it and that's when I sing. I'm either singing out loud, bellowing a tune or there's one going on in my head, comforting me. Its always your voice. I hear you in a lilting refrain of 'Mo Ghile Mear' or 'She is far from the land', and images of walking on the hills of the Beara peninsula with the sun glistening on the Atlantic either side of us, or trawling through the market in Skibbereen or sessions in Ma Murphy's appear before me.

It both breaks my heart and gives me courage to keep going.

So don't stop singing, Caelan and till I write again

Mo Grá Dhuit,

Pádraig

   even small birds fly free

Biddy Mulligan's, Five Points, NYC

May 1848

In which Mary O'Brien tries to make sense of her predicament and accept her unborn child

Mary O'Brien is in despair. Not for the first time in her life but this time it feels like the end of something. After an all too short number of weeks when she adjusts to her new surrounding, loves the camaraderie, comfort and company of the other girls, reality impinges and she understands she has to face up to it. She is now showing; Five months gone. And dreads the day when madam sends her packing. The other girls have done well protecting her but she can see now that they are also fearful for her. Apprehensive of what they are convinced awaits her. Biddy Mulligan is a hard woman and does not believe in charity. If 'her girls' are not earning she has no place for them. The fact that Mary has got away with it for so long is a miracle but in her heart of hearts, she knows it cannot last.

The joy of feeling her child kick and tumble inside her, The inexplicable and ineffable nature of the event itself she is barely able to register, such is her fear for the future. In the early hours of the morning, when the customers have left and the girls grab sleep in their cramped dormitory, she lies awake. The spectre of Kincaid haunts her continuously. She recoils from the thought that she will not be able to look at her baby when the day comes, let alone nurse the poor child. Such is her disgust and disdain for that man and the trauma she relives whenever the event itself looms in her consciousness, a violation so thorough that it has ripped from her any sense of who she was before that day in Lackendarragh woods.

Thoughts clamour in her mind's eye during those lonely hours between wakefulness and oblivion. 'Why me?' 'Did I give him cause?' Should I have struggled?' 'Why was Cormac so passive?' 'Did he also lust like Kincaid?' 'Are all men the same?' 'How can I ever tell Da?' 'How can I love this child?' 'A product of such a man?' 'Everyone knows that a son or daughter is like the parent?'

In those long nights, what was previously a comfort becomes a curse; She herself had Ma (whom she never knew but was told about) and Da as her parents and the splendour of that becomes something to oppress her. What a 'Da' she is bequeathing to her child in Kincaid.

Annie Joyce remains strong for her. "Era, sure, of course I'll be there for you Mary," she says one day, when Mary is feeling particularly low,

"Our family motto 'Bás Roimh Easonóir' (death before dishonour) is a promise of that. So don't worry, mo chroí, I will fight tooth and nail to keep you here. I'll down tools or indeed not even stroke 'one', if it comes to that."

And with that quip, both of them are reduced to howls of laughter.

In the first week of July though, the dreaded summons arrives. One of the girls is despatched to tell Mary that Biddie Mulligan wants to see her in her room. She rises from her bed with a sinking feeling in the pit of her stomach, her legs unsteady as she makes her way to the stately room at the end of the corridor.

She is surprised when she knocks and opens Biddie's door to see a nun in her full habit engaged in an intense conversation with Biddie.

"There you are Mary and aren't you the very lucky girl. Not that I think you deserve it. But this sister here has offered to take you off my hands, paying me the $30 I will lose through missing your service."

Mary is taken aback at this sudden turn of events and turns to look at the nun sitting by the window; A striking woman in her twenties, with bright blue eyes, an engaging smile, startlingly pretty, her face framed like a portrait by the navy blue veil she is wearing.

"I'm Sister Agnes, and it's lovely to meet you Mary. Conas tá tú, a stóir," she says with not a cloud of judgement in her manner. Mary's heart beats so fast she feels faint. "Sure, why don't you get your things and we will be on our way, if you like. There's not much of the day left in it."

Mary hears the musical lilt of a Cork accent in Sister Agnes' voice and immediately feels at home.

Saying goodbye to Annie and the other girls is hard. "Sure, you can come back to see us when the baby's born," Annie says as she gives her a big hug.

Outside Five Points is transformed for her through this young nun's eyes. The noisy shouts of traders seem coarse, the ribald laughter from the bars, the stench and smell assault her in a different way. Mary feels protective of the sister as they make their way down new Bowery to the harbour and pier. They board the Fulton ferry to Brooklyn and as the ferry leaves Manhattan, Mary feels a freedom grow deep inside her. Her mood changes and the late afternoon sun on the river creates bright, glittering diamonds which sparkle and complement her mood. She is full of questions

    even small birds fly free

"How did you hear of me? Did you just stumble on the place by chance? I never expected a sister to come into that house, how can that be?"

They rush out of her like a torrent.

Sister Agnes laughs heartily.

"You have a friend in Pittsburgh, yes? Nóra Flanagan? Sure, she contacted the sisters there. We've been in Pittsburgh a few years now and are just starting off in New York. She told us all about you and how desperate you are."

"Oh my goodness. Nóra, yes I wrote to her. But why did you respond? I don't understand."

"That's a long story, girl. And you'd want to know our history to understand that.[27] But you and girls like you are why we are here. It's been that way from the very beginning in Dublin, sixteen years ago. The woman who started the movement was fifty eight at the time. Can you imagine that? An old woman of fifty eight? Her name was Catherine Macauley. She had been left a fortune by the good people she looked after, Protestants mind you, and built a house right in the centre of posh Dublin with the desire to help young women who were vulnerable. Lots of girls in service in the city are put in the family way by their employers and often ended up homeless. Catherine gave them a home."

Mary is touched deeply by the basic humanity that this young woman espouses and the extraordinary strength of the movement she represents. Something she had never heard about in the Ireland she had left behind.

"She became very popular and lots of other women joined to help. Of course, the archbishop couldn't have that. Us women wandering the streets doing good. They were so threatened, those men, so he commanded Catherine to found a religious order and that's what she did. Fair play to her. No man was going to get in her way."

At this point Sister Agnes drew a deep breath, proud as she is of belonging to this group of extraordinary women.

"And after that we grew and grew very fast and have followed Irish people wherever they were forced to emigrate. England first, then here and we've also just gone to Australia. And you're the very girl we are trying to help. So you can now feel safe Mary. We will take care of you."

Tears begin to roll down Mary's face as she takes in what is happening. When they leave the ferry they make their way along the majestic Brooklyn streets of tall elegant houses. After a short walk from the pier they arrive at the convent house on Willoughby Avenue. Mary is charmed. The tall three story building with its soft features, the delicately-carved oak front door with its stylish fanlight rise above her as if to greet her from the morass in which she has been submerged, the door to safety to be reached by ten wide stone steps framed by an exquisitely wrought iron balustrade.

Sister Agnes turns to her and smiles. "Welcome home, Mary" and reaches for her arm to accompany her up the stoop. Mary stretches for the balustrade as if to a bulwark and grabs the rail to help her up the flight of stone steps as on a journey to heaven and refuge.

When they are halfway up the steps, Mary senses a blur of activity above her as a tall, handsome, Black man comes rushing down the stairs to help with her belongings.

"Shucks, sister, you should have called me to help you with the move," he says, as he gently and courteously relieves Mary of the sack of belongings she is carrying.

Sister Agnes laughs. "Era, I wouldn't have wanted you to be setting all those girls a quiver if you came with me and moved among them, so I went for Mary on my own. This is Samuel, Mary. This lovely man has been sent to look after us. He can fix anything that needs fixing and he keeps our spirits up with his good humour. Samuel, this is Mary. After she has settled in with us, I expect her to be the same kind of tonic that you are, bless you and her."

During this conversation and introduction, Mary is surprised to see that Samuel is blushing from either the unsolicited praise or the embarrassment of their meeting. What she cannot deny however, is a sudden movement in her heart, along with her baby doing a somersault in her womb, such was the effect of this charming man's southern accent. All in all, it was turning into a sweet arrival for her.

The next few days and weeks are a mixture. Mary settles into her home and is busy with the work, cleaning, helping to cook and take care of the few street children the sisters have taken in. It feels natural to her to be in this giving environment. In the nighttime however, panic again visits her and she takes refuge outside, sitting on the steps of the stoop, the night air having cooled from the heat of the day. There she cries her woman's tears, silently, unobtrusively. And it is there that Samuel finds her.

	even small birds fly free

"I've been watching you for a while, to make sure you are all right. Do you mind if I sit with you here. I won't say anything. I have found that it's nearly always better if you don't feel so alone at moments like this," he says the first night he approaches her.

Mary is surprised by this. She has never before known of a man who could see the value of tears, particularly silent ones, hidden ones. All the men she had known including her Da saw tears as a weakness. Sure men could be angry and also understand a woman's rage but tears, sobs, quietly quickening they were frightened by. She wonders at this man who not only was not daunted by them but exudes a kind of calm, peaceful serenity towards her and just sits alongside her as she continues to weep. She also reflects that this kind man has demonstrated no thought or judgement on her because she has been taken in from a brothel.

On the third night he finds her there, she breaks her silence. She tells him of Kincaid. Of her defilement at his hands. And of her fears for her child. Of her apprehension of what she is capable of in rejecting her child. All these things he listens to, attentively, supportively. He does not offer any solutions. He does not try and console or ameliorate any of the pain she is evidently feeling. He just lets her ramble in her thoughts, even if they often spew from her mouth inconsistently and haphazardly. When she finishes, he reaches out to her and gathers her into the crook of his shoulder. She willingly nestles there, breathing him in, feeling the quiet stillness of his heart, resting in his calm assuredness, taking in the warm, masculine smell of his body.

It is not long before Mary finds herself sneaking out to the stoop as night falls, no longer because she wants to cry in silence. If she is able to be honest with herself, it is always in the fervent hope that she will find Samuel there and they can be with one another for a few stolen moments of each day. The feelings she has are unrecognisable to her. A kind of nervous excitement, fluttering in her stomach, an exhilarating explosion of joy whenever she sees him that also reduces her to a weakness. She is a little frightened of it all but cannot stop herself. She finds herself powerfully drawn to this young man who shows kindness and wisdom beyond his years.

What she doesn't know is that Samuel is experiencing the same conflagration of emotions. He also can't wait until the end of each day, living with the fervent and disorienting hope that as night falls she will be there again, this beautiful woman who has taken hold of his heart. He is enormously interested in her story and of the place she hails from and spends most evenings listening to her yarns from that island on the other side of the Atlantic. Tragic accounts not unlike his own.

One evening, Mary becomes bold enough to ask him about himself. "And you, Samuel, how did you end up here."

It's not a thing he ever talks about. The memories are so painful that he seeks solace every day in burying his past deep down, so he can muster the energy to build a life for himself. It's what he owes his dear mother. It's what she asked of him that night when he held her for the very last time before he fled the plantation. But with Mary all the rules and boundaries he constructed for himself are collapsing, disintegrating in front of her charm and vulnerability. He has already found healing in her presence. He already has discovered a hope that can only come when a bond is being constructed between one person and another. And so he lets down his guard and pours out his soul to her.

"I was born in Georgia. My mother is an enslaved woman on a cotton plantation there. She is owned and has been raped and used continuously by the planter, the owner. So, you see, my father is no better than this man Kincaid."

"Oh, Samuel, I am so sorry."

Samuel nods, his eyes, his beautiful eyes holding some tears.

"My mother, Mima is a wonderful woman. I feel loved by her always. That love helps me become my own man. When I hear your story Mary, it opens up to me how much she loved and loves. Her strength enables her to see that her violation, severe as it has been, is that planter's responsibility not hers. She walks tall. She loves and gives without measure. She told me when I was just becoming a man, that she did not and would not allow what this man did to her to dictate how her life turns out or change the measure of her soul."

"Oh gosh, Samuel, I would love to meet her. I think I would get great strength from her. How did she manage all that?'

"Well you will immediately recognise her if you ever get the chance to see her because she carries a shock of auburn hair that sets her apart. She is beautiful, but I suppose every son says that about his mother. But to answer your question, in truth, I don't know how she manages, Mary. But I do know, that somehow, she found the strength within herself to see me as a gift, despite how I was conceived. And as an enslaved woman she also knew that I could be taken from her or she from me at any point and sold, never to be together again. She had seen

          even small birds fly free

this happen to countless women. And witnessed their grief. Yet she continues to love, to open her heart. In the face of knowing that we would part."

Mary is captivated by this. And it sets her reflecting also on her Da's courage, taking her on, loving her, helping her grow. Remembering him at this moment fills her heart with acute pain and sorrow. For herself, for Samuel. For both their parents. Partings, permanent unassailable partings. After thinking on this in silence, a silence that Samuel generously affords her, she is still eager to know more. To see this man as he is, no matter what he has had to endure. She wants to know the whole of him, so that she can love the whole of him, no barrier, no secrets, sharing everything.

"What about you? When did you find out? How did it affect you?"

She is immediately embarrassed by her forthrightness.

"Sorry, I have so many questions. You don't have to tell me, if you don't want to."

"Mary, I love talking to you. It somehow relieves a burden I am carrying. Nobody knows about my story but you. Here, I strive to become someone new. I carry myself in New York as she asked me to, with dignity. But at one level, about Mammy's ordeal, I think I always knew. It's very disturbing what we learn to accept as normal. The whole notion of one person owning another as a piece of property. It's obnoxious. And yet we live with it. Even the notion that one person is superior to another. Because of the colour of a person's skin or as you Irish people have found here, because of where you come from. Despised because of it. But Mammy kept what she had to endure from me very subtly. To protect my young mind, I suppose. One night however, when I was about thirteen, he came to her. The planter. Unabashed and unashamed. Entitled. He hadn't been to her for a long time before that. He had moved on to other women he owned. He liked young women and Mammy was now about twenty five. So, old in his perverted mind. She gave birth to me when she was fourteen."

"Fourteen!" Mary can hardly credit this. "Fourteen. How she managed. Such a strong woman."

Samuel stops for a moment. The words being formed by his tongue, the first time they have ever been uttered, bring with them a deeper revelation of his upbringing and belonging.

"Yes. The other women on the plantation helped her of course. Its how they survive, to this day. It's where their hope comes from. That night when I was thirteen, he came and demanded sex from her, I was paralysed by him, his lustful power, his entitlement. It seemed to me that the very devil had appeared and took hold of the room and I was immobilised by it all. I turned my back on it and shook with fear. Mammy spent days and weeks afterwards helping me, consoling me. Repeating all the counsel she had given for years but now openly, redirecting me. And it worked for a time."

"Oh Samuel, I am so sorry," Mary reaches to hold him and he surrenders to the comfort of her arms. They embrace like this for some time.

Eventually Mary feels brave enough to utter the thoughts that dominate her own circumstances.

"Do you think it's possible Cormac felt the same way as you when Kincaid assaulted me? Is that likely?"

Samuel face changes to an earnestness that she has not seen before.

"I have no doubt about it. What age was he. Fifteen. He would have had no inkling that such evil existed before that moment and he would have been rooted to the spot. Like I was. But you don't get away scot free. For days, months, years after it stays with you, that moment, etched in your consciousness. Ready to sabotage your life. You can be sure Cormac is in turmoil to this day. My Mammy knew this. When I was fifteen she talked to me about making a dash for freedom. She could see the repressed anger grow in me. Even though she coached me daily about forgiveness and letting it go. She could see the adrenalin of a young man, deepening. The sense of not wanting to feel emasculated. A young man standing up to evil. To protect his woman, his mother. And she saw its danger. She knew how this ended. The cruel barbaric treatment dished out to men who rebelled. The torture. The example made of those men to terrorise those who were forced to watch the cruel exhibition of punishment. This she would not have been able to withstand. She had seen how it had broken other women. None of us wanted to submit, to surrender. It's not in our nature. But survival requires other ways. Which in the end, eats into the soul. But you have some understanding of that, don't you? The way Irish people have been treated?"

                    even small birds fly free

Mary feels a shiver run down her spine. The night sky grows darker as the moon is eclipsed by a passing cloud. She could not agree, however, with Samuel's kind statement.

"I would say only a little bit, Samuel. We were not slaves. We were not owned. I cannot imagine the horror of what you describe. But yes, I do have some understanding of this pain. But we have not suffered like that. What is happening down south is unpardonable. I never knew anything about that before I came here to America."

Samuel pauses for a moment. Thoughts of his past assault his consciousness as he continues to remember his mother, her wisdom, her sacrifice, her love for him.

"Mammy devised a strategy. I saw that later. To avoid me rising up and doing something stupid, she spent long nights, coaching me and convincing me that I had to break free. It was her and my only hope. She said she would fervently prefer me to be apart from her, than to be tortured and killed in front of her. And if I love her, she said, I would want the same thing."

"Gosh, that's like Da. He wanted the same thing for me. I know it cost him everything to let me board that ship in Cove. But I think for the first time, listening to what you say, I fully understand why."

Taking a deep breath, Samuel recalls the pivotal event of his life so far.

"One night, Mammy told me she had heard of what was called an 'underground railroad'. Not a real railroad of course but safe places and good people along a route from the south to the north. And she urged me to take it even though she knew then we would never see each other again. We made secret contact with people who knew of it and planned for three weeks. Then I left the plantation at night under the cover of darkness and headed for the Appalachians. My first target was to get to the Great Smokey mountain where I was told there was a station."

"What's a station? Like a railway station."

Samuel laughs. "No, it's what we call safe stops along the way, where good people will hide us, feed us, give us supplies and pass us on to the next people on the journey. It's like a code. To hide the structure from plantation owners. And at these stations, each of the people only know the next people along the way. That way the railroad can be protected in case any one station is raided and discovered."

"Oh my goodness, Samuel, that must have been so frightening, so nerve-wracking."

"Hmmm. Not much worse than you've been through, Mary. The main problem is Pattyrollers."

"Pattyrollers. I never heard of that. What is that?"

"Pattyrollers are a group of men. Dangerous men. They are hired by plantations to hunt down escaped slaves and return them to the plantation. They get paid a ransom and roam everywhere. I came across them a few times on the road. Once when I was hiding in an attic. I could see them going from house to house in the village. I think they got a tip off that there was a safe house in the village. They eventually knocked on the front door of the couple where I was hiding. Very threatening and domineering, they were. Me, in the attic, daring not to breathe. That was the worst moment. Fortunately, my hosts, an older couple, were very clever and strong. They pretended to be unaware of anything and the pattyrollers thought they were a bit senile and moved on. We laughed a lot that night, thinking about it. I think the laughter was mostly relief though."

"Gosh Samuel, your story is just for me. I think I have fallen in love with your mother, dear Mima. Did she really reach out to you like you say and protect you from your father. Did it work? Do you feel loved, accepted? Or do you worry you also carry your father inside you?"

Mary looks at him anxiously, beseechingly, feeling that his answer has huge import for the baby she is carrying.

"I don't worry about that, Mary. My mother made sure of that. I am my mother's son. I have banished him, that man, from my mind. It's important, I have discovered what you focus on. I don't think of him but her. When faced with a choice, it's always what would Mima do in a situation. She is the one I look up to. But as to the answer to the other questions, you yourself are the best judge of that. What do you think? Do you cower from me afraid of that hidden beast? Or do you see or only recognise in me what I have told you about Mima? I don't want an answer. I'm not fishing for one. I think it's only something you can think about for yourself and your own child. The child you are carrying. Is he you or Kincaid? Mima faced the same questions you face all those years ago."

Silence descends on both of them. It's as if time stands still. The moment is held between them and neither wants to break it. Within

         even small birds fly free

that serene instant, their souls are opened out, held. The moment is interrupted, no enhanced when a barn owl suddenly swoops from it's perch on an ailanthus, 'the tree of heaven' two doors away on the street and its slow, graceful flight is picked out by the lantern outside the house five doors further up. In flight they see its heart-shaped face, light brown, ochreous wings and glorious white undersides brilliantly, ephemerally catching the light. Both of their hearts skip a beat at the wonder of this apparition. It provides a memorable and glorious full stop to their conversation and recollections.

Mary cannot sleep when she lies on her bed. She conjures up an image of this wonderful woman, Mima, Samuel's mother. She does her best to imagine her life, the awful constriction. To be enslaved. Owned by someone else and disposed of by that person to meet his whim or desire. And yet Samuel told her of a person who is a hero to him. She feels she must also embrace Mima as a hero for herself as well. And, she must become her own hero.

A searingly beautiful, regenerative, rehabilitative light enters her soul. 'Yes,' she almost cries out, 'That's it. I must escape Kincaid. I will not," 'She repeats to herself again, to add definitive emphasis to her resolution, 'I will not allow this man to determine who I am or who I will become. I will not allow him to affect this wonderful child in my womb. I will echo Mima in my heart. This child will grow like Samuel did under the shelter of her love. I will cover my child with my love. It will be hard. But I am resolved. I will not hide in shame. I will rise up. I will write to Da and tell him my news. Not as a tragedy but as something joyful.'

These thoughts circle in her consciousness, bedding in, developing a deeper conviction. She can feel their effect as if they are concentric rings on an established oak, only this time layered in seconds, minutes, hours as she lies awake, enlivened, awaiting the dawn of a new day.

Glenville

September 1848

In which Peadar O'Brien is in despair and Cormac McCarthy travels to find him.

Throughout the early months of her pregnancy, Peadar is absent to her. The man she has come to know and love is unrecognisable. She wakes some nights to find him gone from their shared bed. The first few times she follows him out the door and discovers him staring at the horizon, some nights in the dark and rain and on others staring at the moon like some ainniseóir. She stumbles on him on a few nights and hears him crying out as in some fierce argument, on the first occasion thinking he has come across someone in the dark and is berating them. In the end, she gives up. She has other things to concern her. And any amount of pleading with him has no effect. He is gormless, almost catatonic.

Eileen has her baby inside her to think of; A gift in her later years and she knows that is her priority now, for this moment. Peadar can wait for later. Anyway, she thinks, half of us have gone mad with the pain, absence and loss which visited us these past three years. Peadar has plenty of company in his strangeness. She, herself, bewildered and apprehensive of bringing another child into this world which has taken so much away. But she is at least satisfied that Peadar settles to the books and accounts for Hudson and is keeping them afloat.

Late one afternoon in September, he is in the fields above Graigue. Chopping a tree he has found which had blown over in the winter storm of the previous November. Cutting up and storing wood for the long nights to come. Taking a break, he looks up and sees a figure walk up towards him from the valley below. The figure looks bowed down, broken. Not too much of a surprise these days, as most of us are, he thinks to himself. But he is curious, nonetheless. Who is this?

From where he stands he can't make out who it is and it is only when the man is about two hundred yards away that recognition dawns. It's Cormac McCarthy. Immediately Peadar is thrown into a conflict of emotions. McCarthy, the boy he has spent countless nights wrestling with, as with demons. And what is he doing here? It's all he can manage not to go rushing at him with his big felling axe, whirling it in the air, like the flaming sword guarding the tree of life.

In truth though, this is the moment when reason returns. The sight of the boy moves him. Almost as if Mary is returning to him. And his

          even small birds fly free

heart breaks inside. The torment, the ongoing melodrama in his head is released and for the first time in months, he takes a deep breath.

Surprisingly, when he is still ten yards away, young Cormac falls to his knees in front of him, in a gesture of forlorn supplication.

Peadar walks towards him.

"Please, sir, I've come to you for forgiveness," Cormac wails.

At that moment, it hits Peadar that all he has imagined, what he has been keeping at bay since Kincaid mocked him, is true. That his beloved daughter was defiled by both these men. Kincaid, he could consider. The beast of a man with no guiding principle or thought but young Cormac?

Stifling his rage, Peadar screams at the child in front of him.

"How could you? With your ma and da just gone. Growing up in our village. With the bonds we formed family to family. Our lifeblood connected on so many levels. And in school, how could you sit in the same small clochán with Mary and then rape her with that brute of a man. Cormac?"

Cormac looks up at him in fear and bewilderment and then crashes to the wet earth in despair. All his phantoms, the figures who have visited him in the dark nights are no comparison to this. This man's anger and anguish. The man who in all the world he looks up to. Now turning on him in disgust and rejection. He cannot bear this.

Peadar can hardly hear him through the sobs and howls. The broken child in front of him prostrate as if cast out from Hades itself. He has never heard sounds like this coming from another human and it is all he can muster to resist gathering him in his arms to offer comfort. It's as if the suffering of the whole valley is being laid on these young shoulders; The death, disease, fracturing of bonds, spirit and culture. The summoning up of all that has been lost, taken, broken, ripped asunder is laid bare in his primeval howling. Peadar is reminded of the time he sat on the wall as his bothán was pulled down, Mary, his dear Mary, beside him. Now, slowly he pieces together the words being uttered incoherently from the young boy's lips. "I didn't, sir.......... I couldn't move, sir............ I could not touch Mary.........But I watched him, sir........I don't know what happened to me.........I was paralysed......... I became unmade..............Not a man anymore but shrunk. To nothing. I know I am so wrong and I need you and her to forgive me."

Slowly, for it took too long, Peadar realises that this poor boy has been witness to the monstrous act perpetrated by Kincaid. No different to himself, Peadar realises, this poor boy was unable to protect Mary from Kincaid's debauched avarice. This lad he has loved has been to hell and is trying to get back. Peadar falls to the ground beside him and holds him tenderly, lovingly, forgivingly as if he is holding the whole valley in his arms. As if he is holding the neighbours who have perished, those who became skeletons in ditches, those who are now struggling in far-off lands, cut asunder. He joins Cormac with his tears and cries of anguish, expurgating as best they can together, the anguish, the terrible visitation of the past three years on all who held this place to be home.

Later, he gathers Cormac up and takes him home. Eileen greets both men and prepares soup. When he has eaten, Peadar tells him of Kincaid's fate and all that has happened since he left the valley. The air is washed clean in the telling. Peadar tells him of Mary's safe passage to New York. There is a moment in the telling when both men remember their meeting in Cork city and the transaction that happened between them. The falseness of it. The subterfuge in which they were both involved at the time. To get Mary away. Both stop in their words and thoughts to think inwardly, deeply of Mary's plight and whether she will be able to live with the memory of what befell her. That moment is held. Their part eclipsed by the terrible cost to her. Silently, individually, both men utter a beseeching prayer to the Almighty for forgiveness for them and succour for her, far away, out of reach of embrace, across the ocean.

Cormac regards in wonder the tenderness, the renewed vulnerable, loving coupling between Eileen and Peadar and sees Eileen big with child. She moves around the kitchen with grace and he is touched by her evident love for the school master. It's then, as if he is asking advice and permission from his own Da, that Cormac tells them of why he finally made the long trip on foot from Sheep's head to Glenville, a journey taking three days.

"I've fallen for a young woman among the Booleymen," he says, "Cailín is her name. I first met her when they came for me on Mayday. And I have been watching her since. For four months now. I haven't the heart to approach her because of my wrongdoing to Mary, sir. I know in order to earn the trust I need to love another woman, I have to come to you and beg forgiveness for my cowardice and desertion of your daughter. So here I am. My future is in your hands."

     even small birds fly free

"Era, Cormac," Both Eileen and Peadar rush together to throw their arms around him. "Bless you child."

"You have my forgiveness and blessing, son," Peadar says, conscious, nonetheless, of Mary, they are restrained in their common joy.

Cormac spends the night there in reminiscences of good times and leaves in the morning with a spring in his step as he returns to what he hopes fervently is a life with the booleymen and his Cailín.

17, Willoughby Avenue,
Brooklyn,
New York

11th July 1848

Dear Da,

I have settled here with the Sisters of Mercy in their convent in Brooklyn. I am working as a housekeeper and cook for them and feel welcomed and am loving it. So I want you to know I am safe.

I hope this reaches you and that you will be able to reply,

All my love

Mary

                     even small birds fly free

The Lodge,
Glenville Manor,
Glenville ,
County Cork.

20th November 1848

Dearest Mary,

So much has happened since you have left and I have at last the chance to write to you.   The most important thing I want to ask is that you forgive me, mo chuisle. I discovered through a dreadful encounter with him, that Kincaid raped you in those terrible weeks before you left. I couldn't protect you and then afterwards, you were not able to tell me. I suppose you couldn't tell me because of the shame of it and not knowing if I could bear it. I am so sorry you were left alone with it and then so soon after, that you had to leave. I wish I could hold you now and say these words to you. But I am so, so glad you are safe and are doing ok. That is a big relief. Thank the Sisters for me. They are a great lot.

As I say, a lot has happened. Kincaid is dead. He came to me one day on the famine relief road works and was looking for Cormac McCarthy to get his horse back. That's when he said the terrible words to me. In his anger at me not telling him where young Cormac was, he spooked his new horse which bolted. He fell to a terrible death. So you can let him go, if you can. He will trouble you no more. You have that as consolation at least.

My other news, which will shock you, is that your Da, in his later years, has fallen in love. Something you always wished for me, I remember. We met on the relief road where we were working and she captured my heart. Eileen is her name. She has had so much heartbreak in her short life. Losing her husband and her two small children to the famine fevers. But we are very happy together. God has given us great joy in the midst of such pain and loss. And to add to it all, Eileen is now with child and you will soon have a baby brother or sister. Isn't that a wonder?

I must also tell you that last week, Cormac McCarthy sought us out. He has been living on Sheep's Head with booleymen. He wanted me to tell you that he is so sorry for not fighting for you when Kincaid had his way with you. Truly he is devastated, Mary. I know it is something he will never forget. He was broken-hearted when he came but with kindness and particularly Eileen's touch, we sent him back on his way with his burden relieved. I know you would have done the same thing. That's all our news for now. We will write again when the baby is born.

All our love,

Da

                    even small birds fly free

Brooklyn,
New York,
January, 1849
Dearest Da,

What wonderful news you have given me. It gladdens my heart that you have fallen in love. It makes me feel safe now, knowing that you are not alone. And a baby on the way? What glorious news that is. I hope everything goes well and that Eileen gains some comfort from her child with you after all she has suffered.

I have much news myself to give you. I have also become a mother. Last August I gave birth to a gorgeous little girl who is the joy of my life. Her name is Cora. Before you do the maths in your head, Kincaid is the biological father. But Da, listen to me that is not the only tale I have to tell.

I have fallen head over heels in love with a wonderful man, Samuel. We got married in September and I am blissfully happy. Samuel is everything I could have hoped for. A kind, compassionate, wise man. He has guided me and been a huge support to me in the last few months. He works here also at the convent.

Samuel escaped from slavery in a plantation in Georgia five years ago. Such bravery. His mother remains a slave there. And in our getting to know one another he told me his story of how his mother was continuously raped by the plantation owner who is Samuel's father. Samuel has helped me understand that I can love my daughter as my own as he was and is loved by his mother. A remarkable woman called Mima. When he tells me about her and how strong she is as a woman, I am inspired. I see a future for myself and dear Cora, because of her.

So Da, I am very happy. Blessed I would say when I consider all the things that befell our neighbours. So don't torture yourself. Put Kincaid in the past as I have done. Look to the wonderful future you have in front of you with Eileen and the child of your later years. Having dear Cora beside me now as I write is a wonderful blessing. I can't imagine that I worried about accepting her (being Kincaid's child). But that's all in the past, thank God. I am also imagining you (without dear Ma) as you held me, all those long years ago. The mixture of pain, absence yet joy is a curious thing that us humans can manage.

So let us rebuild together from a distance what has been taken away from us. Joy happiness love

I love you Da as always

Mary

p.s. If you have Cormac's place, maybe I will write to him.

 even small birds fly free

Louisiana

1850

In which Pádraig O'Donovan fits into life as a slave-catcher, a pattyroller until one fateful day

The swamp is thick with lack of air. The oppressive heat burning their lungs. For days now, they are on the scent. The dogs fiercely pulling on the leads with a rabid, avaricious compulsion. The pattyrollers struggling to keep up. Pádraig O'Donovan, now acclimatised to the work, knows how to pace himself. He has lost the fear of the swamp, and is now cavalier in the pursuit. Something feral was unleashed in him after John Roberts recruited him to his team, and paid off the indenture with a loan to be taken from his earned commission.

The early relief of escaping from canal digging carried him the first weeks and months until he developed a taste for the work. This is matched by Roberts, who is a man metamorphosed when out on the trail. The easy-going lover of Cajun music and great raconteur of tales is transformed into a wily, determined, driven man.

Pádraig is beginning to realise that there is no sport greater than hunting men. He feels it deeply inside and feels it dwarfs the feeling men get when they are hunting other animals. The adrenalin coursing through his body, the camaraderie of the other men is something he has never before experienced and something he did not know existed. He is a transformed man. He, if asked, would say he has found his true vocation.

When the job was explained to him, Pádraig easily acquiesced to Robert's logic. "Our whole economic system, our culture, our heritage, our lifestyle is built on slavery," he explained that evening in the Bayou Inn. "Look around you at the Haitians here and imagine the chaos unleashed if our slaves rebelled and caused a revolution like happened down there. The economic turmoil would bring the country down."

Pádraig listened attentively to this insightful man. He recognised he had so much to learn.

"And the British, with their empire and hypocrisy, want to fan the flames here too. Anything to destabilise the growing power we possess. Mischief-makers that's all they have ever been. So don't give them too much mind with their emancipation talk. They are full of cant."

Whether through his wiliness or plain speaking, Roberts seems to know exactly how to get the cogs in Pádraig's mind working. Reinforcing his embedded hatred of the Crown.

"Look Paddy," Roberts continues, "Slaves will not survive outside of the plantation. That's their natural, safe home in this country. Planters provide them with all they need. But to ensure that survives, we have to take care of the obstinate, belligerent fuckers. Teach them a lesson. It really is for the good of all. It's that simple. Forget those abolitionists in the north. They know fuck-all about the realities of our lives down here. Preserving our heritage and capturing renegades is a mission that I gladly take on for my country. I believe it's that important. Our future prosperity and ongoing unity depend on it. And I want to make America great."

At that time, when the conversation was taking place in the bar, Pádraig wondered how Roberts could speak so freely about these things in such a public place. He later learned that what Roberts was saying was the prevailing view and nobody was likely to challenge him.

"I mean just look at them. How can they survive. As soon as they set foot abroad from the plantation, the colour of their skin would finish them off. No-one will employ them, rent them a place to live. They will be outcasts. And any move that threatens someone, particularly our womenfolk will end in a lynching. No, I tell you Paddy the plantation is the safest place for them and we are doing them a service by enforcing that message. It's for their own safety. And don't be fooled by what you see here in New Orleans and the freedom the Black man has in this city. Here is an island. Outside things are very, very different."

When he is back in New Orleans, Pádraig's growing conviction of his place in his new country is further affirmed by the slogans he sees from the Southern Democrats. "This is a white man's country, let the white man rule." He sees that the only passage available to him as a 'despised, Catholic, disease-ridden Irish immigrant' is to exploit his own white skin and assimilate. This looking for his place to fit into the world, what he sees as 'reality', is always the thing that comes naturally for Pádraig. And that he has found his place in Robert's pattyrollers fulfils this. He sees the Southern Democrats wooing his and other Irish votes and gladly accedes to their cause.

Fuelled by these thoughts and discussions, Pádraig easily accepts his role as policeman and temporary jailer. He also recognises the lawful position conferred on pattyrollers in their jobs through the fugitive slave

	even small birds fly free

act[28]. So the celebration all of them feel when they capture an errant Negro is something he joins in with gladly. However, he recoils when exposed to the punishment meted out and turns his back on the humiliations dispensed as a slave is returned back to the owner. But he learns to see this as part of the job, a necessary deterrent for others. He would do it differently if he was in charge but he accepts that he is not the leader nor does he wish to be.

Suddenly his thoughts are interrupted and he is back on the hunt, on the trail. His ears pick up the faintest quiver a few hundred yards to his left. It's one of the things he realises he has been gifted through the work. A keen sense of awareness and particularly, hearing. Roberts often commends him for it and all the others keep half an eye on him when on the trail, particularly deep in the swamp.

The dogs have lost the scent through the water-soaked ground. He raises his hand quietly. And the others stop moving immediately. Slowly, gracefully like a wolf with its prey, Pádraig moves towards the sound. When he is no more than ten yards way, a frightened, sprightly being bolts from its hiding place, for all the world like a hare from its form. Pádraig immediately accelerates and his long legs and lithe body moves over the swampy ground as if he is gliding on water. Within fifty yards he reaches the fugitive and throws his body to bring yet another runaway to the ground.

He is surprised to discover a soft, svelte body beneath him, wriggling furiously. Keeping a firm hold, he stands up to discover the angry, frightened, yet unbearably sweet face of a fifteen year old girl, clawing, writhing and squirming furiously with him to get free. Her eyes, her brown, terrified eyes. "Oh my God," he thinks to himself, groaning inwardly in anguish, "those eyes. They're the same as Aoife's."

The apparition of himself bent over his little sister and holding her in his arms as life faded from her on that last, long, never to be forgotten night in the Skibbereen bothán, all of five years ago, the first year of an Gorta, dominates his consciousness as he beholds this girl, this vision in front of him.

This girl's face, the memory, the dreadful recall of it, is what he will, from this moment on, spend the rest of his chosen path seeking to banish. He turns from her quickly but all too late, as reinforcements and the team take care of the girl, shackling her abruptly in irons.

He is left alone, in a catatonic state, his vivid reflections dominating his consciousness, casting a debilitating, disabling, overwhelming pall over his future.

Boston

1849

In which Caelan O'Donovan prospers as an apprentice photographer and on a terrible day in a fight with the No-Nothings loses his dear friend Seán Mulcahy.

After what can only be described as a short, six month apprenticeship, Ambrose Cutting takes on Caelan O'Donovan as his apprentice.

"I have no son of my own, young man. And I want to be able to ensure that everything I have learned survives me. This is the future. These images here. They can change the course of history."

They are reviewing photos taken by Cutting. A winsome print of Horace Greeley, the newspaper man had caught their eye. "Pictures tell a story and influence people. If we are to bring sense to this nation and abolish its addiction to slavery, pictures will be one of the main methods of achieving this. I see you have an eye. I see you can reach in with a camera and capture a person's soul. Their beliefs and convictions. That's powerful. And I want to help you get better at it."

Caelan is so grateful. He leaves his work on the docks and starts with Cutting, taking on commissions to bring to print, scenes and portraits which are sold to newspapers to enhance their written features.

On a late Fall evening in 1850, he is walking home, back to Batterymarch Street. He sees a huge kerfuffle breaking out in front of him on High Street at the entrance to Batterymarch. He runs towards it, anxiously and finds his neighbours engaged in a huge and vicious fight with the No-nothings. Fists and clubs are swinging in the fray and he throws himself into the brawl. The noise and ferocious fighting consumes him. The battle lasts about an hour and together they manage to hold off the mob, intent as they were to create mayhem on the street.

When they finally repel the invaders, Caelan looks around for Seán. To gain reassurance that he has acquitted himself well. When he doesn't see him, he asks a neighbour.

"Oh they attacked us from both ends. Half of us are down at Milk Street."

"We'd better go down there to help them then," Caelan shouts and leads a charge of men down Batterymarch, rushing past the faces of their anxious women and children. 'We shouldn't be living like this,' Caelan thinks but his mind fixes on finding Seán.

When they arrive on Milk Street, the fight is over and he breathes a sigh of relief, scanning the faces for Seán. He asks again where he is, to the men gathered, who are breathing heavily from the combat. One young lad, Caelan can't remember his name, says he saw Seán chase a bunch of No-nothings down the side of the Liberty Tree building. Caelan immediately gathers some of his neighbours and they race to the building and disappear down the alleyway.

As they turn the corner they all stop suddenly, struck as they are by a group of three who are kneeling on the ground beside a prostrate figure. Caelan recognises immediately it is Seán and runs fiercely towards him. There is blood everywhere. Caelan cannot believe that so much blood can spill out of just one man. He kneels down beside Seán and gathers him in his arms, looking at the pale, almost lifeless face of his dear friend.

"Tá mé ag fáil bháis, a Caelan. Tabhair aire do Bridie agus mo bhuachaillí agus cailíní beaga. Tóg amach as an áit thréigthe seo iad." (I am dying, Caelan. Take care of Bridie and my little boys and girls. Take them out of this God-forsaken place.)

These last words burn in Caelan's heart. That it has come to this. He continues to hold his friend gently as life leaves him, the many, many brutal knife wounds he has sustained giving him no chance. Seán is gone. The suddenness shocks Caelan and yet he has no time to grieve. He knows he has to find strength now like he has never needed it before.

When it is over, his neighbours find a large plank of wood and tenderly place Seán's body on it and carry him home as a dead hero on his shield. Caelan walks on ahead having asked the men to give him time to speak to Bridie and prepare her and the children.

At the gate of their dwelling, he sees her, a long way off. He recognises she knows immediately. It's written on her face. Her body forlorn, as the children beside her hold on to her frame for comfort. It's like he doesn't need to say anything, but he knows he must. Inanely, he bursts out,

"He's gone, Bridie. I'm so sorry."

He is not prepared for her rushing at him, fists flailing as she thumps him on his chest, repeatedly, with terrible, heart-breaking blows."No, no, no, no, no," She screams. Her cries, her screams, as of a wild animal in its death throes. Neighbours gather the children and Caelan tries to hold Bridie, who is flailing in his arms. Eventually one of her friends,

Nuala, gently releases her and takes her away.Caelan watches as the woman he has given his heart to, the woman he loves deeply, is led away, broken, barely able to walk.

part three
the american civil war

antebellum

Sullivan Street, New York City

1849

In which Samuel is faced with Mary's trauma and despair and seeks to console and hold her.

Samuel Williams

Most days she breaks down and it is heartrending to watch her. 'I love the very bones of her'. It's an expression she taught me. But it's difficult and sometimes frightening to behold her in her anguish. I have to conclude that when a man takes a woman against her will, he breaks and violates something deep inside her and the damage and what that man has laid waste renders her very being in two. I have to control my rage for this man, Kincaid. Watching her also opens out a place within me where I think of the same desecration of my mother. However, I must remain strong for her, my dear Mary.

It was very bad during the late stage of her pregnancy. Then she would wake in the middle of the night and sob. I tried my best not to be terrified by this. The degree of her agony and distress made me fear for her sanity. I felt helpless. No words reassured. I found myself holding her as grief racked her very soul. Even though I feel I have lived so many lives in my short twenty years, I have never faced anything like this. I must become a man now.

Some days she is assaulted within by an inchoate rage. Bubbling up inside of her, she will lose herself to it. At those moments, I know not to take what she says or does personally. But sadly much of her fury is directed against herself. I hear her cry out, cursing herself. She tells me afterwards when she calms down that she feels complicit. That somehow she had surrendered too easily to Kincaid. "That Langer," she screams using an expression I had never heard. But I don't need interpretation such is the venom with which she spits out the word. On a few occasions she has thrown herself against the wall and repeatedly sought to bash her head against it. I have to restrain her then, as gently as I can but she exercises so much force, I am exhausted afterwards. I hold her until she becomes spent, listless in my arms, gently subsiding to quiet tears.

One day, after a particularly tremulous night, when she lay quietly beside me, I asked her, with trepidation. "What is it you need from me, Mary?"

She took time to phrase the words. "I want to be able to show myself, to reveal myself to you. I need you to love me so deeply that I am not

 even small birds fly free

afraid to show you how ugly I can become. I want, in your arms, just being in your embracing presence to show me scars I didn't even know I have. I don't want you to make them go away. In those moments, I need you to help me nurse my own wounds and afterwards to cherish the bruises that are left behind." I had no answer. Only Mary can say if I measure up. I want to. I hope I do.

She is such a brave woman. I see that in the way she gathers herself afterwards. That's not to say she doesn't look and feel vulnerable and fragile. She is. There seems to be an exposed friability in her gut for days after her breakdowns and I am very vigilant particularly then that she is not confronted by too much. A difficult task where we live. We are surrounded here in lower Manhattan by misery, sickness and disease. Every day tragedy is visited on our neighbours, some to whom we have become very close.

I try to help Mary to narrow her focus. To stay strong and safe for herself and not to waste energy in engaging in the misery of others. But in all truth, that flies against her nature. She is innately a compassionate, sensitive soul. It's also why I love and adore her. So I watch her ride the storm. Day by day. Hour by hour. She tells me often, 'She has to become her own heroine'. And I can see that visibly.

Lots of people equate vulnerability with weakness. And I say, perish that thought. I have not much time for such people. I think they are oblivious to how frangible we all are when faced with disaster.

We have moved to be close to my people here in this corner of the city. And the women have been wonderful. I think they have adopted us. As a young couple they want so much to help us realise our future. Many, of course, have experienced and come through hell on earth and are that much stronger, wiser and surprisingly tender as a result. They love Mary and have taken to her as their own and I swell with pride when I see their solicitude towards her. It's not unusual for the women to help out with basic things and we share so much in common.

I am so grateful for this support as I'm not sure I am strong enough on my own to hold Mary up. Sometimes, it feels I love her too much and it's very hard to look at her when I see such torment. But when she comes through such bouts, she often tenderly touches me and thanks me. "Thank you, Samuel," she says, "Thank you for not trying to explain anything away. Thank you for silently holding me. I get so much comfort from your embrace. You enfold me and I can let myself go."

When Cora was born, I noticed a change in her. A determination. As if a storm had passed and a bright new day dawned. Cora is beautiful. She's a gift to us both and we both became instantly obsessed with her. Of course it would be foolish to say that it is all plain sailing. It isn't. For Mary, for both of us, the responsibility to this tiny child occasionally overwhelms us. We are still so young. But I see Mary move differently. She gains courage from I don't know where and I love watching her with our child.

She often tells me of Peadar, her dad. He seems like an exceptional human being. She tells me her mother, the love of his life, died giving birth to her. And she feels his strength flowing through her now as she faces her own tryst with destiny having conceived a child through such devastating circumstances and with such a man as Kincaid. But it seems as each day goes by, her own father eclipses this man and there is a strength and fortitude in her that is a wonder to behold.

So I also want to record. To tell myself. That of all men I am blessed. Blessed to love and be loved by such a woman. She has become my life and I want to support her. I have found work on the docks. And am good at it. It's not easy as I am looked on by others in the gang suspiciously. But I keep my head down, work hard and do my best for Mary, for our child Cora and our future together.

   even small birds fly free

26, Sullivan Street
New York,
January, 1850
Dearest Da,

I hope you and Eileen and baby Shay are in good health. I miss you so much and would love to see you all. I have huge news as well. Cora has a little brother. Born just a few weeks ago. A beautiful baby boy. We named him Abe. Samuel and I got married last year. He is a wonderful man. You would immediately love him, I'm sure. And be proud of him. He educated himself. Just like you did all those years ago. Goodness knows how he managed it but he is now a wise, learned articulate man. I am so proud of him.

When I look at him, at the way he takes care of me, Cora and Abe, I am reminded of how you must have been all those years ago. I am now full of admiration for you as I cannot imagine how you gave so much, suffering as you were then, from the loss of Mammy. It is one of the reasons I am so happy that you have found a new life with Eileen and are able to be with Shay together. You are blessed now and I am glad.

Life is not easy here. But we are happy. So I don't want to worry you. We moved to a tiny apartment on Sullivan Street. You, of course, may think of New York as glamourous. That's the reports that people send home. But it's far from glamour we are. The streets around here are crowded and the places to rent are mostly foul. There is a smell that comes from the tanning factories and slaughterhouses which is particularly hard in the hot summers. But it's the winters here that are the hardest of all. The wind goes right through you, It's no place for the old.[1] *In truth, I nearly died the first night I was here only a group of girls from home (who have remained my best friends) saved me, appearing like a flock of angels. But that's a tale for another time. The whole area was built on a swamp and the houses are all beginning to lose their shape and sink into the ground. The owners here are fierce, avaricious men who stick people in all sorts of hovels and demand ridiculous rents. It's tough to watch people from Ireland continually arrive, green behind the ears*[2] *and get taken for a ride.*

But I have Samuel, such a hard-working, conscientious man looking out for us and I feel very safe and secure. We managed to get a small, one-roomed apartment which has a window to the front. That's so important as we can get clean air. Most of the rooms in buildings are window-less and the air is rank, which leads to disease and sickness. We are lucky. And I can keep the children healthy, thank God. Thanks to the money Samuel brings in from work.

Antebellum

I continue to work with the Sisters. They have started an orphanage for homeless street children and I work there. Basic work, cleaning and cooking. There are thousands of homeless children in the area. Scrabbling to survive. Little urchins with no adult to care for them. They are very vulnerable. It would break your heart. The Sisters take in as many as they can and provide them with shelter, food and education.

They let me take Cora and Abe (now) with me and so I have become very independent. The Sisters also love Samuel and support us. I don't know if you are aware but Negroes experience a lot of discrimination here. It's so hard to find work. Most jobs are barred for them and it is dangerous to challenge that. The men, and mostly our own countrymen, gang up against them,. It makes me feel very ashamed. But Samuel shrugs it off. The women are different though and see no harm in us being together and I get a lot of support from the girls I have come to know and love.

Samuel, meanwhile, has done well. He got a job as a stevedore on the docks. It doesn't surprise me. He is such a hard worker, big and strong, but also has an active mind, intelligent, wise. No wonder they want to employ him. The wages aren't great. But we manage. We are resourceful. And we are a great support to one another.

Little Cora is nearly two and is bright and cheery. She is such fun to be with and loves her little baby brother. She learns new words every day and is, amazingly, a great conversationalist. Can you imagine. She is all the time trying out new things and always wants me to know and be aware of what she sees. Pointing things out as we walk to work. She also greets our neighbours with a smile and a wave and she has become very popular among those who live close by. The great thing is, and I feared the opposite of this so much, that I do not see her father in her at all. She reminds me so much of you and she adores Samuel. All is well.

The friendly, supportive neighbourhood is also the great thing about where we live. There is a strong sense of community. There are many Negro families on our street and they have accepted me as one of their own. The way we relate to one another reminds me so much of Graigue, and our little village at home. We share a lot together and when one or the other of us goes through a hard time, we can always rely on one another for support.

So, Da, I wanted to be honest with you. And not want to paint the Shangri-La picture posted by others from the old country. You are much better off where you are, much though I miss you. At the same time, I want to assure you that we are a strong unit. We will survive and prosper here, despite all the difficulties. Of this I am sure. You can count on us.

                        even small birds fly free

I send my love to you, Eileen and Shay (my little brother)
Mary, Samuel, Cora and Abe
XXXX

Oak Plantation, Natchez, Mississippi,

May, 1851

In which Pádraig O'Donovan finally understands the country in which he has come to live.

As soon as Pádraig O'Donovan settles into plantation life, everything makes sense. He begins to understand America and his place within it. The revelation excites him, as an opportunity. He recognises the hand of that great coloniser, England. Only here, as distinct from Ireland, the caste system which they have a preternatural ability to construct is ordered on very different lines. He, of course, knows their scheme. In his homeland, his family were firmly trapped as an underclass, landless, without rights, considered racially inferior. This he had acquiesced to; Why he had struggled so hard to get his idealistic, revolutionary brother out of the country, lest he perish in an impossible rebellion. He knows enough about life not to contest the inevitable but surrender to hegemony.

However, in America it is egregiously obvious that things are constructed differently. And extraordinarily, more brutal. A caste system based on the colour of one's skin.[3] Here, Negroes are firmly consigned as the racially inferior underclass, enslaved for life; Men, women and children, whole families. While in Ireland, a small country, no-one is able to escape his origins and so are trapped as an underclass; Here, Pádraig realises, that because of his white skin, he can mimic the gentry, the elite, eventually hide his origins and lay claim to a position of progress. He sees it as a gift to be cherished.

This insightful revelation he will keep quietly to himself as he becomes familiar with the norms and yardsticks of how things work. The long suffering of his people finally bringing some reward. An opportunity for advancement. As a pragmatic man, he will not let this pass him by.

Employed as an Overseer, he immediately observes that he is not automatically in favour. In any conflict, Planters will side with their slaves. The slave a valuable commodity, revolt always a threat. He, despised by both slave and master, a necessary evil, will be dispensable, disposable. He must earn respect. A delicate balance between kowtowing and assertion.

He discerns instability, uncertainty, ambivalence everywhere. The Planter, entitled, often precocious, dissolute. His set-upon wife, continually enduring the birth of half-caste children spawned by her husband's flagrant and frequent insemination of young female slaves; She is

          even small birds fly free

unpredictable, ready to pivot and rage in her ongoing humiliations and Pádraig must remain vigilant. The slaves, subdued yet dangerous, always ready to challenge him if he strays over a line he must learn to differentiate.

It is for this reason he keeps himself to himself. He will exercise restraint in his governance, be meticulous in his accounts and will not use his position and command to take advantage of any of the young Negro women, even though he is in awe of their beauty. He will not succumb. He knows instinctively that this is a line he should not cross. It will harbour resentment.

Although the Planter[4] would prefer he has a wife, Pádraig will not pursue this line either. He feels unable to trust anyone else in this delicate dance and knows that taking a wife will fix him in his status. He has ambitions to rise, to assimilate, to graduate, to buy some land, procure some slaves of his own, ape the behaviour of the class he can only gaze on from afar. Soon in this vast country he will become unrecognisable, and rise to appanage and privilege. With concentrated effort, diligent observation, attention to detail he knows he can advance.

Fortunately he has alongside him his slave driver, July[5]. Outfitted with high leather boots, greatcoat and armed with a whip, his great, burly frame commands compliance. Benefitting from meting out discipline to errant slaves, he is diligent in their whipping. Although Pádraig issues the punishment, he always absents himself during its execution. The effect of witness not meant for him but for the other slaves to absorb. The ire of the slave population of seventy men and women largely directed at July, one of their own. But July is a wily fox and Pádraig knows he must be wary and alert. He also watches and learns from July; How this Negro negotiates his position with aplomb.

In the witching hour, however, Pádraig is often tormented, reduced. The visions which haunt his soul and trouble his spirit, usually begin with the memory of the lithe young woman he sprang upon and apprehended in the swamp, her eyes so full of fear and innocence, evoking Aoife, his sister; His night-time tryst with evil begins there; Visions inhabit his consciousness; The Planter commanding the female slave to sing as her husband is taken away to be sold at the 'Forks in the Road' market, her three children, wailing and clinging to her skirts. The incongruity deeply disturbing him.

When morning comes, however, his resolve returns as the chilling hallucinations which haunt him become evanescent, evaporate as the sun rises. He will settle this. To have his future, he needs the Negro in his assigned place. This, he grasps, will allow his white skin to prosper.

                                            even small birds fly free

Oak Plantation
Natchez,
Mississippi
June 1851

Dear Caelan,

I am well and settled at last you will be glad to know. I have served my time with the pattyrollers and am glad it's over. There a peculiar irony here. I loved been out in the wild. I loved giving chase. The thrill of the hunt. I discovered that my senses are more alert than most and I became a good and invaluable tracker. Because of my efforts, many slaves were returned to their masters and safety. So I did well.

As you already know, I think the plantation is the best place for Negroes. The country is not safe for a coloured man or woman. There is no place for them to settle and they cannot adapt to modern life. No-one will give them work. They are not trusted and of course are easily visible. Outside of the plantation, they will starve. Why they want to escape, I don't know. And I believe there is a big relief among many when they are caught by us. They don't need to run any more.

But over the time with the pattyrollers, I began to be filled with disquiet. The others seemed different to me. And particularly John Roberts. The face and character of the man I knew from Alexis Coffee House is transformed when on the trail. There is a cruelty and hatred in him and others towards the Negro that I found very distressing. Often times, I was the principal tracker to expose and find the escapee and when he or she was apprehended, I had to turn my back on the vicious beatings meted out. They always ensured no permanent damage was done. The slave is a valuable commodity after all. But Roberts made sure enough pain was inflicted. He would remonstrate to us that it was necessary 'to teach a severe lesson'. Why this is so, I couldn't figure out. It seems to me that when we came about an escapee, such was their terrible, emaciated, starving condition, that I felt they would be more than glad to give up and get back home to their family. They had suffered enough already. In the end, I bowed to his years of experience.

I am more convinced than ever, now, of the good the Plantation affords us all. As I continually say to you, the Negro is so much better off there. And can't survive outside of it. So Planters are to be praised for providing this security. And of course it gives us all, slaves included, an economy to which we can be proud. I am tired of hearing the propaganda from England which tries to poison minds and bring revolt here. I see English peoples' typical, perfidious nature in these statements. Happy to advance slavery when they were in charge of this country. Losing their once, fine colony, they try their level best to destabilise this new, great nation. I wish you in the North would only see through what they are trying to do.

So the upshot of everything is that I have been very lucky. And I tried to use a bit of intelligence and nous along with my luck. We regularly returned our slaves to the market near here. The 'Forks of the Road' market. Where they are either sold on or returned to their owner. What an amazing place, full of barter and prosperity. And when we rested there before our next commission, I ingratiated myself, (can't think of a better phrase), to a local planter who had recently bought a plantation here called Oak Plantation. He told me he always stayed away from pattyrollers as possible employees. "You're rough types," he said, "Difficult to control." But somehow he began to like me and eventually on meeting him on my third trip back to the market, he took me on as an Overseer.

So here I am on the plantation. Managing the slaves and overseeing their work. And it is a huge relief. I have stability at last and think I will be here for some time. The Negroes here are like one, big, extended family. So much of how they behave I recognise from our old families back home in County Cork. They look after one another, have a strong moral code and I could not be more happy.

I read, with interest, how your life is growing there. Your interest in photography alarms me however. I am not sure that something like that has a future and think you would be better off finding yourself in some traditional, more secure work. We both know what it is like to be without and how things can turn very quickly, so I worry about you. And pray that you will abandon this outlandish pursuit.

I fear you remain gullible, Caelan. And that this man Cutting is taking advantage of you. Don't rely on him or trust him. My big sadness is that I am not there in Boston alongside you. To protect you from yourself. I hope the next time I hear from you, I will learn that you have moved on. Isn't there plenty of work on the docks or in building trade? That'd be perfect for you.

Know I pray for you every day, Caelan, and hope to hear better news from you soon,

Love

Pádraig

                          even small birds fly free

Rochester, New York

July 4th, 1852

In which Caelan O'Donovan prospers as a photo-journalist and feature writer and meets with Frederick Douglass.

Caelan is nervous. He knows this is a big assignment. He has grown in confidence over the years, mentored by Ambrose Cutting, but he is always anxious when a facing a new project, capturing the image with his equipment. When he began, Ambrose had taught him gently. The projects inanimate but important nonetheless. Buildings, public spaces. These were his main subjects. He loved the challenge of capturing the light and shade, bringing depth, clarity, a kind of distinction to the mundane nature of his subjects. Ambrose often grinned approvingly at the work and complimented Caelan accordingly.

"I think you are ready for something different, lad, something to get your teeth into. I'll see what I can do." he said, chuckling to himself.

About this time, Cutting met Alonzo Hartwell, an exceptional wood engraver and the collaboration between Cutting, Caelan and Alonzo means that nothing is lost when the images they capture are sent to print.

Caelan discovers his life is full of questions. He grasps that his earlier appreciation of this new world that so enraptured him on his arrival four years before, is an elaborate fiction. The highfalutin charter of 'all men being created equal' a conceit. An ideal maybe, but long since divorced from reality. He can see in his own life, amongst his own people, that this is abjectly apparent. Left as they are in ghettos. He struggles daily to come to terms with the brutal death of his friend, Seán. In the intervening years, he tries to expurgate this with his devotion to Bridie and their kids. Fulfilling the dying wish of his friend, he willingly gives his life and his increasing income to separate them from the poverty in which they were trapped.

He bought a house on Moore Street, a stately wood-panelled frontage built with the optimism and grandeur of this city and they have come with him to live there. He took a small room for himself and gave the family free reign over the rest of the house. He is away often for his work, and the sheer joy of returning never leaves him. When he sees Bridie again, after an absence, his heart always leaps inside him, reducing him to a vulnerable wreck. She never notices of course or appears not to and in any case, the children, increasingly turning into young adults, besiege him always on his arrival, eclipsing the moment and hiding his blushing chagrin.

Initially the overwhelming assault of the children is to discover what delights he has for them, the presents he always seeks diligently to brighten their lives. Each gift perspicaciously chosen to compliment and identify the characters of each one individually. Nowadays, however, it is replaced by genuine joy, love and affection, unconditionally offered, as they wait to hear about his adventures, his achievements, his publications.

They spend evenings together on the wide verandah laughing, chatting, telling stories, all the while Caelan seeking those moments when he can be with Bridie on her own, alone. Her beauty, which first enamoured him, is now enhanced by the grace in which she lives her life, his knowing of her as they live alongside one another, her care for her children, the dignity and forbearance with which she has adjusted after the death of her husband and father of their children.

In the winter months, they sit together in front of the roaring fire. Caelan plays songs they know so well on the melodeon and the sound of children and Bridie singing the well-rehearsed words together is nothing short of heaven to him.

His work engages him. Cutting leads him towards creating image profiles and he is commissioned to chronicle the major actors and events of the day. Boston is alive with the imperative of abolition and the city is divided. The enslavement of peoples absorbs his revolutionary spirit. This, above all, he sees as the original stain on the charter that first captured his spirit. Seeing the power of the camera and its extraordinary capacity to hold attention, he is set free in a way that allows him to come home to himself. Here in this city, he finds a capacity to affect change, in a way he never found in Ireland. Those days with Pádraig never leave him, the frustration, the ranting that he felt forced to express in lieu of any effective avenue of revolt, allows him to, now, see a future in this, as yet unmade, country. He devours the rhetoric of the abolitionist as his source of inspiration, enhancing and complementing his own thirst for justice.

After some time, his work is noticed. Within his portraits, he captures unequivocally the spirit, the nuance, the character, the import of his various subjects. His pictures replace a thousand words, such is their graphic and inspired quality. It appears effortless. He has an eye.

                    even small birds fly free

Somehow when he looks through the lens, he can see light, shade, colour, yet mostly character and energy, the essential characteristics of his subjects are laid bare before him. He sees their vulnerabilities and exposes the frailty and essential truths, hidden in their blustering words and rehearsed phrases.

Some of the editors of magazines to which he contributes, request him to accompany his work with bylines. They tell him that what he is unmasking, revealing, is not seen by those who often feature alongside him as reporters. Their words bring a divergence, a distraction to the essential authenticity hidden in his portraits. "I would prefer if you wrote something about what you see, Caelan," they would say. And as a consequence, over time, these bylines evolve into features. Full scale portraits in picture and word. Giving him free reign to interpret the world, what he sees in his subjects' unguarded moments, however they are disguised and what he hears and discerns in their bombast and deception. He shapes his conclusions into lyrical, well-chosen phrases and image forming a challenge, a gauntlet to this fledgling nation to repent and reflect on its founding principles, however idealistic and out-of-reach they may appear to be.

He hears from many and particularly his many detractors (of which there is a sizeable and exponential rise), the phrase this 'Great Country'. And he knows the falseness of this claim. He wonders if it's his truculence, which has been burnt into him. Blasted into him through the suffering of his own family and his people. A hatred of hegemonic opinion. Of imperialism and privilege in all its forms. The sense of entitlement so obvious and evident among the elite of the society into which he is immersed.

This is a distrust born deep from his infancy of the oppressor whose callous and flippant rule destroyed so many of his own people. Wherever it has come from, he cannot join the cheerleaders. He loves the country that has become his home but as an idea. As a place that from the moment of his disembarkation, presents a potential for growth and freedom. But the opportunities afforded are conditioned on race, colour, ethnicity. The ideals portrayed not a reality. Not by a long chalk. This he sees. His reading, his reflection clearly evinces that this county is not great and has never been so.

The avarice for land which displaces Native Peoples appals him. Driven onwards by the day. Reports of capricious treaties disinheriting those who have lived here long before Europeans arrived. It reminds him of his homeland and the forced march by Cromwell driving his own people to Connacht. He realises how idiosyncratic this is but it's his only point of reference. And it impels him. He is appalled by the adoption of the idea of Manifest Destiny, where an increasing majority of white people assume its their right to conquer and usurp the land, driving the peoples who have lived there for centuries out west and in many cases to their extinction. It resonates deeply with him and fuels his daily search for sincerity in his work. He is galvanised.

Yet he also remains perplexed by it all. How did a people who arrived in this land, often as refugees of a pogrom of sorts in European countries so quickly forget their own terror and inflict a similar dread on the peoples they had come to live among? How are they able to forget their own trauma and suffering in order to invalidate the suffering of those driven out before them?

Daily he rehearses the debate on the state of the Union. The expansion of the country. The challenge placed in front of its people by the institution of enslavement. Of Slavery. Of binding a peoples, families, individuals, children to be owned by another human being. The sacrilege of it. Two hundred and fifty years of this abomination and now in the expansion of the union, the ever present greed to move west, the plantation owners and their political hacks want to extend this atrocity westward beyond the Mason and Dixon line. All the way down to Mexico, if they have their way. The debate threatening the break-up of the Union as sides are taken North and South. He realises that he must try and temper his anger, his sense of the injustice and frame his pieces in cogent, articulate pieces illustrated with graphic, trenchant portraits which confer nobility, integrity to his argument.

Which leads him to his present state. He has been asked by the editor of the fledgling and increasingly popular journal, Harper's New Monthly Magazine, to do a feature on Frederick Douglass. This, now renowned, former Slave, who through his oratory is a leading figure in the abolitionist movement. Caelan is in Rochester, New York and it is two days after the great celebration marking the Independence of the country. Only yesterday he was present when Douglass spoke. Douglass, who had been asked to present on the day itself choosing not to do so, in protest. He appeared the day following Independence Day in Corinthian Hall. A hugely elevated dais, garlanded with the union flag and flowers, exalting the man above those who heard him. Watching him on the

 even small birds fly free

podium, Caelan was struck by his immense dignity, magnetic charisma yet searing frailty, despite his tall frame and robust figure.

Douglass had not held back in his oratory, which had galvanised Caelan like nothing before. Phrases elegantly constructed rained down on the audience, blow by blow. As he spoke about the celebration of independence.

"I am not included within the pale of glorious anniversary! Your high independence only reveals the immeasurable distance between us."

Caelan, immediately became aware of restlessness, had heard distinct murmurings among the audience as they began to sit uncomfortably in their seats.

"The sunlight that brought light and healing to you, has brought stripes and death to me. This Fourth July is yours, not mine. You may rejoice, I must mourn…"

The memory of the previous day's laughter, merriment, celebration and family reunion quickly evaporating among those gathered as this big man held forth and held nothing back. Dwelling on each word, each sentence, taking his time, ensuring the full import of his statements and conviction were revealed.

"What, to the American slave, is your 4th of July? I answer; a day that reveals to him, more than all other days in the year, the gross injustice and cruelty to which he is the constant victim."

Now Caelan realised as he listened, there is no escape. The logic, the graphic imagery, the power of the words, the charisma of the man, swept the room like a pentecostal flame. Speaking of his enslaved brothers and sisters he yowled,

"To him, your celebration is a sham; your boasted liberty, an unholy license; your national greatness, swelling vanity; your sounds of rejoicing are empty and heartless; your denunciation of tyrants, brass fronted impudence; your shouts of liberty and equality, hollow mockery; your prayers and hymns, your sermons and thanksgivings, with all your religious parade and solemnity, are, to Him, mere bombast, fraud, deception, impiety, and hypocrisy — a thin veil to cover up crimes which would disgrace a nation of savages."

It is at this point that Caelan realised why Douglass had chosen not to speak on Independence Day. How wise. Then he would have been competing with the overwhelming sense of pride and entitlement so cherished by his audience. This day, the day after, with a surfeit of food, wine and good will, he has an audience lain prone and vulnerable in front of him. If ever there was an opportunity for this country to wake up to its original sin, this was it.

At the end of the speech, Caelan was reeling as he observed the crowd shocked and stunned.

He realises today after reflecting on the words overnight, that the gallery had not expected to be assaulted in their comfortable status in quite that way. Of course all are abolitionists. But the stark truth of the imperative had never been so piercingly delivered to puncture their own self-righteousness. Douglass had placed everyone in the frame. There was no succour in their alliances and proclamations, no dodging the realities placed in front of them.

Today he is to meet the man and is walking down Alexander Street to the small unostentatious dwelling in which he has his home. As he approaches the building, carrying his equipment over his shoulder, he sees Douglass reclining in an easy chair on the front balcony. Douglass does not see him and Caelan has an opportunity to focus on his subject ensconced in the stark simplicity of his life, away from the acclaim and glamour. He seems reduced to Caelan, troubled.

It is just a moment of naked exposure and susceptibility. The instance is over in a flash, as Douglass sees him, rises from his chair and rushes towards him with a wide grin to offer assistance in carrying the heavy equipment. They greet one another and Caelan is immediately struck by the warmth of the man, his kindly nature.

"I have been so looking forward to meeting you Caelan," Douglass says, shaking his hand vigorously, "Your reputation proceeds you. I have read some of your work and seen your pictures and I love the way you are capturing scenes and people and having an impact on our common story. And you are Irish. This gives a chance to return the wonderful hospitality afforded by your people when I visited some years ago. Where in that country are you from?"

Caelan is taken aback. Of all the first moments he had wondered and been anxious about, this never featured. The expansiveness of the great man envelops and overawes him.

"I'm from Skibbereen, sir,"

"Ah, County Cork. The good people of Cork city were very kind to me. Of course I was an oddity. Very few had seen a Black man before. But somehow, I felt very much at home. Although, they stared. It seemed they did so with a serene and welcoming level of curiosity. I found it

 even small birds fly free

enchanting. In fact, I would say, Ireland made me. I underwent a transformation there. I began to live a new life from that moment. Instead of the bright blue sky of America, I am covered with the soft grey fog of the Emerald Isle," he chuckles to himself, "I began to breathe, and lo! The chattel became a man"

"I'm so glad, sir."

"It wasn't an easy trip, Caelan. I saw a lot of suffering. Things I couldn't understand. How the people of the richest empire the world has ever seen could be left starving, desolate and derelict. It didn't make sense. But even then, I received such warmth and encouragement. You know I met your great man?"

"O'Connell, you mean?"

"Yes Caelan. He was, maybe still is, my hero. Lord have mercy on his soul. If I can command half of the power that man held in his voice and rhetoric, I think we will see slavery abolished. Anyway, on to the business in hand, how would you like the day to proceed."

"Well, in truth sir, this is a perfect way to start. I like to get to know my subjects. We have a word in the Irish language. 'Ráiméis'. It means we just spend time together. Relaxed. Speaking nonsense if that's what befalls but just seeing what happens. That is the best way for me to capture you. To see your true nature."

"Oh, now you're scaring me, Caelan. I'm not sure any of us are ready for that kind of exposure."

They laugh together an easy laugh. And spend the rest of the day in tranquil company. Caelan remembers special moments.

"You are a privileged people, Caelan. The same as my people."

"How can that be, sir? Your people and my people have suffered so much."

"Exactly because of that. We know the nature of suffering. How it cleanses the soul of its illusions. As a peoples we have been on what is called the wrong side of history. But it prepares us. We can learn compassion. Provided we are not bitter."

Caelan stops then and looks at the man before him. He asks him to hold his position as he takes his image. Looking through the lens, he penetrates into the inner sanctum and it takes his breath away. His mind is a blur. How can it be? How can this man who has endured so much, project such inner peace and nobility? Caelan is humbled in his art and hopes the skill he has learned to capture the focus, light, angle will do justice to the revelation apparent to his soul.

"People in the ascendancy. The white man. The imperialist. The coloniser. He has no idea who he is. And his people, groomed as they are in their lie of superiority. The notion that they are bringing civilisation to us feckless people. These people are lost. And to find themselves they must go through such painful self examination. Very, very few are capable of that. Most shrug their shoulders and say 'but that's just history, its nothing to do with me'. When in truth it has everything to do with the composition of their soul and their reflections. Do you know, if the Negro did not exist, if my kind were not there in front of them, they would have to invent me, to justify who they are, what they have become."

They are sitting in the living room of the house. The fire blazing in the hearth, enriching with its glow the wood-panelled walls. Ensconced on walnut armchairs, Douglass becomes expansive,

"In thinking of America, I sometimes find myself admiring her bright blue sky, her grand old woods, her fertile fields, her beautiful rivers, her mighty lakes, and star-crowned mountains. Do you know what I mean, Caelan?"

"I sure do,"

"But my rapture is soon checked, my joy is soon turned to mourning. When I remember that all is cursed with the infernal actions of slaveholding, robbery and wrong. When I remember that with the waters of her noblest rivers, the tears of my brethren are borne to the ocean, disregarded and forgotten, and that her most fertile fields drink daily of the warm blood of my outraged sisters, I am filled with unutterable loathing."

Caelan sees an unbearable sadness overtake the man and wonders how he can continue to sustain his fight.

Later in the day, they share stories and intimate details of their own lives. Caelan talks about his brother, Pádraig. And his perplexity of how Pádraig has adapted to life in America.

"It's like I hardly know him anymore. He'll always be my brother, of course. He took up with the pattyrollers to escape his indenture working in the swamps. I couldn't believe it. The pattyrollers! Hunting down people!!!"

"Don't get me started on that, Caelan. Can you believe it? By an act of the American Congress, slavery has been nationalised in its most

 even small birds fly free

horrible and revolting form. By this act, Mason & Dixon's line has been obliterated; New York has become like Virginia; and the power to hold, hunt, and sell men, women and children, as slaves, remains no longer a mere state institution, but is now an institution of the whole United States. Where those who have escaped go, may also go the merciless slave-hunter. Where these are, man is not sacred. He is a bird for the sportsman's gun. By that most foul and fiendish of all human decrees, the liberty and person of every man are put in peril. The broad republican domain is hunting ground for men. Not just for thieves and robbers, enemies of society, merely, but for men guilty of no crime, whatsoever."

Caelan watches the man before him in full flow. The conviction burning inside him. And he cringes in shame at the memory of his dear brother, an accomplice in this malfeasance.

"An American judge gets ten dollars for every victim he consigns to slavery, and five, when he fails to do so. The oath of any two villains is sufficient, under this hell-black enactment, to send the most pious and exemplary Black man into the remorseless jaws of slavery! His own testimony is nothing. He can bring no witnesses for himself. This Fugitive Slave Law stands alone in the annals of tyrannical legislation. I doubt there is another nation on earth, having the brass and the baseness to put such a law on the statute-book."

Such is the force of the argument, that Caelan thinks of himself as an accomplice in its use, by extension, through his brother. He feels utterly lost. In meekness he says,

"Lately, he has told me he has left the pattyrollers. And now has taken up employment on a plantation. But in his letters, he has all this justification for what he does. Its like he has been drugged, brainwashed. I try my best to help him see but he is obdurate in his position."

Douglass stops for a long while and pauses in reflection. His hands joined as if in supplication. Seeking some way inside himself to reconcile, to accommodate the extraordinary complexity of what it means to be a man.

"Bless you, Caelan. Your brother's experience is not unusual. And in the end, it is not for us to judge. Despite our conviction. Until we are in another's situation, we cannot know. I have seen many men and some women in the plantation and even here in the north, Negroes, who do things that I find hard to comprehend. Turning on their own. Sadly what some people only possess is the will to survive at all costs. Nothing else matters to them. Compromise after compromise, leading to desertion and betrayal. I suspect your brother may be of that ilk. He has forced himself to fit in. Is it because of how he sees his past? Or the people who now influence him? Or his own need to feel accepted, safe? Who knows? In his case, he has his white skin as a passport. The most important thing for you is to continue to love him. Hold him. Gently support him with his horrible dilemma. He is not able to come home to himself where he is right now. Some day he may be able to. You need to be there waiting."

Towards the evening, as night draws in, Caelan takes his leave of Douglass. Touched in soul and spirit, he senses the images he has captured, will illuminate the words growing within him and shape a feature which will enrich the debate further. But more importantly, he registers he has been in touch with greatness. A power that will inspire his future work. And he is grateful that his work has given him this opportunity. He rushes home to tell Bridie. He can't wait to see her face as he reveals to her all that has happened.

Prospect Cottage,
Georgetown
Washington DC
December 1857

Dear Pádraig,

You will be surprised to hear that I have moved. I am now in Washington, right in the heart of the debate on the future of the country. But it's not only work that brings me here. Although that is central. There are, of course, many opportunities for me here. And despite your reservations about the precariousness of my chosen profession, I am thriving and have been for years now.

Editors seem to like my work and I keep getting commissions and it has required me to travel a lot and be away from Boston. Lately most of my work is here at the Capitol, where all are drawn. The main actors of the day, we would say. And I need to be here among them to record what I see and give my analysis. It is tremendously exciting work and it fulfils me. I am growing in resolution day by day. To frame argument about the inhumane conditions that are reported from plantations and the outrage of slavery; Of one man owning another. I know this doesn't sit easy with you but this is my life now.

I managed to get rooms with a writer. A fiercely strong woman called Emma Southworth[6]. I am very lucky. I came across her when she asked me to look at a short story she was writing called 'The Irish refugee'. And when the time came for me to make my move south from Boston, she offered me a room. It suits us both. She does not have a lot of money. Her husband, like too many these days, abandoned her and her two children, and went to South America to seek his fortune. So the little rent she charges improves her income. And don't be worrying about her reputation with her offering a room to a man. She doesn't care two figs about that and is committed fully to women's independence.

But in truth I am not telling you the full story. I am in love with Bridie Mulcahy. Hopelessly so in fact. Indeed from the first moment I met her, boarding the ship from Liverpool. As you know, she is married with six children, now all pretty much grown up. Gráinne is eighteen, a beautiful young woman; Both sets of twins are almost ready for work and the youngest, Patrick a sweet boy entering his teenage years is fast becoming a talented musician. You may remember her husband Seán was murdered by the No-Nothings in a riot nearly ten years ago. I promised him as he lay in my arms with his last breath leaving his body, that I would look after his family. And I have done so.

Over the years, it has become unbearable. I suppose it was easier when the children were young and all her and to a degree, my focus was on them. But they are largely independent which leaves me with Bridie. And I am undone.

Antebellum   167

I have been away a lot because of work. Every time I leave, I leave a piece of my heart with her. When I return home, she is there, present but unattainable. And my heart dissolves. And I am captured once again. By her beauty. By her simple, gracious spirit. I have never met anyone like her. And never will.

The heartache, which never goes away, has started to interfere with my work. It is proving a huge distraction. Sometimes forcing me to end assignments early. So much do I miss her and want to be in her presence. Nothing has passed between us. She is blissfully oblivious of my deep love and passion for her. A passion that is all consuming. And I feel two things. One that I could not face the heartache of telling her how I feel. I think it would shake her and I would lose her friendship and the companionship of her children. And I also feel it would be unfair on Seán, Lord have mercy on his soul. He is the love of her life and remains so to this day. It fills me with admiration the way she carries on through her own heartache and grief and is continually there for their daughters and sons.

So on my last trip away I came to my senses. I knew I had to make a choice. For my profession. It's so important for me. And to avoid self-immolation and the destruction of a deep friendship. It came as a shock to her of course. I don't think she would have anticipated that at all. Of course, I hastened to assure her that nothing changes. The house is still hers and I can continue to send money for its upkeep and the family needs. My work pays so well.

So that is the state in which you find me. Grief-struck of course but in a way liberated. The memory of walking away that last time burnt into my soul. But I can throw myself into my work without encumbrances. That is a salve for my spirit. It's not all doom and gloom.

The cottage in which I have a room is in a beautiful setting. Its half hidden from the street by Elm trees, yet set on the hill above the Potomac, the verandah which surrounds is bathed in the evening glow at Sunset. Its a perfect place to reflect and write. I also have a little developing shed in the garden.

So I am good too Pádraig. No need to worry about me

Lots of love,

Nollaig Shona agus athbliain faoi mhaise,

Caelan

        even small birds fly free

Boston

January 1859

Bridie Mulcahy

In which Bridie Mulcahy is heartbroken.

I am heartbroken. And it is a shock to me. Caelan has left. Coming to me as he did a couple of weeks ago, to tell me he needed to move to Washington. Of course, I immediately understood. Why wouldn't I? He's been getting on great guns in his work. Conquering all and sundry. And I can see the passion in it. But I didn't understand why the news hit me like a ferocious blow to my gut. I was almost reduced by it and had to make a quick excuse to retire to the bathroom where I became violently sick. It took me sometime to compose myself and return.

He, of course, looked at me solicitously when I came back. I brushed it off by saying that I had eaten something that morning which obviously didn't agree with me. He countered saying that nothing would change. He would continue to look after us. We now would have the whole house to ourselves and he was glad of that. And would continue with his monthly stipend.

Of course, I knew at that moment that this was not the reason why his revelation hit me so hard and it was only when I lay in bed that night that I came to a full recognition. And the realisation has meant many sleepless nights since.

I am in love with Caelan O'Donovan. And it is a love that has overtaken my whole being. And I now know that this has been the case since I first laid eyes on him when he kindly approached me on the quayside in Liverpool, ten years ago. How could I have been so blind? But it's probably a godsend. I don't think I could have got on with anything if I had known before. So maybe it's a mercy.

But this pain now besieges me. What is it? Just the memory of him reduces me. And he's only gone a couple of weeks. Is it his Cork blas? The sweet lilt in his voice reminding me of so many things, home, the life before, the innocent bliss of it. His way of walking. Betraying jaunty enthusiasm. His peculiar friendly disposition. From home. From our country. I know now that it has meant so much to me. It has helped me deal with the loss of everything. The way we lived before it all fell apart. The Great Hunger devouring all. The easy, common dúchas we shared. I know now he helped me settle here. Absorb and adjust to the transition and losses. What can I say?

I have to wake up now. I can't let this grief get the better of me. Two men I love gone from my life. I will be grateful. That's what I will be. That I have known two wonderful men and love them both is a blessing. Many would be happy with this.

And I will change. I will become an American. I have to let go all of the past. With Caelan gone, there will be no easy way to recollect it anyway. And it's gone. Yes, I will become an American. And that will make my future here more clear. It's what the boys and girls need from me anyway.

So I will resolve to let Caelan go. And pray for him. That the work in which he is immersed will prosper and that he will continue to find a voice and an eye for those who have no representative and are marginalised. This may heal my aching heart. Please God. Oh God, this is so hard.

     even small birds fly free

Five Points, New York City,
February 1860

In which Abraham Lincoln visits Five Points and has a short conversation with street bystanders, Mary O'Brien, Samuel and their two children.

Whenever Caelan came across the Illinois congressman Abe Lincoln, he was continually taken aback. The first impression of an awkward man, a tall ungainly frame with a long angular bent face. 'This fellow will have trouble making an impression,' he felt. However, this opinion was dispelled on hearing him speak, every time.

Today, Caelan is in New York to cover an event in which the congressman himself is the main attraction and is galvanised, once again, by the sheer charisma of Lincoln's voice. In what is definitely a pitch to become presidential nominee for the Republican party, he excels. Forcefully challenging the existence of slavery as unconstitutional, he uses his wit and intelligence to convince his audience that the words of the constitution fly in the face of its existence and certainly its intended expansion. It is abundantly evident the audience is enraptured and Caelan's media colleagues are electrified and intoxicated with an unbounded enthusiasm for the man, which he has not seen before. The speech is a triumph.

Through some local contacts, Caelan hears that, after this event in the Cooper Institute in the Bowery, Lincoln is going on a walking tour of Five Points[7]. This is indeed a surprise and interesting revelation. Caelan knows the area well having been asked over the years to document his people's experience there and he uses this to get quickly, by horse and cart, and instal himself in a prime position at Five Points, the first floor of a grocery store, opposite the House of Industry, a children's orphanage.

As he sets himself up, he battles with the feelings he always experiences on arrival at this part of Manhattan. The slum conditions appal him. It's difficult for him to look at the people, his own people there. Very much reduced in their circumstances. Memory and pain assaulting him in equal measure. Today, however, he sees them through different eyes and recognises their spirit and enduring forbearance. And he understands why Lincoln would want to walk among them. After his triumph in the hall. This is this man's electorate, his people. Is Caelan witnessing the beginning of a revolution? The people seem to think so and he recognises something in the air when Lincoln arrives. Caelan captures the joy and exhilaration bountifully evident as caps are thrown in the air. A celebration, just like at home. He smiles to himself at this. Maybe there is something to watch out for in this Illinois congressman after all. Maybe he is the future.

After visiting the House of Industry, Caelan watches closely as Lincoln files past onlookers, stopping and entering long conversations with those gathered to cheer him on.   His eyes are drawn to a young couple, sweetly holding hands with their two small children by their side, a tableau depicting a future. Lincoln stops to talk to the man. Caelan is struck by the image of the two men, the husband of the couple, a tall, stately Black man with a beautiful, handsome face standing face to face with the esteemed congressman. They shake hands and are engaged in deep conversation. Lincoln also greets the young woman, the wife of the Black man and their children. Caelan sees Irish blood in her, a sweet, freckled, pretty face. Auburn hair and sparkling green eyes. There is something thrilling in this triptych. It looks so normal. So dignified and inspiring and yet so out of the ordinary. Surely, this is the world to come.

Samuel Williams has been eagerly awaiting this day. Enthusiastically engaged in the movement to abolish slavery; Seeing that as his best hope of being reunited with his mother, he has followed the career path of many of the major voices of the day and has high hopes for the congressman from Illinois, Abraham Lincoln. He has even given his son the congressman's name. When he heard Lincoln was coming to visit Five Points, he was beside himself in anticipation.

He, Mary and the children are on the sidewalk when Lincoln passes and stops by them. Reaching out, Lincoln asks,

"Hello there, my good man. Do you mind if I ask your story? I want to get the know the people I hope to represent."

The words come gushing out of Samuel. This is a moment he has rehearsed for so long. An opportunity to talk to someone in the axis of power who may effect change. He is eloquent in the telling and he can see that Lincoln is deeply moved when Samuel describes his mother, her position, his escape north and the abomination of the Fugitive Slave Law. At the end of the conversation Lincoln reaches for his hand and assures him he will do his best.

When the moment is over and the congressman has moved on, Samuel slumps to the floor. "Mary, Mary, Is this it? Is this the beginning of the end? I have such a strong feeling that the man means it. And I think he

            even small birds fly free

may very well have the power, have it within him to change everything. But, dear Mary, it's hard to keep believing. Keep hoping."

Mary reaches down and embraces Samuel tenderly. Her man, Her glorious, noble, dignified, gorgeous man. She wants above all to be his strength. To be his shield. To give him succour when the winds of change blow against his dreams, when an icy pall descends on the nation and on his life. Above all, she wants to kindle within him, the hope, the unfailing faith, that one day he will see his mother again, hold her in his strong arms and console her, introduce her to his daughter and son.

As Samuel sinks into her arms, Mary hums softly to him, to encourage him, to nurture this new hope instilled in his heart and soul through the encounter, to prophesy towards a future which this hope signifies is in their grasp. She hums a song, a hymn, which Samuel taught her, a hymn which above all rings out in defiance at the abomination of men owning men, of Samuel's mother incarcerated on a plantation in Georgia, not knowing her son is alive, and not knowing her new family. As a prayer she sings softly as a lullaby to him, seated on the pavement of Worth Street,

My country, 'tis of Thee,
Sweet Land of Liberty
Of thee I sing;
Land where my fathers died,
Land of the pilgrims' pride,
From every mountain side
Let Freedom ring.

What she does not know, and cannot know, is that the future for these two men, who meet fatefully on this day, will change immeasurably within a few short years. A father will lose a son, and a son will lose a father and the whole country will be plunged into an internecine conflict, a conniption of enmity, hatred, violence and death which will leave hundreds of thousands of fathers without sons and sons without fathers in a ruinous and traumatic war. A bloody conflict of countrymen against countrymen not just four years in its execution but as a tumultuous consequence to two hundred and forty four long years of enslavement, of violence, forced family disintegration and men owning men, women and children as patrimony, as mere chattel. The cataclysmic eruption delivering emancipation without equality and sadly, little change in the mindset of incumbents on both sides, who will continue to groom their descendants in their pernicious view of ascendency.

the civil war

November 6ᵗʰ 1860

In which Samuel, Pádraig, Mary and Caelan react to the Big Man from Springfield's election to the office of President[1]

Chicago Tribune

THE VICTORY.

**Republicanism Triumphant over
Fraud, Fusion, Cotton,
Disunion and
Treason.**

HONEST OLD ABE

ELECTED.

ALL NEW ENGLAND FOR LINCOLN

NEW YORK FOR LINCOLN.

**PENNSYLVANIA, OHIO AND
INDIANA FOR LINCOLN.**

Illinois for Lincoln.

The Legislature Probably Safe.

REJOICE AND BE GLAD!

Samuel Williams

I am beside myself with joy. The news has the whole city at fever pitch. Lincoln has made it. He's the incoming president. Is this what hope feels like? The long years of waiting distilled down into this one cataclysmic event. The new President will surely change this country. It cannot be otherwise. He looked into my eyes, didn't he? Earlier in the year. Barely a few months ago. I saw there fervent conviction, and the handshake, strong, sure, warm; As equals. I am careful though not to show too much emotion among the Irish labourers on the docks. I have quietly observed their affiliation to the Democrats and I worry that they may not greet any enthusiasm on my part with their approval. The new Republican party has swept the board and they won't like that. Trapped in their own small world and fight for survival, I don't think they can see how momentous this is. And if they did, I am not sure they would be happy, such is their insecurity, their latent antagonism against us. So as always, even though I'm bubbling up inside, I will keep this to myself. I will continue to be wary moving among the team. The Irish can be threatened very easily, Mary tells me; They don't feel secure here. Too may skirmishes with the 'know-nothings.' I owe my reticence and circumspection to her. She advises me to be on my guard at all times. They can turn any minute, she says. I can't wait to get home though, to celebrate.

Pádraig O'Donovan

Paddy O'Donovan is and has been a frequent visitor to the verandah of the main house. The Planter had long recognised Paddy's keen intellect and careful manner. A man to be trusted. He rarely takes his fiddle with him, though. He doesn't want to be seen in a stage-Irishy way. A nincompoop for their entertainment. On the odd occasion when he does, he woos the womenfolk with his virtuosity. This helps to keep his elevated position intact.

Today, receiving the tempestuous news from the ballot, both men are incensed. That 'long streak of misery' from Illinois is about to destroy everything in a reckless political gamble. His election is a shot from a gun. He wants to dictate to them how they should live. Destroy their livelihoods.

There is no doubt now that the country will be divided. There is no room for compromise. Both men actively discuss plans. Paddy's expertise will be useful. The Planter reassures him that he will be more valuable in the confederate army than on the plantation. "I have July", the Planter reassures him. "He will keep the work going. I will recommend you to Beauregard[2]. I'm sure he will be in the command group when it comes. There is nothing now for us here but to leave the Union, Paddy and fight for our future. I'm depending on you to do your bit."

"I'm grateful sir and honoured," Paddy replies. Inside he thinks how strange his life has panned out. Now he is the militant one. Not his brother. Now he has the motive. He will fight and give his all for this land that he has come to love, that is now his home. 'It's a strange thing,' he thinks, 'how my time with the pattyrollers and my overseer post here has equipped me for tough days ahead.' He is excited and later in the evening finds it difficult to sleep as he contemplates the new future which is being laid out in front of him.

Mary O'Brien

I am anxious today like I have never been. This news, which everyone is greeting like Christmas has come, fills me with foreboding. I can see what people are excited about. Didn't we meet and shake hands with the great man himself. Honest Abe, they call him. But I see in people's manner, behind their eyes that they are also not happy. Not everyone. This presidency will turn the world upside down and God knows do I know how that feels. There are dark days ahead and I cannot rise to the pervasive hoopla all around me. I fear for Samuel. This splits everything down the middle and people are threatened and when that happens, everything falls apart. The Irish migrants here are suspicious of Samuel and me. It's why I feel safer here among the Negroes on Sullivan Street. Everyone is going on about the precious Union but it is our union, Samuel and I, that I worry about being under attack. I will hold my family close now. It's time for vigilance like never before.

Caelan O'Donovan

Today I know I must delve into my deepest reserves to frame a piece which will establish once and for all the momentous nature of the news we have received. Honest Abe has made it. And the country has an opportunity to rise up and claim the heritage it so proudly proclaims. But I am nervous. Will I find the words which will do justice to what is in my heart? To what is so glaringly obvious in what is before us? I see what I will write today as a culmination of all that I have learnt. Of all that has been passed on to me. Strangely, I feel Ma and Da and Aoife by my side, supportively cheering me on. How I miss them. And yet my thoughts stray also to Pádraig and wonder how he will greet today. I fear for him. I feel I have lost him. That he has been engulfed, traduced by those where he lives. In a way, I want to write for him too. To convince. And others. The Irish labourers I have come to know and write about in Boston and New York. I have seen their fear and insecurity up close. Their alliance with the Democrats who promise them everything. I want to write to help all see how things can be different and we do not have to fear. It is a time for courage and sensitive argument. I miss Bridie now more than ever. If I had her by my side at this moment then

even small birds fly free

I would have within me from her comforting presence the wherewithal to face what is before me. But enough of this now. I must block everything out and write like never before.

The Atlantic Monthly November 1860[2]

'Can the Country find its way back home'
By Caelan O'Donovan

When I strolled on these shores for the first time twelve years ago, I ambled with a light step. I, like many of my countrymen and women, had escaped oppression of the fiercest kind which brought death and disease to my family and a million others. Leaving nearly two million others no other option but to flee. Arriving here in the beautiful city of Boston on a glorious summer's day lifted my spirits. I sang in my heart the great words of the constitution;
'We hold these truths to be self-evident, that all men are created equal, that they are endowed by their Creator with certain unalienable Rights, that among these are Life, Liberty and the pursuit of Happiness.'
These words and the tune I made-up in my head galvanised me. I can make my home here, I thought, these principles marry with my own.

The years since have provided me with a rude awakening. I discovered that the country is built on exploitation of a people it refuses to call citizens, turning them into property. I have loaned my voice, such as it is, to the cause of liberty for the Negro. To the encroachment of the notion on our national life of a man being the property of another. The very idea that a man or woman can be a thing in Georgia and yet a human being in Massachusetts flies in the face of all logic and yet our elected representatives have danced on pinheads over this for the last decade.

The news that Abraham Lincoln is elected to the Presidency changes all of this. It has been our good fortune that a question has been thrust upon the Nation which has forced us to reconsider the primal principles of government. Principles which appeal to conscience as well as reason. Bringing the vision of the Declaration of Independence to the test of experience in our thought, life and action, leading to a conviction of understanding and soul.

It will not do for Lincoln to confine himself now to mere political argument, for the matter then becomes one of expediency, with two defensible sides to it; He must go deeper, to the radical question of Right and Wrong, or surrender the chief advantage of his position.

I am told often and by many to keep quiet. That my words and those of other newspapermen sow division and threaten the Union. On the contrary, the true danger to popular forms of government begins when public opinion ceases because the people are incompetent or unwilling to think. In a democracy it is the duty of every citizen to think; But unless the thinking result in a definite opinion, and the opinion leads to considerate action, they are nothing.

The moment asks of us an unavoidable question. What kind of country do we

even small birds fly free

want to be? Do we continue to flaunt those words which elevate and enlighten our constitution, the abiding principle that all men are equal? Or do we consign ourselves to the abomination where one man can own another and his wife, family, progeny and not only own but whip and separate at will and for profit? Is the aberration of the Fugitive Slave Act which turns the whole country into a jail for the Negro our common future?

I for one do not want to live in such a country. And I believe a good proportion of my new countrymen assent to my voice. If this heralds a deep division and issues in a violent conflict with those who are irredeemably wedded to a future of man as property, then what is our alternative? To compromise with the evil of slavery? To the detriment of our common soul? Reducing our voice and influence in the world to a sham? That slow, enervating sickness will poison our future worse than any threat of the break-up of the Union.

We must face the naysayers down. Those that through greed and privilege have quietened their conscience and deadened their souls and deprived other human beings a present and a future over two and half centuries. This is the clarion call of the election of 'Honest Abe'. This is our opportunity. To find a way home to the uplifting, inspiring words and principles of our constitution; All Men are Created Equal.

Fort Sumter

18th April 1861

In which Samuel, Mary, Pádraig and Caelan react to the inception of the Civil War

<<Beginning at 4:30 a.m. on April 12, the Confederates bombarded the fort from artillery batteries surrounding the harbour. Although the Union garrison returned fire, they were significantly outgunned and, after 34 hours, Major Anderson agreed to evacuate. There were no deaths on either side as a direct result of this engagement, although a gun explosion during the surrender ceremonies on April 14 caused the death of two U.S. Army soldiers. REUTERS>>

Samuel Williams

When Samuel Williams hears the news of the confederacy attack on the Union Fort it is like a huge boil being lanced; Painful yet also bringing relief. It has begun. It's not a surprise to him. He knows these southerners inside out as only someone who has languished under them can. He knew they would react like this. There is no reasoning with them. Full of conviction of the rightness of their position, they are ready to do anything to preserve the life that they have gathered for themselves. And recognising their obstinate, obdurate nature, he knows they will extract great pain from those who would seek to oppose them.

Of the North, the Union, he is not so sure. He wonders if the ordinary man has stomach for the battle ahead. Or even knows anything about what he is facing. In the conversations he overhears on the docks and the jubilant shouts of the men ready to go to war for their precious Union, he does not see the same visceral reaction he knows will inhabit the people he has lived amongst in the South. Full of swagger and daredevilry, those dockers seem blithely ignorant of what is at stake and what is to come to pass.

Samuel has been acutely disappointed in Lincoln. The man he used to think of as upright, reliable, full of justice and conviction is very much reduced in his eyes. Trying to accommodate those in the south, he has made compromise after compromise trying to protect his precious Union. Bargaining to accept the continued existence of slavery in states where it is ongoing, to prevent its expansion to the New Territories. Samuel feels any preservation of something that is rotten to the core is not worth the effort. Better to let the thing fall apart.

Lincoln however has got a bloody nose with the secession of states and the formation of a Confederacy. South Carolina, closely followed

 even small birds fly free

by Louisiana, Mississippi, Alabama, Georgia, Florida, Texas have all broken away in the months since he has become President and North Carolina, Arkansas, Tennessee and Virginia are on the brink. Now Fort Sumpter in South Carolina has been attacked and Union troops overcome with ease. The country has descended into war and are not even able to say out loud what it's all about. It's laughable if it wasn't so tragic.

The South, the new Confederacy of States is justifying its secession seeking its legitimacy on the core principle that a man has a God-given right to own another man and his progeny for life, based purely on the colour of skin. To anyone with sense it is preposterous. But it's not the issue on which Lincoln is prepared to go to war. No, the man, betraying all his finer instincts, is calling to arms to preserve the Union and prevent the disintegration of this vast land into a conglomerate, a hodgepodge, a mishmash of newly made up countries. Samuel thinks this loosely affiliated confederation of southern states will not last long before self interests pull it apart. But to bully them to give up by prosecuting a war on them just to preserve some mythical idea of 'union'?; Samuel thinks will not solve anything.

What's clear to him, however, is that he and others of his people are not included in either the debate or the war. The ultimate irony is that a war propagated on a disguise, avoiding like a taboo, the key divergence between the protagonists, the right to own slaves, will achieve nothing. Nothing but hatred, recrimination, bloodshed and death. And so he is left with feelings of despair and disappointment. The kind that can come from lionising a man only to see his true colours emerge. Abraham Lincoln is that man and it fills him with sadness.[3] He has lost his great hope.

Pádraig O'Donovan

He is out in the cotton fields when he hears the news. A beautiful spring morning, with a slight breeze carrying coolness. The soft, melodic timbre of the Negros singing as they work. He is overjoyed. Just twenty four hours and they cave in. He feels the Northerners are soft and will have no stomach for the fight.

When he first heard that Lincoln had sneaked in and grabbed the presidency, the vote being split among Democrats north and south, handing the initiative to the Republican party, he was in despair. He feared then for his future. But in recent months, things have changed and he begins to see a solidarity emerging among southern states to preserve the status quo. The forming of a confederacy of states heartens him and he knows now that he will have a part to play. He can't wait. On hearing the news he whoops with an exclamation of joy and pride. He leaves July in charge and races into Natchez on his horse to join in the celebration and tumult.

Within a few days, things become clear to him. The pathway opens up. He comes across a posting in the New Orleans Daily Crescent newspaper which reads ""We understand that our friend, Gen. C.R. Wheat, is about to raise a company of volunteers, to serve in the Army of Louisiana. His headquarters are on 64, Charles Street, where we advise all friends of a glorious cause to repair and enlist." Immediately he recognises his destiny. He confers with the Planter, takes his leave with an excellently worded letter of commendation and makes his way down to New Orleans.

On arrival in the city he is intoxicated by remembrances. The vibrant smells and sounds, the clammy heat, the sweet scent of southern magnolia, the musky, fruity sensual smell of Jasmine, the open-air fires boiling pots of stew enriched by a concoction of spices, garlic and lemon ready to add flavour to crawfish, crab or shrimp. He feels alive. He feels like he has come home.

With his experience in the Pattyrollers standing him in good stead, with his letter of commendation he is enlisted as captain to take charge of a motley crew of Irish ship hands, dock workers, stevedores and immediately feels like he belongs. The rapport instant. They recognise him as one of their own and he already feels loyalty and comradeship growing. They will become a band of brothers. Ready to die for the land that gave them opportunity.

It isn't long before he is togged out and feeling smart, superior and fearless in the proscribed uniform; Dark green wool Zouave jackets with red cotton trim, distinctive red fezzes with red tassels, red flannel band collar shirts with five white porcelain buttons. He loves the outlandishly baggy Wedgwood blue and cream, vertically striped, heavy cotton ship pantaloons which will become the signature of his Company. He is also provided with blue and white horizontally striped stockings and white canvas leggings. But most important of all, the Company acquires for themselves a shipment of coveted Mississippi rifles. He is ready to make his name. This oncoming war his opportunity. What he has been waiting for. And he is more excited than he has ever been in his life.

 even small birds fly free

They are given leave for two days before their forced march north. "Get it out of your system, boys" he says, "and report back here in forty eight hours". He has no doubt that they will return, such is their excitement and fervour. Paddy, dressed in his uniform, strides into town as a king. He makes his way, inevitably, to the Coffee House and is immediately caught up in the atmosphere. All the restraint he has felt on the plantation surrounded by beautiful women dissolves and he finds himself in the centre of everything. The freedom of New Orleans assails him. Here there are no barriers. Black men and women mingle confidently and add a 'je ne sais quoi' to the ambience of the place. He is approached by a handsome Black man, a saxophonist, who greets him warmly and having heard he plays, invites him to join the ensemble. Strangely he feels at home immediately in this motley crew.

One of the others hands him a fiddle. Filled with bourbon, he throws himself into the strange, plaintiff cajun rhythm and the cadence of his apprenticeship in jigs and reels pays off and he adds to the enveloping sound. The bar is alive with dancing.

In the middle of it all, he sees a beautiful woman. Her flesh blue black, her eyes shining in merriment and abandonment as she flings herself sensually into the beat and tempo. The colours of her dress, vibrant, a clash of extravagance adding an unrestrained quality to her whirling shape. He is smitten. He does not know what overtakes him, is it the alchemy of the city, his years of celibacy, the glamour of his uniform or her sheer beauty but when his set finishes, he timorously approaches her. Solene her name and she greets him tenderly and warmly and sweeps him up onto the dance floor. He is captivated. All the exotic charm, beauty, glory and splendour of New Orleans are captured in her sinuous grace. When they stop to rest and talk, their connection is immediate and enhanced through the desire flowing between them. Pádraig sees mirth and winsomeness in her eyes and his attraction to her is instant and unfettered.

As the night enters the early morning, the New Orleans air cools and they step outside to look at the sky. "I didn't know how much I love this city until now. Until my return this time," He says. He is nervous in her company. And struggles to find words. He is so unused to talking with a woman. His forced celibacy for ten years bringing an uncommon, awkward, maladroit frisson to their exchange. Eventually he stumbles on the words.

"I am going away in three days. To fight for the South. I would love to spend the time in between with you. Am I asking too much?"

"Oh Pádraig, you are so sweet. What's a girl to do," she laughs and grabs him by the hand to return inside to the music and revelry.

All through the night and into the next day, they are together. She gives herself to him generously, sensuously, amorously, and he has never known anything like it. Her perspicacious intelligence; Her freedom in emotion, body and spirit transports him. He shares himself deeply with her, his losses, particularly Aoife. Leaving home, his country behind and the struggles he had to adapt. She does not judge him when he talks of his time with the pattyrollers but listens quietly with concern and affection. It's like a confessional for him.

Solene in turn tells him she understands and tells him of her people. Free people of colour.[4] Originally from Haiti, they have settled in New Orleans, their freedom and rights protected there. "We are not saints either, my people. Many have had slaves of their own. So I cannot stand in judgement. Things have changed among us now. The French were much more liberal in their approach to us. But America is changing and we are slowly being ostracised. White people cannot cope with us. A lot of the freedoms and status we held under the French are under attack. Many of my family have left and emigrated to Europe. But I love it here. I am ashamed now with how we treated other Black people in the past. I see that. But I cannot stand in judgement of you."

Her words assail and oppugn his long held beliefs. But its disturbance is put to rest by her magnanimity, her generosity of soul, their gentle lovemaking. Time stands still for them in the hotel room they have commandeered for themselves. Lovers in dangerous times. For Paddy it's a voyage of discovery. Immersing himself in the tender ministrations of this beautiful woman, delighting in the form and physicality of her glorious body exalts, apotheocizes, deifies her in his eyes. He takes refuge in his native language to articulate what is happening to him. He has found his 'anam cara', his soul friend.

On the last morning, early, at five o clock, he wakes, with a start, alongside her naked body and is caught up in sheer wonder. Her soulfulness and her life-affirming figure and form has turned his world upside down. All his interaction with coloured men and women before this have been distant, inhumane, treating those with whom he has been

    even small birds fly free

in contact as inferior, base, a property to be used. Solene has upended all these categories. And he is left unreconciled with his world view which he has, up to this moment, comfortably embraced. As she silently sleeps alongside him, he imagines in a sleep of angels, he, contrarily, is thrown into utter confusion.

Then, as if struck by a thunderbolt, he realises he is in love with her, his Solene. Deeply, irrevocably joined with her. So much so, he cannot bear to be parted from her. He is shocked and at the same moment fear overtakes him as he realises the implication of his changed state. Consternation, dread and terror grip his very being. He has a desperate choice to make.

Solene wakes to see him looking at her in this altered state. "What's up', She whispers.

With tears, he says, "I have just discovered I have fallen in love with you hook, line and sinker, Solene. I realise that you are the woman I would love to spend my life with. It's so sudden. I am unbalanced."

She smiles sweetly at his words and holds his hand tenderly, wide awake now.

"But I also can't do it. I cannot marry you. And it's what I want. But I don't have your courage. I can't live with you here. I can't look at you every day and see how constrained your life is and will become. How people see a Black person in this country. How I have seen Black people until I have met you. I adore you. I adore these moments we have been together. But I cannot imagine a future for us. Not here. Not in this land. I have not your daring and audacity. It fills me with fear and apprehension."

Paddy feels a sick, gnawing consternation grow in his stomach. He did not expect this. The long ten years of his apprenticeship to rise in his social status upended by this unexpected happening. Solene, for her part, looks at him kindly. Her love and affection for him undiminished.

"Do you want me to leave?" She asks.

"No. Solene. I must leave before my resolve fails me. I am so sorry. This is breaking my heart."

He quietly rises from bed and slips into his uniform. A uniform which brought him so much pride and joy, now he begins to despise for the dilemma it has caused.

He reaches for her as she stands to say goodbye and he hugs her gently. Her soft, tender hands cradle his neck and it is a touch that burns into his consciousness. A sweet, precious scar that will fix this moment in time for him, on into his lonely future.

"Be safe, Pádraig. I will always love you. Thank you for this special time." she says with quiet dignity.

It is all too much for him. With restraint, borne from years of self reliance and an innate survival skill, he does not break down or cry. He lets her go, his Solene, the only love he will ever know.

He turns then and trusts his legs to manage the walk across the room, out the door, out of Solene's life. On the stairs he pulls on his boots and as he does he breaks, huge heaving sobs engulfing him. After some time, he gathers himself and with a face like flint makes his way back to the barracks. Although hurting, he has a war to fight and stripes to win. Without looking behind him, he strides through the streets of New Orleans, which have now acquired a bitter, oppressive quality, and makes his way to the barracks ready to assume his commission and go to into battle for the glorious South

          even small birds fly free

So it has begun. This morning's news. Southerners are on the attack. I find it curious how in the North nobody is talking about the real reason for this conflict. They talk about their Union but not about slavery. I see the Negro men here and they are frustrated. They are champing at the bit to be involved. This is the first time that they could strike a blow for emancipation and have the weight of government on their side. I know they would give their all. Most live with the haunting memory of families, mothers and sisters particularly, separated and still caught up in that dreadful system. What soldiers they would be. But such is the nature of prejudice that prevails here, they are not allowed. I see dear Samuel stymied, thwarted and precluded from taking part and it is difficult to see the pain of his powerlessness. This morning's news doesn't help. The easy surrender of Union forces demonstrating clearly that the North can't match the South with the same fire in their bellies. This is not going to be over soon. No, not for a long time.

The Atlantic Monthly April 1861
'Dilly-dallying has cost the Country'
By Caelan O'Donovan

There is no need for protracted discussion in any democracy when a minority is displeased with an election result and forthwith thinks it has the right to rebellion.[5] To suggest an election is stolen and propose an alternative president is nothing less than an assault on the American people. Treason is treason. Sadly, the Republican party has spent too many long hours seeking compromise with these traitors and seeking guarantees around the abomination of slavery. President Lincoln has suffered as a consequence of divisions within his own party.

Compromise is inconceivable with people who have established an alternative government and nominated an anti-president in Jefferson Davis. If the delay is a result of negotiations with border states to avoid fracturing the Union further, the message should have been loud and clear. To flirt with secession is to dabble with danger.

There is a clear distinction between revolution and rebellion and this chasmic difference should have been clearly asseverated. The Republican party had effected a peaceful revolution in the November election. It had stood up to an oligarchy who, since the foundation of the state, has abused the functions of government in the institution of slavery, a tyrannical rule which had usurped the lives of millions of Negroes. Rebellion always goes backwards, is morally bankrupt. The delay has given these traitors time for their secession to assume the proportion and dignity of a revolution; Of a rebellion too powerful to be crushed.

In November the message was clear. There was a change of government which will sound a death knell to slavery. The insurrectionists by their secession have defied the will of the people of the United States. Their actions have bellowed loud and clear to all. Either it's their way or war. This cannot and should not stand. There is no room for equivocation. What their rebellion and treason have demonstrated is that there is no, nor can there ever be, moderation in slavery. They are antithetical, polar opposites, incompatible.

There was never and can ever be conciliation here. And the delay in seeking one has only benefitted the rebels. It has given them time to consolidate their organisation and propound that their actions had merit to the watching world. England and France particularly looking on with curious amusement at our procrastinations. At this point, I quote the esteemed writer of the London Times, William Russell; *'What on earth is the matter with the American people? Do they really covet the world's ridicule as well as their own social and political*

even small birds fly free

ruin? Every man who can carry a bucket of water or remove a brick is wanted. Yet government leaders persistently refuse to receive as soldiers the slaves, the very class of men which has a deeper interest in the defeat and humiliation of the rebels than all others. Such is the pride, the stupid prejudice and folly that rules the hour. Little did I conceive of the greatness of the defeat, the magnitude of the disaster which has entailed upon the United States, so short-lived has been the American Union that men who saw it rise may live to see it fall.'

The shot fired by the so called 'venerable' Edward Ruflin at Fort Sumter has ended all prorogation. We wake to a different and altogether clearer path. As the shot heard around the world from Concord's north bridge eighty seven years ago which gave us independence, the cannon fired on us, fires our soul and will culminate in a victorious response and a nation in which we can be proud.

While it is legitimate to be reluctant to engage in war and especially war against ones own people, a greater evil would be to submit to the concessions demanded by traitors. We now need to show strength of will and courage. They will be fighting for self interest. We will be fighting for principles that make government and civil society worth contending. We must convince all that treason against the ballot box is even more pernicious than treason against any throne. The bill of rights transcends and abrogates all and stands firmly against a right to anarchy which is being issued in through this cannon shot and the secession of states.

However long this war which has now been declared, it will be worth it rather than succumb to the tyranny of the secessionists. Such a war will bring a radical change in the system of African slavery and produce a nation and a flag in which we can be duly proud. A symbol of a principled nation, a beacon for the world.

New Orleans
May 1861

Dear Caelan,

I have enlisted in the Louisiana Tigers[6] and have been made Captain. The men in my company are all Irish so I feel very much at home with them. We are excited to be going to war for what we stand for. We strongly believe that the northern states should not be dictating to us how we should live and so we are ready to fight for our new homeland.

I am sure this will be over soon. One big battle and I am convinced the namby-pamby northerners will realise that we are not to be messed with. My men are tough. They have had a hard life here, most working on the docks and their strength and ability to endure pain is immense. I am proud to be associated with them. They are wild of course and it takes all my will power to control them. But when I point them in the right direction, they are fierce as the tigers we are named after.

You would be delighted to see me in my captain's uniform. Very colourful. I should get one of your photographer class of people to take an image so I can send to you. I hope you will see in the next few months how strongly we are set up here and that you will come around to the opinion that one group of states should not be in position to dictate to others how they should live.

I fear you are all enthralled with the liberals in the cities there. It's well for them in their rich lives to have fancy notions. The men I live among are poor and are looking for an opportunity to build something for themselves. The fact that we have had no problem enlisting volunteers will tell you that. But you should know it yourself. How we have had to flee our homeland because of the oppressive uncaring rule of the English. I despair that the liberals being egged on by England in the hope that this great new country will fail have decided to dig their heels in.

But never mind. This will all be over soon. We, I am sure, will whip their asses and we can all go back to our lives without the meddling interference of the republicans or abolitionists.

I know you will see this in time. I'm also glad that you now have your dedication to your profession and won't be joining the other crazy northerners in opposing us.

I hope you keep well

Pádraig

 even small birds fly free

Washington

May 1861

Dear Pádraig,

Please keep well. I am worried about you as you are seduced into this crazy venture. It grieves me actually. I fail to understand how you and so many other Irishmen are prepared to take up arms to preserve such a devilish system as slavery. I thought that all our suffering, for centuries really, would ensure that you and our countryfolk would understand what it is like to be oppressed like the Negro is.

I want you to keep safe. But now I can only hope that. This thing that has begun cannot finish in one big battle as you name it. The rift that is present in the country is a chasm. The acts of secession by the various states, treason. And treason in any country is punishable by death. I say all this dramatically to hope that you will come to your senses. I remember you prevailing on me in Ireland not to join the Young Irelanders. You were afraid for me. But then I had every right. It was to join a movement to throw off an oppressor who had usurped our right for self government. This is different. The southern states which seceded voluntarily joined the Union in the first place. And vowed to serve voluntarily. To turn and wage war because these states did not like the outcome of a presidential election, a first principle in any democracy, is nothing short of being a traitorous act, treason. But the main thing is what is behind the secession and rebellion but the abominable practice of slavery. Surely this is of no benefit to you or any of your company. Why oh why are you enlisting to give support to such tyranny. I have seen here in the north how it seems easy for a great majority of people to reduce the Negro to a thing. Easy because they have no contact, no real interaction with the person, the Negro. I have been blessed in my work to become friends and close companions with many Black men and women and I can say wholeheartedly that I have been overwhelmed, by and large, by the people I have come to know. Individual acts of generosity, open expressions of vulnerability, continual empathy and identification which has meant so much. Their suffering has many equivalents with the personal history of so many Irish men and women. Loss of family, home, facing prejudice and hostility. I have been blessed in the company of many.

So my wish for you dear Pádraig, as I know my arguments have had no influence on your thinking, is that you meet and befriend and know and come to love a Black man or woman and find yourself opened up by such intimate contact.

Stay safe, your brother as always,

Caelan

The Civil War

The Atlantic Monthly July 1861
The Battle at Manasses Chutzpah, Chaos and Slaughter

By Caelan O'Donovan

Yesterday this thing that has overtaken us, came home with a rude awakening. We are at war with one another. The buoyant expectancy that had coursed through the hearts of the Union during the last few weeks has come crashing down. What most thought would end in a crushing victory for our brave men and a return to normality has ended in a rout and very near disaster.

As I made my way to cover the battle at Manasses, I was astonished to see ladies and gentlemen in their carriages, with picnic baskets prepared, opera glasses in hand to watch from vantage points what they assumed would be a glorious victory.[7] Filled with notions of a Napoleonic triumph by the Union, one assumes these bystanders were seeking a tale they could whisper to their grandchildren.

But the day ended in chaos. Where first all signs showed that our army was making strides and throwing the rebels back, it all came to a sudden end when rebels, led by Jackson, stopped the advance. As if federal forces were throwing themselves against a wall of stone that would not budge. From that moment the day turned. The rebels took Union guns and turned them against our men and with that their advance began. Charging down the hill from their positions, screaming like a mob of furies, a howl from hell erupted, pierced the valley and sent shivers down my spine.

I watched in horror as chaos ensued. The Union army breaking and splintering and running backwards in fear and trembling, engulfing the onlooking spectators with their champagne and vittles. I saw the 12th New York regiment rush pell-mell out of the wood. Frightened soldiers fleeing for their lives. Other soldiers threw down their weapons and ran from the battlefield, sweeping up civilians in the retreat. In that moment, all seemed to be lost. The day which had begun with such exuberant anticipation ending in despair. Some of the fleeing army did not stop running until they reached Washington, there to bury their trauma and shame in an alcoholic binge.

But it would be wrong to consider this outcome a disaster. We not only deserved it but needed it. Far from being disheartened, it should give us new confidence in our cause. For if the victory that was expected was ours today, nothing would be resolved. The Union, such as it is, would be preserved as Lincoln has prayed for. But it would be a flawed Union. Slavery would still exist and this abomination would still course through our common life as an original sin.

No. What faces us now is reality. This is not going to be a short Napoleonic

   even small birds fly free

campaign. What we have entered is a battle for the soul of the nation. And it will take all our resolve, all our courage, all our strength to win the true objective of what is now before us. The ending of a man owning another and treating him and his family as a thing.

Our mission now to cleanse our lives. God has given us work to do not only for ourselves, but for coming generations of men. To reclaim the principle inspired by our declaration of independence that all men are created equal. Thus all the North must join in vowing that to gain this end, no sacrifice can be too precious or too costly.

Pádraig O'Donovan

Captain O'Donovan moves with his company to Camp Moore in Kentwood just one hundred miles north of New Orleans soon after their furlough. The activities, boring as they are, serve to dull Paddy's yearning for Solene and his transformed circumstances. He finds it easy to engage with the men, understand their origin and story and becomes a popular leader. After a hard days slog, drilling, marching they often gather around the camp fire. Paddy plays some fiddle tunes for them regularly and this further bonds their sense of brotherhood and identity as a unit.

Within weeks, they are shipped north by train, rumbling over the countryside. The vastness of the country becoming apparent as they ride, day after day. Travelling up the Mississippi to Corinth and then across Tennessee and Alabama into Northern Virginia, the beauty and diversity of the terrain fills their hearts and consolidates their commitment to fight for their homeland. Vast tracks of blue-ridged Appalachian forests populated with huge pine tress, sweeping verdant valleys, rivers streaming, cascading and plunging by as the journey ever northward. Paddy is moved deeply by this glorious lush landscape.

All of his men seem filled with notions of valour and the glory that await them. Stories abound and promises are made. High in spirit, their sense of identity as a unit grows, day by day. Paddy is told they are headed for Manasses, a huge railway junction which needs to be held against Union forces. "It's their gateway to Richmond," he is informed in a briefing. Paddy is thrilled with expectation of such an important role. Richmond, the pride of the South, will be held. General Lee will have overall command. The level of excitement grows daily as they trundle north slowly.

When they arrive at Manasses and are preparing for the promised, great battle, Paddy spends long evenings among his men. Many of them are now becoming engulfed with the momentous nature of what faces them. Their mood altering as the days pass. Quite a few come to him for help to write home. Suddenly he sees vulnerability in men where before he has only recognised bravado, pluck and machismo. The stories they tell him about those with whom they want to correspond deeply affect him. Facing this pivotal moment in their lives, some men desperately want to set things right.

The fresh faced young man, barely twenty, who tells him that he loves a girl in his home territory, a small farm in the wetlands of the Amite river. He has never declared his love and now he is afraid he never will be able to do so. He spends great effort telling Paddy what she looks like, possibly to capture the beauty he sees in her, to evoke her presence.

There are a number of boy men who want to talk to him about their mothers, making themselves very vulnerable to him as they describe how much they miss her endearing presence, her comforting touch. Some of the men want help to write to wives and sweethearts. All have a look of deep regret, fear and longing that is questioning their rash rush to enlist. Even the hard bitten, flinty, stone-faced Irish dockers and stevedores, men he saw as hard as nails are reduced by thoughts of the coming terror. One wants to make amends with his father, a relationship that seems to have been orchestrated through brutality and roughness, telling Paddy he does not want to take this history with him to the grave. Many talk about Ireland, their losses, the pain they have endured since their exile. It seems as if the day looming ahead of all has crystallised their lives and reflections.

As he lies later in his bed, Paddy is overwhelmed with his own thoughts and demons. Try as he does he cannot get Solene from his mind. The decision he made to walk away did not leave him free as he hoped it would at the time but distracted, troubled. Her beauty, kindness and generosity forever upending his received prejudice, interrogating quietly, cross examining thoroughly, his ambition for this war. And then there is Caelan. Determined in his heart he tries to write what he feels, but in reality as he puts pen to paper he fails. He gives up. He will write afterwards. To write now will only further disrupt the conviction he needs to lead his men.

   even small birds fly free

On the morning of the battle of Bull Run, he is nervous. He has responsibility for his men but is completely unprepared. In an effort to calm his soul he rises and rallies his company. As day breaks, the morning air is clear and bright and bird song is heard from copses nearby. It's a near perfect day. They are to hold the left hand side of Stone bridge. His company makes a series of skirmishes across the river attacking enemy lines but are met with resistance and draw back. Then chaos erupts and they are shot at by their own side. This he is completely thrown by and cannot understand. Did they not see the uniform? He sees three of his men fall and is helpless. The lovesick young man from Amite river farm one of them. He desperately tries to get his men to hold their fire and is partly successful but within minutes they draw fire from the Yankees.

His men are bewildered and set upon. And he is trying to bring order into a very dangerous situation. The noise of grapeshot, canister and cannon balls being shot and exploding all around them instilling terror. Cannon balls come as thick as hail and grape, bomb and canister sweep his ranks every minute. The oppressive smell of gunpowder and sulphur filling the air with the pungent aroma of rotting eggs. The fields which had been serene, filled with a transcendent light and birdsong in the early morning has proved ephemeral and are now crammed with dread, the sweat of fear. Consternation reigns. He musters his men again and again to throw themselves at Union lines. The hand-to-hand combat fierce. Bayonets at the ready, he sees the faces of the men they are engaging as demonic, filled with hate and fear. Paddy is in hell as he tries to keep a grip of his sanity. For a full half an hour, it did not seem as though men were fighting, it was ghouls from hell mingling in the conflict, cursing, yelling, cutting, shrieking.

Time and again, he rallies and marshals his men and throws them into the fray. The opposing force of the Yankees outnumber his company. His few hundred against the might of thousands. "Tigers, go in once more. Go in my sons, I'll be goddamned if these sons of bitches can ever whip us Tigers." His men respond time and again to his courage and call. Paddy throws caution to the winds. He ceases to care and is swept up in the pitch of the moment.

He sees his men switch to use their bowie knives. The reloading of their guns too slow. Plunging themselves into arm-to-arm, face-to-face hostility, he can see his men generate fear and terror in Yankee faces. Slaughter descending all around him. The pristine fields soaked in blood and corpse and the screaming of wounded men. But it is the yells of his own company that assail him. A deep and yet high-pitched scream and bellow which captures the roar of a lion and feral scream of a fox. It is terrifying. His men adapt and tie twine to their knives and expertly throw them at oncoming Yankees, striking them and retrieving to go again.

He calls for a retreat and they take refuge on Matthew's hill. The battle is going against them as Union forces, superior in number march on relentlessly. Late in the afternoon, reinforcements arrive in the First Brigade led by Thomas Jackson. Paddy thinks the day is lost. They are facing numbers which are too great. But as the afternoon deepens towards evening, he notices a shift and is amazed at the fortitude of Jackson's brigade and the hesitancy of the Yankees. One of his company shouts out. "Look at Jackson. He's in their among his men. He is standing there like a stone wall refusing to budge." All take courage from this and the tide begins to turn.

Within minutes a concerted attack down the hill begins and the sound of the confederate yell which he has heard in parts in their own skirmishes, resounds across the valley. A terrifying shriek and growl. As if uttered by Beelzebub himself. They rush forward to rout the Yankees, like maniacs released from hell. They see the troops before them, which a half an hour before had looked like a supreme unconquerable force, break up, turn and flee, many of them dropping their weapons in flight. It is a rout. He sees his men cheer and race down the hill across Bull Run and through the enemy camps. To his surprise at the end of the camp all stop. The whole confederate army pauses and gives up the chase, convinced that the day is won and enough has been done. He is confused by the decision to stall but quickly gathers his men. They become busy in pilfering what they can from the deserted Union campsite.

Paddy sits on a rock, draws a bandana across his sweaty brow, takes out a cigar, lights and inhales deeply. He feels his senses sharpen, his frayed nerves are soothed, and his trembling hands are given something to do. The action and cigar embodying the warm presence of an old friend, who has seen him through many trying times before. But none like this. His company eventually gather around him, clapping him and paying their tribute to his bravery and leadership. Inwardly, he swells with pride. The day is won.

Later in the evening everything changes. The stench of death rising from the fields they have traversed assault his senses. Stinking bodies

                    even small birds fly free

on the hills. Irrevocably drawn to it, trying to make sense of it, Paddy leaves the encampment and walks back over the battleground. Rotting bodies, many now being ravaged by wild boar fill the ground. Men become indistinguishable from animals. He cannot come to terms with this. He accidentally steps on a dead man's foot, and feels his boot touch like a piece of pickled pork, hard yet fleshy. He jumps back in alarm. He covers his mouth with his bandana to be able to endure the reek and stench. With ultimate irony, he sees the faces of the dead and is shaken by their colour. Not discolouring to purple as he had imagined but all of them have turned into a deep bluish black, giving each corpse with black hair the appearance of a Negro. Like a verdict from the Almighty.

Dear Caelan,

We did it and I'm so proud. You would be too. To lead my men on such an important occasion was a real privilege and we were not found wanting. You will have heard about how we put the run on the Yankee soldiers who fled away from us like scared cats. It was a tough day but all the hardships were worth it in the end. We have great leaders and the battle finished for us with loud cheers and beaming smiles.

It will be interesting to hear from you. To see if the event changed your mind. But we have definitely sent out a message that we mean business.

I lost some good men in the fighting and that put a bit of a damper on everything. But they can know they died for a great cause, defending their homeland.

General Lee is an inspiration to us all. The best soldier in the whole of the country before, he decided to fight for us because he is at heart a Virginian. He represents the spirit that most of us feel. Our home state has our first loyalty and if we are being attacked then you can be certain we will put up an enormous fight.

I had to dash this off to you. You wanted to know how I am and I also wanted to help you change your mind about the whole damn thing.

Your brother,

Pádraig

     even small birds fly free

Sullivan Street,
New York
September 1861

Dear Da and Eileen and Shay,

I know you will be hearing regularly about the war in your newspapers. And I suppose you are worried about us. We are ok. As you know Samuel is not allowed to be involved in the conflict. And although that is a blessing of sorts, he also remains very frustrated. He has to put up with a lot at work. Most of the Irish labourers here are very against Lincoln. They are mostly democrats. There are huge numbers of our people also involved in the battles.

We know now that it is not going to be over soon. The casualty lists are terrible. The whole country is in shock with the numbers of dead and reports of the fighting are fierce, cruel and inhumane. I feel so sorry for mothers. Some places have lost many young men as battalions are filled with recruits from the same area. And if a battalion is caught in a bad place whole villages can lose a huge bulk of their menfolk. I find it all very distressing. But we must accept. Although the objective is put about that we are fighting to save the Union, we know underneath it all that if slavery is not abolished nothing will change. It's why Lincoln is so hated by our people here as they are afraid that if abolition happens they fear they will face huge opposition for jobs from Negroes freed in the south. It's madness of course but it's in all the newspapers they read.

A typical example is The Pilot. Last week it led with the headline 'If Lincoln had sold out to the radical abolitionists of his party, the war would be prolonged as the South would resist. Abolition would cause a flood of black workers to the north. Negroes did not want to be emancipated. They were devoted to their owners and satisfied with their lot in life.' Such nonsense. But it feeds the fear and paranoia of our people here. Samuel is careful but he continually walks a fine line among them.

So you are well out of it. Your life there so much simpler and I am glad you have a family to support and engage you. As for me, I qualified in my nursing course thanks to the Sisters of Mercy. I have now got a job nursing in the Northern Dispensary in the west village. It's about a 30 minute walk away. People here measure distance by blocks. The streets are all designed in square blocks and you can guess how far one place is from another by simply learning that it is so many blocks away. My work is five blocks from home. We take care of the city's poor there and although it can be at times very distressing, I am very fulfilled in my work.

Cora has got work. She is such a bright young woman and managed to land a job at AT Stewart's dry goods store. They have just expanded and she works in a fancy new building called 'The Marble Palace'. Samuel and I are very proud of her. She is a beautiful, intelligent and wise girl. Abe is still at school with the Sisters. So as you can see, we are well set up.

So don't worry about us, Da. Love to all,

Mary

even small birds fly free

Glenville,
County Cork
October 1861

Dearest Mary,

It's always so lovely to get your letters and to know you and your family are well. You are right. The newspapers here are full of your war and it is hard not to worry. And I must say it is sad to hear that so many Irish emigrants are against Lincoln and what he is trying to do. You would imagine that having suffered so much themselves in their long journey and the losses they experienced to get to where they are, they would immediately know and identify with the suffering and lack of freedom of the Negro. But we also know what fear can do to people. And you are right. Newspapers have a lot to answer for.

Here we are well. There is the beginnings of a movement towards land reform of which I am very hopeful. Of course there is a long way to go. But I can see some time in the future that it may be possible for our people to own land again.

I have started teaching again. It's Shay's need that began that and Mr. Hudson has given me the freedom. I can handle his accounts on the weekends. He also gave me a small room and its great to see the children young and old in their learning. There is of course a real appetite to learn English. So many of the folk around here have relatives scattered everywhere, England, Australia, South Africa, America and Canada, so they all want to learn it to stay in touch. And many who have remained behind have moved to Dublin. My fear now would be that we will lose our beautiful tongue. And that would be a shame. There is not a tongue like it anywhere in the world. One of the oldest languages and the most descriptive. Did you know there are a full thirty two words just to name a field. Our ancestors kept us so in touch with nature and I fear that in our movement to the big cities of the world, our sensitivity to the earth and the thin veil which separates us from the spiritual world will die in us.

I understand that most of our people who emigrated stay in the cities and I also wonder if we have been traumatised by the land deserting us, turning its back on us, during the terrible five years of An Gorta Mór.

But here am I like an old man going on about things, like a bad seanachaí. Shay keeps me grounded. I love entering his world of imagination. And I learn something new from him every day. He has been really healing for Eileen too.

The Civil War   203

Although of course nothing can replace her dreadful loss of her first two. She is such a brave woman. She is my hero actually. I think she lives every day for them. Carrying them in her heart. Oisín and Ciara. Keeping them alive and in touch with our world. It's very moving when she shares her stories of them with Shay.

We have a small patch of land and you will be delighted to know we get a good crop of vegetables each year. So with my small income from teaching, the free cottage and the income from the Landlord, we are even prosperous. It's hard to imagine isn't it.

Of course, I also keep in my heart our neighbours who are no more. And I see people in the town who are languishing, traumatised, without hope with family and loved ones gone. There are not many céilí's these days. Slowly but surely, life is returning, even if it's not the same. Its been over ten years now and in truth it feels a lifetime ago.

You are very much in our hearts and prayers, Mary. You, Samuel, who seems a fine man and your children. I'm so glad you have community with his people there. Is ar scáth a chéile a mhaireann na daoine.[8]

Slán go foill,

Da

     even small birds fly free

Sullivan Street

In which Samuel, Mary become fearful of the Fugitive Slave Act and the Dred Scott decision

End of Summer 1862

Under Mayor Fernando Wood[10], New York becomes a strange place in the fall of 1862 and Samuel Williams becomes increasingly conscious of the vulnerability of his family. The mood of the city a foment. Most of the Irish immigrants have no understanding of what this war is about. Whipped up by newspapers and the Democratic party, Wood a leading protagonist, New York becomes a very dangerous place for a Negro. Slave catchers abound and everyone remains vigilant. Samuel has joined the New York Vigilance Committee and is active in his local neighbourhood. Many of their neighbours have left Manhattan, some moving to Brooklyn, most fleeing north for safety to Canada.

Mary becomes increasingly terrified. The Dred Scott decision which removes citizenship from her husband and all Black men, women and children also puts her son Abe in danger. She is learning how to keep him safe in the midst of this tumult. The summer is over and he will begin work in the fall. She awakes in the night, in the lonely hours and is filled with poignant reflections of the moments she shared with her son, going back to his early childhood, his days at school, helping her cook in the kitchen, lying with him on his bed, retelling stories her Da would recount to her. Those moments seem ephemeral now. Never to return. The mixture of joy at their recollection and sadness at their loss, leaves her sometimes sobbing beside the man she loves. It's as if innocence has perished from their shared life.

Abe, now a strapping twelve year old boy, is an apprentice with a joiner in Brooklyn. She loves both of her children but somehow the sweet vulnerability of this young man makes her heart ache. She knows she would kill for him. Such is the depth of her love. To see him walk away to the ferry in the morning is to watch her heart walk alone, vulnerable, unprotected in this, now perilous, city.

Fear grips her often and Samuel tries to console her. But logic defies consolation. Through her love for this man she has passed over. To the nightmare world of what it means to be Black in America. She has become associated through love and kinship with a despised caste. Her Da's logical thinking exercises her. The question 'would it have been better never to have met Samuel and so avoid this torment?' is unthinkable and soundly defeated. She cannot envisage a life without this wonderful man. Who has won her heart and soul. Slowly, confidently, inexorably, she begins to accept her lot and puts her faith in God for the safety of her lovely boy. It is a long winter.

even small birds fly free

The Atlantic Monthly September 1862

The Battle at Antietam

By Caelan O'Donovan

They came to me the day before. It's now regular like clockwork, like bees to a honey pot. A sizeable portion of the thirteen dollars they receive monthly in their hands as they ask me for a portrait. Why they do it, I can only guess. Is it that in the horrors they have witnessed they fear their souls are being extinguished? Do they have some premonition of their end? Are they trying to retain the identity within their family or village? Most of the pictures will be despatched immediately to home with a sentimentally, poignant note hastily written on the back.

I take my time with each. It's the most I can do. Peering through the lens into their very being. I find there pain of remembrances, trauma. Maybe sometimes I am projecting things onto them. Things I have seen on the battlefield as I scan from safety through my binoculars. Men firing into each other's faces, not five feet apart. Bayonet-trusts, sabre-strokes, pistol shots…oaths, yells, curses, hurrahs, shouting…men going down on their hands and knees, spinning round like tops, throwing out their arms, gulping up blood, falling legless, armless, headless. Ghastly heaps of dead men. Seconds are centuries, minutes ages as I grip the glasses firmly, unable to shake free from the horror I view.

So these moments with them I seek to transform. To develop rapport, intimacy, an act of being seen, a place of rest. Often the men want to be taken together, I guess as an outward expression of the bonds they have created, bands of brothers, often from the same towns or villages in Pennsylvania, or Connecticut or Ohio; Many many places. Physically they still look young, that I cannot deny. I would hasten a guess that most were no more than nineteen, yet to look into their faces is to see a shell, hallowed out, empty of all but pain, trapped in this tryst with destiny.

And so I take their picture, their pictures, with the best of my ability, trying to find there some vestige of their identity, some token to give to their mothers or sweethearts, something to cling onto, that he exists, that they can see him with hearts of longing. These few hours in their presence exhaust me. I look on them fondly wondering how many of

them will be alive at the end of the next day.

I write this a turbulent day later. Evening has fallen. The familiar cries of scavenging animals ring across the battlefield. Its been like this for thirty six hours now. The bodies which were left lying after the various skirmishes, their prey. Even though I have borne witness to much brutality over the past fourteen long months, the battle at Antietam stands out. Soldiers on both sides fought with a kind of madness -- a demonic fury, heedless of the normal instincts of self- preservation.

At noon on the day of battle, when I crested Sky hill, I could see with my field glasses the bloodshed which raged on the northern edge of a massive cornfield; One of the worst killing places. In one corner, surgeons hastily dressing mortal wounds with corn husks trying to help scores of hideously wounded and dying men. The casualties staggering.

As the sun set on the day, the dead were almost wholly unburied, and

                             even small birds fly free

the stench arising from them was such as to breed a pestilence. Stretched along, in one straight line, ready for interment at least a thousand blackened, bloated corpses, with blood and gas protruding from every orifice, and maggots holding high carnival over their heads. Days after the battle, hundreds of Confederate corpses still lie rotting on the field.

I made it my mission to see if I could find those men who had come to me with their sunken, fearful eyes the day before the carnage commenced. I found only two. The rest of their comrades are gone, swept away by this increasingly terrible war. Numbers are being counted and offered as an illusion of bogus certainty and control in the aftermath of this conflict which has transformed the apparent limits of human brutality. They are counted, too, because there are just so many bodies to count. Numbers seem the only way to capture what is most dramatically new about this war: the very size of the cataclysm and its human cost.

But it is essential to reflect. These numbers are not like ordinary figures, but every number stands for the pale, upturned face of a dead soldier. These are not cold abstractions, but each possesses a human face, so poignantly captured by the image I took of so many the day before their demise. While it may be possible to imagine one man killed; or ten men killed; or, perhaps, a score of men killed, to comprehend the dire meaning of the thousands which perished here, whose every unit represents a soldier's bloody grave, these figures are too large.[11]

The war rolls on across our land and for what? To preserve our Union? The time has surely come for Lincoln to speak out about not only the treachery that has propelled this carnage but to speak clearly about ending the abomination of one man owning another.

Boston

In which Brigid and Caelan arrive at a denouement

September 1862

Caelan is a spent force when he returns to Washington. Awaiting him is a letter from Bridie. Asking him to come home. He realises on receiving it that it's exactly what he needs. To be with the one person who can give him solace. He hasn't been to Boston in six months. Despite his misgivings about returning to the agony of his unrequited passion, he knows that in her home, for it is largely inhabited by her spirit now, he can find rest. And the children will be there. Now adults. To take his mind away from the burdens he has borne, to lift his spirit. He doesn't stay long in the Capital, files some features, gets woodcuts made of his most poignant pictures and catches the rail network through New York to his home town.

Arriving in Boston, a weight disappears from his shoulders. It's as if what he has experienced has been a mirage. Elsewhere in this vast country, horrors abound and yet here men and women continue their daily lives apparently oblivious of the upheaval and disturbance. The quiet streets have a calming effect on him.

When he arrives at the house on Moore Street, he is surprised to find Bridie alone. This he did not foresee. But then again the girls are older now. The sight of her anew sets his pulse skipping, his heart aflame. It has been too long. And he has seen so much in the intervening time. Here in front of him is his heartsease. He is overcome by her beauty, shaken to his core. Try as he has done to forget her, here she is in front of him, transporting him back to the Liverpool docks where first he became smitten by her pretty face and lithe figure. Is it possible to forget how beautiful she is? Reaching to give her an embrace however, he notices a stiffness in her, a certain restraint, a reserve. He has not time to reflect on this before she leads him to the kitchen. For a cup of tea and this being the season, some barmbrack[12]. He is amused by the memory of the tradition. The time of the year. Samhain on its way.

"You know yourself," Bridie says, "I had to make it for the girls. They get very excited with what they will find in their slice. Nobody got the ring or the pea yet."

"How have you been, Bridie, You're looking grand. I hope that speaks about how life is treating you."

 even small birds fly free

Bridie is taken aback by his Cork blas. The sweet nature of the man's face. She has prepared for him but yet the effect is still unexpected.

"I'm grand Caelan, but more importantly how's yourself. With all your long travels and hard roads."

"It's been fierce hard, Bridie." As Gaeilge, Caelan recounts the struggles and trauma of the last while. It pours out of him as a gushing torrent, as a river after a torrential flood. Of how he had to protect his heart with the great losses he has witnessed, the horror of war. Bridie listens to him, the words in Irish pregnant with poignancy and terror, she reaches across to hold his hand when she fears he will break, afraid for him, for his sensitive soul, set among the madness that has taken hold, to recount its progression. He is grateful. It's the first time he has unburdened himself and glad that in her he can do so, vulnerably, openly. Healing he finds there.

When he finishes, there is a long silence. However, this time instead of the comfort they normally experience together in their shared stillness, an air of disquiet surrounds them. An unusual tension. Finally, Bridie breaks the stillness.

"I have some news, Caelan. It's why I'm glad you've come. Why I sent for you. But with you here now, I'm nervous."

"Era, Bridie, we know each other too well. There's nothing to be nervous around the two of us. Haven't we seen it all?"

Bridie takes a deep breath and looks into his eyes. The man she adores.

"I'm to be married, Caelan. To a lovely man. A widower. He's a little bit older. But I know he cares for me very much."

For some reason, of all the things that Caelan thinks Bridie might say, this is the furthest from his thoughts. And now that it is said, he cannot explain why. Surely it is something that is to be expected? He is dumbstruck and shaken. Transfixed. Wordless. Unable to greet his dear friend with words of approval. Bridie notices his shock and thinks it is something else.

"Oh, it means you get your home back, Caelan. I am not expecting to live here. His name is Charles Eliot. He's quite well off and owns a large house on Beacon Hill. So we will all move there. He is from a family that has deep roots here in the city and the country. A widower. He has two girls of his own, now grown up. My lot love them. We are to be one big, happy bunch. So you see, I am to become an American, after all.

With this Bridie laughs.

Through her laugh Caelan recovers and says, "Well, Bridie I couldn't be more happy for you and the Páistí. Congratulations."

As if to ease the tension, the barmbrack intervenes and Bridie bites down on something hard and retrieves the ring wrapped in fine paper. She unwraps the ring, a sentinel of marriage within the year and they both become convulsed in laughter, at odds with the discomfort of the previous few minutes.

"Well, can you believe that?" Finally Bridie says, and then awkwardly, to take the spotlight from herself, "And what about yourself, Caelan, surely you have met someone in all these years, with all your travels. Someone who has captured your heart?"

At this, everything breaks. The pretence dissolves. As Bridie looks at him, she knows, recognises, sees finally even before he speaks. The shocking transparency of his longing and pain evident in his eyes.

"I gave my heart away all of fourteen years ago to a beautiful woman on the quayside in Liverpool and no-one I have met since can hold a candle to her. You are the only the woman I have ever loved. You are the love of my life. It's why I moved away. It's why I can be glad for you now. It's all I have desired that you are happy and taken care of."

The revelation hits Bridie like a sudden storm, an eruption of emotion, a fissure in their small cosmos. How has she not seen this?

"Oh, Caelan. Oh Caelan. How did I not know this? I love you beyond words too. It broke my heart when you left. It was only then I realised how much you are inside of me."

She throws herself into his arms. There, wrapped around one another, everything seems to make sense. Through tears and closeness they are transported into intimacy, touch, kiss, flesh on flesh, exploration previously unthinkable becomes natural, self-evident. The kindness, mutual concern, shared thoughts and care exercised over years for the other now seeking urgent, fervent expression in their physicality as they reach to explore one another. Without thought, instinctively, they seek one another out with joy, unrestrainedly, caught in the unexpectedness of shared love and inexpressible desire. How, they do not recall, such was the nature of their blind obsession, their ardour, they move to her bedroom and spend the night together, filled with the sheer delight and

     even small birds fly free

joy of finally finding full conjugation, consummation of their burgeoning love.

In the morning, as the September sun streams through the window, they wake in one another's arms. All is changed in the bright light of this new day. And wordlessly, both realise this together. It is Bridie who speaks it first.

"Caelan, dear Caelan, this is impossible. We can't do this. I can't get in the way of your first and real love. You are driven to travel, to be present, to record the events of this nation. I am here, solid, strong for my children. I cannot bear your absence in my life, when you are meant to be most present. My destiny lies elsewhere. And so does yours. I know I have to give you up to be happy. And for you to be content and satiated with your drive and mission."

Try as he does in his thoughts, Caelan cannot refute her conclusion. He knows this too. The time they have been apart has given him room to focus, unrestrained by any commitments. He looks at her with silent approval. Pain evident in both their verdicts.

"I know you are right, Bridie. I can't give you what you need. What your children need. Oh how I love you. How being parted from you cuts me to the quick. I will have to let you go. If I can bear it. But in this letting go, I want you to be at peace, fulfilled. You understand I cannot come to your wedding. In time, I will visit and pay my respects to Mr. Eliot. I am so glad we had last evening. It will stay with me for the rest of my life. You will be with me for the rest of my life"

They spend the morning in quiet togetherness as he packs and gets ready to return to Washington. As she reaches to say goodbye to him, she suddenly stops and turns hurriedly. "I have something for you," she says as she rushes up the stairs. When she returns, she places a small stone in his hand. It's a pebble smooth as marble, a light brown colour, unremarkable. "It's from the River Bride, near my old home in Glenville" she says, "I took it with me when we were leaving. To remember. I want you to have it. It's our roots and it will remind you always how entwined we are. Mo Anam Cara" Caelan does not know what to say. Such a simple, small gift that rends his soul. They say their goodbyes sensitively, discretely achieved behind the closed door of their shared house.

On making his way to Causeway Street terminal, Caelan picked up the Daily Globe. Strikingly the headlines screams out:

IMPORTANT PROCLAMATION.

The War to Restore the Constitution.

Freedom of slaves in the Rebel Slates

on and after January First, 1863.

BY THE PRESIDENT OF THE U.S. OF AMERICA.

Avidly, he consumes the emancipation proclamation. The words ring in his consciousness like the peals of a thousand church bells. "*I do order and declare that all persons held as slaves within said designated States, and parts of States, are, and henceforward shall be free*" It is a sign for him. The President has finally spoken, nails his colours to the mast. Now, he thinks, we have turned the corner, the real work can begin to establish this country in line with the aspirations of its founders. All men created equal. He has work to do. The pain of walking away from Bridie is eclipsed by his surrender to this, his life's work and vocation.

even small birds fly free

Sullivan Street,
New York
September 1862

Dear Da and Eileen and Shay,

What a relief. You will have heard through the newspapers that our President has issued a proclamation which ends slavery. It also upends the Fugitive Slave Act and Dred Scott decision. This will come into force on the first of January so all my fears for Samuel and Abe will end on that day. It fills me with great joy and is an answer to fervent prayer.

Of course, Samuel wants to enlist in the army immediately. Such a brave man. But I prevailed on him that, for the moment, he waits. I need him here for Abe to guide him through the first years of that young boys adult life. I can only guess what it means to be Black in this country and I know that Samuel is still needed to guide Abe in this. But it won't be for long more I guess. Maybe a year. Then he can enlist. But it would be my fervent hope that this war would be over by then. Such carnage and loss of life. It seems death and destruction reigns here.

So we are all well. And I send you our love.

Mary

xxx

Glenville,
County Cork
October 1862

Dearest Mary,

We rejoice with you and indeed see it as a gracious answer to prayer. I am glad Samuel will stay with you a while longer. He seems such a good man. While I understand his desire to serve in this great battle for the rights of his people, I also am glad he sees his first priority to his family. His time will come.

We have news of our own. Eileen has given birth to a baby boy, Seán. A delightful child he wakes each day with a smile. Already his personality and influence is changing us as a family. As you can imagine we have been through so much together and before we met that there is an intensity in our shared life that is not always healthy. Seán defuses this with his bright humour and light spirit. It is wonderful to behold.

His older brother Shay was a little sick last week and Seán continually wanted to touch him. It led Shay to say 'It's terrible feeling sick, but it would be so much worse if Seán was not here." We smiled as it is a sentiment we all share.

So rest in this new found relief. You and your family are always in our hearts and prayers and lots of love coming from your now two brothers. Bet you never imagined something like that happening in your life courtesy of your auld fella,

Love

Da, Eileen, Shay and Seán

  even small birds fly free

The Atlantic Monthly January, 1863

Reading Emancipation Proclamation,
Port Royal

By Caelan O'Donovan

For this momentous day in our country's history, I made my way south by steamer to Port Royal, in South Carolina, a place central to the conquest for which we all fervently hope. I felt it symbolic to be geographically placed among the people who would benefit most from this moment.

For some time at the old Fort Plantation, led by Col. Thomas Wentworth Higginson, a unit of former slaves and freed men are being trained ready for battle and for this extraordinary day. It seemed to me the right place to be.

About ten o'clock in the morning, people began to gather by land and sea. All avenues of approach were thronged. The crowd were chiefly coloured women, with gay handkerchiefs on their heads, and a sprinkling of men, with that respectable look they have when dressed for Sunday church.

There were many white visitors also; Society women on horseback and in carriages, superintendents and teachers, officers and cavalrymen. The companies of soldiers were marched to the platform, which held the dignitaries. The Negro people filled up all the vacant openings in the beautiful grove around. Above, shielding the sky, great oak trees with their trailing branches and moss framed the expanse of the blue river beyond the assembled crowd. The location itself a portend for the wonder that was about to be enacted.

The services began at half-past eleven with a simple prayer.

Then the President's Proclamation was read. Amidst all the legalese of the reading those profound words *'all persons held as slaves….shall be henceforth and forever free.'*

The flag presented and raised. There was nothing surprising in this. The programme, dignified and proper.

What took place next, took my breath away. And stunned the assembled crowd. The very moment the speaker had finished and the flag raised, there suddenly arose, close beside the platform, a strong male voice, (but rather cracked and elderly), into which two women's voices instantly blended, singing, as if by an impulse that could no more be silenced than the morning melody of the lark:

"My Country, 'tis of thee,
Sweet land of liberty,
Of thee I sing!

Everyone looked around, to see from where this singing came, this interruption, completely outside the order of service. And sweetly, like a slow hum amplifying the sentiments, others of the Negro people joined in, their voices evocative, recalling and supplanting, transforming forever, the songs sung as they struggled under the mantle of slavery

Land where my fathers died,
Land of the pilgrims' pride,
From every mountain side
Let Freedom ring!"

Firmly and irrepressibly the quavering voices sang on, verse after verse. Some white people on the platform began to sing with them, but quickly, Colonel Higginson motioned them to silence.

My native country, thee,
Land of the noble free,
Thy name I love;
I love thy rocks and rills,
Thy woods and templed hills;
My heart with rapture thrills,
Like that above

I never saw anything so electric; it made all other words cheap; it seemed the choked voice of a race at last unloosed. Nothing could be more wonderfully unconscious; art could not have dreamed of a tribute to the day of jubilee that should be so affecting; History will not believe it.

Let music swell the breeze,
And ring from all the trees
Sweet Freedom's song;
Let mortal tongues awake;
Let all that breathe partake;
Let rocks their silence break,
The sound prolong.

When I reflect on it now I well up, as on that very, blessed day, after the singing stopped, tears were everywhere. Just think of it. The first day these former enslaved people ever had a country, the first flag they had ever seen which promised anything to their people, and here, while mere spectators stood in silence, they interrupted and claimed the

                    even small birds fly free

service as their own, these simple souls bursting out from their hearts, a claim hidden for centuries. Whatever about the people that ruled, they knew the land, an expression of their God welcomed then and profoundly they demonstrated, in a chorus, that this is the real truth, ineffably and irrefutably real, the land and God is also theirs.

It also demonstrates in one profound, exquisite moment, the extraordinary civility and capacity for forgiveness of a people, a people oppressed for centuries. Truly we are blessed that they want to call themselves Americans.

Southern States & Gettysburg

In which Paddy O'Donovan is thwarted and descends into despair

June, July 1863

Sheer exhaustion had already incapacitated Paddy O'Donovan when he finally succumbed to a shrapnel wound during the battle of Chancellorsville. He is given two weeks furlough to recover. With papers in hand, he makes his way south to New Orleans. His only thought to find Solene. Memories of her have filled his heart, mind and imagination for two years. It is what has kept him going. A semblance of sanity in the midst of madness. Now with this first opportunity, he is determined to find her. He travels not knowing whether she will even remember him. But he knows he must give it a chance. He cannot move on in his life without some reconciliation.

He is dreaming of course. New Orleans and Natchez are under Union control, in enemy hands for a full year. Although he knows this, he still hopes that he can pass unnoticed through the lines. But as he travels through the various states, Virginia, Tennessee, Alabama, Mississippi, he sees paranoia, suspicion, treachery, chaos, lawlessness everywhere and he understands that to try and cross over is lunacy and will also carry a severe threat to the woman he adores.

When he arrives near Jackson, he gives up and spends days sinking further into dark thoughts. Like a deep ache in his being, he finds himself standing over an abyss. She is gone from him now, he knows. A thing he finds difficult to bear. The accumulation of shielding himself from recall of what he has seen, witnessed on battlefields, gruesome deaths of his friends, companions, brothers in arms now flash before his eyes and leave him in a comatose state. To have stopped still becomes his enemy. While he continued in the fray, mustering his company he had risen every day to banish these thoughts. Now, in the absence of duty, they assail him on every side. The one hope he had nurtured, seeing Solene, making his capacity to survive worthwhile, is finally and irrevocably dashed.

The Planter visits and remonstrates with him. Raising him from his stupor and with weary legs and even wearier heart, Paddy girds his loins and travels north once again to rejoin his company. Remarkably on the route, he is transformed in the way he sees people in the states he travels through. Having let go of Solene he sees her everywhere. In the Black men and women, he passes on his travels he now recognises

 even small birds fly free

beyond his previous dismissals, their individual beauty, dignity, capacity and yearning for freedom. He is reproached at every turn. How did he not see this before? How did he not recognise the great evil of slavery? What had overcome him and why had it taken him so long? Long into the night, his thoughts overwhelm him. It's a kind of cleansing. And he is grateful to the woman who has made this possible. In her absence, her presence fills him with peace and quiet acceptance. He has lived a charade. The desire to survive at all costs since the terrible visitation of the Great Hunger has blunted his capacity to see and live with a clear eye. Then, he reflects a part of him knew and a part of him which overrun, blinded. Now he has woken up to chaos, destruction, devastation. And he realises he is the true and only author of his own torment. There are tears but also a silent reconciliation with the woman who has taken his heart.

One night in Fredericksburg in a cheap boarding house, he hears his name being shouted out across a busy bar. There in the corner is John Roberts, surrounded by his gang of pattyrollers. "Hey Paddy, would you look at you? What in God's name are you doing here? C'mon over and join us for a bevvy." He joins the group and is taken aback by the change in Roberts. His face now rough, a cruelty in his mouth and a darkness in his eyes. As the beers flow, the men brazenly recount their stories. Roberts leading the way, his men willing courtiers. Tales of barbarity and cruelty. Vividly and unashamedly, giving vent to what they have done now to the slaves, men and women they have captured. It seems the owners want severe lessons taught to quench the possibility of revolt on plantations. Roberts seems to revel in it and is a changed man. The person Pádraig met all those years ago in the Coffee House in New Orleans metamorphosed in the intervening years. Pádraig cannot hear the words being flung about with such abandon and malice. He finds himself becoming overwhelmed with nausea and in a mad rush, flees to the door of the saloon. Outside, he retches and retches, the contents of his stomach and more spraying out onto the gutter and his boots. The memory of his own time in the pattyrollers dominating his consciousness and amplified by the horrible images perpetrated by the stories he has just heard. When he is finished puking, he turns from the bar, staggers away to find another place to lay his head.

When he arrives back with the Louisiana infantry, there is a further shock to his confidence. He is informed that the Tigers have been disbanded and the remaining cohort reassigned. He is apprised that as a valuable veteran, he will take charge of newly conscripted troops and forge them into a fighting force akin to his first charges.

Paddy is disheartened when he finally meets his company. He has not the capacity to see beyond their resistance and reluctance to conscription and their unwillingness to settle into discipline. Nevertheless he perseveres. As a matter of routine. There is no chemistry or rapport between the men. The urgency to galvanise them is great as he knows that a decisive battle is ahead. But he is forlorn, equipped with the knowledge of the immanence of danger which he cannot communicate to these naive young men.

In officers' meetings, he is aware of a great uplift in spirits elsewhere in the army after the victory at Chancellorsville, and General Lee's desire for further incursion into the north to secure a strong negotiating position, playing politics with his men. Despite this strategic knowledge, Paddy has no appetite for the fight.

His company is part of the regiment that cross the Potomac at Blackford's Ford in the middle of June, marching into fertile Pennsylvania but his disquiet grows daily. He sees how unprepared his men are for what lies ahead. In the quiet of the evening, in his quarters, on the last day of June, he sits to write to his brother. This time he will pour his heart out. As he begins the letter, his thoughts circle back to the years they were together and the years, too many, they have been apart. There are tears as he remembers Ma and Da and Aoife and how his brother and himself consoled one another, then, affection pouring between them, never evident usually in their ordinary interaction. The desperate year that followed in Skibbereen watching the town and its people disintegrate. The camaraderie they shared as they travelled to Kerry seeking a way to emigrate and the great loss that issued into their lives.

He can hardly countenance the time in between when they have viewed this country through a different prism. But now in the stark light of his losses and what awaits him, he knows there is no room for counterfeit bluster. He must come clean. This he does. Fully aware that as he writes, he is composing both his epitaph and obituary.

     even small birds fly free

Gettysburg,
Pennsylvania
30th June 1863

Dearest Caelan,

Tomorrow is the day I'm going to die. Over the last two years, I have recognised the signs too clearly. In the beginning, I used to notice a kind of mawkishness among some of my men; An unusual sentimentality wholly out of touch with their character. But too often this resulted in that person not making it through the next day. Many of them wrote letters similar to the one I am writing to you now. And because they needed help, I was far too often a part of their last words and phrases.

All were men I loved. In a way I could not imagine loving another man. Each of us had become so close to one another that we would die for one another. Of course you can imagine that because so many of my company have been drawn from the same community, Irish emigres who fled along with us from the devastation we lived through and endured, it became abhorrent to each of us that we would be found wanting on the battlefield.

You have often written to me to ask me what sustains me and the men I fight alongside for a cause that you feel to be completely immoral, evil, cruel and oppressive. Well, the reality is, we don't fight for this. We don't think of this. We only think of one another. We have always and will continue to fight for one another. In the heart of the conflict, that is all that matters to us. That we will be faithful to one another. That cowardice will be banished from our midst.

What has changed here is the Generals have disbanded my company, The Louisiana Tigers. There were too many losses[9] and in their great wisdom I have been reassigned to take charge and get ready a bunch of raw recruits. My men have been amalgamated elsewhere, carrying our name with them. I will do my best in my new assignment. But these recruits are not ready. And I know the battlefields well now and know that tomorrow will be my last hurrah there. So dear Caelan, I want to tell you everything that is going on in my heart.

This great country has changed us, you and me. And we have been at odds with one another. But just recently, I have come to the realisation that I am wrong. In a letter two years ago, you wrote that you wish that I would meet and get to know a Black man or woman and become close. That was so prescient of you. Not long after I received that letter, I met a free woman of colour in

The Civil War   223

New Orleans. Solene is her name. I fell hopelessly in love with her, remarkably in the few days we were together. I have never felt anything like this and the love we shared has sustained me since. At the time, I knew she is the love of my life, but I lacked courage and left suddenly to go back to my regiment and to begin this dreadful war. I have not seen her since.

Recently, on furlough, I tried to cross over to New Orleans to find her, but in the end gave up, not because I lacked courage or determination, but because I would draw suspicion and hostility towards her, such is the divided nature of this country now. And leave her in great danger. So I am resigned never to see her again. It breaks my heart but at the same time, I am grateful for the love we shared and the time we had together.

Since I let her go, the scales dropped from my eyes and I see now the great evil that has blighted this country for centuries in the enslavement of men, women and children. I see how easily I and others have been duped into fighting a war that makes no sense and is destructive. This I am resigned to. I now go into battle without conviction. Like a lamb to slaughter. Maybe my death will be an atonement for my part in this great original sin.

I don't want you to think I am unhappy. On the contrary, I have received a great cleansing of the soul and to be resigned is a great blessing. Without Solene, my life would not amount to much anyway and I do not want you to grieve too hard for me. Caelan, you are my brother and I love you. All my solicitous instructions to you over the years were solely to protect you. I could not lose you as we have both lost Ma, Da and Aoife. I am glad you came with me to America.

I am wrong in my counsel to you to get a different job. I see now your role is to tell stories. To write and record through your pictures a different more uplifting narrative for this country than the one in which so many are locked into. May the words flow from you as you travel and give voice to the hearts of those who are particularly oppressed. The only blessing of our own dear country, Ireland's tortured history is that we can see oppression clearly. Once, as in my case not yours, the scales have dropped from our eyes,

I love you. Grieve not, I go in peace

Pádraig

                              even small birds fly free

On the first of July, 1863, Pádraig O'Donovan disappears without trace, like so many hundreds of thousands of Americans did in those fateful few short years; Lost without trace, left dying in hundreds of fields across the country; Their individual identity forever blurred, their existence melded together, their bodies offered up as grotesque sacrifices to be consumed by wild animals. Fifty thousand of these men lying in fields at Gettysburg at the end of first three days of July 1863. Pádraig O'Donovan anonymous among them.

New York

In which Mary O'Brien's worst fears are realised

July 13th 1863

Samuel Williams has been nervous for weeks. The Federal Draft Law had taken place on Saturday. He has seen how this inflames his white co-workers, particularly the Irish. The only ones who can escape being called up to fight are those who can afford the three hundred dollars to buy themselves out and Negroes who are exempt. The newspapers have been stoking his co-workers up since the emancipation proclamation, saying New York will now be flooded with cheap Negro labour and their jobs will be under threat. The uneasy tension he has always experienced on the docks has turned to hatred and enmity. The war in the eyes of the Irish has become a war for the Negro, and they are violently angry that they are being called to fight it.

Today, things seem to have got out of hand. He hears reports as he works of events taking place downtown; Riots and government buildings being attacked[13]. Later in the early afternoon, he hears of a mob attacking and burning to the ground, the Coloured Orphan Asylum on Fifth Avenue. It's then he decides to leave the docks to find his way home to Five Points area. But as he moves up the Old Slip, he is confronted by a gang of twenty Irish men carrying cudgels.

Mary has just arrived home after her early morning shift from the clinic when she hears a dreadful scream from outside on the street. It's Bessie, her neighbour. "Mary, Mary, come quickly, they've got him." All of her fears catch in her throat as she thinks of Abe. She should not have let him go to work this morning.

She runs down the stairs as fast as she can and on reaching the street Bessie says, "It's Samuel. A bunch of Irish thugs have attacked him on the Old Slip." Fear grips her as she runs and runs. Down Sullivan Street to Canal Street, block after block, through Five Points. Friends, Irish and Negro, see her and join her, her heart beating, her pulse racing, running, running, wondering, thinking, 'am I too late', her man, her man. Where she finds the strength she does not know, but thirty minutes later, she turns the corner into the Old Slip to see at the end a violent angry mob, jeering and roaring at a spectacle, she can hardly credit, hardly take in, a Black man dangling by a rope from a lamppost, a reality she is not able to absorb, a thing too abhorrent to contemplate, but in that one hundred yards of running, running, the dawning realisation

     even small birds fly free

that it is her lovely man, her Samuel, swinging lifelessly there, horror of horrors, her heart broken, bursting from her chest, fear engulfing, terror unleashed.

Johnny the barman from McSorleys and two traders from Hart's Alley are by her side and as the mob part they scale the lamppost and cut him down, gently, reverently laying his body on the ground, lifeless with staring, vacant eyes.

"Samuel, Samuel, oh Samuel," wails Mary as she holds him, covers him, desperately trying to revive the man she loves, unable to take in what is happening, its ultimate finality. The mob circle around her, distracted by the spectacle. Suddenly, abruptly Mary rises, fiercely and faces them, eyeing each with a terrible accusatory stare,

"Who are you? Who the feck are you? What have you become?," She roars with an eloquence that defies each and every one of them. "What has this country done to you? In just a short decade it has turned you into hateful people, murderers. What has my dear Samuel done to you? How have you, a people that has suffered such pain, such oppression, such tyranny, become the oppressors? How has this country turned you into a people who can hate just because of the colour of a man's skin? What is the matter with you? Shame on you? Shame on You? Shame on you?"

With that she sinks to the ground again to her man, to hold her beloved Samuel. "I am sorry, Samuel, my dear one, mo chara, mo stóirín, mo chuisle, that it is my people who have hated you so much to take you away from me. Forgive me, forgive me, forgive me," and she descends into deep, guttural, gut-wrenching sobs.

The mob disperse, disgraced, mortified, silently, sullenly. Her friends cover her. Slowly and with dignity the women console her, hold her. A door is found on which Samuel is gently lain and the men carry him as in a funeral procession back to Five Points.

City Hospital, Memphis, Tennessee

In which Mary O'Brien's is surprised by joy

September 1863

The weeks following Samuel's death are a blur to Mary O'Brien. Her only conscious thought to keep her son Abe safe. The course of her emotions are a terror. She no longer feels safe in this city. She is unable to bear the loss of her husband so consumed is she with fear for her son. For their part, Cora and Abe try to comfort their mother despite their own unbearable anguish. Neighbours rally around to keep the family nourished.

But Mary is consumed. With a visceral hatred for Irish men. Hearing the accent sends a fury through her veins, a nauseous, electrifying convulsion in her stomach. Her thoughts then become immersed, obsessed with how she can get even. How she can repay. At other times, she is left bewildered. How can the people she grew up among, felt she knew so well, turn into what she now sees. Bigoted, hateful people swallowed up in their own miserly existence. Who are these people? she wonders, and her mind and memory wanders back to Cormac McCarthy and the way he stood by at her violation. There is a pattern here, she thinks. These people are not trustworthy. Of all people arriving on these shores, they should have been the first to recognise the oppression of Negroes and rise up en masse in protest against it. But no, here they are joining, even leading the chorus of tyranny. Disreputable, disreputable people.

As the days move to weeks, Mary arrives at a firm conclusion. Struggling with her remembrance of pleading with Samuel not to join the military she now is left with self recriminations. What if she had acceded to his request. He would still be alive now! Try as she does she cannot eliminate from her consciousness the fact that she denied her man the right to go and fight for his own freedom in this war that is tearing everyone apart.

And then there is the place in which they live. Surrounded by Irish emigres. Full of anger and hatred towards them, she feels unable to allow Abe out of her sight. Irish people are everywhere in this part of the city, now her principal enemy, consumed as they are with hatred for Black men and women. How has it come to this? She is left with tremors as she thinks of this and is woken often in the middle of the night by vivid hallucinatory phantoms.

  even small birds fly free

She arrives at the conclusion of her reflections at the end of August. It feels to her as if Samuel himself has guided her, his soft, calm voice in her ear both a comfort and a source of wisdom. "Go," she hears him say, "Flee this city. Join this struggle for a new America." She enquires at the clinic and is supported by the doctors there to be transferred to a Union hospital in Memphis. Following General Grant's army. She hears it is a place of refuge for escaped slaves. There she knows she will be able to put her considerable skills to use in treating those wounded in battle. And it will help assuage the crippling guilt she feels for denying Samuel. She takes the opportunity only on one condition. That Abe will travel with her. The doctors send recommendations with her for Abe as a handyman/orderly. She will be able to keep her boy safe surrounded by the Union Army. It is the only place her logic will give her peace.

Most of her friends counsel her not to do this. Flee to Canada, they urge. But Mary sees this as desertion. If that could be considered an option she knows Samuel would have suggested it much before. In faithfulness to him, to his memory, she is convinced she is doing the correct thing. After long conversations, it is agreed Cora will stay in the city. In love with her work, she has found lodgings with one of her friend's family on Reade Street, just around the corner from the Marble Palace. And so in early September, they make their tearful goodbyes and Mary and Abe set off on their journey to Memphis where they are to be assigned work in the City Hospital.

On arrival at the hospital, Mary is quickly entrusted with a ward and is immediately in the throes of cleaning the seriously infected wounds of injured soldiers. Packing the wounds with bromide soaked bandages, she moves from patient to patient with the touch of an angel. The horrific nature of the work galvanises her. So many of the men grieving for the loss of a limb, an arm a leg. In the middle of the night when she makes her rounds she is often alongside a young man as they share tears for their individual, unsustainable losses. Taking care of others, looking after the most desolate becomes a panacea for her own internal wound of loss and grief. She serves Samuel in each of these men, and with the same devoted care she would have served him.

Abe meanwhile is quickly put to work, chopping, delivering and stacking wood for the many fires, used in cooking and sterilising equipment. He is in his element and feels grown, surrounded as he is by other Black men. He is adopted by them as a mascot and thrives.

Days pass into weeks and both settle into their new life. Mary enquires about the contraband camps[14]. Places where escaped slaves have fled as refugees, seeking the protection of the Union army from slave catchers and confederates. One of these encampments is on President's Island, a walk of five miles away. She decides to visit. On her first day's break in October she gets up early in the morning and makes her way to the small ferry crossing. Alighting on the island she is surprised to find makeshift shelters and camps filled with hundreds of freed people, many in emaciated condition, without basic clothing and shelter. She meets volunteers who are working among the people, helping them in basics. Mary is galvanised by the effort and commits to return on all her free days.

On the second visit she brings Abe. Who immediately falls in love with the place. Is energised and believes this is his calling. Mary pleads with her commanding officer and Abe is reassigned there. He quickly develops rapport with the other volunteers and with his already burgeoning carpentry skills he is put to work building shelters for the refugees who arrive daily. Mary is thrilled to see him thrive and grow and feels secure in letting him be there, knowing she can visit weekly.

For her part, Mary writes to friends in New York who organise relief efforts and parcels are sent which arrive daily for her, full of clothing, basic provisions, bandages and medicines. She is helped ferry these to the island by horse and cart once a week.

The winter arrives and is thankfully not as bitter as the ones she endured in New York. Abe is very busy fixing shelters, helping to keep people warm. At the beginning of 1864, Mary visits and finds Abe on the south side of the island building a new shelter. She is always glad to see him. As she approaches she sees among the group of six refugees a Black woman with a thatch of auburn hair. A shock of powerful recognition courses through her as this woman turns. Looking into the woman's face she sees her Samuel looking back. For a moment, she is rendered immobile, transfixed, paralysed. The woman gazes at her inquiringly. Abe seeing his mother asks, "Ma, what's the matter?"

"Are you Mima?," Mary can barely get the words from her mouth.

"Yes dear, that's my name. Do I know you?"

Mary flings herself into the woman's arms and sobs and sobs. All the pain, the anguish, the searing loss she feels and has felt is exhumed in this one moment. For her part Mima greets the embrace and emotional outpouring with a calm, serene assurance. Holding Mary's light frame

     even small birds fly free

tenderly and compassionately, whispering soft phrases in her ear. Abe is shaken to the core, bewildered, not knowing what is taking place. Then suddenly it dawns on him. This woman is his grandmother, his dear Da's mother. To Mima's confusion he also rushes to embrace her.

"This is your grandson Abe, Mima," Mary announces. The introduction hastens the telling of the fateful story of Samuel's death, imparted through tears. Mima listens and holds Mary's hand

"Thank you, my dear, for giving my boy a home and your heart. It's all I could have hoped for."

They spend the day together, Mima devouring news of her son's life and family. Abe adoringly at her side. Towards evening Mary leaves the island for her work but Abe takes his grandmother to his shelter. "Here," he tells her, "We will set up home together. Won't it be great."

The following weeks are ones of great healing. Mima listens as Mary pours out her heart, the bitterness she has stored there. Quietly, softly Mima turns her narrative around.

"The people who did this don't deserve a place in your heart dear. They are small people; their lives have become narrow, pinched. A poison has infected them. If you hold hatred towards them, if you don't forgive they will set up a home there and destroy you. I know this. I have had to work very hard to clean up my house from the very vicious men and women who have sought to live there."

"But how can I do that? I have no desire to forgive them. I hate them for what they have done. I want to punish them if I ever could find out how."

"Forgiveness is not a feeling Mary, dearest. It's a decision. It's not easy dear. That I know. I can only tell you how I did it. You remember the story of Christ on the cross, hanging there in agony and he says 'Father forgive them for they don't know what they do?' That for me became the way. You see he is right. They didn't know. Nor did the people who hurt me. Nor do those people who killed Samuel. They didn't know Samuel. They didn't know his heart, his life, his family, his kindness, his thirst for justice, his humility, his loving kindness. All of these things are a mystery to them. Also they don't know your love, your pain, your heartache, what you have been through as an Irish refugee fleeing death and sickness. All these things they did not consciously know when they did what they did. They have closed that part of themselves down. So you can forgive them because they didn't know."

"How do I start? I don't know where to begin."

"Well, I didn't want to when I started either. I just said the words out loud many times during the day. Like a repetitious phrase almost with no meaning. *I forgive you because you didn't know what you were doing.* Many times a day. Whenever hatred started to call. I would add sometimes things like 'you didn't know how you broke my heart, you didn't know what this means to me, on and on. In the end, and surprisingly, the thing eventually started to mean something to me and I felt proud. I was cleaning my house. I was not letting these people decide how my life was going to be. I needed to do it to keep myself clean for Samuel. If I didn't. If I held on to hatred, he would have grown into it and then I would have lost him. He would have used that imparted hatred and poison to gain revenge and where we were living they would have killed him for sure."

As the two women grew closer and became one another's kith and kin, these conversations nurtured their bond and brought healing to Mary. Slowly over the months of 1864, Mary began to discard her hatred. For his part Abe swelled with pride alongside his grandmother. The bond developing between them growing daily; they becoming like peas in a pod.

 even small birds fly free

Washington

Caelan O'Donovan is changed forever

1864 -

When Caelan O'Donovan receives his brother Pádraig's letter he lets out a wail that signals an end of things. His heart is broken. The searing honesty and pain contained in the words on the page reduce him. His brother is gone. And he realises too late, he didn't know him. Not in this way. He lies awake at night, thinking about his own declarations to his brother over the last ten years. Mixed with reflections on his essays and articles, his rhetoric now become empty phrases. From this moment on, because of his brother's revelations, he can truly now say he knows nothing. His mortification humbling even humiliating.

The war rumbles on, carving deeper wounds into the nation's psyche, but Caelan is long past caring. He cannot find words. His brother's death symbolic of the dissolution and extinction of his own dreams for this land. The people and country going to hell in a handcart.

He still rises daily to take portraits. But his enthusiasm, energy, vitality is gone. The images he produces are prosaic and lacking in any insight. The year for him goes by in a flash, motionless, becalmed as he is in the doldrums. For the country as a whole the ongoing war is a long, slow, excruciating purgatory.

Caelan has told Bridie about the death of his brother and receives many imploring letters asking him to visit. To take a break. Having sold his house, he has no appetite to stay in her new home and he declines the offers and continues to wallow in his misery.

At the beginning of 1865, he relents. He does not know why or what prompts it but he writes to Bridie to say he will visit just after New Year. A journey normally undertaken with trepidation, he completes routinely. He is greeted with joy by the children, all gathered around him. Their evident pleasure in seeing him takes the awkwardness out of the situation with Bridie and her new husband and he is able to grasp the hand of Charles Elliot warmly. Bridie hugs him gently and he is immediately made to feel at home.

Later in the evening, they have time together, alone. Caelan, as has always been the case, is able to unburden himself to Bridie and thoughts spill out of him, his despair which is leaving him bereft. Maybe it's because he can converse with her 'as Gaeilge[16]', but he is able to explain the impact of receiving the letter to her and it's repercussion on him, on his world view, on the life he now sees ahead of him. She listens kindly and gently. In the end, she asks if she could also read the letter herself and he reaches into his satchel and hands her the pages now soiled and creased from their often use.

She takes her time. Understanding the starkness of it. Taking in the horror of the hundreds of thousands of such letters written over the past four years. When she is finished she looks up at him and acknowledges its devastating impact. Silence rests between them. A place to recollect. To take in, accept, acquiesce. Finally she says,

"Caelan, I want you to read one part of the letter again. Is that OK?"

Caelan nods, unable to look at her.

"Pádraig says here quite clearly, '*I see now your role is to tell stories. To write and record through your pictures a different more uplifting narrative for this country than the one in which so many are locked into. May the words flow from you as you travel and give voice to the hearts of those who are particularly oppressed.*' He recognises you and is giving you his blessing. I think you have to look at this as important. He is gone from you in this world now, but he has left behind his stamp of approval. He has changed in this too and sees you as a storyteller. You know what an important role that is in our own culture back home in Ireland. Do you think you are able to take up that challenge here? To translate that anointing into American life?"

Somehow in his grief and heartbreak, Caelan had not seen this part of the letter before. At this moment, something profound happens within him. He realises that he owes it to Pádraig to honour these words. He realises he must carry on. In the same way as Seán Mulcahy left him with a road to follow, he now sees his brother Pádraig has done the same.

Not long afterwards, Bridie excuses herself and leaves him to his thoughts by the fireside. The flames of the log fire glow in the dark. He has always found that mesmerising but more so at this moment. He recognises once again the magnetism of gazing into the flames of a fire, the inspiration found there, releasing thoughts and visions that would otherwise remain hidden.

Yes, he will be a storyteller. But not in the same way as before. Broken now, he realises that his commentary before, his writing and pronouncements were often sanctimonious, full of self righteousness, lacking in compassion. Long into the night, he thinks about his brother.

 even small birds fly free

He thinks about all those who have died in battle on both sides. He reflects on the leaders on both sides of this divisive conflict who have taken these young men into battle. But now the reflection is different. He does not have answers, only perplexity, curiosity. He can only think of his bafflement at the human condition. Where before this would lead him to make strong pronouncements, vehement convictions, now his reflections lead him to puzzlement. With horror he realises that the statements he made with utter conviction to Pádraig in his many letters possibly only served to harden his brother's position, to the detriment of his life and choices.

The next few days are glorious in the company of the combined families and he finds it joyous. The hope obvious in their lives fills him with renewed vigour. Bridie's evident contentment a delight and a relief. He returns to Washington to begin his new life as a storyteller.

In the following years his reflections and stories are more opaque, not strident. Asking questions, a kind of disconcerting enquiry as to the state of the nation and its people. As a consequence, most magazines drop him from their books and he finds a place only in small local publications for his ruminations. His portraits and photos always search beyond but in this he is equally not sought by many for events or records. Most want simplicity not depth, mystery. Those that book him are the few unusual people who share his perplexity.

When the war ends, he is left with even deeper misgivings. Where others are buoyant, he is left uncertain. He cannot arrive at any conclusion. When Lincoln is assassinated days later, the line in the constitution flares up at him as a syllogism. *The right of the people to keep and bear arms* assaults him. He is left with the question. A country coming into being through a violent uprising what does it foretell? Does it mean that a gun lies at the heart of its civil life and future? Does it spawn violence as a way of ending conflict? Does it legitimise an individual's right to settle a dilemma in his or her mind by eliminating the source and object of that disquiet?

He is unable to come to any conclusion. He wonders at his own early temptation to join the Young Irelanders and their quest for a violent uprising against the English imperial power. Would his own native country, if it follows America in an attempt to violently overthrow its imperial master, also end up like this country in the throes of a civil war? Does a violent revolution firmly place murderous intent at the heart of a society, growing there like an infectious disease until it poisons the whole? All the questions that enter his ken are framed now in front of two people, Pádraig's thoughts and his. As a consequence, very few magazine and newspaper publications take up his musings and he disappears from public life. As far as that career is concerned he has become a spent force.

Following Pádraig's mandate he becomes a journeyman storyteller. He equips his covered wagon with a bed and cooking equipment to complement his dark room. He travels first to Gettysburg to pay his respects, to, if he can, commune with his brother. But there he finds only emptiness and excruciating sorrow. As the years pass, he hears of a substantial government programme costing millions of dollars to recover the bodies of Union soldiers and give each a dignified ceremony. Sites are designed to honour the dead, but there is no such programme for those who fought on the confederate side. This leaves him with huge questions, reflections. Pádraig's assertion that those men who wore the grey uniform died for one another and not its traitorous cause. He wonders whether this decision on behalf of the government will sow a bitterness in the southern states.

He travels through these states witnessing devastation and decay everywhere. His purpose of making it to New Orleans to see if he can locate Solene but try as he does he cannot find her. Perhaps just as well, he thinks. Better that she remains this mystical body which at one time galvanised his brother and also gave him some fleeting respite, a brief glimpse of heaven, in the short life he lived, desperately struggling always to survive.

He travels west and increasingly his observations leave him confounded and bewildered. The Apache wars and the California gold rush he covers with stories of greed and distrust. His easy manner and non-judgemental nature, his fearlessness means he is comfortable everywhere. He writes of his encounters with pan-handlers, Buffalo Soldiers[17], Apache warriors. His stories are mystical parables, no longer pronouncements of judgements. He gazes into the heart of man and cannot understand, comprehend the hatred and brutality.

In bars in the new frontier, he finds strangers, hard bitten, cynical, who have long since left behind any notion of absolutes, of right and wrong. The gun the arbiter of conflict. One desperado sums it up "Ain't nothing scarier than a man with a gun, ain't nuttin more helpless than a man without one." He doesn't care about danger and experiences no fear and is able to be in the most perilous situations as a still point. The

   even small birds fly free

closer he comes to what he would before call evil, he recognises it as an absence, not a presence, and in his storytelling he tries to communicate this to those who can hear. It is a long time since he holds the constitution he first fell in love with as a burning light of optimism. The words leave him now with deep misgivings such is the reality he witnesses all around.

His discombobulation with what he sees leads him to return and remain in the southern states, those states that seceded. He witnesses no repentance there for the carnage visited on the nation. With the best will in the world he sees the federal government enact new laws to guarantee those who had been enslaved their rights, including the right to vote. But the resistance is formidable and within ten years, the government gives up. He sees the rise of the Ku Klux Klan and their viciousness further astounds him. He makes contact with them and his equanimity affords him to have easy, forthright conversations with many in their ranks. These discourses he later frames into simple records.

Twelve years after the assassination of the President, the 1877 election results in massive Black voter suppression and a compromise is negotiated which allows for the Republican President to be inaugurated, providing federal troops are withdrawn from southern states. The effect of this is to bring to an end the period of reconstruction. The more tragic, calamitous, ruinous the situation becomes in the country, the less its citizens look within. Southern states have the gall to call it the era of Redemption, when in fact it is a call to return to the old order of things, a return to supremacy and the removal of rights from Black citizens. He no longer has a voice to protest. It has been a long time since he possessed the conviction that dissent in this way is effective. He just records stories he is told by people who are affected by the abandoning of reconstruction and by the spread of Jim Crow laws[18] segregating Black Americans. Some of these stories find their way into local journals.

Most of the articles are lost to history. He understands by now that people have no appetite to know where they have come from. History, even recent, being something arcane. Abstruse, irrelevant. The war, and its mass slaughter settling nothing, leaving a deep wound in the nation's animus. The reason why it was fought recedes and the nation continues with its long held caste system which denies the rights of and opportunities for its Negro citizens.

A wanderer to the end, Caelan O'Donovan dies alone, in a small log cabin he buys and retreats to, on Pine mountain in Kentucky. His last days a cloister away from man, surrounded by rolling hills and an expanse of forest. At peace, maybe and possibly with answers to the questions he was never, while alive, been able to fathom.

A few years after his death, at the turn of the twentieth century, his short stories gained a kind of notoriety for their simple record of an era that had passed, especially given his extreme sensitivity to detail and non judgemental appreciation of the lives cast for the people he described. The publisher of the book in undergoing research about who Caelan was, came across the Trapper and his wife who discovered Caelan in his bed the day after he died. "He was an exceptionally kind and sensitive soul, Caelan. He kept himself to himself. But had a lovely spirit. The strange thing was when we found him," the man told him, "He had a firm grip of a small pebble in his right hand which was laid across his heart. An unremarkable stone, really, but we realised that it must have been precious to him, so we buried it with him."

When Bridie Mulcahy hears of Caelan's death she is forlorn. Her hope resides that he found serenity. She grieves quietly unable to share her loss with anyone such is the secret of their shared love. Her children weep with her.

She becomes a matriarch of her family, a woman who remarkably shepherded her six small children on a coffin ship from Ireland to New York.

In 1997, one hundred and fifty years after the Great Hunger, Tony Blair, then British Prime Minister issues the following statement: *The Famine was a defining event in the history of Ireland and of Britain. It has left deep scars. That one million people should have died in what was then part of the richest and most powerful nation in the world is something that still causes pain as we reflect on it today. Those who governed in London at the time failed their people through standing by while a crop failure turned into a massive human tragedy.*

That same year, thirty seven of Bridie Mulcahy's five-times great-grandchildren, one of whom is a U.S. senator return to Glenville[19] and for one night in the Glenville Manor House hold a feast to remember those that perished or left home forever from the village and celebrate the achievement of Bridie Mulcahy in ferrying her family to the new world.

 even small birds fly free

1700, Bergen Street,
Weeksville,
Brooklyn
January 1865

Dear Da and Eileen Shay and Seán,

I have not been able to write to you before now. Such has been my grief. My dear Samuel is no more. He was killed by an Irish mob nearly two years ago. As you can imagine, I have been consumed by anger, sadness and hatred since. But I am alright now. I have been held by a fierce grace. And I find now I can tell you the full story.

At the height of the war the government organised a draft to drive recruitment up. This was after Lincoln had issued his proclamation. Irish people in New York were outraged. They saw the war as a drive to free Black people from slavery and they were told by the local papers that this would mean their jobs and livelihoods were under threat. It shows you how far I have come that I can write that. Because I cannot and will never excuse them for what they did. I am still to this day left with questions as to how our own people have been changed by America so much that they have adopted the American position of hatred and discrimination towards the Black man and woman.

They rioted on the weekend of the draft and Samuel was set upon by a mob on his way home from the docks. The hung him from a lamppost. I still live in agony at the thoughts of his last minutes. It truly broke me. I know you will also be shocked to hear this. It was a terrible thing to tell Cora and Abe. But as I say, I and they have also been touched by a fierce grace.

Not long after Samuel's death, I volunteered with Abe to work in a Union hospital near Memphis. I wanted to get away from New York. It was not safe there for Abe. And I also could not abide being around Irish people who were everywhere in Manhattan. The accent sent a wave of revulsion through me.

The hospital work provided some healing for me and I ventured out on my days off to a contraband camp near the Union army. These camps were places that escaped enslaved people could find refuge and I felt I could help there as well. All the time I was trying to do my best for Samuel's memory, for I had asked him not to join the army when it became possible for him to do so after the emancipation proclamation. Abe joined me in the work and it became natural for him. He's become a wonderful carpenter joiner.

The Civil War

In the end Abe moved to the camp to work full time. I felt safe with him being there as the Union army provided protection.

Then an extraordinary thing happened. Samuel's mother Mima arrived at the camp as a refugee and I recognised her because of her red hair. We had a tearful, sad and joyous reunion and she is with us since that day. When the war ended we returned north and have settled here in Brooklyn as you can see. It is a Negro neighbourhood and I feel very comfortable and safe here.

Mima is wonderful. A warm tender woman, she has helped me enormously to forgive and find healing. There is still a huge wound in my heart and soul. Like the rings of a tree after a forest fire, I can date the traumas that life has visited me. But I am determined with God's help, to not allow Kincaid or the Irish mob to live inside me. I need prayer and courage continually to manage this. But I am glad to say that I am surrounded by love, Cora, Abe, Mima and our dear neighbours.

I am sad to have to pass this news on to you. I know you and Eileen too will be anguished. But I am convinced as well that telling you now rather than before is right. Before you would have felt helpless. Now you can rest that I am recovering and am in good hands. I remember your words to me;

Ar scáth a chéile a mhaireann na daoine. Or as I say to my American children 'It's in each other's shadow that we flourish."

Much much love to you Da, Eileen, Shay and Seán,

Your Mary

Glenville,
County Cork
June 1865

Dearest Mary, Cora, Abe and Mima,

What heartbreaking news you have sent us. I am so sorry that you have had to go through this, Mary mo chuisle. I so wish to hold you now and wish I had been with you then. I am glad you have love and support in your life. You are a brave woman and I am so proud of you my daughter. You are so like your mother.

That you had to suffer this at the hands of our own people is especially grievous. But the reality is that Irish people are not special, are not exceptional. We are the same as everyone else with our good and our bad and with fears and selfishness the same as others. To think otherwise is a kind of arrogance and will surely let us down.

But there is also truth in what you say. To turn as they have, they must really be afraid and I can only think and remember that as a people, we have been visited, not in the small hours of the night, by a nightmare of annihilation but in the noonday it became a reality of personal and national trauma for so many of us. Such has been the wound of an Gorta Mór. But when all that's said, it's still hard to understand how our people who have suffered like this and endured such hardships over centuries can then turn and so easily join in the oppression of another race who have done us no harm.

But these thoughts do not help anyway. Mima sounds like a tour de force. What a grace to have met Samuel and now her. And to see their lives and sacrifices bearing fruit in your own son. Give him and Cora my love. How I would have loved to meet them but in my dwindling years, I'm sixty three this year, that's not going to happen. You have to hold them for me.

Eileen and I are blessed by our two, Shay and Seán. Two gorgeous intelligent little boys. We are happy and content and are glad to say there is little drama in our lives after those tumultuous years. You are in my heart always my dear. Not a day goes by when I don't think of you and your family.

Beannacht Dé oraibh go léir

Da   XXXX

Mary O'Brien continues to live close to her family in the Weeksville community in Brooklyn. Mima Williams lives with Mary and is adopted by the community there as a matriarch, full of wisdom and bright humour. Mary works as a nurse in the Long Island hospital, Mima a seamstress working from home. Cora and Abe both marry and give her grandchildren, six in total, who become the apple of her eye.

Even though the decades they are together are replete with happy memories, it is not without difficulties. Developments change Weeksville, hills are flattened, Brooklyn bridge is built, the area is absorbed and eventually the community is broken and is forced to move on.

The Irish grow to be a powerful force in New York and Abe, along with other Black men, experience animosity, hatred and discrimination. Abe is not able to achieve his mother's equanimity. The memory of his father's brutal death at their hands never leaves him. Filling him with a visceral hatred which eventually he overcomes by burying deep within him. Although he loves his mother, he distances himself from news of his Irish relatives. The long term effect of this in his family is that his Irish ancestry disappears from his life and the lives of his children and grandchildren.

Cora is a faithful companion to her mother all these years, as sisters rather than mother and daughter, they share much together. At the end of both Mima and Mary's lives, Cora takes care of both women. Cora loves her brother Abe fiercely. She sees in him all the qualities of the most important men in their lives, their mother's father, Peadar and his Da, Samuel. From her mother's stories, she recognises the intelligence, wisdom, compassion that shine through stories of Peadar in her brother. It grieves her that Abe is not able to embrace this heritage as his own. She loves the strong kindness he has, a rich gift from his Da, and the courage that burns through her brother's life and actions. After some time she accepts that Abe is not interested in his Irish family and she is left to continue that communication as a solitary exercise.

Peadar O'Brien does not live long enough to see his and Eileen's sons, Shay and Seán grow into strong, intelligent, thoughtful men. Seán, a lawyer, radically involved in supporting the rights, under newly framed Land Law Acts, of Irish tenant farmers to purchase the land they farm; While Shay becomes a teacher like his father in Kanturk primary school, falls in love with and marries Maura Bride, whole family own the local pub 'Nead an Iolair' (The Eagle's Nest) in the nearby village of Nad.

    even small birds fly free

epilogue

The Forge, Ahakista, Sheep's Head County Cork

In which Cormac McCarthy receives a surprise letter from America

April 9th, 1902

When the postman Séamus gets off his bicycle at the Forge it takes Cormac McCarthy, the blacksmith, by surprise. It's been quite a day since he has received any letters.

"I've got a good one for you, Cormac, my boy," Séamus rattles off. "All the way from Americaaaaay," he sings.

"Era, go away out of that," Cormac jokes back. "Sure who would I know across the ocean. Isn't it so that I have spent my life here staying out of trouble and minding my own business."

"Well that's true enough, Cormac me old stock, me old segotia. Sure if it wasn't for your wife and six children we'd all think you are some sort of a class of a hermit or holy man. With your pilgrimages up the mountain and all. And the songs ye sing to us at Samhain. The strange world you bring to us through them. But there's no denying black and white and here I have a letter all the way from New York with a Yankee stamp. Sure, maybe it's the president hisself looking for advice."

Cormac is amused by the conversation as he retreats with the letter into the garden at the back of the Forge overlooking Kitchen Cove. He has long known that he is a strange kettle of fish to everyone around. But he also knows that he is loved and respected and that is more a tribute to the openness of the people than any qualities he might have.

He takes his seat on the iron bench he has crafted in the forge many years before. It was one of his first dabbles into ornate design and he still loves to look at it, with its woven circles and curlicues. It's one of his favourite spots and on this bright, crisp April morning, the air is sweet and the blue sky transposes the ocean into a luxurious apple green. He sits on the oak length of the seat. This is his favourite place and he opens the letter. What he finds there astounds him.

 even small birds fly free

22, Leroy Street,
Greenwich Village
New York City
January 1st 1902

Dear Mr. McCarthy,

This will be a surprise to you, I'm sure. You won't know me but you may remember my dear mother, Mary O'Brien. You lived in the same small village in Cork before the Great Hunger. Ma died three months ago RIP. She is a great loss to me. I loved her so very much. Towards the end of her life she talked to me more about her youth in Ireland. And that is when she asked me to make a promise to write to you.

You see, sir, I am her daughter and I was conceived that traumatic day in the woods near her home by that scoundrel, Robert Kincaid. I'm glad to report to you that I have never considered that man to be my real father. I was blessed to be loved and reared by my mother's husband called Samuel Williams. The kindest, most thoughtful man you would ever wish to meet.

Ma told me of the circumstances of that day and how you, as a mere boy, were witness to everything. And she has thought about you over the years and she believed, knowing you, that you would suffer with the memory. My Da, Samuel, helped her with this as he, as a former slave, was forced to witness the rape of his mother, and know that he was also the issue of such a rape. His mother, Mima, helped him overcome this and wash that man from his life and he in turn was able to help my Ma wash Kincaid out of her life.

Ma was always tough and strong. We had terrible heartache in our lives. My Da, her husband, Samuel was lynched and killed by a marauding Irish mob during the 1863 riots. In truth, I don't think we ever recovered from that but we have had a good life here too.

Anyway the reason I am writing is that Ma wanted you to know that she has not held anything in her heart against you from that day. She even said that she wanted to ease any pain that you may still harbour. She would say that even from that awful event came one of the most precious gifts she ever received, little old me.

I'll end my story there,

Best wishes,

Cora Fitzgerald (nee O'Brien)

Cormac has to read this letter many times to let the full weight of the words sink in. The emotion is overwhelming. He finds himself being transfigured to become once again this young man thrown back into that awful event. To hear Mary's side. To know what has happened to her since. To know of the existence of a child, now woman, from that day fills him with consternation. What does he, as a man, know of the life of a woman? What she has to carry? What she has to bear? And then this woman, with grace and kindness, to reach out to him across the ocean and across the years. This leads him to break. A huge burden lifting from his shoulders. That pivotal moment in his life, years ago, from which all else flowed he is now able to reassign differently. But it will take time. He leaves the seat and goes into his house to see Cailín, his long-suffering wife. She sees his face and knows, such is the bond that has grown between them over the decades.

"I'm for the hills, mo Chuisle. Just for a few days. I need to absorb this."

He packs a few things, some provisions and saddles his horse, Stóirín. This ritual always reminding him of Capaleen the beloved animal who brought him here all those years ago, sadly now long gone. It's a day of wistfulness, he thinks to himself. He makes his way out of the village until he finds his track up to the hut he has built on a small hill by Goats Path overlooking Glanlough. It's where he makes his twice yearly pilgrimage in Spring and Autumn, earning the title 'hermit" as Séamus had quipped earlier in the day. He has the look of one, he thinks. Not through any deliberate effort on his part. More a result of his physical work and the walks he takes over the mountains. He has the physical agility of a mountain goat and his gaunt, lean body lends him a severe look. But it is his straggly, white beard and long white hair that gives him a look of the ancient Celtic monks who spent their lives perched on some craggy rock out in the Atlantic ocean. Others would say it's his soft blue eyes that countermands all that severity and makes him a kindly, compassionate, approachable man.

Within an hour he arrives at the hut overlooking the waters of Glanlough. He will spend a few days here. It's where the dead still appear to him and he can commune. Over the years he has taken solace in the Old Testament. It's only there in stories told of pestilence and disaster that he can find any meaning for the devastation his country has endured in recent times.

even small birds fly free

He loves and admires the fortitude of the prophets, tried and tested beyond measure, beyond at least what he thinks he can endure. Having been exposed to an evil man so young, he admires the prophets' stance against corruption and greed. He sees them as strong, principled and unbending. They are not like tall grasses which lean whichever way the wind blows. His grief at his own capitulation, drives him to study their character, each and every one and love their unbending nature, fierceness, compassion and grace.

Cora's letter discloses to him the trials and tribulations of his people who emigrated to far off places, seeking hospitality, welcome and a home. What they found he can only imagine but his reading certainly has informed him that those that travelled to America were plunged into a country at war with itself.

That first night he dreams. But this time among the faces he is familiar with, those whom he remembers abandoned at roadsides over fifty years before, is Mary again, only now her face is rested and her sea-green eyes are no longer reproachful, but kindly, gentle, tender-hearted. He is astonished by her courage and fortitude in arriving at a place of forgiveness for the wrongs that she has endured and he wakes with soft tears rolling down his cheeks.

He rises early in the morning with the prophet Isaiah in his head. It is a bright, crisp day again and as the sun makes its way up over Bantry Bay, the mist rises ethereally from the lake below, carrying with it the soul travellers of the long gone, swept away in the Great Hunger. Their suffering is deeply etched in his spirit as kith and kin. He also sees those who fled in his imagination, carved with the suffering of emigration and loss, as refugees, at the mercy of others. And bringing it all to mind, a cry rises from deep within his being, a bellow to the hills, a roar, a yowl and out of this emanates a sweet song, in the sean-nós style, a song over the nation, carrying itself north from its tip here in Sheep's Head, over the county of Cork, and north through Limerick, Clare, Galway all the way to Malin Head in Donegal; East to Kerry and west to Waterford, Wexford and up the coast to Clochán na bhFomhórach[1] in Antrim; A psalm for the whole country. A prayer held within it; That from this great wound and suffering would come a resolve within his people now and on into centuries to come, that people they would welcome and nurture the stranger seeking refuge, that as a people they would not visit the same heartlessness on those who would cry to them for help. The song arising plaintively from his lungs pierces the sky and as he continues, a chorus of the long dead take up the refrain, anticipating and sharing his words, oaths deeply imbedded in these ghosts as a prayer too: It is held and passed on as a blessing, an antiphony between the living and the dead for generations yet unborn.

The small birds, the ones he has always loved, join in, the wren, the thrush, the robin, blackbird, and especially the lark fly free above him and amplify the chorus as together they chant

my people my people
you who carry within you
the memory of pestilential hunger and disease,
the helpless holding of your dead child,
coffin-less burials in mass graves,
with no wake or farewell,
You who had to leave in frenzied haste,
with sorrow, tears and a broken heart
locked in a hold over a pitiless ocean
to be flung onto a strange soil
And met with violence, hatred and vitriol
as wretched refuse on an American shore

let us not be like that
let us not be like that
deny bread to the hungry
let us not be like that

let us not be like that
let us not be like that
close our hearts to the homeless
let us not be like that

let us not be like that
let us not be like that
withhold a welcome to the refugee

let us not be like that
for if we are to heal
if we are to recover
if we are to be restored

we must loose, not tie, the bonds of wickedness
undo, not place, heavy burdens
let those that are oppressed fly free

even small birds fly free

share our bread with the hungry
bring the homeless poor into our house
when we see someone naked, vulnerable, cover them
and not turn our back on those that suffer like we have
the stranger, the outcast, the refugee

if we do this
if we do this
if we do this

then shall our light break forth like the morning
our own healing will spring up speedily
our dark days will disappear
and our light will rise from obscurity

if we honour this
if we honour this
if we honour this

if we open our soul to the hungry
and give solace to those who are afflicted
we will become like a well watered garden
like a natural spring whose waters fail not

if we pledge this
if we pledge this
if we pledge this

then there will rise among us
those that shall rebuild the old places
and raise again the foundations of many generations
our dúchas will be preserved
and we will restore the paths
on which we can walk

Footnotes

Notes to - The Humble Prátaí

1. Dúchas The Irish word "duchas" can have a few different meanings depending on the context. It can mean "heritage," "tradition," or "native place." It's a word that encompasses a sense of belonging and connection to one's roots and cultural heritage.

2. "He is my hero, my dashing darling

   He is my Caesar, dashing darling

   Rest or pleasure I did not get

   Since he went far away, my dashing darling"

3. mo stóir = my sweetheart

4. A 'Bothán' is a labourer's dwelling, a small, basic, one-roomed cottage, typically built on half an acre to grow potatoes and was rented from the local landlord.

5. Seanachaí - Bearer of old lore; A traditional Irish storyteller or historian

6. In Celtic Ireland, Samhain is the division of the year between the lighter half (summer) and the darker half (winter). At Samhain, it is believed the division between this world and the other-world is at its thinnest, allowing spirits to pass through.

7. prátaí = potatoes

8. seanmháthair = grandmother

9. The Penal Laws. Throughout most of the eighteenth century, Ireland was governed under a series of codes which have become known collectively as the Penal Laws. Under the terms of these Laws, Catholics were not permitted to vote or serve in Parliament or hold public office in any of the municipal corporations, or live within the limits of incorporated towns; They were forbidden to practice law or hold a post in the military or civil service. Catholics were forbidden to open or teach in a school, serve as private tutors, attend university, or educate their sons abroad. They were forbidden to take part in the manufacture or sale of arms, newspapers, or books, or possess or carry arms. No Catholic might own a horse worth more than five pounds. Except in the linen trade, they might take on no more than two apprentices, and Protestants might not take on Catholic apprentices. Catholics might not buy, inherit, or receive gifts of land from Protestants, nor rent land worth more than thirty shillings a year, nor lease land for longer than thirty-one years, nor make a profit from land of more than one-third of the rent paid; No Catholic estate could be entailed but instead had to be divided at death among all the children. By converting to Protestantism a Catholic son could dispossess his father and disinherit all his brothers. A Protestant landowner lost his civil rights if he married a Catholic, a Protestant heiress her inheritance. All bishops of the Catholic Church were ordered to leave the country under penalty of death if they remained or returned; No priest might enter the country from anywhere, and only one priest was permitted per parish, forbidden to set foot outside it without special permission. Like all Irish, Catholics paid taxes to support the Protestant Church of Ireland. Catholic orphans were to be brought up as Protestants. As can be seen, the Penal Laws regulated every aspect of Irish life, civil, domestic, and spiritual. In effect they established Ireland as a country in which Irish Catholics formed an oppressed race.

10. The '98 uprising. In 1798, the United Irishmen, a society influenced by ideas from the American and French revolutions rebelled against the establishment and led by Presbyterians angry at being shut out of power by the ruling Anglican establishment and joined by Catholics sought to form an independent republic in Ireland.

small birds fly free

Notes to - Death of the Liberator

1. "What's the story, my pulse." The expression 'mo chuisle' says his daughter is the pulse of his heart

2. Tithing, a tenth of income. Since 1830, Catholic peasants or tenant farmers across much of Ireland had been withholding tithes they were obliged to pay to the local vicar of the Anglican Church of Ireland parish. Archdeacon William Ryder was the Rector of the parish of Gortroe, County Cork and also a resident magistrate. His tithes were due on 1st November 1834. On 18th December, the 4th Royal Irish Dragoon Guards under Major Waller; The 29th Worcestershire Regiment under Lieutenant Tait; were led by Archdeacon Ryder, Captain Richard Boyle Bagley, RM, and William Cooke Collins, a Justice of the Peace. The party was met at Bartlemy, a crossroads hamlet, by a military escort, comprising 12 mounted troops and the Irish Constabulary under Captain Pepper. A crowd of 250 local people barricaded the plot of Widow Ryan who "owed" 40 shillings in tithes. The soldiers advanced to collect either the money or produce of equal value. The Riot Act was read. When resistance was met, Waller ordered the soldiers to open fire. Eleven were killed at the scene and 45 injured. The crowd dispersed and Ryan paid her tithe. Nine of the injured died later.

3. Mo Chroí - my heart.

4. Daniel O'Connell. It is difficult to overestimate the effect of Daniel O'Connell on Irish people during this time. Possibly the greatest politician of the 19th century, he was the original master of non-violent protest attracting "Monster" meetings of over a million supporters. A fierce advocate of abolishing the enslavement of people, (Frederick Douglass was an ardent admirer and met O'Connell in Ireland in 1847), O'Connell inspired 20th century icons Mahatma Gandhi and Martin Luther King. The hour-long cheering of his election in 1828 can be compared to Bobby Kennedy's appearance at the Democratic convention of 1964. His death was greeted with the same outpouring of grief as the deaths of Martin Luther King and Bobby Kennedy.

5. A clochán (plural clocháin) or beehive hut is a dry-stone hut with a corbeled roof, commonly associated with the south-western Irish seaboard. The precise construction date of most of these structures is unknown with the buildings belonging to a long-established Celtic tradition, though there is at present no direct evidence to date the surviving examples before c. 700 CE.[1] Some associated with religious sites may be pre-Romanesque, some consider that the most fully intact structures date after the 12th century or later.[2][3] It is where monks lived

Notes to - Taking what I want

1   Irish Poor Law Extension Act which became law on June 8, 1847, placed the entire cost and responsibility of Famine relief directly upon Ireland's property owners. The English now intended to wash their hands of the 'Irish problem' no matter what lay ahead. The assistant to the Treasury and responsible for Ireland, Charles Trevelyan supported this measure in the belief that enforced financial self-sufficiency was the only hope for ever improving Ireland. But in reality, many of Ireland's landlords were deeply in debt with little or no cash income and were teetering on the verge of bankruptcy. The new Poor Law would require them to raise an estimated £10 million in tax revenue to support Ireland's paupers, an impossible task. Subsequently and consequently, they used the law to evict tenants instead.

small birds fly free

Notes to chapter 4 - The Tumbling of Lives

1.   Gleann an Phréacháin. The Valley of the Crows. From ancient times Glenville was called this. Anglicised and changed to its current name. Mariella Hoffmann has written what could be considered as a companion book about this village. Called **Crow Glen - The Spirituality of an Irish Village**, I quote from its pages: '*The Village has been called Crow Glen since human time began. Many hundreds of navy-black crows live in the canopies of the giant beeches. The crows each stand a foot tall on the ground, with broad triangular beaks the colour of sea-rocks. When the beeches are in leaf, their interlocked canopies form a dense-green, bouncy cloud that runs the length of the Village. The crows' homes sit on top, dotted a few yards from each other. Their heavy nests are three feet wide and a foot deep, thick and solid-woven, the edges left untidy. This strip of high-rise real-estate for crows runs well beyond both the crossroad above and the one below. Mysteriously, the crows have always flown away together in unison every morning, and returned together at dusk. I have never known where they go or why. When they come drifting back in on the twilight, many hundreds of black, outstretched bodies block out the village sky. They circle in big, slow, collective, overlapping wheels. This circling is smooth and lazy but their thousands of raw, criss-crossed caws are urgent, contradictory, deafening. All this lasts for about fifteen minutes until each has relocated their own nest and sat down heavily into it, jabbering angrily at their neighbours. Those in adjoining trees continue to pass comment loudly to each other for another five or ten minutes until dusk folds over them like a cloak, settling them into an invisible group silence.*'

2.   Booleying is an Irish term for transhumance – the agricultural tradition of taking cattle up to the high open lands to graze during the summer months. In Ireland, there are large areas of the countryside which have some value during the better part of the year but none at all during the winter and spring e.g. the mountains and moorlands. In the cold season they are barren and desolate, but when the milder part of the year comes they provide grazing which may be sparse but is very sweet. Some of the family went and lived with the cows on the mountain. Some sort of dwelling was built there for them. They would get together at night and pass the long Summer nights with a song, a story, and a tune. They milked the cows morning and evening and made the butter which could be stored until the men from the home farm came for it once a week.

3.   The port, which has had three names, was first called "Cove" in 1750. It was renamed by the British as Queenstown in 1849 to commemorate a visit by Queen Victoria to Ireland. In 1921 when the Irish Free State was established the name was changed to Cobh, in its Irish form, which in my youth, I learned the Yanks called Cob H.

Notes to chapter 5 - Leaving it all behind

1.   Apes. The formed opinion of Irish people by the media. Middle-class public opinion in England at the time of the Famine served to influence government policies. Public opinion was formed by London's newspaper, The Times, the most influential newspaper of the day. Much of the information upon which these stories were based was supplied by Wood, the Treasurer and Trevelyan who used this powerful medium to their own advantage. The racist attitudes of the English toward the Irish are overwhelmingly played out. English ideologies of providentialism and moralism, along with these racist attitudes resulted and justified the limited aid and disastrous policies by the English government. The ideology of providentialism espoused that the Famine disaster was the work of divine providence; the potato blight, in other words, was a result of God's plan to reform Irish society. Moralism naturally follows providentialism in the belief that the Irish suffered a moral deficiency of character, therefore calling upon themselves the wrath of God in the form of famine. Charles Trevelyan, an influential policy maker and assistant head of the treasury during the Famine, was a proponent of these ideologies. A Punch cartoon titled 'The English Labourer's Burden', which portrays a very Ape-like Irish character grinning atop a humble, noble, and miserable Englishmen's shoulders is a good example of the type of racial profiling.   The Times printed such text as, "we have to change the very nature of a people who are born and bred, from time immemorial, in inveterate indolence, improvidence, disorder, and consequent destitution". Races that had a stable temperament and positive personality traits, like the English, were deemed predestined to succeed. Conversely, Races with a volatile temperament and 'negative' personality traits like the Celtic Irish were doomed to a primitive, even barbarous existence.

2.   Indian Corn as a food substitute. Sir Robert Peel Prime Minister (1841-46) brought inexpensive Indian corn (maize) directly from America to be distributed in Ireland. But problems arose as soon as the maize arrived in Ireland. It needed to be ground into digestible corn meal and there weren't enough mills available. Mills that did process the maize discovered the pebble-like grain had to be ground twice. The corn meal itself also caused problems. A working man might eat up to fourteen pounds (six kilograms)of potatoes each day. Indian corn was an unsatisfactory substitute. Peasants nicknamed the bright yellow substance 'Peel's brimstone.' It was difficult to cook, hard to digest and caused diarrhoea. It lacked Vitamin C and resulted in scurvy, a condition previously unknown in Ireland due to the normal consumption of potatoes rich in Vitamin C.

3.   O'Connell's monster meetings. On the night of Saturday, October 7, 1843, a proclamation was issued from Dublin Castle banning the meeting called by Daniel O'Connell north of the city at Clontarf for the following day. Sir Robert Peel called the proposed meeting "an attempt to overthrow the constitution of the British Empire as by law established". Two warships steamed into Dublin Harbour, carrying around 3,000 British troops to ensure the mass rally in favour of Repeal of the Union did not take place. The nationalist newspaper, the Freeman's Journal alleged that the troops had been summoned to "cut the people down" and "run riot in the blood of the innocent". O'Connell, had always insisted that his movement was non-violent. He frantically moved to call it off to prevent, "the slaughter of the people". The following day passed without incident. The Repeal camp was deeply split. Many, particularly those 'Young Irelanders', blamed O'Connell for capitulation to the threat of force and for his unwillingness to confront the English government. They would break from him acrimoniously the following year. With the cancelling of the Clontarf meeting, O'Connell's strategy of mass mobilisation in pursuit of Irish self government was over. He himself was arrested on charges of 'seditious conspiracy' three days later.

Providentialism and Christian political economy. Most schools of thought interpreted the Famine disaster in the light of their own diagnoses of the 'Irish problem' and plans for Irish reconstruction. The very scale of the crisis tended to push each towards an inflexible insistence on their own panaceas. These economic ideologies were in turn variously affected by a pervasive religious mode of Thought-Providentialism, the doctrine that human affairs are regulated by divine agency for human good. More an interpretative language of the coercion acts than a unified body of thought, Providentialism took several forms. What is relevant is the extent to which ideological

                              small birds fly free

stances on the Famine were validated and intensified by the widespread belief that the potato blight had been sent by God for an ascertainable purpose. Ultra-Protestants predictably saw the blight as divine vengeance against Irish Catholicism and on the British state that had recently committed such 'national sins' as endowing the Catholic seminary at Maynooth. Many more interpreted the 'visitation' as a warning against personal and national pride and extravagance, and as an inducement to engage in charitable works.

The Christian duty of charity continued to dominate the actions of groups like the Quakers, but for many in Britain, philanthropic feelings existed alongside a strong desire to see the fundamental changes in Ireland they believed would prevent the need for continuous private generosity. What gave Providentialism some degree of ideological coherence was the existence of a Christian political economy that had evolved alongside the classical tradition in economics. Clerical economists had a profound influence over a British social elite that was imbued with the ethos of evangelical Protestantism. They urged governments to remove restrictions to economic freedom less to promote economic growth, than to subject individuals to the moral discipline of the 'natural economic laws' instituted by God. 'Direct' acts of Providence, such as the potato blight, could be interpreted in this tradition as special 'mercies'. Sir Robert Peel's tying of the potato blight of 1845 to the policy of removing the Corn Laws can be read in this light. The British obsession with free trade in food from 1846 reflected the power of this ideological connection. Many of the Christian political economists were conservative, and had most influence over Peel and his followers. Popularised and radicalised forms of the doctrine had a greater impact on the early-Victorian middle classes and their political leaders. Providentialism blended with Manchester-school economics to produce a moralistic reading of the Irish crisis, that put the blame for the state of society squarely on the moral failings of Irishmen of all classes. Consequently the Famine was welcomed as a God-given opportunity to enforce a policy that would transform Irish behaviour.

4. Whiggery. Moralism was embraced by Whig-liberals such as Earl Grey, Charles Wood, George Grey and the civil servant Charles Trevelyan, who sought to place themselves at the head of radical public opinion, and who were deeply infused with evangelical piety. To Trevelyan the blight was 'the cure ... applied by the direct stroke of an all wise Providence in a manner as unexpected and unthought of as it is likely to be effectual'.

5. Seanair - Grandfather

6. Charlock/prashock (praiseach buí) found on road sides, field margins and waste ground. It was once a pernicious weed, though is somewhat rarer now since the introduction of herbicides. It was a staple food during the hungry months when the old potatoes were finished and the new season crop was not yet ready. The weed was mixed with oats to form a gruel, which is why the Irish word praiseach still means porridge today. Its connection to food shortage and starvation has tarnished its reputation, but it is nevertheless a delicious and versatile vegetable that can be stir-fried like spinach, boiled like kale, or puréed like nettles to form a soup. Its flowering stems can be steamed like broccoli. You can also sprout the seeds and use them as a superfood garnish, or else mill the dry seeds and use like mustard.

7. Couch/scutch grass (broimfhéar) whose roots and rhizomes are "succulent, sweet and nutritious, and taste like liquorice". Scutch roots were widely used during the first World War for their anti-inflammatory properties and can be ground up to produce a flour for bread-making.

8. The Gregory Clause. One provision of the Irish Poor Law Extension Act in June 1847, the so-called Gregory Clause (named after William Gregory, an MP for Dublin who suggested it) exempted from relief anybody who owned more than a quarter of an acre of land. This clause was widely misinterpreted, and some who should have qualified for relief were refused. Many unscrupulous landlords used the Gregory Clause as an excuse to evict thousands of unwanted cottiers from their estates. Those made homeless by these evictions were forced to join the workhouses or to build woefully inadequate shelters on other people's land.

9. Dia Dhaoibh a chairde. God be with you my friends.

10. Chartist's riots. Chartism was a working-class movement for political reform in the United Kingdom that erupted from 1838 to 1857 and was strongest in 1839, 1842 and 1848. It took its

name from the People's Charter of 1838 and was a national protest movement, with particular strongholds of support in Northern England, the East Midlands, the Staffordshire Potteries, the Black Country and the South Wales Valleys, where working people depended on single industries and were subject to wild swings in economic activity. Somerville joined the Royal Scots Greys in December 1831. In May 1832, during the disturbances caused by the Chartists reform bill, Somerville wrote to a newspaper claiming that the army would primarily protect property and stop citizens exercising their rights. Officers in the army wanted to punish him but because he had not broken the law they ordered him at riding school to ride an unruly horse. When he dismounted and refused to remount he was courtmartialed and punished with 100 lashes. He was supported by newspapers and MPs as they believed he had been punished for his political opinions. The court of inquiry acquitted his commanding officer but Somerville's questioning of the officers aroused suspicions that he had been flogged for the letter. He purchased his discharge from the army after a subscription was raised.

small birds fly free

Notes to - In the Mountains

1   Gasún = Young Boy

2   A booley house was a single room dwelling built of stone in remote mountain areas. It was a simple dwelling with a heather roof, a small window and a doorway. There is physical evidence of the booleying in Ireland. On the Coomkeen route of the Sheep's Head Way, there is a little glen high up on the mountain, a setting for a ruined small stone house which could well have been used by those herding the cattle on the summer pasturage in bygone days. It's a beautiful sheltered site, guarded by two ancient thorn trees. It's even possible for the purposes of this story to call the location 'Cormac's Lament'

Notes to - From Nowhere to Anywhere

1.   The Famine road by the Bride river. I am deeply grateful to Mike Murphy, historian at University College Cork, although he is not aware of this. He first led me in his research which I viewed on line to set my story in Graigue and Glenville, neighbouring townships in Cork county. The Famine Road described in this chapter is still there visible in its horror. In the video 'Mapping Famine Roads' on YouTube at the point 21.50 you can see the work in which evicted and starving people were involved. The whole film is worth viewing.

2.   The road to nowhere. Years after the famine, the surgeon William Wilde recalled the summer of 1846 in an image that evokes Samuel Beckett's 'Waiting for Godot'. "Each morning," wrote Wilde, "ghosts of men [would] travel several miles" through an untred landscape of untended fields and decapitated hills "to break up a comparatively good old road, or commence an unnecessary new one, leading from nowhere to anywhere."

3.   mo muirnín - My darling or sweetheart.

small birds fly free

Notes to - The Wretched Refuse

1.   The Royal Irish Constabulary. The RIC was under the authority of the British administration in Ireland. It was a quasi-military police force. Unlike police elsewhere in the United Kingdom, RIC constables were routinely armed (including with carbines) and billeted in barracks, and the force had a militaristic structure. It policed Ireland during a period of agrarian unrest and Irish nationalist agitation.

2.   Young Ireland (Irish: Éire Óg) was a political and cultural movement in the 1840s committed to an all-Ireland struggle for independence and democratic reform. Grouped around the Dublin weekly, The Nation, it took issue with the compromises and clericalism of the larger national movement, Daniel O'Connell's Repeal Association, from which it seceded in 1847. Following an abortive insurrection and the exiling of most of its leading figures in 1848, the movement split between those who carried the commitment to "physical force" forward into the Irish Republican Brotherhood, and those who sought to build a "League of North and South" linking an independent Irish parliamentary party to tenant agitation for land reform.

3.   Strokestown House was the family home of the Cromwellian "adventurer" family - the Pakenham Mahons - from the 1600s until 1979. By the early 18th century, the estate comprised over 11,000 acres (4,500 ha), scattered throughout north east Roscommon, put together from the later seventeenth century as a result of land acquisitions by Captain Nicholas Mahon around 1660. Later, his great-grandson, Maurice Mahon, purchased several additional lands, following elevation to the Peerage of Ireland as the first Baron Hartland in 1800. Many evictions of poor tenant farmers occurred during the Great Famine. The Mahon family alone in 1847 evicted 3,000 people. The killing of Major Denis Mahon in November 1847 was a direct reaction to the large scale deaths of those sent on famine ships to Canada by the Strokestown estate.

4.   The Religious Society of Friends, Quakers or simply 'Friends' as they are also known, are a Christian group who are well remembered in Ireland for their compassionate assistance to victims of the Great Irish Famine. At the time of the famine, there were approximately 3,000 Friends in Ireland out of a population of 8.5 million. However, the impact of their work far outweighed their numbers and the gratitude of people in Ireland resonates today. The Quakers were a practical and solution focussed Society who not only distributed aid but also sought long-term solutions to the situation which Ireland found itself in during this bleak time in Ireland's history. They were highly organised and through a network of committees managed to create a structured system of relief to the areas hardest hit by famine in Ireland. Although often remembered for their work in creating 'soup kitchens' across parts of the country most affected by the devastation of famine, they did much more than this. They did not seek to convert people to their beliefs which was common amongst other faiths at the time but offered help and assistance to anyone in need. They also managed to give those suffering the effects of famine in Ireland a voice by spreading awareness of the true conditions in Ireland at this time, generating aid and assistance from abroad.

5.   Soupers. Souperism was a phenomenon of the Irish Great Famine. Protestant Bible Societies set up schools in which starving children were fed, on the condition of receiving Protestant religious instruction at the same time. Its practitioners were reviled by the Catholic families who had to choose between Protestantism and starvation. People who converted for food were known as "soupers", "jumpers", and "cat breacs". In the words of their peers, they "took the soup". Although souperism was a rare phenomenon, it had a lasting effect on the popular memory of the Famine. It blemished the relief work by Protestants who gave aid without proselytizing, and

the rumour of souperism may have discouraged starving Catholics from attending soup kitchens for fear of betraying their faith.

6.   Mo Stór - My darling.

7.   The Know-Nothing party, or byname of American Party, is a U.S. political party which flourished in the 1850s. It was an outgrowth of the strong anti-immigrant and especially anti-Roman Catholic sentiment that started to manifest itself during the 1840s. A rising tide of immigrants, primarily Germans in the Midwest and Irish in the East, seemed to pose a threat to the economic and political security of native-born Protestant Americans. In 1849, the secret Order of the Star-Spangled Banner formed in New York City, and soon after lodges formed in nearly every other major American city. Members, when asked about their nativist organisations, were supposed to reply that they knew nothing, hence the name. As its membership and importance grew in the 1850s, the group slowly shed its clandestine character and took the official name American Party. As a national political entity, it called for restrictions on immigration, the exclusion of the foreign-born from voting or holding public office in the United States, and for a 21-year residency requirement for citizenship.

8.   Grains unloaded. According to economist Cormac O' Grada, more than 26 million bushels of grain were exported from Ireland to England in 1845, a "famine" year. Even greater exports are documented in the Spring 1997 issue of History Ireland by Christine Kinealy of the University of Liverpool. Her research shows that nearly 4,000 vessels carrying food left Ireland for ports in England during "Black '47" while 400,000 Irish men, women and children died of starvation. Shipping records indicate that 9,992 Irish calves were exported to England during 1847, a 33 percent increase from the previous year. At the same time, more than 4,000 horses and ponies were exported. In fact, the export of all livestock from Ireland to England increased during the famine except for pigs. However, the export of ham and bacon did increase. Other exports from Ireland during the "famine" included peas, beans, onions, rabbits, salmon, oysters, herring, lard, honey and even potatoes. Dr. Kinealy's research also shows that 1,336,220 gallons of grain-derived alcohol were exported from Ireland to England during the first nine months of 1847. In addition, a phenomenal 822,681 gallons of butter left starving Ireland for tables in England during the same period. If the figures for the other three months were comparable, more than 1 million gallons of butter were exported during the worst year of mass starvation in Ireland. The food was shipped from ports in some of the worst famine-stricken areas of Ireland, and British regiments guarded the ports and granaries to guarantee British merchants and absentee landlords their 'free-market' profits.

9.   Refugees sent back. On June 21, 1847, the British government, intending to aid besieged Liverpool, passed a tough new law allowing local authorities to deport homeless Irish back to Ireland. Within days, the first boatloads of paupers were being returned to Dublin and Cork, then abandoned on the docks. Orders for removal were issued by the hundreds. About 15,000 Irish people were dragged out of filthy cellars and lodging houses and sent home even if they were ill with fever.

10. Asylum admissions. While historical scholarship has produced an impressive volume of research and literature on the experiences of Irish migrants and the "Irish problem" in nineteenth century Britain, it is only recently that this has come to focus on what one historian of Irish psychiatry has described as one of the "most traumatic aspects" of Irish migration, the high incidence of mental breakdown and confinement in asylums amongst Irish migrants to Britain and other destinations after the Famine. Boosted by Famine migration, almost one-quarter of the population of Liverpool was Irish-born by 1851, and a large number of these migrants moved

                    small birds fly free

onwards – often via the workhouse and to a lesser extent the prison – into Lancashire's asylums. John Walton's study of the patient population of Lancaster Moor Asylum indicated that in 1851, 22 per cent of patients had migrated from Ireland. By the late 1850s around half of the admissions to Liverpool's Rainhill Asylum were recorded as Irish-born. According to the 1861 census, 18.9 per cent of Liverpool's resident population was Irish-born, suggesting that the proportion of Irish in Rainhill was almost double the proportion of Irish-born in Liverpool. Irish patients had also spilled out into the county's other public asylums, workhouse lunacy wards and private asylums. Asylum superintendents emphasized in their annual reports that much of this patient intake was made up of recent migrants from Ireland, despite the fact that migration reduced to a steadier flow between 1851 and 1871 after the huge influx of the Great Famine. In what is likely to have been one of the largest – and most enduring – migrations of a particular ethnic group into any asylum system at any point in history, the doctors charged with managing these institutions were alarmed by this numerical onslaught, which aggravated problems of overcrowding and limited resources. Many Irish patients arrived at these institutions in poor physical condition, their bodies and minds undermined by destitution and extreme hardship and ravaged by the effects of "bad" living. At the same time, despite their physical degradation, Irish patients were regarded as highly disruptive and difficult to manage. They were also likely to have been highly mobile prior to admission, but, once in the asylum system, very difficult to shift out again.

11. Life on coffin ships. The Liverpool vessel "America", which sailed to New Orleans with 493 passengers, had only one cooking hearth, five by three feet, for all of its passengers, so that each family was allowed to cook its meals only once in four days

12. Loss of life on coffin ships. The "Blanche", arrived with approximately 500 passengers and reported 25 deaths on the voyage; eventually 144 of the remainder were taken to the Charity Hospital. The ship's captain refused to accept the blame for conditions on his ship and gave assurance that things were not as bad as they might seem: "Of all this number I lost, 25 by death—certainly not an excessive mortality under the lamentable circumstances," he stated, "and it ought to be remarked that not one English passenger died; though under the same circumstances, and having the same diet as the rest, who were from Ireland. Nor did I lose one of my crew." The captain suggested that the mortality of the Irish might have resulted from the effect of 'debility and previous habits'.

13. Building the levees. The Irish had been settling in New Orleans long before the waves of immigration which began in the 1800's. Numerous nationalities settled in New Orleans during the French and Spanish colonial periods and continued to arrive during the early years following the Purchase of Louisiana in 1803. While few Irish families migrated to the colony during the French period, a larger number began to arrive from Spain or her colonies after the coming of Governor Alejandro O'Reilly in 1769. The great majority of Irish immigrants, however, were very poor, and in 1826 Reverend Timothy Flint wrote feelingly of the "multitudes of the poor Catholic Irish, with their ruddy faces, without proper nursing, in crowded apartments ...swept away with unpitying fury" by epidemic and other diseases. An important wave of Irish immigrants came to New Orleans in 1832, when construction began on the New Basin Canal, which was to connect Lake Pontchartrain with New Orleans. Serious labour shortages during this period, caused by thousands of deaths from yellow fever and cholera, led the Canal Bank and Trust Company to actively encourage the importation of Irish and German labour. Slaves were considered too valuable for such dangerous work. The average wages of workers on the canal was $20 a month plus living quarters, food, and all the whiskey the men needed. Tyrone Power, the Irish actor, spoke of his countrymen working "under fierce sun, in pestilential swamps -

wading among stumps of trees…….mid-deep in black mud, clearing the spaces pumped out by powerful steam-engines wheeling, digging, hewing, or bearing burdens it made one's shoulders ache to look upon." They lived, many with their families, in open log shelters half submerged in the swamps, "worse lodged than the cattle of the field…….They ate the coarsest food and drank heavily. The mortality rate was extremely high, and the priest was the labourers' only comfort. The Irish inhabitants of New Orleans before the late 1840's were few, however, in comparison to the large numbers who came with the heavy waves of Irish immigration during the Great Famine. Though many of these arrivals continued their journey up the Mississippi, others remained, and in 1850, the Irish constituted 20,200 of the total New Orleans population of 129,747. The Irish were the largest immigrant group in the city, the Germans were the second largest. Though a minority, the Irish in New Orleans were of great significance in the social, political, and economic life of the city. The "Irish Channel," where many of the immigrants settled, was a notoriously dangerous section of town, and more than one policeman was killed there. Political conflicts over the illegal use of the Irish vote precipitated bloody riots in the city. The health of the citizens suffered as the Irish brought in dreaded diseases. In spite of the problems presented by the thousands of newcomers to the city, they made a valuable contribution to the labour force at a time when workers were greatly needed for internal improvements. The Irish in New Orleans were in many ways typical of their fellow countrymen in the United States. The most significant difference was the greater suffering from severe epidemics which the Irish who settled in the marshy, disease-plagued southern city experienced. In other respects, however, the problems and contributions of the Irish in New Orleans and those in other large cities of the nation were much the same. They had left their homeland for the same reasons and had endured similar hardships on their voyage to the new country. On arrival, they congregated in filthy slums, where they did not forget their native land, for they joined Irish organisations, kept abreast of events in Ireland, and, in spite of their poverty, sent generous contributions back to their homeland. Participating in politics, they became the target of the Know-Nothing Party. The Irish in New Orleans, like those in other areas of the United States, came to America at a time when labourers were needed and helped to fill that need.

14. What is Cajun music and where did it come from? The French colonised Canada beginning in 1604, with many settling in what is now Nova Scotia but was then called Acadie. The word Cajun comes from the word Acadian. Canada, however, was a contested area, settled by both the English and the French. The English army took Acadie in 1713. They forced the French settlers to swear an oath of loyalty to the British crown. Those who refused were deported beginning in 1755. They were taken to various destinations: back to France, to New England, and to other French possessions, such as Haiti and Louisiana. Many Acadians arrived in Louisiana in 1765 through 1785. Although Louisiana had been transferred to Spain in 1762, everyday life continued to be lived in French. The Spanish government even brought 1600 Acadians from France to Louisiana in 1785. Few Acadians stayed in the port of arrival, New Orleans. Some settled in the regions south and northwest of New Orleans and along the Teche, Lafourche and Vermilion Bayous. Far more went further west to the marshes and prairies of south central Louisiana. They became hunters and trappers and farmers. It is a popular misconception that most Cajuns live on the bayous and in the marshes, poling their pirogues (small canoe made from a single tree trunk) and hunting alligators. Far more became farmers in the grand triangular prairie that stretches from Lafayette north to Ville Platte and west to Lake Charles. The music these people brought was simple. It was made by singing, humming, and rhythmic clapping and stamping. Instruments were brought to the colony, with a violinist's death recorded in 1782.

small birds fly free

Early instrumental music was played primarily on violins, singly or in pairs. One violin played lead and the second a backing rhythm. A simple rhythm instrument was created out of bent metal bars from hay or rice rakes: the triangle or 'tit fer', meaning little iron. Alan Lomax described the music of Poitou, the region in France most Acadians came from, as solo unaccompanied ballads, lyric songs with complex texts, unaccompanied air playing on fiddles and wind instruments, unison group performances of ceremonial songs, and dance orchestras where string and wind duos play tunes in unison or in an accompanying relationship. The earliest Acadian songs were long ballads originally from France. They told of hard life and suffering. Acadians brought from Canada influences from their neighbours, Native Americans and the Scots-Irish. Jigs, reels, and contradances became part of their repertoire. In their new home, Louisiana, they absorbed more from their new neighbours, Spanish, Germans and people from the Caribbean. Cajun music is first and foremost, social music. Life was hard toiling in the fields, and it was a welcome relief to hear that Boudreaux or Landry was having a bal de maison, a house dance, on a Saturday night. Families appeared and furniture was moved to make room for dancing. Children were put aside and encouraged to sleep, giving the name fais do-do, or go to sleep, to these dances. Musicians wrote original songs telling of their life in the new world. The song J'ai passe devant ta porte tells of the suddenness of death from accident and disease. The singer tells of passing by his beloved's door and hearing no answer to his call. Going inside he sees the candles burning around his love's corpse.

15. What is a Patty Roller? Slave patrols—traditionally known as patrollers, patterrollers, patty-rollers or paddy rollers by enslaved persons of African descent—were organised groups of armed men who monitored and enforced discipline upon slaves in the antebellum U.S. southern states. The slave patrols' function was to police enslaved persons, especially those who escaped or were viewed as defiant. They also formed river patrols to prevent escape by boat. Policing the movements of black people, slave patrols were explicit in their design to empower the white population. They were first established in South Carolina in 1704, and the idea spread throughout the colonies before their use diminished following the Civil War in the 1860s.

16. Púca are shape-shifting troublemakers. Legends say that the púca can change into horses, goats, cats, donkeys, bulls, dogs, foxes, wolves, and hares, though always with jet-black fur. Horses bearing sleek coats, wild manes and flaming eyes are the most common animal shape of these mischievous fairies. When in human form, these fairies still bear animalistic characteristics. Though stories about the púca are vague and varied, one common similarity is the púca's love of mischief. Mischief can take many forms, but one favourite with the púca seems to be taking their preferred animal form of a great black horse and enticing the unwitting rider on its back for a wild and terrible horseback ride through the night. Usually, this person has been on the drink, and even if they haven't, the púca bewitches them, leaving them with a bad feeling and hazy recollections of a night poorly spent. As you can imagine, that would frighten anyone – though little actual harm is done.

Sometimes the púca can serve as a protective entity, helping farmers with the crops, offering presents, or intervening ahead of a terrible accident to prevent harm, though stories of kindly púca are much overshadowed by those of mischief, bad luck, or even doom.

Then again, there are some stories darker still, calling the creatures blood-thirsty and accusing the púca of being evil creatures that hunted and killed humans. It seems the stories are as varied as the púca themselves.

17. Five Points - About 300 years ago, Lower Manhattan was adorned by a pretty five-acre lake known as the Collect. The first steamboat was tested there. Locals would gather to skate on its

ice in the winter and picnic along its shores in the summer. By the mid-1700's, however, the Collect was already rimmed with slaughterhouses and tanneries. The effusions from these bloody businesses were poured directly into the lake and more industries, more trash, quickly followed. By 1800 the Collect was a reeking cesspool. By 1813 it had been entirely filled in and by 1825 something entirely new stood on the site -- America's first real slum, Five Points. No other plot of land would so fire the national imagination in the 19th century. Five Points would not only define the idea of an urban ghetto, but fix the very terms of how a nation argues about the poor. Yet such is the rush of American history that it is barely remembered today. The two most important works on the history of New York published in the 1990's -- The Encyclopaedia of New York City and 'Gotham' -- both misidentify something as simple as the streets whose confluence created the five-cornered intersection that gave the neighbourhood its name. Physically, Five Points was mostly what is now known as Little Italy, Chinatown and the blocks of monolithic courthouses that seem to anchor Manhattan. Metaphysically, it constituted hallowed ground in the American story, occupied by successive waves of freed slaves and Irish, Italian and Chinese immigrants. With the exception of its more celebrated neighbour, the Lower East Side, no part of the country has been a place of the poor, the immigrant and the aspiring for as long as Five Points. Five Points came into being almost at the same moment as America's raucous new penny press, and the newspapers dwelt interminably upon its alleged violence and depravity. Readers were thrilled and repulsed by tales of murder, mayhem and sexual license. By the late 1830's, Five Points was already infamous enough that tourists from around the world made regular ''slumming'' trips; visitors included a Russian grand duke, Davy Crockett, Charles Dickens and Abraham Lincoln. They shivered enjoyably before the countless bars and liquor stores and brazen bordellos; the squalid, lightless tenements and -- most depraved of all! -- The sight of blacks and whites intermingling freely. Like every American slum since, Five Points became a hobby horse for social theorists. Southern politicians blamed race mixing for its depravity. Northern Republicans pointed out that it voted overwhelmingly Democratic. Protestant missionaries scrapped over whether its failings could be attributed to poor living conditions or poor morals -- or to the Roman Catholicism of the Irish immigrants who dominated the area by the 1840's. Was Five Points really so bad? Yes, Five Points was violent and crime-ridden. Yet the neighbourhood's murder rates were probably well below what we would expect from a slum today (not least because the residents had very limited access to firearms). Yes, there was plenty of prostitution and public drunkenness. To quote an inebriated woman telling a health official who asked her why she drank, ''If you lived in this place you would ask for whiskey instead of milk.'' But most Five Points residents -- like most residents of modern American slums -- seem to have worked like demons, sent everything they could back to their relatives in the old country and, in at least some cases, saved up astonishing amounts of money. The overwhelming reality of Five Points, and the one thing that all observers seem to have gotten right, was the misery. The endless drudgery and the low pay. The appalling sanitation and the firetrap tenements. The plagues of cholera, measles, diphtheria and typhus that struck hardest at children and infants. Still, Five Points also produced a vibrant popular culture all its own, from child street musicians to the notorious Civil War draft riot, from the first Chinese in New York to William Henry Lane, a k a Master Juba, the teenage African-American phenomenon who probably invented tap dancing by combining Irish and African folk traditions.

18. The Dead Rabbits - This crew of Irish immigrants was one of the most feared gangs to emerge from Five Points. The Dead Rabbits was the name of an Irish American criminal street gang active in Lower Manhattan in the 1830s to 1850s. The Dead Rabbits were so named after a dead

small birds fly free

rabbit was thrown into the centre of the room during a Roach Guards gang meeting (previous gang), prompting some members to treat this as an omen, withdraw, and form an independent gang. Their battle symbol was a dead rabbit on a pike. They often clashed with Nativist political groups who viewed Irish Catholics as a threatening and criminal subculture. The Dead Rabbits were given the nicknames the "Mulberry Boys" and the "Mulberry Street Boys" by the New York City Police Department because they were known to have operated along Mulberry Street in Five Points. Throughout the 1850s, the Dead Rabbits excelled at robbery, pick-pocketing and brawling—particularly with their sworn enemies, the Bowery Boys. The group was made up mostly of young men, but it wasn't unheard of for women to join in on the violence. According to legend, one of the most feared Dead Rabbits was "Hell-Cat Maggie," a woman who reportedly filed her teeth to points and wore brass fingernails into battle. While the Rabbits mostly dabbled in petty crime, they were also famous for the events of July 4, 1857, when one of their street fights with the Bowery Boys turned into a bloody riot that killed a dozen people. They famously feature in Martin Scorsese's film 'Gangs of New York'

19. The Forty Thieves - One of Gotham's earliest known criminal outfits, the Forty Thieves operated between the 1820s and 1850s in Five Points neighbourhood of Manhattan. This band of Irish thugs, pickpockets and ne'er-do-wells first came together in a grocery store and dive bar owned by a woman named Rosanna Peers. Under the leadership of Edward Coleman—a notorious rogue who was later hanged for beating his wife to death—what started as a motley group of petty criminals soon blossomed into a feared street gang with its own rules and organizational structure. Members of the Forty Thieves reportedly had quotas that required them to steal a certain amount of goods each day or face expulsion. What's more, the gang even franchised itself in the form of the "Forty Little Thieves," a collection of juvenile apprentices who served as pickpockets and lookouts.

20. The Bowery Boys were a nativist, anti-Catholic, and anti-Irish criminal gang based in the Bowery neighbourhood of Manhattan, New York City in the early-mid-19th century. In contrast with the Irish immigrant tenement of Five Points, one of the worst city slums in the United States, the Bowery was a more prosperous working-class community. One of the most storied gangs of New York, the Bowery Boys clashed with the Irish Five Points gangs during the 1840s, 50s and 60s. Unlike some of their criminal counterparts, most of the Bowery Boys dressed in elegant clothing and held legitimate employment as printers, mechanics and other apprentice tradesmen. But when they weren't on the job, these young hoodlums haunted the saloons and back alleys of the Bowery and engaged in bloody turf wars with rival gangs like the Dead Rabbits. The Bowery Boys often acted more as a political club than a mob, and many of their brawls were with supporters of rival politicians. The gang would sometimes even station its members at polling places to intimidate voters into supporting a particular candidate. In return, the gang's home district would receive money and preferential treatment once the politician was in office. The also featured in Scorsese's 'Gangs of New York' lead famously by Daniel Day Lewis playing Bill the Butcher.

21. Van Diemen's land. From the early 1800s to the 1853 abolition of penal transportation (known simply as "transportation"), Van Diemen's Land was the primary penal colony in Australia. Following the suspension of transportation to New South Wales, all transported convicts were sent to Van Diemen's Land. In total, some 73,000 convicts were transported to Van Diemen's Land or about 40% of all convicts sent to Australia. Male convicts served their sentences as assigned labour to free settlers or in gangs assigned to public works. Only the most difficult convicts (mostly re-offenders) were sent to the Tasman Peninsula prison known as Port Arthur. Female convicts were assigned as servants in free settler households or sent to a female factory

(women's workhouse prison). There were five female factories in Van Diemen's Land. When Ireland's greatest disaster struck, the dependence on the potato was fully exposed, when a series of crop failures from 1845 to 1849 plunged Ireland into the Great Famine, millions of people faced the prospect of a slow death through starvation. An agent of a landlord in Queen's county could "scarcely believe that men, women and children were actually dying of starvation in thousands. Yet so it was. They died on the roads~ and they died in the fields; they wandered into the towns, and died in the streets; they closed their cabin doors~ and lay down upon their beds, and died of starvation in their houses. Prior to 1846 the number of persons sentenced to transportation averaged 673 each year but in 1848· the number had reached 2,687. For many the gaols became a refuge; Food provided in prisons was better than that in the workhouses. The extent of the disaster can be measured by the loss of population. By 1851 the total population had declined by twenty per cent and the rural population by almost twenty-five per cent. Under these conditions, it is hardly surprising that crime increased. The Irish authorities reported in 1849 an "unprecedented increase of crime consequent upon the destitution and sufferings endured by the lower classes during four consecutive years," thus courting transportation and the Irish administration was overwhelmed with the numbers in prison. The Famine had particular relevance for convicts transported from Ireland to Van Diemen's Land. Fifty one per cent of the women and forty five per cent of men had been tried during famine years. Almost all male convicts who arrived after 1850 had been convicted during the famine years.

22. The story of Bridie Mulcahy and her six children is inspired by a real and remarkable event, recounted in a companion book to this novel. 'Crow Glen, The Spiritual Universe of an Irish Village, by Marella Hoffman. Marella recounts learning of a woman Johanna Carney who took her eight children aboard a coffin ship to America in 1847. The book celebrates County Cork.

23. Batterymarch Street. The roughest welcome for the refugees would be in Boston, Massachusetts, an Anglo-Saxon city with a population of about 115,000. It was a place run by descendants of English Puritans, men who could proudly recite their lineage back to 1620 and the Mayflower ship. Now, some two hundred thirty years later, their city was undergoing nothing short of an unwanted "social revolution" as described by Ephraim Peabody, member of an old Yankee family. In 1847, the first big year of Famine emigration, the city was swamped with 37,000 Irish Catholics arriving by sea and land. Proper Bostonians pointed and laughed at the first Irish immigrants stepping off ships wearing clothes twenty years out of fashion. They watched as the newly arrived Irishmen settled with their families into enclaves that became exclusively Irish near the Boston waterfront along Batterymarch and Broad Streets, then in the North End section and in East Boston. Irishmen took any unskilled jobs they could find such as cleaning yards and stables, unloading ships, and pushing carts. And once again, they fell victim to unscrupulous landlords. This time it was Boston landlords who sub-divided former Yankee dwellings into cheap housing, charging Irish families up to $1.50 a week to live in a single nine-by-eleven foot room with no water, sanitation, ventilation or daylight. In Boston, as well as other American cities in the mid-1800's, there was no enforcement of sanitary regulations and no building or fire safety codes. Landlords could do as they pleased. A single family three-story house along the waterfront that once belonged to a prosperous Yankee merchant could be divided-up room by room into housing for a hundred Irish people, bringing a nice profit. The overflow Irish emigrants would settle into the gardens, back yards and alleys surrounding the house, living in wooden shacks. Demand for housing of any quality was extraordinary. People lived in musty cellars with low ceilings that partially flooded with every tide. Old warehouses and other buildings within the Irish enclave were hastily converted into rooming houses using flimsy wooden partitions that provided no

small birds fly free

privacy. A Boston Committee of Internal Health studying the situation described the resulting Irish slum as "a perfect hive of human beings, without comforts and mostly without common necessaries; in many cases huddled together like brutes, without regard to age or sex or sense of decency. Under such circumstances self-respect, forethought, all the high and noble virtues soon die out, and sullen indifference and despair or disorder, intemperance and utter degradation reign supreme." The unsanitary conditions were breeding grounds for disease, particularly cholera. Sixty percent of the Irish children born in Boston during this period didn't live to see their sixth birthday. Adult Irish emigrants lived on average just six years after stepping off the boat onto American soil. Those who were not ill were driven to despair. Rowdy behaviour fuelled by alcohol and boredom spilled out into the streets of Boston and the city witnessed a staggering increase in crime, up to 400 percent for such crimes as aggravated assault. Men and boys cooped up in tiny rooms and without employment or schooling got into serious trouble. An estimated 1500 children roamed the streets every day begging and making mischief. There were only a limited number of unskilled jobs available. Intense rivalry quickly developed between the Irish emigrants and working class Bostonians over these jobs. In Ireland, a working man might earn eight cents a day. In America, he could earn up to a dollar a day, a tremendous improvement. Bostonians feared being undercut by hungry Irish emigrants willing to work for less than the going rate. Their resentment, combined with growing anti-Irish and anti-Catholic sentiment among all classes in Boston led to 'No Irish Need Apply' signs being posted in shop windows, factory gates and workshop doors throughout the city.

24. Rachel, the story from the book of Genesis. Soon after his arrival in Harran, Jacob fell in love with the "beautiful and lovely" Rachel, daughter of his cousin Laban (Genesis 29:17). Laban warmly welcomed him to his family, but asked a steep price for Rachel's hand in marriage: Jacob would first have to work as a shepherd for seven years, tending Laban's flocks. The annual wage for a shepherd in the Bronze Age was about 10 shekels; hence, seven years of labour was a stiff demand. But Jacob, a fugitive from Esau, was in no position to bargain. When the seven years were fulfilled at last, Jacob spent his wedding night only to discover at dawn that it wasn't Rachel, but her elder sister Leah whom Laban had delivered to Jacob's tent. Laban explained that according to tribal custom, the oldest daughter should be married first (Genesis 29:26). If Jacob wanted to marry Rachel as well, he would owe Laban another seven years of labour.

25. Ambrose Cutting. The keen history buffs of my readers will notice I have taken a slight liberty in the narrative. Wet plate photography was not invented until 1851, but for the purposes of the story, I have Caelan stumbling on it in 1849 - two years early. James Ambrose Cutting (1814–1867) was an American photographer and inventor, sometimes called the inventor of the Ambrotype photographic process. He grew up in poverty on a farm in Haverhill, New Hampshire. At age 28, he invented a new type of beehive in 1842, and on the money from selling his patents moved to Boston, Massachusetts. He created ambrotype photograph through sensitising a polished plate of glass by the wet plate collodion process and exposing the plate in a camera to produce a negative image. The wet plate collodion process was invented just a few years before by Frederick Scott Archer and widely used for glass negatives, but in an ambrotype the collodion image is used as a positive, instead of a negative. When dry, the glass plate was then backed either with black paint, metal, cloth, or paper; this black backing made light areas of the negative appear darker, turning the negative image into a positive. Some ambrotypes were made with ruby or dark green glass to simulate the effect of a backing without using one. Ambrotypes often were hand-coloured, most commonly with dabs of red paint on the cheeks of the sitter. They were housed in wood or thermoplastic cases (also called 'Union cases'), like the daguerreotype

photographs with which they are often confused; an ambrotype is easily distinguished from a daguerreotype because its surface is not reflective, as daguerreotype surfaces are. Ambrotypes were most popular during the mid- to late-1850s but continued to be available through the 1890s. In 1854, Cutting took out three patents relating to the process of creating images on glass using the wet plate collodion process. While Cutting is sometimes referred to as the inventor of the ambrotype, his three photographic patents of 1854 refer only to improvements in the process, rather than the idea of the collodion positive itself. Ambrotypes (black-backed collodion positives) are reported to have been made at least as early as 1852 by Frederick Scott Archer.

26. Wet-collodion process, also called collodion process is an early photographic technique invented by Englishman Frederick Scott Archer in 1851. The process involved adding a soluble iodide to a solution of collodion (cellulose nitrate) and coating a glass plate with the mixture. In the darkroom, the plate was immersed in a solution of silver nitrate to form silver iodide. The plate, still wet, was exposed in the camera. It was then developed by pouring a solution of pyrogallic acid over it and was fixed with a strong solution of sodium thiosulfate, for which potassium cyanide was later substituted. Immediate developing and fixing were necessary because, after the collodion film had dried, it became waterproof and the reagent solutions could not penetrate it. The process was valued for the level of detail and clarity it allowed. A modification of the process, in which an underexposed negative was backed with black paper or velvet to form what was called an ambrotype, became very popular from the mid- to late 19th century, as did a version on black lacquered metal known as a tintype, or ferrotype.

27. Catherine McAuley started the Mercy movement in Dublin in 1831 at the age of 52. A remarkable fact, given that the average lifespan in the early nineteenth century was 49. To begin such a major contribution at that point in her life speaks immensely of who she was. The previous twenty years of her life had been spent caring for an elderly couple and managing their household. They left her a substantial financial inheritance which she used to buy a house in the centre of Georgian Dublin, where she took care of vulnerable women and street children. The movement from its early years took hold of the vision of 'Mercy' and this was passed on and translated into life and work. Most organisations and movements are founded by a charismatic individual. For many organisations, to emerge out of the shadow of the charismatic leader is a significant challenge which many do not fully achieve. The charismatic leader casts a long shadow. With the Mercy movement, it appears that the vision of Mercy promulgated was the significant factor which gave energy and vitality to its growth and not the personal charisma of Catherine McAuley. It can be assumed that her long sojourn in hidden service prior to founding the work, gave her the capacity to pass on the inspiration without getting in its way. The beginning of the movement is also exceptional given the context of early nineteenth century Dublin. Catherine McAuley gathered women together and inspired them to reach out and provide shelter to vulnerable women - many who had come to the city to seek work in households and became exposed to the sexual predations of male householders. She and the other women also reached out to poor families in the city and provided education and shelter for their children. They were an unaligned and organic group. As such they constituted a real threat to the status quo. A women, more than a century ahead of her time, Catherine McAuley did not seek the blessing or permission of the establishment to begin her work. Provocatively siting her centre in the heart of Georgian Dublin, the rich could not escape seeing the poor and their poverty. She was a subversive and challenged the prevailing hegemony of ignorance by asserting in action the right of all to education. However, in the end, she was forced to compromise as the institution of the church was threatened and she submitted to founding a religious order. This seems to demonstrate her practical nature. In the end, she

small birds fly free

refused to fully conform and introduced a fourth vow among her members to "service", lest they forget among the trappings and paraphernalia of religious life, what it was all about. Within 20 years, and in a time without global travel or communication, the movement had spread to Britain, United States, Australia, and New Zealand, largely following the Irish diaspora who entered the new world as marginalised, third class, desperately poor citizens, often a result of the Famine - An Gorta Mór. The strength of the movement is that it did not focus on cross-cultural work and remained untainted by the imperialist vision of many nineteenth and twentieth century missions. Mercy sisters reached out to the poor and marginalised within their own communities wherever they had migrated.

28. The Fugitive Slave Act was a congressional statute passed in 1850 that permitted for the seizure and return of runaway slaves who escaped from one state and fled into another. The Act, as a part of the Compromise of 1850, required that the U.S. government actively intervene to help slave owners regain control over their slaves. This act dictated that fugitive slaves were neither allowed to testify on their own behalf, nor were they allowed to have a trial by jury. This was "justified" through legislators' claims that African Americans could not be United States citizens and thus were not afforded any protections. Moreover, federal marshals who refused to enforce the law and individuals who helped slaves to escape were heavily penalised and were fined $1,000. Furthermore, special commissioners were given concurrent jurisdiction with U.S. courts enforcing this act. This was determined to be wildly corrupt, for these special commissioners were paid $10 to rule in favour of slave owners, but they only received $5 if they sided with slaves. Between 1850 and 1860, 343 fugitive slaves appeared before these special commission, and of those, 332 were returned to slavery in the South. The severity of this statute inspired an increased number of abolitionists, the development of a more efficient Underground Railroad, and the establishment of new personal-liberty laws in the North. These personal liberty laws were enacted in eight Northern States and prohibited state officials from assisting in returning fugitive slaves to the South. This prominent resistance to the Fugitive Slave Act of 1850 incited further hostility between the North and the South and bolstered the controversy over slavery. Anti-Fugitive Slave Act riots erupted all over the North in 1851. The Fugitive Slave Acts were not repealed until June 28, 1864. The effect of the Act is best captured in the words of Frederick Douglass in his 4th July speech in Rochester, ny, 1852: "But a still more inhuman, disgraceful, and scandalous state of things remains to be presented. By an act of the American Congress, not yet two years old, slavery has been nationalised in its most horrible and revolting form. By that act, Mason & Dixon's line has been obliterated; New York has become as Virginia; and the power to hold, hunt, and sell men, women, and children as slaves remains no longer a mere state institution, but is now an institution of the whole United States. The power is co-extensive with the Star-Spangled Banner and American Christianity. Where these go, may also go the merciless slave-hunter. Where these are, man is not sacred. He is a bird for the sportsman's gun. By that most foul and fiendish of all human decrees, the liberty and person of every man are put in peril. Your broad republican domain is hunting ground for men. Not for thieves and robbers, enemies of society, merely, but for men guilty of no crime. Your lawmakers have commanded all good citizens to engage in this hellish sport. Your President, your Secretary of State, your lords, nobles and ecclesiastics enforce, as a duty you owe to your free and glorious country, and to your God, that you do this accursed thing. Not fewer than forty Americans have, within the past two years, been hunted down and, without a moment's warning, hurried away in chains, and consigned to slavery and excruciating torture. Some of these have had wives and children, dependent on them for bread; but of this, no account was made. The right of the hunter to his prey stands superior

to the right of marriage, and to all rights in this republic, the rights of God included! For Black men there are neither law, justice, humanity, not religion. The Fugitive Slave Law makes makes mercy to them a crime; and bribes the judge who tries them. An American judge gets ten dollars for every victim he consigns to slavery, and five, when he fails to do so. The oath of any two villains is sufficient, under this hell-black enactment, to send the most pious and exemplary black man into the remorseless jaws of slavery! His own testimony is nothing. He can bring no witnesses for himself. The minister of American justice is bound by the law to hear but one side; and that side, is the side of the oppressor. Let this damning fact be perpetually told. Let it be thundered around the world, that, in tyrant-killing, king-hating, people-loving, democratic, Christian America, the seats of justice are filled with judges, who hold their offices under an open and palpable bribe, and are bound, in deciding in the case of a man's liberty, to hear only his accusers! In glaring violation of justice, in shameless disregard of the forms of administering law, in cunning arrangement to entrap the defenceless, and in diabolical intent, this Fugitive Slave Law stands alone in the annals of tyrannical legislation. I doubt if there be another nation on the globe, having the brass and the baseness to put such a law on the statute-book. If any man in this assembly thinks differently from me in this matter, and feels able to disprove my statements, I will gladly confront him at any suitable time and place he may select. I take this law to be one of the grossest infringements of Christian Liberty, and, if the churches and ministers of our country were not stupidly blind, or most wickedly indifferent, they, too, would so regard it."

Notes to - Antebellum

1.'No place for the old." For the observant, of course this is a line from that evocative Shane McGowan song, Fairytale of New York. Was Shane also thinking of his countrymen's early arrivals when he wrote it? In any case I would like to print Nick Cave's obituary here to remember a much-loved man. Those who have read my first novel will have noticed a nod to the Pogues in that as well.

2."I first met Shane in 1989 when the music paper NME thought it would be a good idea to bring us two together alongside Mark E Smith from the Fall for a so-called "summit meeting". I was excited because I was a fan, completely in awe of Shane's songwriting. Unfortunately, it was my first day out of rehab, and it probably wasn't the greatest idea to spend the day with two people who were not known for their moderation. It was pure mayhem from the outset. Not the most auspicious start to a friendship, but Shane and I did become close friends soon afterwards. When we initially started to hang out, we often went out to bars and clubs. It was a little difficult, because I'd temporarily stopped taking drugs and drinking, but we liked each other's company. I don't think he was used to being around someone who didn't drink. He essentially didn't trust anyone who wasn't completely shit-faced. At some point, when I eventually started drinking again, we met in a bar and he asked me what I wanted. I ordered a double vodka and his eyes just lit up. It was like he was a little kid and it was Christmas Day. And that was that. We spent the next years going out, fucking around, getting wasted. Sometimes I'd call round his flat in King's Cross and he'd be watching Scarface or one of those violent Kitano cop thrillers. I remember being concerned that he wasn't writing songs. Once, when I asked him about it, he crawled across the floor and started rooting in the pile of rubbish until he found a scrap of paper. It was the lyrics to a song called St John of Gods. A beautiful title. Beautiful words. To me, his songs were such precious things, deep works of art, really, but he didn't treat them like that. While I laboured away at my desk, day after day, to produce what I could, Shane's words were delivered to him on a beer tray with a whiskey chaser. What I really envied about Shane's lyric writing was that he was doing something extraordinary with the classic songwriting form. His way of writing was steeped in the tradition of Irish balladry. It was in no way modern, whereas my songs, back then, were more of their time: darker and fractured and experimental. There was little compassion in them. No true understanding of the "ordinary". I don't think I could have written a lyric like "The wind goes right through you/ It's no place for the old" [from Fairytale of New York]. It speaks volumes. You can feel the wind and the ice in the air but also the sense of learned empathy and deep compassion Shane had for people.

3.I loved his voice, too. It was the perfect vehicle for his chaotic, poetic soul. And I loved the way he comported himself when he was singing live. There was a nonchalance about it. I remember watching the Pogues do a soundcheck somewhere at a festival in France. He just walked up to the mic and sang A Pair of Brown Eyes with his hands shoved in his pockets, this gorgeous, racked voice coming out of him like he was a cypher for the angels. It was a rare privilege to witness something like that. Shane saw it as a solemn duty to be permanently fucked up and, for most of his life, he was happy to be the way he was. I never heard him complain about having a hangover or feeling bad. He just got on with it. He was never regretful. And I respected that about him, but sometimes it was difficult. There were times when he was so reduced he was barely functioning and, as a friend, that was heartbreaking to see. There's a myth that there are these "special" people, who do everything to excess and somehow carry on being creative, but it's just not true. It was sad to see Shane lose his extraordinary gifts and become so diminished over time, but that doesn't stop you loving someone.

At the end of the day, though, it is his genius we should remember rather than all the other stuff. He wrote a bunch of songs that are truly great. That's a hell of a lot more than most songwriters manage. His best lyrics have a truly lived-in nature to them. His beautiful soul is baked in to every word, every phrase of A Rainy Night in Soho or The Old Main Drag. They are rooted in earned experience. Those profoundly beautiful words coming out of such a broken soul. He had something that we lesser writers have to work hard to even get close to. An effortless, God-given talent. When my friendship with him began, it was based on a deep admiration for his songwriting. I was a fan, pure and simple, and I will always be that. But the enduring nature of our relationship grew out of a great love for the man himself. Shane was not like other people. Regardless of what condition he was in, he had a goodness about him and a depth of feeling about the poetic nature of our human condition that was immeasurable. There was a truth to him, a clarity of soul that was of the purest kind. You can't hide something like that. The whole world could see it, which is why he was so deeply loved by so many."

4. Green behind the ears": the untold story by Ben Zimmer. In my Word Routes column over on the Visual Thesaurus website, I recently took a look at a peculiar turn of phrase used by Barack Obama in the Oct. 7 presidential debate: "Now, Senator McCain suggests that somehow, you know, I'm green behind the ears…" My initial assessment was that Obama had created an idiom blend, combining the more established expression "wet behind the ears" with the metaphorical extension of green implying immaturity. But as it turns out, the story of "green behind the ears" has some unexpected intricacies, including a surprising parallel in German. First, I'm not entirely sure "idiom blend" is the right term to describe what is happening here. In canonical idiom blends (as described by Cutting & Bock, Mark Liberman, Neal Whitman, and others), two elements from idiomatic phrases are combined in a "one from Column A – one from Column B" style. Thus It's not rocket science + It's not brain surgery = It's not rocket surgery He's under the gun + He's behind the eight ball = He's under the eight ball That's another kettle of fish + That's another can of worms = That's another kettle of worms In the case of "green behind the ears," there's no obvious idiomatic phrase involving the word green for "wet behind the ears" to combine with in this fashion. The closest I can think of is "green around the gills," but that relates to a different sense of green: 'queasy-looking' rather than 'immature, inexperienced.' The queasy connotation of "green around the gills" does seem to be a contributing element to an early example I found for "green behind the ears," in the 1911 book The Complete Oxford Man by A. Hamilton Gibbs: When these people have the needle what a remarkable change comes over them. Some tremble and look green behind the ears. But in the other examples of "green behind the ears" I've collected, up to and including Obama's usage, green appears to take the place of wet (or not dry) in the traditional "behind the ears" idiom without involving another competing phrase. Rather, it's simply providing a new metaphorical basis for the expression, moving away from the founding image of "a newly born animal, as a colt or a calf, on which the last spot to become dry after birth is the little depression behind either ear" (as Charles Earle Funk explained the expression in his 1948 book A Hog On Ice). In my Word Routes column, I suggest that the replacement of wet with green doesn't necessarily imply an accidental mix-up or a humorous play on words. Rather, it could be a serious historical transformation of the idiom, since the original image of wet-eared livestock might not be a familiar one to many in our urbanised world. In this regard it's similar to egg-corn substitutions like free reign, since the equestrian idiom of free rein has become less relevant as the automobile has replaced the horse as our favoured mode of transportation..

                              small birds fly free

The plot thickened when an anonymous Visual Thesaurus commenter pointed out that German has the exact same idiomatic variations:. (noch) nicht trocken hinter den Ohren = not (yet) dry behind the ears. (noch) feucht hinter den Ohren = (still) wet behind the ears. (noch) grün hinter den Ohren = (still) green behind the ears.

5.   Caste system. I am indebted in my research to Isabel Wilkerson's book 'Caste - The Origins of Our Discontent'. The Guardian review says:- Wilkerson's is essentially a two-tier caste system – dominant or white and subordinate or non-white. The signal of rank in the American hierarchy is caste's "faithful servant", race. Caste and race continually bleed into each other; Wilkerson defines a racist as someone who harms, mocks or institutionalises inferiority on the basis of race. A casteist is someone who upholds or benefits from an ingrained system of hierarchy, never challenging its assumptions. Wilkerson's choice of examining caste rather than race is a valuable one; this book is not about biology, social history or science, but about structural power. Caste is a "hologram", she explains, an "insidious" force that operates outside of hatred or intolerance, animated by practice and reflex. It's not just the far right or trigger-happy cops; even the "good" can be casteists – such as the guest at a Tina Brown book party who asked the then state senator Barack Obama to get them a drink. Since its inception, the American caste system has reinvented itself in terrifying and hideous ways. "Before there was a United States of America," Wilkerson writes, "there was enslavement. Theirs was a living death passed down for twelve generations." Caste is a dark history of the inexhaustible scope of human violence. Enslaved Africans were seen as incapable of injury, worked to the bone and starved, and routinely subjected to torture and rape. The American caste system, like India or Germany's, was constructed and practised openly; it did not hide its savagery. Even Hitler recorded his admiration for the uniquely American "knack for maintaining an air of robust innocence in the wake of mass death". Wilkerson reminds us that the Nazis, though inspired by America's race laws, ultimately thought they went too far. Wilkerson threads microhistories into the larger, horrendous tapestry. She describes local lynching trees, schools letting out early so children could accompany their parents to watch murder, advertised by newspapers as though they were sporting events. Photographers brought portable printing presses to sell photos of the hanged men as souvenirs. Lynching postcards were a thriving industry at the turn of the 20th century, wish-you-were-here's of the severed, half-burned head of Will James, lynched in Illinois in 1909 or of burned torsos from Waco. "This is the barbeque we had last night," a Texan wrote to his mother on the back on one such card. Writing of the South, where the purest form of American caste is practised, Wilkerson writes about a country trembling with indignation when asked to simply acknowledge that black lives matter. Congress has steadfastly refused even to debate reparations for the descendants of the people they enslaved, refusing for 30 years to pass HR 40, a bill that would do nothing more than table a discussion on the matter. The author unearths much disquieting material in 'Caste'. We know that during the Jim Crow era, Black Americans were forced to drink from separate water fountains, but before they were given fountains, Wilkerson writes, they had to drink from horse troughs. Caste as a concept can be dizzying, but Wilkerson makes plain the deeply embedded infrastructure of American hierarchy. Caste is why Robert E Lee, the Confederate general who went to war against his own country for the right to enslave other humans can be honoured by 230 memorials across the land. It is why Alabama was the last state in the union to throw out its law banning interracial marriage, which it did in 2000, 36 years after the Civil Rights Act ended segregation. And it is why Lyndon B Johnson, who signed that act into law, was the last Democrat ever to win the presidency with the majority of the white electorate. Based on my reflection, I propose

Footnotes

that Irish migrants in the mid nineteenth century were the first Europeans to legitimise the caste system and use it to their advantage. Other Europeans, Germans and Italians followed suit.

6.   I deliberately in this story do not name the Planter. He is amorphous and represents a class of vile, rapacious, individuals who owned vast tracks of land and owned and and oppressed other human beings for centuries.

7. Slave driver. From the Man in the Middle by Randall Miller. Wise planters of the antebellum South never relaxed their search for talent among their slaves. The ambitious, intelligent, and proficient were winnowed out and recruited for positions of trust and responsibility. These privileged bondsmen—artisans, house servants, foremen—served as intermediaries between the master and his enslaved people; they exercised considerable power; they learned vital skills of survival in a complex, often hostile world. Knowing, as they did, the master's needs and vulnerabilities, they were the most dangerous of slaves; but they were also the most necessary.

None of these men in the middle has been more misunderstood than the slave driver, policeman of the fields and the quarters. To enforce discipline and guarantee performance in the fields, planters enlisted slave foremen or drivers. On large plantations they worked as assistants to the white overseers; on smaller units they served immediately under the master. Generally, they were of an imposing physical presence capable of commanding respect from the other slaves. Ex-slaves described the drivers as, for example, "a great, big cullud man," "a large tall, black man," "a burly fellow … severe in the extreme." Armed with a whip and outfitted in high leather boots and greatcoat, all emblematic of plantation authority, the driver exuded an aura of power. The English traveler, Basil Hall, thought the driver had power more symbolic than real. The slaves knew better. With hardly repressed anger, ex-slave Adelaine Marshall condemned the black foremen at the Brevard plantation in Texas for "all de time whippin' and stroppin' de niggers to make dem work harder." Many other former slaves echoed this theme of driver brutality; accounts of mutilations, lacerations, burnings, and whippings fill the pages of the slave narratives. But physical coercion alone never moved slaves to industry. The drivers, therefore, were selected as men able to bargain, bribe, cajole, flatter, and only as a last resort, to flog the slaves to perform their tasks and refrain from acts destructive of order in the quarters.

Masters often conferred with their black slave drivers on matters of farming, or on social arrangements in the quarters, and often deferred to their advice. As the driver matured and became more knowledgeable, his relationship with his master became one of mutual regard, in sharp contrast to the master's less settled and more transient relationship with white overseers.

White overseers as well were frequently governed by the driver's counsel, although the relationship between these two species of foreman was sometimes strained. The overseer's insistence on steady work from the slaves, and the driver's interest in protecting his people from white abuses, placed the driver in the agonising dilemma of torn loyalties and interest. In this conflict the driver often appealed to the master and won his support. A chorus of complaint from white Southern overseers alleged that planters trusted the black driver more than the overseer. The charge seems to have been justified. John Hartwell Cocke of Virginia regarded his driver as his "humble friend," but held overseers at arm's length. The astute agricultural reformer and planter, James H. Hammond, unabashedly acknowledged that he disregarded his overseer's testimony in many instances and instead heeded his driver, whom Hammond considered a "confidential servant" especially enjoined to guard against "any excesses or omissions of the overseer." Planters dismissed overseers as an expendable breed, and, indeed, overseers rarely lasted more than two

                        small birds fly free

or three seasons with any single master. The driver, however, stayed on indefinitely as the master's man, and some masters came to depend on him to an extraordinary degree.

8.   E.D.E.N. Southworth (1819-1899) was the author of more than 60 novels and was the most widely read American novelist of last half of the 19th century. She invariably signed herself Mrs. E.D.E.N. Southworth, though she began writing in 1844 to support herself and her children after Mr. Southworth deserted her four years into their marriage. In 1844, when Emma was pregnant with their second child, Frederick abandoned his family to seek his fortune in South America. This was not uncommon in the 19th century. With divorce unthinkable, many men just escaped to the frontier if they wanted out of a marriage, keeping the divorce rate low, but having the same effect on those they left behind. Faced with the task of raising and supporting her children alone, E.D.E.N. Southworth returned to Washington, DC to resume her teaching career. She wrote: *I found myself broken in spirit, health, and purse – a widow in fate but not in fact – with my babes looking up to me for a support I could not give them. It was in these darkest days of my woman's life, that my author's life commenced.*

Her annual salary of $250 was a very meagre family income. Perhaps to distract herself from her troubles, Southworth began writing fiction. She turned in a short story at a local book store she frequented, asking that it be submitted somewhere for publication. "The Irish Refugee" was published by the Baltimore Saturday Visitor in 1846. Southworth's own experiences gave her sensibilities that would resonate with her female contemporaries who yearned to lead independent lives. In an era when debates over human rights dominated the political and social landscape, Southworth wrote fiction celebrating strong women who transcend or ignore class distinctions and stand firm against oppression of any sort.

9.   Lincoln visits Five Points. February 27, 1860 was the date Lincoln delivered his famous speech at Cooper Union, explaining his position on slavery—and wowing New Yorkers who were not so familiar with this Republican presidential candidate from the Midwest. That afternoon, however, he spoke in front of a very different audience: destitute children who lived at Five Points House of Industry. At the time, Five Points was Manhattan's most crime-ridden, impoverished slum. The House of Industry was a charity that mainly housed and assisted poor and orphaned kids. As Lincoln peeked in on one of the Sunday School classes, a teacher asked the tall, skinny lawyer to say a few words to his students, writes Tyler Anbinder, author of Five Points. Lincoln at first declined, insisting he could offer no words of advice to such destitute children. But his companion, Illinois congressman Elihu B. Washburne, insisted that Lincoln speak, suggesting that he describe the hard times of his own youth. Lincoln reluctantly consented, telling the students, as Washburne later recalled, that '*I had been poor; that I remembered when my toes stuck out through my broken shoes in the winter; when my arms were out at the elbows; when I shivered with the cold. And I told them there was only one rule. That was, always do the very best you can . . . if they would follow that rule, they would get along somehow.*' By now, Lincoln's eyes had filled with tears, and he could not continue.

Notes to - The Civil War

1. Lincoln elected. Yesterday, the start of the most exciting day in the history of Springfield, Ill., could not wait for the sun. At 3 a.m., somebody got Election Day started with volleys of cannon fire, and after that there were incessant and spontaneous eruptions of cheering and singing all day long. A moment of delirium erupted in mid-afternoon, when the city's favourite citizen emerged from his law office and went to vote, taking care to slice his name off the top of the ballot so as to prevent accusations that he had voted for himself.

After the sun went down, he joined other Republican stalwarts in the Capitol building, where they eagerly received the early returns that were trotted over from the telegraph office.

There were no surprises: the long-settled Yankees in Maine and New Hampshire and pioneering Germans of Michigan and Wisconsin delivered the expected victories. And then came news from Illinois: "We have stood fine. Victory has come." And then from Indiana: "Indiana over twenty thousand for honest Old Abe."

The throngs in the streets cheered every report, every step towards the electoral college number, but news from the big Eastern states was coming painfully slowly, and finally the candidate and his closest associates decamped the capitol and invaded the narrow offices of the Illinois and Mississippi Telegraph Company. The advisers paced the floorboards, jumping at every eruption of the rapid clacking of Morse's machine, while the nominee parked on the couch, seemingly at ease with either outcome awaiting him.

It wasn't until after 10 that reports of victory in Pennsylvania arrived in the form a telegram from the canny vote-counter Simon Cameron, the political boss of the Keystone State, who tucked within his state's tallies joyfully positive news about New York: "Hon. Abe Lincoln, seventy thousand for you. New York safe. Glory enough."

Not until 2 a.m. did official results from New York arrive, and the expected close contest in the make-or-break state never appeared: the one-time rail-splitter won by 50,000 votes. His men cheered, and broke out into an impromptu rendition of "Ain't You Glad You Joined the Republicans?" Outside, pandemonium had been unleashed, but Abraham Lincoln partook of none it, and instead put on his hat and walked home to bed.

"The Republican pulse continues to beat high," exulted a correspondent for The New York Times. "Chanticleer is perched on the back of the American Eagle, and with flapping wings and a sonorous note proclaims his joy at the victory. The return for the first Napoleon from Elba did not create a greater excitement than the returns for the present election."

Well should he sing, for the days of song will end soon enough. Mr. Lincoln is indeed the president-elect, but barely by a whisker, and what exactly one means by "the United States" any more is apt to become a topic of some heated discussion. Lincoln won his parlay, taking 16 of the 17 Northern states that he set his sights upon, including the hard-fought New York, and most by a solid majority.

But there were states where he was more lucky than popular, like California, where all four candidates polled significant numbers. Lincoln won only 32.3 percent of the ballots, but managed to eke out a victory and capture the state's four electoral votes by the wafer-thin margin of 734 votes. A similar, if slightly less dramatic story played out in Oregon, where Lincoln's victory margin was fewer than 1,200 votes. In his home state of Illinois, facing Mr. Douglas, Mr. Lincoln won by fewer than 12,000 out of 350,000 votes cast, a clear win but hardly a romp.

small birds fly free

The South, of course, presents a vastly different picture. In the states of Alabama, Arkansas, Florida, Georgia, Louisiana. Mississippi, North Carolina, Tennessee and Texas Mr. Lincoln received a combined total of no votes. None. True, his name wasn't even listed on the ballot, but that seems to be a mere technical oversight that would have had no great consequence. After all, in Virginia, the largest and wealthiest southern state, Mr. Lincoln was on the ballot, and there he tallied a total of 1,887 votes, or just 1.1 percent of the total cast. The results were even worse in Kentucky, his place of birth. One might have thought that sheer native pride should have earned him more than 1,364 of the 146,216 votes cast, but perhaps Kentuckians resented that he deserted them at such a tender age.

All told, Mr. Lincoln will assume the presidency in March on the strength of his muscular 180 electoral votes, and despite the puny 39.8 percent of the popular vote he accumulated.

The narrowness of this fragile mandate (if that word can even be used) naturally invites speculation about what might have been. The year began with Mr. Douglas standing, like Franklin Pierce and James Buchanan before him, as an electable anti-slavery Northerner who could be depended on to maintain southern prerogatives. But from the moment last April when fire-eating Southern Democrats made it clear that they would rather punish Mr. Douglas for his vote on the Kansas-Nebraska Act two years ago than win the White House in the fall, it was ordained that the Little Giant, so long touted as a certain president-to-be, was steering a doomed vessel.

Yet there were times when his campaign picked up speed, and at such moments Mr. Douglas seemed very close to capturing enough support to thwart Mr. Lincoln's northern sweep and deny him his electoral college majority. Had that happened, Mr. Douglas would be sitting solidly in second place. He would have demonstrated support both north and south, and he would offer the South preservation of the status quo. That might well have been enough to pacify the reckless Southern Democrats who shunned him in the spring, and to win their support in the House of Representatives.

But for every Douglas surge there was a Douglas blunder. Final tallies show that wherever Mr. Douglas actually campaigned in New York, he won more votes than President Buchanan took when he captured the state four years ago. But instead of investing his time in the Empire State, Mr. Douglas headed into the inhospitable South, where he did the seemingly impossible — he managed to make southern voters dislike him even more than they already did. Appearing before a crowd in Virginia, he was asked if the election of Mr. Lincoln would justify secession. A politician of Mr. Douglas's experience should have known how to handle this kind of question with finesse, but instead he offered the one answer certain to damage him. No, he told the crowd. He might have stopped at that, but perhaps figuring that, having jumped the fence, he may as well have a picnic, he told the crowd, It is the duty of the president of the United States to enforce the laws of the United States, and if Mr. Lincoln is the winner, I will do all in my power to help the government do so. With that answer, Mr. Douglas dismissed the purported right to secede that the south so cherishes, and surrendered his claim as the only man who could be counted on to keep the union together.

Now that task falls to a president who received fewer than four votes in 10; a president who is purely the creature of only one section of the country; a president who, apart from one undistinguished term in the House of Representatives a decade ago (and a period in the state legislature), has no experience in public office; a president who comes from a Republican party that has been stitched together from various interests, who will be asked to work with a Congress whose two houses are controlled by Democrats.

Footnotes

2.   Pierre Gustave Toutant Beauregard was a Louisiana-born author, civil servant, politician, inventor, and first prominent general for the Confederacy. Beauregard was trained as a civil engineer at the United States Military Academy and served with distinction as an engineer in the Mexican-American War. Following an extremely brief tenure as the superintendent of the Military Academy in 1861, he became the first Confederate brigadier general and commanded the defence of Charleston, South Carolina, for the start of the Civil War at Fort Sumter on April 12, 1861. Three months later he was the victor at the First Battle of Bull Run. Beauregard commanded armies in the Western Theatre, including the Battle of Shiloh in Tennessee, and the Siege of Corinth in Northern Mississippi. He returned to Charleston and defended it from repeated naval and land attacks in 1863. His arguably greatest achievement was saving the city of Petersburg, Virginia, and thus also the Confederate capital of Richmond, from assaults by overwhelmingly superior Union Army forces in June of 1864. However, his influence over Confederate strategy was marred by his poor relationships with Confederate President Jefferson Davis and other generals. In April 1865, Beauregard and his commander, General Joseph E. Johnston, convinced Davis and the remaining cabinet members that the war needed to end, and the majority of the remaining confederate armies were surrendered to Sherman.

3.   Lincoln's compromise. The fire eaters in South Carolina have already announced that they will immediately introduce a bill of secession. But that has been something they have been itching to do for years; as any doctor or fireman will tell you, sometimes the best way to end a fever or a blaze is to just let the thing burn out. Not everyone in the South is a slave owner, and not every slave owner is a disunionist. If any of the firebrands would take the time to listen to what Mr. Lincoln has actually said, they would see that he is no raving abolitionist like Sen. William Seward and his ilk. (Indeed, anti-slavery activist Wendell Phillips sneeringly calls Mr. Lincoln a "huckster" and William Lloyd Garrison says he has "not one drop of anti-slavery blood in his veins.")

Mr. Lincoln has made his position clear: while he is against slavery and calls it evil, he would not do anything — more to the point, that he is powerless under the Constitution to do anything — to end slavery where the Constitution already permits it. The line that he has drawn is against an expansion of slavery in the territories, but look at a map: there are no more territories held by the United States in North America that are in dispute. On every other matter relating to slavery he has been silent. And ultimately, they ought to realise that Mr. Lincoln may not be an experienced politician, or have strong political support, but that by training and avocation, he is a lawyer, and a good one. And almost every lawyer will tell you that it is cheaper to settle a matter quietly than to fight it out in court.

4.   Free people of colour. During the antebellum period, Louisiana's free people of colour enjoyed a relatively high level of acceptance and prosperity, a legacy of the state's French and Spanish founders, but as the American Civil War approached, white society increasingly turned against them. Most heavily concentrated in New Orleans, many worked as artisans and professionals. Significant numbers were also found in Baton Rouge, St. Landry Parish, and the Natchitoches area, where some were plantation owners and slaveholders. It is for their contributions to the arts that Louisiana's free people of colour have come to be best known, with many distinguishing themselves as authors, artists, and musicians. Only in the last few decades have historians themselves begun to appreciate the complexity of free black communities and their significance to our understanding not just of the past, but also the present. The fact that free people of colour, particularly in the South, never made it into the mainstream narrative of American history is

                    small birds fly free

extraordinary considering their status was one of the most talked about issues of the first half of the nineteenth century. Even where their numbers were small, they made significant contributions to the economies and cultures of the communities in which they lived, and, as a group, exerted a strong influence on government policy and public opinion at a time of increasing polarisation over the issue of slavery. Nor did their story lose its relevance once the abolition of slavery had rendered all Americans legally free. Discrimination against freedmen, blacks who had never known slavery, and Creoles of Colour in the postbellum South led many of them to seek a better life elsewhere, where many of mixed-race heritage were able to "pass" in their new communities. As a result of their exodus, southern black communities were deprived of talented leaders, businessmen, role models, and cultural brokers at the time when they were most needed. Those who remained, however, cooperated with other African Americans in the long struggle for civil rights.

5.   This editorial is inspired by and follows the gist of an editorial published in the Atlantic at the time. There is an extraordinary synergy between the events of 1860 and Lincoln's election and the fact that a significant portion of the electorate refused to recognise the ballot and Joe Biden's election in 2020. The consequence of that division becomes catastrophic to the US in the following years. The aftermath of the Trump led rebellion is yet to be determined.

6.   Louisiana Tigers. Irish soldiers could be found in most Louisiana divisions. However, several were particularly notable for their large Irish numbers. Among them were the Emmet and Montgomery Guards of the 1st Louisiana Volunteers; the 7th Louisiana Volunteers with a company from Donaldsonville which was over 90 percent Irish; the 10th with five companies dominated by the Irish; the 1st Battalion of the Louisiana Volunteers, frequently referred to as the Louisiana Tigers filled by New Orleans Irish, and the 6th Louisiana Volunteers: Of the 980 men in the 6th at least 468 were born in Ireland and 100 more had common Irish surnames.

The Irish had a reputation for bravery, violence and rowdiness. High consumption of alcohol was customarily followed by brawls. "Four or five drinking Irishmen were in the habit of coming into camp late at night and in a drunken condition making life hideous" one soldier complained. Captain Monaghan reported that one of his own men, James McCormack, was killed by one of Wheat's Tiger's after a dispute between the men. Monaghan had the killer tracked down and brought back to camp for trial.

The Louisiana Tigers were a tough lot, and they did not take orders easily. The men demanded frequently that their commanding officers prove themselves before they would obey them. Lt. Col. Charles de Choiseul, a French Creole, experienced this first hand when he was asked to take over the Louisiana Tigers temporarily from Major Chatham Roberdeau Wheat while the Major was recovering from a wound. When he heard of this appointment, Choiseul wrote to a friend, "I am a victim of circumstances, not of my own will. … Whether the Tigers will devour me, or whether I will succeed in taming them, remains to be seen." As he feared, the men openly challenged his authority. Tension escalated quickly, and Choiseul had to threaten to shoot any man who "raised a finger". Predictably, the threat resulted in one of the Tigers challenging him. As Choiseul recalled a "big double fisted ugly looking fellow came at me and said 'God damn you, shoot me." So Choiseul complied and shot the man at point blank range. The bullet knocked out a several teeth and the lower jaw of the soldier as well as cut his tongue. With authority now persuasively restored, the Tigers accepted Choiseul.

The Louisiana Tigers spread fear not only among Yankee soldiers but even other confederate divisions and civilians. One soldier in Alabama stated "I was actually afraid of them, afraid I would meet them somewhere and that they would do me like they did Tom Lane of my company; Knock me down and stamp me half to death."

However, with this reputation for fierceness came also one of extreme bravery. General Thomas "Stonewall" Jackson considered his Irish the essential part of the "foot cavalry". Courageous acts, such as refusing to retreat even after they had run out of ammunition in the Second Battle of Bull Run, substantiated this reputation.

A variety of reasons motivated the Irish recruits to join these units. Money certainly played a part. The $10 enlistment bounties were a real boon to any working man. However, other motives existed. Singular to the Irish, was the comparison of British oppression of the Irish with the view that the Civil War was simply Northern attempts at subjugating the South.

I believe the North is about to wage a brutal and unholy war on a people who have done them no wrong, in violation of the government. They no longer acknowledge that all government derives its validity from the consent of the governed. They are about to invade our peaceful homes, destroy our property, and inaugurate a servile insurrection, murder our men and dishonour our women. We propose no invasion of the North, no attack on them, and only ask to be left alone. They cannot conquer us but would turn the wolf from their own door by letting this idle, brutal mob come here to be destroyed. . . . Our army is for protection, Lincoln's to subjugate and enslave the whole Southern people and divide the property among his vulgar unprincipled mob.

To any Irish national, the words "North" could easily be substituted for "British" and "South" swapped for "Irish". Ardent Irish nationalist and journalist, John Mitchel's own son (also named John) fought, and ultimately died, for the Confederate Cause. He conveyed this sentiment shortly before his death in 1864 "I die willingly for the South, but oh, that it had been for Ireland".

While many Irish saw parallels with the fight for the Confederate cause and the fight against British oppression, they also viewed the abolition of slavery as detrimental to their economic and social standing in the South. In the predominant racial hierarchy of the Deep South, even the poorest Irish person was legally better off than any person of colour. Abolition of slavery they were led to believe would bring the grim reality of increased competition for jobs and fears that an over-supplied labor market would lower wages.

Finally, support for the confederacy was also a means, they thought, of displaying patriotism, and their reputation for fierce fighting earned them respect from other Louisianans. Like many Southerners, most Irish recruits saw the war simply in terms of defending their own home and protecting their interests, economic and otherwise. America in general, and New Orleans in particular, had offered Irish immigrants a chance at prosperity unimaginable at home. The majority of the Irish people in the city had just spent the last ten to twenty years constructing new lives for themselves, creating communities, and building churches, school and orphanages. All of these factors, in their opinion at the time, were worth fighting for.

7. Battle of Bull Run. On the morning of July 21, 1861, civilians from Washington rode out to Centreville, Virginia, to watch a Union army made up of very green recruits—they signed up for a 90-day war—march boldly into combat. Men, women, and even children came to witness the predicted Union victory, bringing along picnic baskets and opera glasses. Bull Run soon became known as the "picnic battle." Among the civilian ranks were some of Congress's most powerful senators—many of whom had called for just such a campaign. They quickly learned that war can be unpredictable.

The Union army performed well that morning, but by early afternoon the Confederates had brought in reinforcements, forcing an intense battle over a space known as Henry Hill. When

small birds fly free

Union generals finally called retreat around 4:00 p.m., the frightened soldiers fled for their lives. "I saw the 12th New York regiment rush pell-mell out of the wood," commented one reporter. Soldiers threw down their weapons and ran from the battlefield, sweeping up civilians in the retreat.

Near the battlefield, a group of senators was eating lunch. They heard a loud noise and looked around to see the road filled with soldiers, horses, and wagons—all headed in the wrong direction. "Turn back, turn back, we're whipped," Union soldiers cried as they ran past the spectators. Startled, Michigan senator Zachariah Chandler tried to block the road to stop the retreat. Senator Ben Wade of Ohio, sensing a disastrous defeat, picked up a discarded rifle and threatened to shoot any soldier who ran. While Senator Henry Wilson distributed sandwiches, a Confederate shell destroyed his buggy, forcing him to escape on a stray mule. Iowa senator James Grimes barely avoided capture and vowed never to go near another battlefield.

Senators returned to Washington "with gloomy faces," noted one reporter, where they delivered eyewitness accounts to a stunned President Lincoln. Only one member of Congress, New York representative Alfred Ely, made it to Richmond that day—as a prisoner of war. The Union army's defeat at Bull Run shocked and sobered members of Congress, making it painfully clear that the war would last much longer than 90 days and be harder fought than anyone had expected. It certainly would be no picnic.

8.   An Irish proverb: "Is ar scáth a chéile a mhaireann na daoine." This translates as: "It is in each other's shadow(community) that we flourish."

9.   At the start of the war, the Louisiana Tigers had 12,000 men; four years later only 373 remained - a death rate of 97%.

10. Fernando Wood, Mayor of New York. As the Civil War pitted North against South, New York became a city of divided loyalties and complex class, racial, and economic interests. While most New Yorkers supported the war at its outset, significant forces urged conciliation with the Confederacy. From Wall Street financiers, to commercial shippers, to merchants selling manufactured goods to a South that produced little of its own, the New York City economy depended heavily on southern cotton. In response to the divisive Compromise of 1850, a group of merchants formed the Union Safety Committee, which pledged "to resist every attempt to alienate any portion of our country from the rest." During the war years, Mayor Fernando Wood, a "Peace Democrat," led opposition to the war in the city, which grew as the wartime economy floundered and casualties mounted.

By 1860, one of every four of New York City's 800,000 residents was an Irish-born immigrant. While many laboured in several of the city's skilled trades, the vast majority of Irish immigrants worked as unskilled labourers on the docks, as ditch diggers and street pavers, and as cartmen and coal heavers. In several of these occupations they competed directly with African-American workers. African Americans had lived and worked in New York City--some as slaves, some as free people--since well before the Revolutionary War, and had established churches, newspapers, literary societies, and free schools. Black workers lived in close proximity to white workers in racially mixed communities that dotted the lower half of Manhattan.

When the Civil War began in 1861, large numbers of New York City's white workers did not embrace the fight to preserve the Union. Many resented the war effort, which brought economic hardship and increasing unemployment to working-class neighbourhoods. Competition for jobs between Irish and Black workers, already intense before the war, increased dramatically, and racial tensions mounted in work places and in working-class neighbourhoods throughout the city.

Among New Yorkers, African Americans and middle-class and wealthy Republicans tended to support abolition; most of the white working-class did not, fearing competition for jobs from thousands of newly emancipated slaves.

Lincoln's famous speech at Cooper Institute in February 1860 calling to limit the extension – but not the end – of slavery was a critical campaign speech that helped him secure the Republican Party nomination for President. In November, he was elected, and, in December, South Carolina was the first state to secede from the Union. Lincoln's speech was strongly attacked by New York city business leaders and the Democratic Party, many assailing him with the racist slogan, "Black Republican." More important, Lincoln's election sparked a strong movement in the city, led by Mayor Fernando Wood, to join the South and secede from the Union. Although slavery was formally abolished in New York State in 1827, the slave trade lived on in the city until the Civil War because New York was the capital of the Southern slave economy.

The city's business community of major banks, insurance companies and shipping industry financed and facilitated the cotton trade. Many of the leaders of this community played a decisive role in city social life and politics, including control over the powerful Democratic Party. Together, they backed the authority of the Constitution's "Fugitive Slave Clause" – and later Fugitive Slave Acts (1793 and 1850) — guaranteeing slavery. Equally critical, city police, leading lawyers and judges (state and federal), with the support of the growing Irish immigrant community, colluded with organised slave "kidnappers."

The slave trade functioned in two complementary ways. First, northern free Blacks — including young children — as well as self-emancipated former slaves who fled to New York from the slave states lived in fear of being kidnapped by organised slave catchers (often city police officers) and transported south into slavery. Second, "slaver" ships regularly stopped in New York harbour with numerous African slaves hidden on board as cargo to be sold as part of a lucrative, if illegal, business. In pre-Civil War New York, the police were underpaid and made money through accepting bribes as well as by securing lucrative rewards from seizing and sending alleged "fugitive" Black people to the South or a fee for the sale of a captured free Black person into slavery. Because the courts were run by the Democrats, graft and corruption were accepted judicial procedures. Any Black person could be seized — walking on the street, working on the docks, at home in the middle of the night and even kids on their way to school – and accused of being an allegedly run-away slave. Most judges were notorious racists who thought little of Black people and were eager to go along with police charges. The city's powerful pro-slavery movement based its support for Southern slavery and slave kidnapping on the Constitution's "Fugitive Slave Clause" (i.e., Article 4, Section 2, Clause 3). It stipulated that "no person held to service or labour" would be released from bondage in the event they escaped to a free state, thus requiring northern free cities like New York to return self-emancipated persons to their southern enslavers.

11. Casualties in Major Battles of Civil War

Battle of Gettysburg, Pennsylvania July 1-3, 1863 Casualties: **51,112**
(23,049 Union and 28,063 Confederate)
Battle of Chickamauga, Georgia September 19-20, 1863 Casualties: **34,624**
(16,170 Union and 18,454 Confederate)
Battle of Chancellorsville, Virginia May 1-4, 1863 Casualties: **30,099**
(17,278 Union and 12,821 Confederate)
Battle of Spotsylvania, Virginia May 8-19, 1864 Casualties: **27,399**

                                    small birds fly free

(18,399 Union and 9,000 Confederate)
Battle of Antietam, Maryland September 17, 1862 Casualties: **26,134**
(12,410 Union and 13,724 Confederate)
Battle of The Wilderness, Virginia May 5-7, 1864 Casualties: **25,416**
(17,666 Union and 7,750 Confederate)
Battle of Second Manasses, Virginia August 29-30, 1862 Casualties: **25,251**
(16,054 Union and 9,197 Confederate)
Battle of Stone's River, Tennessee December 31, 1862 Casualties: **24,645**
(12,906 Union and 11,739 Confederate)
Battle of Shiloh, Tennessee April 6-7, 1862   Casualties: **23,741**
(13,047 Union and 10,694 Confederate)
Battle of Fort Donelson, Tennessee February 13-16, 1862 Casualties: **19,455**
(2,832 Union and 16,623 Confederate)

12. Barmbrack is the centre of an Irish Halloween custom. The Halloween Brack traditionally contained various objects baked into the bread and was used as a sort of fortune-telling game. In the brack were: a pea, a stick, a piece of cloth, a small coin (originally a silver sixpence), a ring, and a bean. Each item, when received in the slice, was supposed to carry a meaning to the person concerned: The pea, the person would not marry that year; The stick, would have an unhappy marriage or continually be in disputes; The cloth or rag, would have bad luck or be poor; The coin, would enjoy good fortune or be rich; The ring, would be wed within the year; The bean, would have a future without money.

13. The New York City Draft Riots remain today the single largest urban civilian insurrection in United States history. By the start of the Civil War in April 1861, New York City Mayor Fernando Wood called for the city to secede from the Union and join the Confederacy, but the response from most New Yorkers was unenthusiastic. Nonetheless, two years later when the U.S. government instituted the first military draft, anti-government sentiment particularly among the city's large Irish-born population, grew quickly. One could escape the draft by paying a $300 fine (about $5,500 today). The rich were able to afford the fines, while the disenfranchised and poor white men, who in New York City were often Irish, were forced to enlist because they were frequently the sole source of income for their families.

When the draft came to New York City in July 1863, anti-government anger turned to anti-government and anti-Black violence. The anti-Black violence was driven by the resentment that the Irish would have to compete with freed people for jobs in the city because the Union had embraced emancipation.

On the first day of the draft, July 11, the city was relatively quiet. However, by day three, July 13, tensions boiled over. Volunteer firefighters from Engine Co. No. 33, were known for their violent nature. Angry at their commissioner, they set fire to their own company firehouse which attracted an angry mob. Led by the firefighters, the mob continued down 3rd Avenue, ransacking and burning businesses in their wake. They focused on those enterprises known to employ African Americans including Brooks Brothers, Harper's Weekly, Knickerbockers, and other wealthy businesses. They also attacked the homes of prominent white abolitionists. When the mob reached the Coloured Orphans' Asylum, filled with mostly women and children, it began looting the building before setting it on fire. The 200 children inside were led out of the back by their benefactors and taken to safety.

There were many accounts in New York City newspapers of Black individuals killed during the riot. Although there were an estimated 663 deaths, only 120 were reported to the police. Of those, however, 106 were African Americans. One account of Ebrahim Franklin's death was typical. Franklin was in church, praying. He was a disabled man who made his living working as a carriage driver. He lived with his elderly mother whom he supported. The mob reached him just as he was rising to his feet from his prayers and beat him to his death. They then dragged him outside and hung him in the church yard in front of his mother. Finally, they mutilated his corpse.

14. Contraband camps. For upward of 500,000 enslaved people, the path to freedom during the American Civil War (1861–65) involved a contraband camp. These enclaves were established by people who fled from enslavement to Union-controlled territory. Although some Union officials initially sent them back to the slaveholders, in May 1861 General Benjamin F. Butler refused to return three fugitives, claiming that they were confiscated property of the enemy. His response soon became official policy, as the federal government essentially classified people who had escaped slavery as 'contraband of war' and emancipated them. This encouraged more enslaved people to flee, and 'contraband camps' sprang up in the Deep South, in Washington, D.C., and in such border states as Kentucky and Missouri. It is estimated that upward of 200 camps existed during the war. Union officials, however, were often ill-equipped to provide assistance, and a refugee crisis developed. Shortages of food and clothing were not uncommon, and poor sanitary conditions contributed to mortality rates that reportedly approached 50 percent. Although often reduced to a footnote, the camps played important roles. Their inhabitants made vital contributions to the war effort, from growing crops to working as cooks. And many of the African Americans who fought for the Union were recruited from the camps. In addition, the contraband camps helped formerly enslaved people transition to independence. Notably, the establishment of schools, churches, and hospitals contributed to the rise of Black communities.

15. As Gaeilge - 'In the Irish language'.

16. Buffalo Soldiers were United States Army regiments composed exclusively of African American soldiers, formed during the 19th century to serve on the American frontier. On September 21, 1866, the 10th Cavalry Regiment was formed at Fort Leavenworth, Kansas. The nickname "Buffalo Soldiers" was purportedly given to the regiments by the Native American tribes who fought against them during the American Indian Wars, and the term eventually became synonymous with all of the African American regiments that were established in 1866, including the 9th Cavalry Regiment, 10th Cavalry Regiment, 24th Infantry Regiment, 25th Infantry Regiment and 38th Infantry Regiment. Although numerous African American Union Army regiments were raised during the Civil War (referred to collectively as the United States Coloured Troops), "Buffalo Soldiers" were established by the U.S Congress as the first all-black Army regiments in peacetime. The regiments were racially segregated, as the U.S. military would not desegregate until 1948.

17. Jim Crow laws were a collection of state and local statutes that legalised racial segregation. Named after a Black minstrel show character, the laws, which existed for about 100 years, from the post-Civil War era until 1968, were meant to marginalise African Americans by denying them the right to vote, hold jobs, get an education or other opportunities. Those who attempted to defy Jim Crow laws often faced arrest, fines, jail sentences, violence and death.

18. This story I was told by the village historian Norma Buckley and is movingly recounted in a companion book, I discovered in writing my novel. Written by Marella Hoffman '*Crow Glen - The spirituality of an Irish Village*' is an odyssey through big time in a small place, unfolds 1,000 years of history in Crow Glen, the village of Glenville, County Cork. Returning to her native place, an emigrant ethnographer uses original oral history recordings, archival documents

small birds fly free

and collective memoir to reveal the layers of Irish history in this microcosm. The Fianna, pre-Christian nature worship, the Bards, the Famine, the War of Independence, locals' Catholic practices on the body, in the home and in the landscape - all are resuscitated out of the land, the archives and folk memory. There are circles of emigration and return. Irish Americans come back to the village 170 years after their ancestors' coffin-ship exodus during An Gorta Mór. Their memories engage a rich dialogue with those of the villagers today. The book tells of Fagan, the hedge-school teacher; and some of the country's greatest Irish-language Bards who worked in Crow Glen. Nineteenth-century locals continued Crow Glen's Bardic tradition with witty songs and biting satires that celebrate the landscape, regulate feuds and remember emigrants. In this book, the land speaks too. Lyrenamon, Mullanabowree, Toorgariffe - exotic place names stud the area's black soil like jewels. Townlands speak their original Irish-language meanings, yielding messages about how our ancestors lived there.

Notes to - Epilogue

1.   Clochán na bhFomhórach - Commonly called 'The Giants Causeway. According to legend, the columns are the remains of a causeway built by a giant. The story goes that the Irish giant Fionn mac Cumhaill (Finn MacCool), from the Fenian Cycle of Gaelic mythology, was challenged to a fight by the Scottish giant Benandonner. Fionn accepted the challenge and built the causeway across the North Channel so that the two could meet. In one version of the story, Fionn defeats Benandonner. In another, Fionn hides from Benandonner when he realises that his foe is much bigger than he is. Fionn's wife, Sadhbh, disguises Fionn as a baby and tucks him in a cradle. When Benandonner sees the size of the "baby", he reckons that its father, Fionn, must be a giant among giants. He flees back to Scotland in fright, destroying the causeway behind him so that Fionn would be unable to chase him down. Across the sea, there are identical basalt columns (a part of the same ancient lava flow) at Fingal's Cave on the Scottish isle of Staffa, and it is possible that the story was influenced by this.

Acknowledgements

I wrote this story to understand who we are. I have been intrigued by the Iroquois tribe maxim that one must travel three generations back in order to find one's way forward. Although the Irish Famine (An Gorta Mór) is more than three generations, it dealt a severe wound to our culture and consciousness and I wanted to explore it. The story led me to America and the American civil war and the enslavement of men that precipitated it. I wanted to explore the Irish connection and how Irish refugees settled in America, particularly as generations later, far too many Americans who claim Irish heritage joined Trump's coterie of sycophants.

I could not have achieved the end result, a published novel, without the aid of a dear friend Pierre Peyrot and my brother, Anthony. Both read the drafts I sent to them carefully over the five years it took to write. Their feedback and direction made the story immeasurably better. And I am very grateful.

I also owe a debt to a number of authors who inspired and educated me. Particularly Isabel Wilkerson whose seminal book 'Caste - the origin of our discontents' gave a framework to race in America. I have been equally animated by the novels of Percival Everett and adored Honorée Fanonne Jeffers 'The Love Songs of W.E.B. du Bois'.

Even though it is published second, 'even small birds fly free' is the first book in a trilogy. 'The Drowning of Innocence' published in 2017 is the second book in what I hope will one day be complete with a novel on contemporary Ireland. I have written these stories for my grandchildren now numbering four, who keep me grounded in the present moment. Such a precious gift. I love being with them and love them beyond words.

Finally I want to pay tribute to Emily Catherine who painted the cover of both novels. She interpreted the story in an image and is a powerful artist. The painting is of a starling in whose eye is captured Fastnet Rock (Ireland's teardrop), the last piece of Ireland the refugees sailing to America would have seen.

I hope the story met your expectations. You can write to me padraigogorman@gmail.com

Pádraig O'Gorman
December 2024
www.padraigogorman.ie